Margaret Mayo say.

w... ...and made up stories, right from ...
age. Not her! Margaret was a voracious reader but
never invented stories, until the morning of June 14th
1974 when she woke up with an idea for a short story.
The story grew until it turned into a full length novel,
and after a few rewrites, it was accepted by Mills &
Boon. Two years and eight books later, Margaret gave
up full-time work for good. And her love of writing
goes on!

Robyn Grady has sold millions of books worldwide,
and features regularly on bestsellers lists and at award
ceremonies, including The National Readers Choice,
The Booksellers Best and Australia's prestigious
Romantic Book of the Year. When she's not tapping
out her next story, she enjoys the challenge of raising
three very different daughters as well as dreaming
about shooting the breeze with Stephen King during a
month-long Mediterranean cruise. Contact her at
www.robyngrady.com

Sarah Morgan is a *USA Today* and *Sunday Times*
bestselling author of contemporary romance and
women's fiction. She has sold more than 16 million
copies of her books and her trademark humour and
warmth have gained her fans across the globe. Sarah
lives with her family near London, England, where the
rain frequently keeps her trapped in her office. Visit her
at www.sar... ...organ.com

The Italian Mavericks

COLLECTION

Italian Mavericks: New Year Temptation

MARGARET MAYO

ROBYN GRADY

SARAH MORGAN

MILLS & BOON

First Published in Great Britain 2019
By Mills & Boon, an imprint of HarperCollins *Publishers*
1 London Bridge Street, London, SE1 9GF

ITALIAN MAVERICKS: NEW YEAR TEMPTATION © 2019
Harlequin Books S.A.

Her Husband's Christmas Bargain © 2004 Margaret Mayo
Confessions of a Millionaire's Mistress © 2008 Robyn Grady
The Italian's New-Year Marriage Wish © 2007 Harlequin Books S.A.

Special thanks and acknowledgement are given to Sarah Morgan for her contribution to *The Brides of Penhally Bay* series

ISBN: 978-0-263-27993-1

1219

Printed and bound in Spain
by CPI, Barcelona

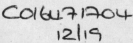

C016471704
12/19

HER HUSBAND'S CHRISTMAS BARGAIN

MARGARET MAYO

CHAPTER ONE

IT WASN'T! It was! It *was* Megan. Luigi Costanzo had overheard the child telling Santa that all she wanted for Christmas was a daddy. It had aroused his curiosity, even caused a faint stir somewhere deep within him, and he'd watched her as she returned to her mother. She was a pretty little girl with long blonde hair and big blue eyes, but it was the shock of seeing who was her parent that caused him to do a double take.

Megan!

His Megan!

Megan, whom he hadn't seen for almost four years.

What the hell?

Luigi looked from mother to daughter and his eyes narrowed. Megan still had the same shoulder-length blonde hair, the same slender figure; nothing about her had changed. She didn't even look any older. He swung on his heel, snapping his fingers at his nearest employee. 'Please follow that woman and report back to me with her address.'

'Yes, sir.'

If the young man was surprised he didn't show it. He spurted into immediate action. There was no arguing with the new owner of Gerards. He'd had everyone on their toes ever since he took over a few months ago.

'Sweetheart, what did you ask for?' Megan looked down at her beloved daughter, who was skipping happily along at her side. There hadn't really been time to visit Santa's

5

grotto but Charlotte had pleaded so eloquently that Megan couldn't find it in her heart to refuse. There was always another train, even if it meant travelling home at the height of the rush hour.

'For a daddy.'

Megan hid her surprise, smiling indulgently instead. 'I don't think Santa supplies daddies. You were supposed to ask for a toy.' Her heart felt heavy as she spoke. Charlotte was right, she did need a father, and if Luigi had been different…

Megan halted her thoughts. It was no good letting them run along those lines. She had been an idiot for marrying him, for allowing her parents to convince her that she could do no better. He was a man with big ambition; she would never want for anything, they had said.

She could understand their reasoning because money had been the bane of their lives, her father never able to hold down a job for long due to ill health, so for that reason she hadn't told her parents that she was leaving Luigi. She had simply disappeared, telephoning them later so that they would know she was safe, but not giving them her address. They had not been happy, telling her that she was making a big mistake. But Megan didn't think so.

Luigi's chief aim in life was making money, and he was very good at it. His wife was someone to clean his home, and cook and wash for him, and to make love to whenever the urge drove him. But there was no love in his heart; she had found that out after the first few months of marriage. She doubted he was capable of feeling any such emotion. Whereas she had loved him with a passion that had sometimes scared her.

With an effort she pushed him out of her mind, concentrating instead on her chatterbox daughter. Santa had given her a parcel and they played a guessing game all the way home as to what was inside.

Home was a rented terraced house in Greenwich, which she shared with Jenny Wilson whom she'd met when she first arrived in London. As soon as they were indoors Charlotte ripped the wrapping paper off her gift. If Megan was disappointed her daughter wasn't. She was delighted with her soldier doll.

'Look, Mummy, I can pretend he's my daddy. Wasn't Santa kind?'

It was a clear case of the boys and girls presents getting muddled but Megan hadn't the heart to tell Charlotte this. 'He certainly is, sweetheart. What are you going to call him?'

'Daddy, of course,' said Charlotte scornfully. 'Come on, Daddy, come and play with me.'

It broke Megan's heart to see her daughter being so passionate about a doll. She hadn't realised that Charlotte missed having a father. Where had the idea come from? Surely she was too young to know?

Daddy doll was a part of their lives for the next few days and on Sunday morning, when Charlotte jumped into bed beside her, the doll had to come too. Megan was sometimes tempted to conveniently lose the doll, except that she knew her daughter would be heartbroken. The trouble was, all this talk about Daddy dragged up memories she would far rather forget.

When the doorbell rang loudly and insistently she was tempted to ignore it. This was Sunday morning for heaven's sake. No one of any consequence called at this hour. It was probably for Jenny anyway, and she was spending the weekend with her fiancé. But the ringing didn't stop; whoever it was kept their finger on the button with no intention of going away until it was answered.

Impatiently Megan pulled on her dressing gown. 'Stay there and keep the bed warm,' she told her daughter. Someone was going to get a piece of her mind. But that someone robbed her of speech. She felt the colour drain from her face, and her heart skipped a couple of beats before resuming at a startling pace.

The very last person she had expected to see was her husband. After all these years she had thought she was safe. In fact she'd felt extremely secure in the knowledge that he had no idea where she was. Not that she'd expected him to come looking. He might just as well have employed a housekeeper for all the notice he'd ever taken of her.

He was still as handsome as ever, his dark Latin looks improving with age rather than fading. Black hair aggressively short, deep brown eyes intensely disturbing. There was maybe a line or two around their corners but it added rather than detracted from his appearance. His nose was strong and straight and his generous lips were at this moment compressed into a grim line.

Although there was a step up into her house he still stood a couple of inches taller. He was six three compared to her five feet six and she was glad at this moment of the extra few inches the step afforded her. He could be very intimidating when he chose.

And it looked as though this was one of those occasions.

'I've come to claim my daughter.'

The bald statement left Megan gasping. This was her worst nightmare come true. She clung to the door handle for support as her legs threatened to buckle. 'H—how did you know?' She felt a tightness in her throat that threatened to choke her.

'So she is mine!' he claimed triumphantly, a gleam of light entering those dark, dark eyes.

He had tricked her! Megan felt like taking a swipe at him. Or at the very least slamming the door in his face. But what good would that do? He wouldn't go away until he'd got what he came for. She dared not think what that might be.

'Can I come in or shall we negotiate on the doorstep?'

Negotiate? Negotiate what? Visiting rights? Some hope of that. He was no longer a part of her life, their lives, hers and Charlotte's. She ought to have divorced him. How had he found her? The question whirled round and round in her head.

He lived in Derbyshire; he had no connections with London. She had thought she would be safe a hundred and fifty or more miles away in a big anonymous city. So how had he discovered her whereabouts? Had he been looking for her all these years? Somehow she doubted it. He had declared he loved her before they got married but there had been very little show of affection afterwards, certainly not enough for him to take time off from his precious work to scour the country after her.

He looked as though he'd done well for himself. A short black Crombie overcoat, mohair trousers with perfectly pressed pleats, Italian leather shoes. Yes, he wasn't short of a few pennies. Not that he ever had been. But he was far more polished, far more mature and self-confident. Even the way he stood told her that.

There was not an ounce of diffidence. He was here on a mission and expected to get his own way. No, not expected, he would demand it—as his right. She could see it in his expression. Dark eyes overpowered her, making her step back and invite him silently into her private domain.

She didn't want to do it but she had no choice. He was hypnotising her into obeying. Or was it because she didn't want to argue with him in full view of her neighbours? Whichever, she was going along with his wishes and she had the secret fear that she would live to regret it.

He followed her as she opened the door into her lounge-cum-dining room, standing just inside the doorway as she drew back the curtains and let the cold morning light filter in. She folded her arms and looked at him as imperiously as she was able in her purple wool dressing gown. It wasn't exactly the outfit she would have chosen for facing the enemy.

And he *was* her enemy if he thought he was going to take Charlotte away from her. The very notion triggered a protective parent syndrome. Her grey eyes flared hostility and her back stiffened. 'How did you find me?'

'Does it matter?' he asked coolly. 'The issue here is that you have denied me my daughter.'

'And you think you'd have made a good father?' Megan's voice was growing shriller by the second. 'You didn't even show *me* any affection; I had no intention of putting a child through that.'

He drew in a swift disbelieving breath. 'I was working for our future, Megan, in case you'd forgotten.'

'So *I* didn't matter?'

'Of course you mattered. But I thought you understood.'

'Oh, I understood all right,' she retorted. 'You thought I'd be happy taking a back seat while you headed towards making your first million. You believed that the thought of all that money would be sufficient for me to happily keep house while you spent every waking hour making more of the bloody stuff. Well, let me tell you something, dear husband of mine, I'm not interested in money. So long as I have enough to put a roof over mine and Charlotte's head and feed and clothe us, then—'

'So that's my daughter's name—Charlotte. Mmm, I like it,' he cut in with a smile. 'Where is she? I'd like to—'

'She's asleep,' lied Megan, 'and I'd thank you to keep your voice down.'

'I want to see her.'

'And then you'll go away?' she rasped. 'I don't think so. I didn't like it when you said you'd come to *claim* your daughter. What was that supposed to mean? Because I'll tell you this right now, it will be over my dead body that you take her from me.'

Megan could hear herself shrieking and knew that it was no way to conduct herself, but she couldn't help it. He wasn't going to take Charlotte; *he wasn't!* She would fight him tooth and nail.

'What I want,' he said, 'is for you and Charlotte to come and spend Christmas with me.'

Megan stared at him in disbelief, finally shaking her head. 'You really think we'd do that? You think I'd let my daughter spend Christmas with a stranger?'

The jibe hurt; she could see it in his eyes, but she didn't care. How dare he think he could walk in here and take over her life?

'I'm not a stranger *I* am her father,' he rasped, 'and as such I have rights. You must know that. And if necessary I'll implement those rights,' he added harshly. 'If you know what's good for you you'll accept that you have no alternative.'

He moved further into the room, halting a few menacing inches from her. Megan felt every hair on her skin prickle and she wanted to step back but she knew that she must show no fear or he would take advantage. Luigi could be ruthless. If he wanted something he went all out for it. She'd seen it enough times in his business life and knew that he'd be equally determined where his daughter was concerned. She was being hounded into a corner and wasn't sure which way to turn.

When his big hands gripped her shoulders she felt a powerful sensation rush through her—anger, fear, desperation. All three! With a strength she didn't know she possessed, Megan pushed him away. Then out of the corner of her eye, she saw Charlotte sidling into the room—a scared-looking Charlotte.

'Mummy,' her daughter cried plaintively. 'What's that man doing to you?'

Megan immediately gathered the child into her arms. 'Nothing, sweetheart.'

'But I saw him touch you. Were you fighting?'

'Of course not.'

'So who is he? What's he doing here?'

Megan could understand Charlotte's questions because they never had any male visitors except Jenny's boyfriend. There'd been no one in her life since Luigi, not because she'd been short of invitations; she simply wasn't interested. Her daughter filled her every waking hour and Megan was completely happy—or she had been until a few minutes ago. Now she felt her happiness fading and worry begin to take its place.

It was ironic that Luigi should put in an appearance now—when Charlotte was crying out for a daddy. He had unknowingly timed his visit to perfection. And it looked as though he intended to do all in his power to take her beloved baby away from her. It was as clear in her head as water out of a tap that this was what he had in mind. He didn't want her, he wanted Charlotte.

I've come to claim my daughter!

Those were his exact words and they struck chill in her heart as she recalled them. And because of that how could she explain to Charlotte that this was her father? He had no part to play in their lives. Not now, not ever! But how was she to get rid of him?

'It looks as though Mummy isn't going to tell you who I am,' he said, looking down at the girl.

Megan shot him a warning glance because she knew what was going to come next, but her wishes were ignored.

'I'm your father,' he informed in a voice that held no love at all. It was a matter-of-fact statement and Megan could have cheerfully strangled him. He hadn't changed one iota.

Charlotte hung on to Megan's dressing gown, looking up at him shyly with an expression of awe and reverence on her face. 'Did Santa send you?' she asked in a tiny, breathless voice.

At that he smiled. 'Indeed he did. He told me that there was a very special little girl looking for a daddy.'

Charlotte's eyes were enormous as she turned to her mother. It was clear she thought that some miracle had happened. 'Mummy, isn't Santa wonderful?'

Megan forced herself to smile. 'He always does his best, sweetheart, but it's not Christmas yet, you know.' What else could she say? How could she burst her daughter's precious bubble of happiness? And how the hell had Luigi known?

'It's near enough,' said Luigi. 'How would you and your mummy like to come and spend Christmas with me? I have a great big house and you can help dress the Christmas tree and goodness knows how many presents you'll find under it on Christmas Day.'

'Luigi!' Megan whispered through her teeth. This was emotional blackmail at its worst. Yes, he probably would ply Charlotte with presents, but what the little girl wanted more than anything in the world was a father who loved her, a father who showed his affection in every way possible. Buying a child's love was inexcusable. And that was all he would do, all he would ever do.

And Charlotte was completely overwhelmed, hiding behind her mother's skirts, very warily peeping at Luigi.

'How dare you think you can walk in here after all these years and try to take over my life?' said Megan coldly. 'I have plans for Christmas; why should I change them because of a whim on your part?'

'I can assure you it's no whim,' he told her brusquely. 'I want both you and my daughter back where you belong. I'm giving you no choice.'

Luigi was angry, fiercely angry. His stomach was a tight, knotted ball and he wanted to lash out. He had felt bad enough when Megan left him, but for her to be carrying his child when she did so went beyond the pale. Had she hated him that much? Did she still hate him?

In truth, he hadn't realised that anything had gone wrong with their marriage. Night after sleepless night he'd racked his brains for a possible reason and come up with nothing. He'd thought she was happy, she had no reason not to be. He was a good provider; she'd never been left wanting. He'd worked long hours, yes, but she understood that. It was the only way to get anywhere.

None of her friends or even her parents had known

where she'd gone, and his search had proved fruitless. Not even the police could help him. He had immersed himself more deeply into his work, hoping that one day she would get in touch. Finally, though, he'd had to accept that their marriage was over. And he'd worked even harder.

When he'd seen her in his London store he'd been stunned, and when he had looked closely at the little girl he'd known at once that it was his child. He had an old photograph somewhere of his mother at the same age and there was a distinct likeness.

Megan had denied him his daughter and now she was trying to say that he had no rights to her. Lord, she really must hate him. What the hell had he done to her? Of one thing he was sure; he wasn't going to let her get away with it. She was not going to walk out on him again.

'I have no choice?' she questioned now. 'Believe me, no one, and that includes you, makes me do anything I don't want to do.'

He admired the way she stood up for herself. Her bright eyes and prickly stance reminded him of an animal defending its young. And that was exactly what she was doing. But Charlotte was as much his as Megan's.

'Give me a reason why you don't want to spend Christmas with me.' He was sure she had none, except that she no longer loved him. But that was no excuse for depriving her daughter, *his* daughter. He'd never very much liked children, and he'd always worked over Christmas, but all of a sudden he found himself looking forward to taking a few days off and getting to know this beautiful little girl who kept peeping at him from behind her mother's dressing gown.

He would shower her with presents, she would want

for nothing, and it would be a Christmas filled with all the good things in life.

And after that? asked his conscience.

After that he would keep her with him, of course. It was her rightful place. Both Charlotte and Megan. He would accept nothing less.

'The reason,' she told him swiftly, 'is that Charlotte doesn't know you. And, to be quite honest, I don't want her to get to know you. An absentee father is worse than not having one at all.'

'What do you mean, absentee father?' he asked sharply. 'You were the one who walked out.'

'Because I never saw you, dammit. What sort of a life was that? And I don't want Charlotte suffering the same way.'

'You belong with me,' he growled fiercely. 'Are you forgetting your wedding vows?'

'Mummy, what's the matter?' Charlotte tugged at Megan's dressing gown, forcing her to soften her face and look down at her worried daughter.

'Nothing, sweetheart. I'm just not sure that I want to go and spend Christmas with your—father.' It pained her to say the word.

'I'd like to go,' whispered her daughter, giving him a timid smile.

Luigi felt exultation. The battle was half won. All he needed now was Megan's acceptance.

'It looks as though you're getting your wish,' she finally managed to choke out. 'You've always been the same, haven't you, Luigi? Nothing ever stands in your way. How many million have you made?'

The question surprised him. 'Enough to buy the whole Gerards Group,' he admitted proudly.

'What?' she asked, her eyes narrowing, a deep, incredulous frown dragging her fine brows together. 'I knew you had ambition but I never imagined that you'd do this well—so quickly.' Gerards was a department store *par excellence*. 'Where are you living these days?'

'I have an apartment right here in the City where I spend most of the week, but my house is in Sussex.'

'Did you know I lived here?'

She looked appalled at the very thought and his lips twisted bitterly. 'Not at all. I was checking that everything was running smoothly when I overheard this little girl asking Santa Claus for a daddy. It was such an unusual request that I watched as she ran back to her mother. You can imagine my astonishment when I saw that it was you.'

'And so you put your spies on the job and found out where I lived, is that it?' she demanded, her grey eyes bright now with accusation.

'Wouldn't you have done the same if you'd found out that you had a three-year-old daughter whom you knew nothing about?' he countered harshly. 'I find it hard to believe that you've done this to me.'

Megan shrugged, as if she couldn't care less what he thought.

'I think,' he said, 'you'd better get dressed and start packing.'

'Not on your life,' she retorted. He thought she meant that she wasn't going to come at all until she added, 'There's still a whole week before Christmas. And I have to work for a living. I don't finish until Thursday.'

Beginning to fear that he was losing the battle, Luigi snapped his dark eyes and shot her a condemning glance. 'You won't need to work when you're back with me. Give it up.'

She looked beautifully indignant. 'I beg your pardon?'

'I do not want my wife working, it's as simple as that. And may I ask where you leave Charlotte while you're doing whatever it is you do? I hope she's safe.'

'Of course she's safe,' snapped Megan. 'We have a crèche; I can be with her at a second's notice. And I have to work, otherwise how would I keep myself?'

'You won't need to; you're going to live with me,' he repeated impatiently. 'It's your rightful place.' Now that he'd found out he had a daughter he most definitely wasn't going to allow her to escape again.

Megan sucked in a harsh breath. 'You can't tell me what to do. I'm not one of your minions, Luigi; you'd best remember that. Charlotte and I will come to you on Friday, not a day before. And as soon as Christmas is over we're back here.'

He decided not to make an issue of it in front of Charlotte, but he wasn't happy with the situation and he intended to tell Megan so at the very first opportunity. 'I'll send a car for you,' he announced stiffly.

Megan's chin jerked. 'There's no need. Give me your address and we'll make our own way.' She held his gaze, her grey eyes, tinged with amethyst, were as cold and belligerent as his.

'Don't be ridiculous,' he snapped. 'My car will be here at ten. Make sure you're ready. And, Megan,' he added warningly, 'don't try to run away again.'

'Mummy, I like my new daddy. I wanted to go with him,' Charlotte said, pouting, when Luigi had gone.

Megan was peering through the window, watching as he climbed into a sleek black Mercedes. 'I know you did, sweetheart, but Mummy has to work, I can't take time off or I'll lose my job.'

'Will he come back again?'

'I don't think so.' In fact she prayed he wouldn't. 'But it won't be long before we go to his house.'

'Where does he live?'

'I don't know.'

'Why don't we live with him? Laura's daddy lives with them, and Katie's.'

Megan turned back into the room and gathered her daughter into her arms. 'Sometimes, sweetheart, Mummies and Daddies stop loving each other and they live in separate houses because if they didn't they'd always be arguing.'

'Did you used to argue with Daddy?'

'Not really.'

'So why don't you live together? I want you to. I want my daddy with me all the time.'

How could she explain to a three-year-old that her father was a workaholic and couldn't care less about his family? It wouldn't be the heaven Charlotte thought it would be. Fortunately Jenny phoned at that moment wanting to know if Megan was doing some washing and if so would she throw in her white jeans. By the time their conversation was finished Charlotte had thankfully forgotten her question.

But as far as Megan was concerned her whole day was spoilt. Usually Jenny and her boyfriend lounged about the house and she and Charlotte never had any time to themselves. She had been so looking forward to it. And now all she could think about was Luigi and the fact that they were going to spend Christmas with him.

She ought to have been strong; she should have said no, but how could she deny her daughter what she so obviously wanted? It would be purgatory, she was sure of that. And there was no way on this earth that he could persuade her to move in permanently.

The next four days were sheer hell. She finished her Christmas shopping, not even entertaining the idea of buying Luigi a gift. Why should she? She truly and deeply resented the fact that he was forcing them to spend the festive period with him.

It looked as though another move might be in the cards because she most definitely didn't want to live the rest of her life with a man who hadn't an ounce of love in the whole of his body. It wouldn't even be fair on her daughter to be thrust into such a situation.

Jenny and her fiancé were flying to Paris for Christmas, another reason why Megan had been looking forward to Christmas alone with her daughter, and on Christmas Eve morning it was chaos as they all got ready at once. Finally Jenny and Jake left but Megan had only a short period of breathing space before the car arrived.

She was expecting a polite but indifferent driver and was annoyed to discover that Luigi himself had come to pick them up. Charlotte had been looking through the window and she gave a hoot of delight, though when Megan let him into the house she became suddenly shy again.

'Are you ready?' he asked. He was wearing a suit this morning, an immaculate dark grey with a crisp white shirt and a patterned mustard tie. He was the epitome of the successful businessman, gorgeously handsome to boot, and Megan couldn't stave off a brief flash of the old feelings that had once filled her with such excitement. Had he taken time off work to fetch them? Would he be shooting straight back? It would be good if that were the case because then she and Charlotte could explore his house on their own.

She couldn't help being curious as to where he now lived. Had he sold the house in Derbyshire or did he still own that as well? He had always said how much he loved the Peak District with its beautiful countryside and interesting little villages.

'I'm as ready as I'll ever be,' she admitted.

'So you're still not happy about spending Christmas with me?' he asked, his eyes hard and enquiring on hers.

'No, I'm not.'

'Perhaps I should take Charlotte on her own? Leave you here to—'

'Not on your life!'

He gave a faint smile of satisfaction. Not the sort that reached his eyes and made them crinkle at the corners, not the sort that had once made her reach out to him and kiss him soundly. Nothing like that. It was a getting-his-own-way kind of smile.

'Good, then let's go. Are these your things?'

There wasn't much, two small suitcases. One with their clothes and one with the presents she had bought for her daughter, already wrapped and hidden away from her prying eyes. She saw him look at them doubtfully. 'We'll be coming back for the rest of your stuff after Christmas, I take it?'

'We won't be staying,' she answered evenly. 'Didn't I make myself clear?'

'Perfectly, but I thought you might have changed your mind.'

'I never will,' Megan muttered, keeping her tone low for Charlotte's sake. She didn't want her daughter to hear her sniping at her new-found daddy. But Luigi heard the determination in her tone and his mouth compressed grimly.

He picked up the two cases and headed out to the car. They looked ridiculously small in his hands and as he tossed them into the boot Megan wanted to cry out that she had changed her mind. She had the strongest feeling that if she went with Luigi now it would change her life for ever.

CHAPTER TWO

MEGAN gasped when she saw Luigi's house. They'd left the city behind and headed into the Sussex countryside. He had paused at a set of heavy iron security gates to press a remote control and then driven up a winding drive before coming to a halt in front of a mansion that was perched imposingly at the top of a hill. It was a huge grey stone building with massive Ionic columns forming the front portico, and generous wings flanking the main house on either side.

'*This* is where you live?' she asked incredulously. Charlotte was awestruck too, sitting on the edge of her seat and gazing at the building with wide blue eyes.

'Impressed?' he asked, a dark eyebrow rising expectantly.

'It's not what I imagined,' Megan admitted, but if he thought she was impressed enough to want to move back in with him he was wide of the mark. 'And a little bit grand for one man on his own, wouldn't you say? Unless of course you don't live here alone?'

Her thoughts immediately turned to his very beautiful PA. Was Serena still with him? Was she a permanent part of his life now? When she had first started working for Luigi he had almost constantly sung her praises. So much so that Megan had begun to get suspicious, especially when his long working hours went on late into the night. He had denied it, of course, but her fears had never gone away and it had been part of the reason she had left him.

'I'm alone,' he admitted, much to her relief, because if Serena had been here she would have insisted he take her straight back home. 'For the moment,' he added ominously, looking deeply into her troubled eyes.

Megan ignored it and as they approached the house one of the pair of carved oak doors opened and a dark-suited, white-haired man appeared.

'William, meet my wife, Megan,' said Luigi with a smile. 'And Charlotte, my daughter.'

The man inclined his head. 'Megan, Charlotte,' he acknowledged gravely. 'Shall I show them to their rooms, sir?'

'I'll do it,' said Luigi. 'Tell Cook we're here and we'd like tea in the drawing room.'

Megan was dumbstruck. This was a rags to riches tale in one giant leap. She'd always known he had excellent entrepreneurial skills, but for him to be able to buy Gerards, as well as a house like this in such a short space of time was beyond her comprehension. How had he done it?

And she couldn't help wondering what else he had in mind. A top ranking football club? A luxurious yacht? Exotic holiday homes? It seemed as though the world was his oyster these days. Perhaps he even had these things. But she wasn't disgruntled that she'd missed out because she knew that he would have worked all the hours God gave to get where he was, and that wasn't the sort of lifestyle she wanted.

She and Charlotte were content in their little house, there was always a sense of satisfaction when she paid her bills and cooked and cleaned and provided a happy, carefree environment for her daughter. She wouldn't like to live here, not permanently. It wasn't a home; it was a showpiece.

There wasn't a speck of dust anywhere in the enormous entrance hall, or the shallow, wide staircase they were now ascending. Nothing was out of place. Urns of flowers spilled their heady perfume into the air, while marble statues stood in alcoves and paintings by old masters adorned the walls.

They followed Luigi through long corridors, finally coming to a halt at a suite of rooms, which she presumed to be in one of the wings. He pushed the door open and Megan walked into a blue carpeted room with a four-poster bed draped in matching blue and two armchairs near the window upholstered in cream damask. The curtains at the tall windows were in a cream and blue fabric. It was all very elegant but not her style and Megan felt a faint shudder run through her.

Luigi appeared to be waiting for her to say something, but when she didn't he opened an adjoining door, revealing a further bedroom filled with every imaginable toy possible. Charlotte's eyes widened and she ran inside. 'Are these for me?' she asked in wonderment.

'It's your room,' he told her, 'for as long as you want it.'

'How dare you do this to her,' hissed Megan accusingly as soon as Charlotte had disappeared inside. 'It's nothing short of blackmail. I've not changed my mind. When Christmas is over we're out of here.'

Luigi's lips curved upwards in a knowing smile. 'We'll see about that.'

Meaning over his dead body. Well, that was what she'd do, kill him if necessary. Actually she wouldn't do anything so drastic, but there had to be a way to make him change his mind.

'I'm serious, Luigi,' she told him coldly.

'And I'm serious about you moving back in with me. There's nothing to stop you.'

'Except that I don't love you any more.'

His eyes narrowed suspiciously. 'Is there someone else?'

'There could be.' Why should she tell him that there'd been no one since the day she'd walked out on him? He didn't deserve to know anything.

'Tell me, is there?' he demanded angrily, and he took her by the shoulders and almost shook her. 'Because if there is,' he warned, 'I'm taking Charlotte from you. I won't allow another man to bring up my child.'

Megan was shocked by the ferocity of his tone. 'You're in no position to do anything, so take your hands off me. What I do with my private life is no longer any concern of yours. Charlotte is being well looked after and that's all that need concern you.'

He let out a whoosh of angry air. 'Charlotte needs her father, her biological father. If you're not happy with that then get out. But Charlotte stays.'

Megan couldn't believe he was saying this. A flash of red fury filled her eyes and she lashed out with both fists, raining them on his chest, battering him until she ran out of energy. In response he wrapped his strong arms about her and held her close.

Amazingly Megan felt a stirring of her senses. Lord, this was the last thing she wanted. It had to be anger, a turbulent rage flooding every nerve and tissue. It couldn't be anything else. Could it?

She wrenched away and glared furiously. 'You're a swine, Luigi Costanzo. I can't believe I let myself be bullied into coming here.'

'Bullied?' he challenged. 'Ask your daughter if she was bullied. She's been deprived, that's what. Why else would she ask for a daddy for Christmas? It's appalling what you've done to her, and I intend to make up for the missing years, have no fear about that.'

A cold chill stole through Megan's veins. 'Is that a threat?' she demanded, standing very straight and rigid and glaring at him through stony eyes.

'If you care to take it that way.'

'What exactly are you saying?'

'That even if you don't want to stay I'm keeping Charlotte.'

This was what she had feared, and the very thought filled her with a dread so deep that the air around her thickened until she found it difficult to breathe. She dragged in huge painful gulps of air. He was serious, and he had the clout to do it. And, unfortunately, it left her with no alternative but to move in with him herself.

But she wouldn't let him know yet that he had her over a barrel. She would fight him every inch of the way. Once Christmas was over, when he'd discovered how much of his time a young child demanded, he might change his mind. Megan felt sure that he had no real comprehension of what it was like to bring up a young, extremely active daughter.

'Bold words, Luigi.'

'I mean them.'

'And have you perhaps thought about Charlotte? She might not want to stay here. It's not exactly what I'd call a homely place.'

He frowned. 'You don't like it?'

Megan shrugged. 'It's imposing, I'll admit that. But it's a statement. It says, look at my lifestyle, look how wealthy I am. It doesn't say that you're happy or comfortable.'

'I don't have time to be comfortable.'

'Precisely. And that is what your daughter would require. Time. *Your* time! How would you give her that when you're busy making your millions?'

'It could be arranged.'

'Arranged,' sneered Megan. 'You make it sound like a business proposition. It wouldn't work, Luigi, and you know it. When Charlotte said she wanted a daddy she meant a full-time one, not someone who would try to fit her in when he could.'

Dark eyes flashed hotly in her direction but he was prevented from saying anything else by Charlotte running back into the room. 'Mummy, come and look what I've got.'

It was sheer madness on Luigi's part, decided Megan, as she studied the mounds of toys stacked in Charlotte's room. Did he think that going over the top like this would make up for the missing years? He really had no idea what a child needed. And the more she thought about his intention to claim Charlotte the angrier she became.

'Didn't you say something about tea?' she asked him sharply, wanting to get out of this room and the obscene number of gifts he had loaded on his daughter.

'Wouldn't you like to unpack first? Or shall I ask—'

'I'll do it,' she snapped, wondering whom he was going to suggest do the job for her. It sounded as though he had a whole army of servants at his beck and call. Was he really happy with this kind of lifestyle?

She backed out of the room and snapped open the locks on her case. It took less than two minutes to hang up their few clothes. The other suitcase with the presents in she left safely fastened. And when she presented herself in Charlotte's bedroom again he was still standing where she had left him. A real father would have got down on his knees and played with his daughter, but not Luigi. He was content to watch; he didn't know how to play. Lord, it made her so mad that he'd cocooned himself in a world where money was the prime factor.

They made their way back downstairs to the drawing room. Again it was carpeted in blue, with display cabinets filled with fine pieces of porcelain. There were two very uncomfortable looking, square-armed chairs and a matching sofa, and on a rosewood tea table in front of them was the tea he had ordered.

The china was delicate, the pot covered by a cosy, and tiny biscuits were arranged on a plate. Hardly the sort of refreshment one would offer a three-year-old, thought Megan, but there were three cups and three small plates, so it looked as though she was expected to join them.

Charlotte ate most of the biscuits but she refused the tea. 'Can I have Coke?' she asked politely.

Megan felt quite amused when Luigi was forced to confess that he didn't have any and Charlotte settled for milk instead.

'We could go shopping,' said Charlotte innocently. 'Me and Mummy always go when we run out of anything.'

'I have to go back to work in a minute,' confessed her father.

Typical, thought Megan. Nothing had changed. But actually it was a relief when he'd gone and she and Charlotte could explore the house together. Her daughter ran from room to room, visibly impressed by the size of the place, but it made Megan angry. Was this what success meant to him? Was he trying to buy happiness? If so he was failing dismally.

As far as she was concerned it was a loveless place

and he must rattle round in it. It wasn't a home and she couldn't imagine Charlotte being happy here either. And what annoyed her even more, there wasn't a single Christmas decoration in sight. Why the hell had he invited them for Christmas if he wasn't going to celebrate it?

Megan didn't expect Luigi home for several hours and was surprised when he turned up in the middle of the afternoon with a huge Christmas tree tied on top of his car. Charlotte whooped with delight and all three of them spent the next couple of hours adorning it with the garlands and baubles and strings of flashing lights that he had also brought home.

It reminded Megan of the first Christmas they'd spent together as a married couple. She'd been deliriously happy. They had a home of their own by then and Luigi had walked in on Christmas Eve with a tree, much as he had now. It had taken a long time to dress it because each time she stretched up to hang a bauble he had slid his arms around her and kissed her.

They had called it their loving tree, but as each consecutive Christmas came he worked harder and harder, often not coming home until late on Christmas Eve, and by then Megan had dressed their tree herself. And slowly the magic had gone out of it.

'Look, Mummy, look.' Charlotte was high on her father's shoulders and had just placed the fairy on top of the tree. 'Isn't it beautiful?'

'It's lovely, sweetheart.'

'When's Santa coming?'

'Tonight, when you're in bed.'

'Can I go to bed now?' she asked excitedly.

'No, darling, it's too early.'

'Will he bring my presents here?'

'Of course he will.'

'How will he know I'm here, though?'

'Because he's magic. He knows where all little girls and boys are,' she answered.

Luigi lifted his daughter down and as he did so his eyes met Megan's, and whether it was the magic of the occasion or because she'd been thinking about their first Christmas together, Megan wasn't sure, but she felt a volt of electricity arc through her. She turned swiftly away. It was a warning to be careful. She didn't want to get involved with Luigi again, not at any price. Not unless he changed his lifestyle, and she couldn't see that happening in a hundred years.

It made her increasingly aware how dangerous it had been to come here. She ought to have stood her ground even if it had meant disappointing her daughter. Not that Luigi would have let her. He'd been fully determined to have his daughter for Christmas, with or without her mother.

In fact it might have been safer to let Charlotte come on her own. No! She immediately negated that thought. She would have lost her. Luigi was adamant that he wanted his daughter—permanently. And she was equally as resolute that he would not.

Luigi had felt a warm surge of pleasure as he held his daughter aloft. It was unlike any feeling he'd ever experienced. This was his child, his flesh and blood, something he had created. She was nothing short of a miracle. And he knew that he never wanted to let her go—unlike his handsome Italian father and fun-loving English mother who had never really wanted him, who preferred to go out partying instead of looking after their son.

When he was eight he'd been taken from them and

fostered out. Even then he'd been tossed from one family to another because he'd proved to be too much of a handful. He was full of anger and resentment over the treatment he'd received and several times he'd run away, never settling, never knowing what it was like to be truly loved.

It had made him into the tough person he was today. It had made him decide that he was going to make something of his life. He was quick to learn and very intelligent and at sixteen he had left school and started his first job with an IT firm. In fact he'd had a few little money-earners going long before then.

He'd helped school-friends with their homework and charged them. He had good computer skills and published a teenage magazine that was purchased by dozens of his friends both in school and out. He'd bought and sold all sorts of stuff, anything that would make him a profit. By the time he'd left school he'd amassed almost a thousand pounds. But he'd got his eyes set on a million before he was thirty, and he'd succeeded beyond his wildest dreams. He didn't even know what he was worth these days.

Money gave him security, something he'd never had, and he was hurt that Megan didn't like his house. To him it was the pinnacle of all that he'd worked for.

Charlotte was speaking now. 'Do you think, Mummy, that 'cos I asked Santa for a daddy and he's given me one, he won't leave me anything else?'

'Of course he will, sweetheart,' answered Megan, gathering the child into her arms and giving her a great big hug.

Luigi felt an unbelievable sadness. He'd never experienced a mother's arms around him like that. All he'd ever been to his mother was a nuisance, someone to be fed and clothed and told to keep out of the way, often left in the house for long periods alone.

'I expect he'll leave you lots,' he said to his daughter now, and was hurt when Megan gave him a damning look. What did she expect, that he wouldn't give his daughter anything? That he'd given her enough with the few things he'd put into her room? They were nothing, just a few toys to make her feel at home. Wait until tomorrow, she would be the happiest girl alive.

And Megan too; he had no intention of leaving her out, even though she was making it very clear that she wasn't pleased to see him. All that would change, he felt certain, when she realised how much better it would be for Charlotte to have a father as well as a mother.

He couldn't even begin to understand why Megan had kept their daughter a secret. If he hadn't spotted her in Gerards he might never have known. Charlotte would have grown up and had children, *his* grandchildren, and he would have been none the wiser.

The very thought sent a spurt of anger through him and he knew he had to get to the bottom of it. Was Megan being truthful when she said that she'd left him because of the long hours he worked? Or had there been another man involved? Was there still someone else? The one he had seen coming and going from her house, for instance?

Luigi's lips compressed at the thought that there might be some other man in her life. *And in his daughter's life!* This man could be the reason why Megan had been so adamant about wanting to spend as little time with him as possible. He needed to speak to her about it, about *him*, and soon.

The opportunity presented itself as soon as Charlotte had been bathed and put to bed. He'd stood and watched, marvelling at the bond between mother and daughter. It was something he wanted, something he'd missed out on, and he vowed that whatever it took, however much he had to bribe or force, Megan and Charlotte would become a part of his life—for ever!

At least they were still married, that should make things easier. He wondered why Megan had never got around to divorcing him. On his part it was because he'd never met anyone else he wanted to marry—though there'd been plenty of girls who wanted to marry him. But Megan, what was her story? Did she love the man she shared the house with? What sort of a guy was he that he was content to live with a woman who could never be his in the eyes of the law?

'Asleep at last,' said Megan as she left Charlotte's bedroom and discovered Luigi still lurking. 'She's so excited. Sleeping in a strange house and wondering what Santa's going to bring her is a lot for a little girl.'

'And will it be a lot for her mother, sleeping in a strange house? A house she doesn't particularly like?' he asked, unable to keep the bitterness out of his voice. It had disappointed him that she hadn't been as enthralled as he was. He had expected her to be impressed by how well he'd done. In fact he had hoped that it might prove a deciding factor in bringing them back together.

'I don't expect I'll sleep very much,' she admitted.

'Are you excited about Christmas too?'

'Not on your life,' she retorted. 'I wish I was anywhere but here.'

Luigi felt as though she'd kicked him in the stomach, although, he supposed reluctantly, it had been a big step for Megan to take. She had been honest about why she'd run away and he'd virtually forced her here. Not that he regretted it.

They would both grow to love it, he felt sure. All they needed was time. At least Megan did. Charlotte seemed happy enough, though he wasn't sure whether she'd be so content if her mother didn't stay. In fact he knew she wouldn't. Which made it even more imperative that he persuade Megan to move in with him permanently.

He would need to treat her with kid gloves, which might be difficult because he wasn't used to holding back. And he'd need to show her what she and Charlotte would be missing if she went back to their cramped little house. She'd made it very homely but, given the choice between there and here, he couldn't see there was a choice. This house would win hands down. And he would win too; he would make sure of that.

Couldn't Megan see that Charlotte would be far better off? Not only because of the space in the house, but the grounds as well. There was a copse, a tennis court, a swimming pool, a lake. It was a child's dream. There were even stables, though he had no horses yet. But if Charlotte wanted a pony then it would be hers for the asking.

'It's too early for you to judge whether you're going to be happy here,' he said to Megan now. 'When—'

'It's not altogether the house,' she retorted sharply, 'even though I think it's too pretentious. It's you! You're obsessed with money. You've always been the same. You think you can buy happiness. Well, let me tell you, Mr Rich Guy, you can be happy living in the tiniest hovel, so long as you're with the right person.'

'And you've found the right person?' He couldn't avoid the hard edge to his voice. He wanted to kill the guy, whoever he was. This was his wife.

'I was talking generally.'

She flashed her grey eyes at him and he thought how beautiful she was, still flushed from bathing Charlotte, her hair in slight disarray. His groin stirred and he wanted to pull her into his arms and kiss her—thoroughly. He wanted to prove to her that their love had never gone away; it had simply got lost. 'But there is someone else? I know because you didn't refute it earlier. In fact I've seen him.'

Megan's head jerked, her eyes widened. 'You have?'

'Come and sit down,' he said. 'We need to talk.' He led her downstairs into a cosy little room with panelled walls and a log fire. Red velvet curtains were drawn against the cold winter day and table lamps cast a warm glow. He saw Megan looking around appreciatively. There were a few pieces of antique furniture that he had chosen himself and actually the room was overcrowded, but he quite liked it that way.

'This is my den,' he told her. 'It's—'

'The smallest room in the house,' she finished for him. 'Proving that you don't need a mansion. Big rooms are too impersonal; you can't relax. It's like living in a National Trust property that's open to the public.' She perched herself on the edge of an easy chair.

'So you're saying small is cosy?' He had hoped she would flop down and relax. It looked as though he still had a long way to go. He dropped into the chair opposite so that he could study her to his heart's content, and stretched out his long legs.

'Absolutely.'

'That's why you're happy in your own home?'

'Yes.'

'It's not because you can't afford anything bigger?' Lord, she was more beautiful than ever. What a fool he'd been not to continue his search. He would have promised her the earth if she'd come back to him. Instead he had given up and got on with what really interested him. And it was only now that he realised his mistake.

Megan sucked in a disapproving breath. 'There you go again, bringing money into it. I tell you, money doesn't interest me.'

'You're one on your own, Megan, do you know that?

'Because every other woman you've met has been more interested in your bank balance than you?' she asked sharply.

Her words struck home. It was quite true. He'd never appreciated before he had acquired his wealth how mercenary some girls could be. In one way it pleased him that Megan was different; on the other hand he felt irritated because he wanted her to be excited by what he had achieved.

'It would make life a lot easier for you if you moved in here,' he said, trying his hardest to sound gentle. In reality he wanted to shake her. He had no idea that she could be so stubborn. This was a side of her that had never surfaced in the early years of their marriage.

'No, it wouldn't,' she retorted.

He could see by the glint in her eyes that she meant living with him would be abhorrent, and it hurt. 'You'd never need to work again. That must be every woman's dream?'

'I admit it would be nice not to have to leave Charlotte. On the other hand, she enjoys playing with other children. And soon she'll be at school.'

'Will that make any difference?' he asked tersely. 'What if she becomes ill? Can you take time off work? Would your boss understand? Admit it, Megan, you'd be far better off giving up your job and moving in here.

Unless, of course, it's the boyfriend! Is he the one holding you back?'

'So you have been spying on me?' Megan spat the words loudly and, without giving him time to answer, added, 'How low is that?'

He hadn't considered it low. He'd wanted to find out where she lived, what sort of a lifestyle she had. He wanted to make sure she didn't move again. Was that wrong? 'I must confess that when I discovered your address I did sometimes keep watch. Not that it was my intention to spy, Megan. I was hoping to catch sight of you so that we could talk. I would have preferred it that way rather than knocking on your door and giving you the surprise of your life.'

'Fright of my life, more like,' she riposted.

'So, tell me about your boyfriend. He's clearly not asked you to marry him, otherwise you'd have sought a divorce. What does he mean to you? How long have you known him? Does he have a good job?'

'I think,' said Megan tightly, 'that it's none of your business.'

'You're my wife. It's every bit my business,' he challenged.

'In name only,' she retorted. 'Our marriage was over a long time ago.'

'Then why haven't you applied for a divorce?' he asked. This surely had to be in his favour.

Megan shrugged. 'I never got round to it.'

'Because you were secretly hoping that one day we'd get back together?' he suggested.

'You know that's not true,' Megan thrust. 'And, while we're on the subject, let me make it quite clear that I shall never come back to you. Never! So we might as well start divorce proceedings as soon as Christmas is over.'

Stunned by Megan's statement, Luigi sat forward in his chair and looked at her in consternation. 'Divorce? Now! When we've found each other again? When we have Charlotte to consider?' Despite the warmth from the blazing logs a chill radiated out from his heart until his whole body felt as though it were packed in ice. This was the last thing he'd expected—or wanted! She couldn't have given him a crueller Christmas gift.

'I'm perfectly serious,' she retorted. 'We're not compatible, you and I. We each want different things in life.'

'I want Charlotte.' He was adamant on that point. Whether Megan came with her was her problem, but he wasn't letting the child go. She meant more to him than any amount of money. The thought surprised him because previously the state of his bank balance was the most important thing in his life.

'Charlotte doesn't come without me,' she announced. 'And as I have no—'

'You're not being given a choice,' he warned her testily. 'I've got you here now and you're staying whether you like it or not.'

CHAPTER THREE

'IS THAT a warning?' asked Megan, the air constricting in her throat as it closed tightly over Luigi's words. He sounded deadly serious.

'It's not a warning, it's a fact,' he announced. 'And if you dare to defy me I'll have every court in the country on your back. You've denied me my daughter all these years; you can no longer be allowed to get away with it.'

Panic struck in Megan's heart. Could he do it? Had he the right? Surely the courts would find in her favour? Could she afford to take the risk? Was she stuck in this situation? She felt the colour drain from her face and sank back into the chair. 'I can't believe you'd do this to me.'

'You can't? After what you've done to me?' he countered harshly. 'I think you've got away with too much for too long.'

'What if Charlotte doesn't want to stay here? What if Charlotte doesn't like you after she's seen what a bad father you'll be to her? Don't forget I know how much time you spend away from home. She won't like it, she won't be very forgiving.'

'Then I'll have to spend more time here, won't I?' Dark brown eyes seared steadily into hers. He had beautiful eyes; she had always thought that. The whites were very clear and if you looked closely there was a black line around the brown iris. It gave them extra definition, and as he looked at her now she felt that he was seeing right into her mind.

And he was seeing the doubt, the unhappiness, the fear. And he was waiting for her to speak. 'You know you won't,' she flared. 'Maybe for a while, but you'd soon fall back into your old ways. It's a way of life. You wouldn't know what it was like to spend every evening and weekend with your wife and child. You'd be itching to get back to work, to check that things were running smoothly in your absence. You don't know how to delegate. As a matter of fact you don't even know how to play with Charlotte.'

Her rebuke hit home. A dark red flush swept across his face and the air suddenly went chill. 'If I'd been given a chance then maybe I would,' he shot back. 'You're the one who's being unfair here, not me.'

'I like that,' she tossed fiercely. 'You've more or less said that you're going to hold us prisoner—yet I'm the one who's being unfair? I don't think so.'

Luigi jumped to his feet. 'I'm sure that by the time Christmas is over you'll have had the chance to see for yourself that it makes sense. It's time for us to eat. Come, we mustn't keep Cook waiting.'

'I'm not hungry,' protested Megan.

'You will be when you see what culinary delights Edwina has managed to conjure up. She's a marvel in the kitchen.'

Megan reluctantly allowed herself to follow him into the smallest of the two dining rooms where a walnut table had been set for the two of them. It looked very festive with a holly table decoration and red napkins tucked into gold rings, but Megan guessed that there would have been none of these seasonal trimmings if he were eating alone. He probably wouldn't even have been home yet. He would dine out, or make do with a sandwich at around midnight. That used to be his normal practice.

William, the butler, served their meal and Megan found with surprise that she was hungry, very much so.

They started with mango and lobster on a green salad, a combination Megan had never had before, and she found it truly delicious and complementary. 'Is your cook always this inventive?' she asked between mouthfuls.

'Always,' he agreed. 'She keeps urging me to have dinner parties so that she can show off her prowess.'

'And do you?' Megan dabbed a drop of French dressing from her lip with her napkin, an action Luigi watched closely. His eyes on her mouth reminded her of the time on their honeymoon when they'd shared a bowl of strawberries. He had dipped each one in cream and then held it between his teeth for her to take half. And any cream that was left on her lips he had licked off. It had been a truly sexually exciting experience and she dashed the memory away quickly. It was dangerous allowing such thoughts. Besides, such sensual activities had stopped once they were home and work consumed his every waking hour.

The whole meal was a gastronomic experience, making Megan wonder what Christmas Day itself would be like. Her own cooking skills were limited to plain cooking. She ensured Charlotte had a well-balanced diet, they had no takeaway meals or fast food and they ate plenty of fruit, but she wasn't into this type of cookery.

'You're enjoying your meal?' Luigi had hardly taken his eyes off Megan all the time they were eating.

'Very much so,' she said. 'You've found a treasure in Edwina.'

'You could eat her food all the time if you—'

'And I'd end up piling on weight. No, thank you. I prefer my own simple cooking.'

'Maybe I should give Edwina her marching orders?'

'Maybe you ought to get the message that we're not staying,' Megan retorted coolly.

Luigi's lips compressed and he said no more, but even when their meal was finished he wasn't ready to let her go. 'Where do you normally put Charlotte's presents?'

'I fill a stocking from Santa which I put by the fireplace, and a couple under the tree from me.'

'Then we'd better start,' he said.

Megan frowned. 'It won't take a minute; it's too soon. What if she wakes and comes down?'

'If she wakes we'll hear the monitor. I thought it a wise precaution in a house of this size. We don't want her getting lost and upset.'

We, thought Megan, as though he was already of the opinion that they were back together as husband and wife. But maybe it was a good idea to put the presents out because then she could go to bed early and escape him for a few hours. She really wasn't looking forward to Christmas Day, which was a shame because it was normally the highlight of their year.

It wasn't that easy to get away from him, though. After they'd placed their presents—and she was pleased to note that there was only one from Luigi for his daughter—he invited her to join him for a nightcap. Megan wasn't really in the mood but Luigi was insistent, and she knew he wouldn't let her go until she'd agreed.

She couldn't help wondering how things would have been if she hadn't run out on him. Would he be where he was today or would he have become a doting father and spent a lot more time at home? She would never know and, surprisingly, she felt a faint pang of regret that she'd never stopped to find out.

'Would you have ever told me?' he asked, his eyes steady on hers now as he sipped his Scotch.

'About Charlotte?' How had he known what she was thinking?

'Of course.'

'I don't know,' she answered honestly. 'Maybe one day, if Charlotte began asking about you. Not simply, Why haven't I got a daddy?'

'Then I can thank my lucky stars that I was in the right place at the right time. I could have waited a long, long time to meet my daughter.' And with a swift change of subject, 'You're more beautiful than ever, do you know that? Motherhood suits you.'

'Flattery will get you nowhere,' Megan assured him tartly.

His lips curved upwards into a gentle smile. 'It's not flattery for the sake of it, it's the truth.'

They were back in his den, sitting in companion armchairs, the lights turned low, the fire flickering in the grate. The whole house was centrally heated, and she'd never thought Luigi the type to like old-fashioned comforts, but even so it was very welcome. Maybe the fire was in honour of Christmas. There was one already laid in the drawing room fireplace where the tree had been set up. Tomorrow she could imagine it roaring up the chimney, adding to the magic of Christmas for Charlotte.

'Would you have gone to all this trouble if we hadn't been here?' asked Megan, preferring to steer the conversation back to safer grounds. 'I mean the Christmas tree and the log fires.'

'Truthfully?'

'Truthfully.'

'No,' he answered. 'What would have been the point? This is going to be the best Christmas ever for me—and for you too, I hope.'

'I'm merely here to make Charlotte happy.'

'You're making me happy.'

His voice went down an octave, seeming to vibrate through her bones, and Megan turned her head away, concentrating on her drink, taking large sips of the vodka and orange he had mixed for her. A big mistake; it went straight to her head. Much more of this and she wouldn't be in charge of her senses. 'I've never seen you as the slippers in front of the fire sort of guy.'

'So how do you see me?' he asked with a roguish growl, his eyes reflecting the glow of the embers.

Megan felt them warming her—or was it the fire? Or even the drink? Whichever, she was growing hotter by the second. 'As the tough businessman who's feet never hit the ground. What made you buy Gerards? I thought you were in the IT industry.'

'I still am, but I have my finger in lots of pies. I'll tell you about them some day,' he added dismissively, 'but for the moment I want to talk about you. Why didn't you tell me you were unhappy? Why did you walk out without saying a word?'

'Because I knew you'd stop me,' she retorted, her eyes condemning as she looked at him over the rim of her glass. Her almost empty glass, she realised. 'You'd probably have sworn that you'd change, but I knew differently. And I was right, wasn't I?'

'No one will ever know,' he answered sadly. 'It's hard to accept that I've missed the first three years of my daughter's life—it's something I shall never forgive you for,' he finished harshly as he tossed the last of his drink down his throat. 'Ever!'

Megan finished her drink also and put her glass firmly down on the table. 'I don't want to talk about this. It's late, I'm going to bed.'

As she stood, he too got up, and before she could stop him his arms came around her. 'But you're still my wife, the mother of my daughter, and I'd like a goodnight kiss.'

Megan struggled furiously but he refused to let her go. Instead his mouth came down on hers, one hand behind her head effectively cutting off her escape, the other against the small of her back. It was a long, punishing kiss and it sent resentment reeling through every inch of her body.

There was no escape. The kiss deepened, his arms tightened, and all too soon she felt herself beginning to respond. It was like a replay of when she had met him. She could remember the day very clearly. This handsome, dark-haired, Latin-looking young man had stopped to pick up a bag she'd dropped. Ironically, it had been a few weeks before Christmas and her arms had been full of purchases. When she'd looked into his eyes to thank him she'd been so taken with his good looks that she'd dropped another of her parcels.

'I think,' he said, with a smile that turned her legs to jelly, 'that I'd better help you to your car, or the bus, or wherever you're going. Home, in fact. You've got an extraordinary amount of packages.'

'Christmas presents,' she admitted shyly. 'And I'm catching the bus.'

'I think not,' he said with a laugh, 'not unless you want to lose the lot as you're jumping on or off. I'll run you home; my car's just around the corner.'

'But I don't know you. I—'

'I assure you you'll be perfectly safe. My name's

Luigi Costanzo, I live in Mickleover, near Derby.' He flashed his business card in front of her and then tucked it into one of her bags. And Megan knew instinctively that she could trust him. He had an open, honest face, and he had almost to pass her house to get to his own. It would be silly to refuse.

But still she hesitated.

'I know how you must feel,' he said. 'A complete stranger and all that. The offer's there if you want it, but I'll still walk you to the bus stop if that's what you'd prefer.'

Megan was eighteen and he was much older than the boys she usually hung around with. Mid twenties, she imagined, maybe even older than that. She was enchanted by him. And she found herself agreeing to let him give her a lift.

His car was smart, black and sleek. Whatever his business he was clearly doing well for himself. And he drove her straight to her door, even helping her with her parcels. Her parents' eyes goggled when they saw her with a strange, handsome man, but they were clearly impressed.

Before he left, Luigi asked whether he could see her again. Megan couldn't refuse. By this time she was completely bowled over. Her insides felt as though they had turned to mush—*as they were doing at this moment!*

His kiss was awakening all she'd ever felt, and Megan resented it, struggling even more furiously to free herself, until in the end he let her go. There was a twisted smile on his lips. 'Something tells me that old emotions were stirred there. You're not as immune to me as you'd have me believe.'

'Wishful thinking,' she retorted, her lovely grey eyes glaring icily.

'Mmm, we'll see.'

Megan felt a tightening in her stomach. She didn't like the way he said that. He was going to try again, she knew, and it was the last thing she wanted. Damn! How could she respond to him after all this time? She didn't want to be involved with him again, not ever. He wasn't good for Charlotte. A workaholic father was good for no child. She needed two full-time parents.

'Goodnight!' she tossed stormily and marched out.

She felt Luigi's eyes on her but he didn't call her back, and she ran up the stairs as quickly as she could. It seemed to take an age to reach her room, but finally she found it, and closing the door quietly behind her, she stood a moment reflecting on her reaction to his kiss.

It had shocked her beyond measure. She'd thought herself over him. For her feelings to rise so quickly after all these years was scary to say the least.

Perhaps, she tried to convince herself, it wasn't desire—she refused to use the word love, that had flown out of the window a long time ago—it was pure animal passion. After all, she hadn't been with any other man since Luigi; it was natural she would feel something if he—or any man for that matter—kissed her. She was a young, passionate woman with all the feelings that went with it.

Slowly now she walked across the room to check on Charlotte. Her daughter was fast asleep, a faint smile on her lips as though she was dreaming of something nice. Christmas, probably. Or her father. Megan grimaced. Hopefully not! She didn't want Charlotte getting too attached to him because she had no intention of staying, despite Luigi's threats.

Threats! Was that what he was doing, threatening her? It didn't sound nice, and basically Luigi was a nice guy.

She'd found that out on the day they met. He had been polite and considerate to her parents and they had immediately taken to him, and in the ensuing days a romance had begun that ended in them getting married six months later. In fact her parents had pushed her into it, declaring she would never find anyone else as good.

She had been the envy of all her friends. Nothing had prepared her for the fact that he put work before everything else. At first she'd been proud of how well he was doing. Before he met her he had written a software program that had taken the computer world by storm, and he had become increasingly busy working on further projects. Sometimes she felt that he thought more of his work than he did her. But then he would come home and their lovemaking reached heights unimaginable. He was every woman's dream in bed, making up a hundredfold for all the time they spent apart.

At least that was what she'd thought in the beginning, but as the months and years had rolled by and he'd never showed her any real affection, she had begun to suspect that their acts of love were merely to satisfy his own basic needs, either that or to ease his conscience because he was bedding Serena. The only time he'd ever declared that he loved her was when he asked her to marry him; even then he hadn't sounded comfortable saying it.

She had become increasingly dissatisfied but if she complained about the way he was never at home he would say that he was doing it all for her, making her feel that she was being selfish. It wasn't until she had found herself pregnant that Megan had known she couldn't bring up her child in a household where there was no love or trust.

Bending over her daughter, she smoothed her soft blonde hair back from her face and kissed her. Charlotte stirred but didn't wake. 'Goodnight, my sweet child,' she whispered. 'Happy dreams always.' And that would only happen if they kept well away from Luigi. Megan wanted Charlotte to grow up in an openly loving family. She was always telling her daughter how much she loved her; Luigi would never do that.

Admittedly, Charlotte was excited now, but it wouldn't last. She would soon find out that her father wasn't the sort of parent she expected and wanted. Not in a million years could Megan imagine Luigi picking up his daughter and swinging her around and telling her how much he loved her. It simply wasn't in him.

It could be that she was doing him an injustice, because after all he'd never been shown any love as a child. But she'd shown him love, so why hadn't he returned it? It wasn't hard to let your feelings flood to the surface. At least she didn't find it so. Luigi obviously did. He kept them all tied up in a knot that he didn't know how to undo. He didn't even try. And she had a sneaky feeling that he might try to buy himself into Charlotte's affections.

Her fears proved true when they went downstairs on Christmas morning and she saw a huge pile of presents almost dwarfing the tree. There was every size and shape imaginable and she was furious with Luigi. He stood there waiting for them, looking extremely pleased with himself.

Naturally Charlotte didn't even look at the stocking Megan had so carefully filled, she ran straight across to the tree. 'Are these all for me, Daddy? Has Santa brought me all these?' Her blue eyes were wide with wonder and excitement.

'Your ones from Santa are over here, sweetheart,' said Megan, taking her hand and drawing her across the room. 'He couldn't carry all those in his sleigh, could he?'

'So where did they come from?'

'From me,' said Luigi, a broad smile on his face. 'Some for you and some for your mother.'

Megan frowned her displeasure. What the hell was he trying to prove?

'But I think your mother wants you to open Santa's presents first.'

He had no idea, thought Megan. Every child in the country this morning was opening their gifts from Santa Claus. Didn't he know that? Not because their mothers wanted it; because it was tradition.

Megan dropped down to her knees and watched as Charlotte tore at the wrappings, her tiny hands trembling. 'Oh, look, Mummy, look,' she kept exclaiming.

'What have you got?' asked Luigi, moving to stand beside her, but not getting down to his daughter's level as Megan had done.

'A new dolly, Daddy, and some clothes for her, and—'

But Megan gained the impression that he wasn't really interested. He wanted Charlotte to open the gifts from him; he wanted to see her pleasure and receive her thanks. He wanted to feel good.

And it wasn't long before Charlotte ran across to the tree. And this time Luigi squatted beside her, enjoying the pleasure on her face as she opened her presents. 'Thank you, Daddy,' she said time and time again, hugging him spontaneously, her shyness forgotten for the moment.

He looked uncomfortable at receiving so much affection, thought Megan, and then wondered whether she was being mean. This was Christmas, after all. A time for giving. She oughtn't to criticise.

She was annoyed, though, at the number of presents he'd bought Charlotte. She was a well-adjusted child, aware that there were some things she wanted but couldn't have, so how dare he undermine her values like this?

Then it was her turn. A whole heap of parcels were for her, and when she begrudgingly opened them, trying her hardest to show pleasure when in truth she felt like throwing them back in his face, she couldn't believe how much he'd spent on her. It looked as though he'd bought up the whole ladies' department at Gerards. Jewellery, underwear, handbags, evening dresses, day dresses, nightdresses, and amazingly all in her size. And the whole of the toy department for Charlotte!

'I haven't bought you anything,' she announced, rather more tartly than she should have done.

'That's all right,' he said pleasantly. 'The fact that you're here is good enough for me.' He gave her a meaningful look over Charlotte's head.

Megan was less than impressed and as soon as she could have a private word with him she went in with all guns blazing. 'You had no right buying Charlotte all those things,' she flared. 'Nor me, as a matter of fact. Have you any idea what you're doing to a young, impressionable child? Are you trying to buy her love, for heaven's sake? You do know she'll come to expect this all the time?'

'So?' he enquired, both hands spread wide, palms facing upwards, a big grin on his face.

'It's not good for her.'

'I have a lot to make up.'

'Nonsense. One gift would have done; she'd have been happy.'

'But I can afford it.'

'I don't care. It's wrong, Luigi. Very wrong! And, let me tell you this, when we leave here she's not taking everything. You've gone over the top and I'm angrier than you can possibly imagine.'

'And beautiful with it. Do you know I never saw you really angry when we were living together. I never saw your eyes flash so dramatically, or your skin colour so beautifully.' His voice lowered conspiratorially. 'It makes me want to take you to bed.'

'Something that is never likely to happen,' she spat.

'Wouldn't you like a little sister or brother for Charlotte?' he asked gruffly.

'Not by you,' she charged.

His face flushed a dull, ugly red. 'And not by that swine you're living with either. Tell him to keep his hands off. You belong to me.'

'Since you never came looking for me I don't see how you can make that claim,' she retorted. 'It proves you weren't interested. I'm even more sure now that it's time to start divorce proceedings.'

CHAPTER FOUR

'NOT on your life,' rasped Luigi. She hadn't a cat in hell's chance of him giving her a divorce.

Megan flashed her magnificent eyes. 'You're nothing more than a materialistic, selfish, uncaring brute. You haven't a loving bone in your body and I want rid of you.'

'Well, think again, sweet wife of mine,' he answered grimly. 'Neither of us is going anywhere. Your place is with me.'

'And wasn't your place with me for the three years I spent with you?' she tossed back scornfully.

For goodness' sake! Why couldn't Megan understand that he had done it solely for her benefit? And he wanted her back—*now*. He wanted Charlotte because she was his daughter, but he wanted his wife because he needed her in bed beside him each night.

How he had missed making love to her. No one else had managed to arouse him as deeply as Megan. Right from the day he'd met her he had desired her, in fact they had constantly devoured each other with their passion. He'd been destroyed when she walked out.

Never for one moment had he thought that it was because of the hours he spent working. He'd provided for her every need, she'd wanted for nothing, and they'd made love with amazing frequency no matter how tired he felt, so had that really been the reason? Or was she making excuses?

Had she fallen for someone else? That guy she was

now living with, for instance. Only one thing pleased him about that relationship; Charlotte didn't call him Daddy. Otherwise she wouldn't have wished for a daddy for Christmas.

And what did her boyfriend think about Megan coming here for the holiday period? Was he angry or understanding? He had to be the reason Megan wanted to keep her visit as short as possible. Maybe he ought to talk to him. Tell him he was wasting his time, that Megan belonged to him and he was taking her back.

'Things are different,' he told her now, trying to keep his voice low. 'I don't need to work so hard. I have people who do it for me. Believe me, Megan, you can come up with all the excuses in the world but none of them hold any water.'

'How do I know you're not saying this simply to get me to change my mind?' she demanded fiercely.

Lord, how beautiful she looked on this Christmas morning in her button-through red dress, which fitted her narrow waist and flared elegantly over her hips and thighs. She had gorgeous legs, long and slender, and he couldn't help remembering the times she had wrapped them around him as they made love. He could even imagine the feel of her against him now and he made a half move towards her, his heart hammering against his ribcage.

But the glare in her lovely eyes stopped him. 'We shouldn't be having this conversation,' he said. 'I want this day to be as perfect for you and Charlotte as possible.'

'Some hope of that,' she hissed beneath her breath but he ignored it and turned to his daughter instead, who was skipping from one present to another, unsure of which to play with first. It filled his heart with joy and pride to watch her, and he knew in that moment that he was never going to let her go. He would fight Megan tooth and nail if necessary.

All of a sudden Megan glanced through the window. 'Charlotte, look,' she said urgently, 'it's snowing.'

They all three went to watch as big white flakes settled on the lawn and then melted again just as quickly.

'Can we go outside?' asked Charlotte excitedly.

'Of course, sweetheart,' answered Megan, thankful for the distraction. But Luigi came too and he and Charlotte tried to catch the falling flakes. He was a little awkward at first, playing with her, but after a while he began to relax and ran around the garden while she chased him.

But all too soon the snow stopped, there was not even enough to cover the ground, and they all trooped back indoors. By this time they were thoroughly late for breakfast and Cook tutted as she served their meal. 'I bet it's ruined,' she complained.

'It's not your fault, Edwina,' said Luigi, trying to placate her. 'We didn't want to miss the snow, did we, Charlotte?'

Charlotte, suddenly shy again, shook her head, staring with wide blue eyes at the plump motherly woman who was standing arms akimbo watching to see whether their bacon and eggs were edible.

Megan took a mouthful and smiled. 'It's perfect. Thank you very much, and I'm sorry we held you up.'

The woman suddenly beamed. 'That's all right, lass, it is Christmas after all.'

The whole day passed in a whirl of talking and eating and playing and Megan began to feel that it might not be so bad after all living with Luigi. He was undoubtedly making an effort. The question was, would it last?

It was not until Charlotte was in bed that Megan and Luigi were finally alone.

'Have you enjoyed your day?' she asked as she curled up on a chair in Luigi's den. 'Has Charlotte worn you out? Did you find it easy coping?'

'If you're asking whether I've changed my mind the answer's no,' he retorted sharply, his eyes narrowed on her face. 'I'm even more determined now. This is the ideal place for a child. She's had the time of her life, surely even you can see that?'

'She enjoys herself every day,' flashed Megan, not having expected such a sharp rejoinder. 'A palace or a cottage, it makes no difference. What wouldn't be good for Charlotte is you spoiling her. You've bought her far too many toys, and as for the computer, how old do you think she is, for goodness' sake?'

Luigi shrugged. 'I simply instructed my toy department to pack up whatever they thought suitable for a nearly four-year-old.'

'You did what?' exclaimed Megan disgustedly. 'You didn't even choose one thing yourself? How appalling is that? Did you issue the same instructions for my presents? Damn you, Luigi! You can take the whole lot back after the holiday. I don't need them and I don't want them.'

A muscle jerked in his jaw, telling her that she had hit a raw nerve, but she didn't care; it was true. What sort of a cop out was that?

'Don't be ridiculous,' he snorted. 'You're overreacting. How the hell am I supposed to know what a young child likes?'

'You could have made it your business to find out. Or would that have been too much trouble?' she demanded coldly. 'It seems to me that you've grown too big for your boots. It's easier to pay someone else to do your chores. I don't think I want to hear any more of this. I'm going to my room. I should have known that Christmas would turn out to be a disaster.'

But she hadn't even reached the door before Luigi was on his feet barring her exit. And when she tried to push her way past him he enclosed her in his strong arms. 'I refuse to spend the evening alone,' he told her tersely. 'You're not walking out on me.' And before she could even begin to struggle, before she could even guess his intentions, his mouth possessed hers.

It was Megan's undoing. It sent a whole storm of sensations spiralling through her and although she knew that she ought to push him away she did nothing, she actually revelled in the feelings he created. He always had been a fantastic lover and it took her no more than a few seconds to realise what she'd been missing. Lord, if this kept up she would be begging him to make love to her. What sort of a Christmas present would that be?

And, excitingly, it did keep up. She hadn't the will-power to stop him. Every vein and artery went on to red alert, responding and leaping out of control. She kept telling herself to fight him, to put an end to this joy, but how could she? Her body was starved. She hadn't realised it until this moment but it was now telling her that it wasn't natural to go so long without the attention of a man.

That the man should prove to be Luigi was ironic to say the least, but better the devil you know came the immediate thought, and Megan returned his kiss, parting her lips to allow him entry, moving her body against his, feeling the source of his own passion. He groaned deep within his throat and took advantage of the fact that she wasn't rejecting him.

Just this one kiss, decided Megan, then she would carry on up to her room. Easier said than done. That one kiss lasted for an infinite period of time. That one kiss turned into a full-scale sex alert.

'You're still the sexiest woman in the universe,' Luigi said in a hoarse passion-filled voice. 'I must have been crazy to let you go.'

Not half as crazy as she felt at this moment, decided Megan, her hands on the back of Luigi's head, her fingertips digging in, unconsciously revealing the fact that she didn't want this moment to stop.

Luigi's hands slid down to her bottom and pulled her firmly against him, his deep groans revealing the desire that raged in his tautly honed body. When she didn't object he swung her up into his arms and carried her over to the soft leather sofa.

Megan lay there and looked at him, her breathing unsteady, her grey eyes luminous and filled with a sexual hunger that she hadn't felt in years. Ought she to put a stop to it, or let nature and their animal hunger take its course? Would she live to regret it, or would she view this occasion as a fitting end to their tragic marriage? Maybe she could even use it as a form of revenge? Let Luigi see exactly what he was missing. Allow him this one last chance to make love to her and then leave him high and dry. She smiled at the thought.

'What's funny?' he asked as he sat on the edge of the sofa and stroked a gentle finger over her lips.

'Private thoughts; nothing you'd understand.' Or appreciate, she added silently, nibbling the end of his finger.

He drew in a swift breath. 'How I've missed you,' he murmured, his eyes darkening, his hand sliding possessively over her breast.

It hardened beneath his touch, her nipple leaping into ecstatic response, and Megan closed her eyes, her mind suddenly confused. This was a dangerous game. She ought to get out now while she still had the strength. But already it was too late. Luigi had popped the buttons on her dress and with a speed perhaps born of desperation he sucked first one and then the other nipple into his mouth right through the thin fabric of her bra.

Megan was lost. She had always loved him doing this to her. It created the most exquisite feelings, making her arch towards him, giving freely, wanting everything that he had to offer.

The sane part of her mind told her that she was making a mistake when he moved her from the sofa to the softly carpeted floor, when he stripped off his clothes with indecent haste and then began to undress her somewhat more leisurely. At least that was his intention but Megan couldn't wait. She tore off her dress, swiftly followed by her undies, and they fell on each other with a hunger created by the years they'd spent apart.

Luigi had always been a brilliant lover, she couldn't deny that, and nothing had changed. Although he was desperate he was still solicitous of her needs, making sure that she had no last minute regrets.

How could she when her body raged with desire so deep that it almost hurt? Their bodies moved together in a rhythm as ancient as time and he allowed her to reach her climax first, to revel in wave after wave of exquisite sensation, before he too gave up the fight and wrestled with his own delirious torture.

As the convulsive movements of his body slowed and finally came to a stop he turned to her with a smile. 'Just like old times, eh?'

Megan nodded. How could she deny it? Nevertheless

it wasn't going to happen again. She had succumbed to her bodily needs without consulting her head. A major mistake. Not that she regretted it; how could she regret such feverish passion? She had missed this part of their relationship without even realising it. Her body had become almost barren and now it was alive again.

'Do you still want to go up to your room?'

'No,' she whispered, her throat aching with the pleasure she'd just experienced.

And as they lay there in each other's arms Luigi reached for her again. This time there was no urgency; they were able to take their time rekindling all the delicious excitement that had once been theirs.

When Megan finally lay in her bed she felt as if she were floating on air. Her body had been taken over by forces beyond her control. There was no thought in her mind about escaping back to her own home; her place was here with Luigi.

Luigi, who was in bed beside her!

He'd wanted her to join him in his own bed but Megan had refused. 'What if Charlotte wakes and can't find me? She'll panic.'

'Then,' he'd announced in a deep, sexy growl, 'I'll share yours.' And there had been no hope of saying no to him.

He lay on one elbow now looking at her, a gentle finger exploring the contours of her breasts, his eyes, so dark with pleasure, stirring fresh emotions. Where they all came from Megan had no idea. She couldn't quench her thirst for him. Nor could he, for that matter.

'We have a lot of time to make up,' he murmured, honing in on her thoughts.

Megan smiled, her eyes softening and warming. 'And you propose doing it all at once?'

'I intend to try.'

'How do you suggest we cope with a spirited child tomorrow if we have no sleep?'

'Uh oh!' He slapped a hand to his head. 'I'd forgotten. I'd imagined spending the whole of Boxing Day in bed. Edwina bringing us up our meals while we did our best to catch up on the missing years.'

'Think you could manage?' she taunted, her eyes alight with wicked pleasure. She had never in her wildest dreams imagined that this was how the holiday would turn out. And the most amazing thing was that she didn't mind. She was actually enjoying it. She had shut out of her mind the fact that all too soon Luigi would be back at work and this honeymoon period, if she could call it that, would be over. She was taking every minute as it came and making the most of it. It was the wrong time of the month for her to conceive, so she wasn't even worrying about that.

Luigi couldn't believe his good fortune. He hadn't even had to work on Megan; she had fallen into his arms as naturally as if they had never parted. Elation filled his very soul and there was no doubt in his mind that she would now move in with him and they would become a proper family.

It would change his life. He was a father! He wanted to shout it from the rooftops. And what a gorgeous little girl she was. Megan had done a brilliant job bringing her up so far, and now he would be here to help. Long hours would be a thing of the past. Charlotte needed him. And he needed Megan!

Hungrily he reached for her again but she had fallen asleep. He smiled and with his arm across her body he too drifted into the world of the unconscious.

They were woken by Charlotte's highly excited voice. 'Mummy, wake up! It's snowing again. Daddy, it's snowing. Come and look.'

As they were both naked under the bedcovers they waited until Charlotte had turned to the window before Megan dived for her dressing gown and Luigi whipped a sheet off the bed and tucked it around his loins in double-quick time.

They were laughing as they joined Charlotte and it pleased him that his daughter had made no comment about finding them in bed together. It meant that she'd accepted him unreservedly as her father, and as Megan had welcomed him with open arms too the future looked good.

The snow fell more heavily than the day before and began to stick to the ground. It was so rare to have a white Christmas, thought Megan, that it had to be a good omen. In fact she was glad that she'd let Luigi persuade her to join him.

Later in the day they snowballed each other and made a snowman and Luigi let his hair down more than Megan had ever seen before—except in bed, of course. There were no inhibitions there. He was, if anything, a better lover.

There was the faint niggling doubt in her mind that he had gained extra experience with other girls, but she swept it away—it was her fault if he had—and if he had enhanced his sexual prowess then she ought to be grateful. The many different ways he'd pleasured her had been utterly fantastic. She only had to think about it to experience a resurgence of the feelings that had danced excitedly inside her.

Her eyes sparkled whenever she looked at him and

Luigi gave her slow, intimate smiles that told her he knew exactly what she was thinking. 'Later,' he mouthed and Megan hugged the precious thought to her. She couldn't wait. It was like a replay of when they first met and couldn't get enough of each other.

Before he had become a tycoon and work was more important!

She dismissed the thought as immediately as it entered her head. Luigi was a father now, he had a different set of responsibilities. He wouldn't let Charlotte down.

Neither of them could wait for their daughter's bedtime. Luigi followed Megan to the bathroom and watched her bathing Charlotte. What an amazing mother she was, so gentle, with a glow about her that touched his heart. But his fingers curled into his palms when he recalled how she had cheated him out of seeing his daughter born, of sharing the first few precious years of her life, even preparing for the birth. Not that he was going to let that spoil his pleasure this evening.

He'd been looking forward all day to making love to Megan. She had matched him step for step last night and judging by the way she kept looking at him, her beautiful eyes full of passion and desire, she was quite willing to allow him into her bed again.

And he was not disappointed. From the very moment he slid his arms around her the years they had spent apart dissolved into the mists of time. She was his again, completely, urging herself against him, her hunger as deep as his own.

She kissed him with the sensuality that only a woman deeply in love could give. And it amused him to let her take the lead—for now! She touched and kissed and stroked, enjoying the fact that she could arouse him by a simple kiss, or the lightest touch of her fingertips, her actions becoming more and more urgent until in the end he could contain himself no longer.

'No more,' he growled, laying her on her back and positioning himself over her. Then he took her, instantly and fiercely, and her cries of pleasure matched his as the intense joy of making love filled their hearts and minds. It was a long time before their sweat-slicked bodies stopped writhing in the aftermath of exquisite pleasure, before their breathing returned to normal.

'That was quite something,' he muttered hoarsely. 'Lord, am I glad I found you again.'

Megan didn't answer. She had her eyes closed and a blissful expression on her face. In fact he had never seen her look more beautiful. Every feature was softened, and her skin had a lustrous glow. She looked like a woman who was extremely satisfied. He was sure now that she wouldn't walk away from him again.

They made love twice more before falling asleep in each other's arms. And for the first time in his life Luigi didn't feel the urge to be up at dawn and at his desk. He had a woman at his side whom he had almost lost; he wasn't going to risk it again. He would go, eventually, and he would work sensible hours, but for the moment Megan was more important.

Except that it didn't work out like that.

Halfway through the morning he and Charlotte were snowballing each other once again, when Megan, who had gone indoors for a handkerchief for her daughter, marched out of the house with her face as black as a thundercloud and slammed the phone into his hand. 'A call for you.'

He frowned. 'Who is it?'

'Find out for yourself,' she snapped, and taking Charlotte's hand she dragged her protestingly into the house. He faintly heard her say, 'Come on, let's get packed, we're leaving.'

One half of him wanted to chase after her, find out what was going on, the other needed to know who was on the other end of the phone. Whoever it was had clearly upset his wife.

'Can I speak to Luigi, please?' The woman's husky voice still echoed in Megan's ears.

'May I ask who's calling?'

'Tell him it's Serena,' came the sultry answer. 'And hurry please; I haven't got all day.'

Serena! So she *was* still on the scene! The thought sent her sick to the pit of her stomach. 'How dare you speak to me like that?' retorted Megan. 'I'm not one of his servants.'

'I don't care who you are,' riposted the woman. 'I want Luigi.'

'You want him, do you?' snapped Megan, unable to keep the anger out of her voice. 'Then it's bad luck you're having because he's not available.'

'I think Luigi will be available if you tell him who I am.'

'You think you'd take preference over his wife?' It crucified Megan to think that Luigi had jumped into bed with her while still carrying on an affair with his PA. But she wasn't going to let Serena know that.

'He and his wife are long since parted,' sneered the other woman. 'He's a fool not to have divorced her. How she could walk out on him, I have no idea. He's—'

'Actually she's walked back into his life,' rasped Megan. 'You're speaking to her right now.'

There was a long silence.

'But I'll still get him for you, if that's what you want,' she added, her voice sickly sweet. 'Just one moment.' And she didn't stop to listen to what else the girl had to say. She was sick to the bottom of her heart as she walked out of the house and tossed the phone to him.

His eyes said it all. He was torn two ways. And it told her what she needed to know. If he truly cared about her, if he truly wanted them to get back together, he would have ignored Serena's call and followed her. Instead she heard him speak softly into the phone, turning away so that she wouldn't hear.

CHAPTER FIVE

'Is SERENA still working for you?' Megan didn't really want to know and yet she couldn't stop herself. She wished she could take the question back because it made her sound jealous, and why should she be? As Luigi was no longer a part of her life she couldn't care less how many women he was involved with.

Liar!

It wouldn't have mattered before she slept with him, but it did now. He had treated her as though she were the only one. No, that wasn't strictly true. He had made her *feel* as though she were the only one. A big difference! It could be that he was an artist at it. How did she know what he was like these days? His main aim at the moment was getting custody of his daughter. And if the mother came as part of the package then he was home and dry. A ready built babysitter while he was free to work his long hours and continue his affair.

Megan was furious by the time she'd worked all this out and had already packed before confronting Luigi. She had seen him out of her bedroom window talking into the phone. She had observed the way he stood, the way he moved his head as he listened, the way he moved his hands—as though he was touching Serena in his mind's eye. It all suggested that he was speaking to a woman who meant a great deal to him. It even looked as though he blew her a kiss when he finished.

'As a matter of fact, yes, she is,' he answered easily.

'But you don't need to worry your pretty head about her.'

'I don't?' Megan retorted, her tone so sharp that it was a wonder it didn't slice into him. 'She made it sound pretty clear to me that she was number one priority in your life.'

'In my business life,' he pointed out. 'Serena's my PA. You know that.'

'Really?' Megan allowed her finely shaped brows to ride smoothly upwards, her grey eyes totally disbelieving. 'Is that *all* she is? It wasn't the impression I got. And if you believe I'm going to move back into your life when she is clearly a part of it then think again. All I can say is thank goodness Serena rang because now I know exactly where I stand.'

'Don't be ridiculous, Megan,' barked Luigi. 'Serena means nothing to me. You and Charlotte mean everything.'

'I wonder if you'd be saying that if I hadn't walked out on you?' she accused. 'I wonder whether fatherhood would have made you change your lifestyle? Somehow I don't think so. You feel cheated, yes, and because Charlotte's lawfully your daughter you want her, but that's as far as it goes.'

'Are you suggesting that the last two nights meant nothing to you?' he demanded, his brow thunderously dark, his whole body taut with suppressed emotions.

'All they've done,' she riposted smartly, 'is remind me of what an expert lover you are. But good sex is all it was. It didn't mean anything.' She'd been love-starved, that was what, and she *had* enjoyed it, but it went no further than that.

His dark eyes flashed. 'I don't believe you.'

'Believe what you like,' she tossed back, 'but I'm out of your life for good. Serena's welcome to you.'

'You'd ruin your daughter's happiness?' he accused. 'Her life as well, by depriving her of the father she's just found? Whom she needs, I might add, as much as she needs her mother.' His eyes were glacial, as hard as the ice that had formed in the cracks in the paving outside.

Megan hadn't looked at it from this angle. Would it be bad for Charlotte? Or would it be better to make a clean break now before her daughter really got to know Luigi? She knew the answer even before she began debating it. Charlotte needed her father. It was that simple. She'd been so happy when she discovered she did have a daddy after all. It would be cruel to deprive her of him now. Except that she didn't want a part-time father for Charlotte. Nor indeed a father who bedded other women!

'I'll stay on two conditions,' she told him stonily, reluctantly.

'And they are?' he demanded.

Who would have thought, Megan asked herself, that a few short hours ago they'd been making love? Where had all the pleasure gone? They were facing each other like two sworn enemies out for the kill. She lifted her chin. 'Number one, that you cut your working hours. And number two, there are no other women in your life.'

'Done,' he said easily and far too quickly for her peace of mind.

'I'm serious,' she countered.

'And so am I. You and Charlotte mean everything to me.'

'And Serena?'

He gave a tiny shake of his head, as if to say, Why do you keep questioning me about Serena? 'She's my right hand,' he told her calmly. 'I can't cut her out of my life, she virtually runs it—on a business level, of course,' he added when he saw the accusing glint in Megan's eyes.

'And was business the reason she rang now?' charged Megan. Because it hadn't seemed like that to her. The woman had sounded sickly possessive.

'Of course! Which reminds me—' he shot back his cuff and looked at his watch '—I'm needed. I have to go. And when I return we'll go to your house and collect the rest of your stuff. You will be here?' he added when he saw the doubt in her eyes.

Megan realised with a pang that she had little choice. Charlotte's future security and happiness depended on it.

As Luigi drove to his office he felt faintly uneasy. He wasn't completely sure that Megan would still be there when he got back. On the other hand, the fact that she'd sounded jealous of Serena had to be a good thing. If she *was* jealous then it could mean that she still had feelings for him. It could be to his advantage, except that he would have to tread a fine line. He couldn't afford to let Serena upset Megan.

Serena was excellent at her job, he didn't know what he'd do without her, and he sometimes rewarded her by taking her to dinner or the theatre. That Serena fancied herself in love with him he was fully aware, but the feelings weren't mutual. Even though he had lost all hope of Megan returning he'd never wanted anyone to take her place. He kept his lady friends at a distance and usually they got the message—except for Serena. He wondered exactly what she had said to Megan. Perhaps he should ask her?

But the opportunity didn't present itself. He ran his

whole empire from a top floor suite of prestigious offices in London's regenerated dockland area, where the views on a clear day were far reaching. Today he didn't have time to look out of the windows. A problem had occurred at one of his IT companies where a disgruntled employee had fed a virus into a software programme that had been released for Christmas. It had already begun to reveal itself and he needed to recall all copies before any real damage was done.

It was after eight by the time he arrived home. He had phoned Megan from his car on the way, half-expecting her to be gone, relieved when she wasn't, and not surprised that she sounded angry.

He found her curled up in a chair in the sitting room, so deeply engrossed in a book that she didn't hear him enter. Except that the book was upside down! He smiled faintly and spoke her name and she looked up with a very creditable start.

'So you've finally torn yourself away from Serena,' she accused, her magnificent eyes flashing daggers at him. Their usual grey had become a soft amethyst, reflecting the colour of the purple sweater she wore. He had noticed this before—whichever colour she wore, her eyes seemed to change with it. It fascinated him.

'I did explain on the phone,' he told her patiently. At least he hoped he sounded patient. She didn't make it easy for him. What he would like to do was give her a good shake—except that it would get him nowhere. But patience never had been one of his virtues.

'And was it only this morning that you promised to work less hours?' she continued. 'Such a short memory you have. Why am I surprised?'

'There were extenuating circumstances,' he reminded her sharply. 'Weren't you listening when I—?'

'Oh, yes, I heard everything you said,' Megan cut in with exaggerated calm.

'But you don't believe me? Well, you'd better because it will be spread all over the newspapers tomorrow. We've already had several reporters sniffing around. This could ruin the company.'

'And do you know who did it?'

'Actually, yes. Before leaving he bragged to one of his colleagues that he would bring the company to its knees. It's a pity he wasn't taken seriously. It's going to be one big headache for the next few days, weeks, months maybe.'

'Meaning you'll be working all the hours God gave again?'

'I'll try not to.' But he could see by her expression that she didn't believe him, and he couldn't answer in all honesty that he wouldn't. He was a hands-on type of guy who never believed in passing the buck. 'Let's go and collect your stuff. I'll instruct Amy to keep her eye on Charlotte.'

'At this hour?' she demurred, slowly uncurling her legs and sitting up straight. Amy was the maid, a giggly brunette girl who was always willing to please.

Luigi wondered if Megan had any idea how gorgeous she looked. Her face was bare of make-up and she could have passed for eighteen. His male hormones stirred and he wanted to take her to bed, but he forced sanity to prevail. 'Why not?'

'Of course, you'll be working late again tomorrow,' she scorned. 'It's now or never, isn't it? Maybe it wasn't such a good idea to—'

'You're not changing your mind,' he cut in swiftly and fiercely. No matter what it took, he was determined not to lose Megan again. 'Get your coat; we're leaving now.'

To his relief she did as he asked, running down the stairs a couple of minutes later in a camel-coloured winter coat with a red scarf tossed casually around her neck. It would be warm in his car but it was jolly cold outside, and he guessed her house would be cold too.

'I presume you're going to put your house on the market,' he said, after they'd been driving for a few minutes in silence.

'It's rented,' she corrected him.

'So what's the procedure? Will the landlord accept a lump sum in lieu of notice?'

'I share,' she told him flatly.

Luigi felt his guts tighten. He'd almost forgotten the boyfriend. Oddly, Megan hadn't seemed too concerned about leaving him. It wasn't a nice feeling to realise that he didn't know the way his own wife's mind worked. In fact, had he ever really got to know her? Hadn't he been too immersed in his own business dealings? Physically, they'd both been fulfilled, but mentally and spiritually? A brief sadness filled him. 'What do you think he'll have to say about you moving in with me?'

'He? Oh, Jake. There's not much he can say, is there? I'm still legally married to you.'

She sounded remarkably calm and for some reason it angered him. 'If you think you're still going to see him, then you can forget it,' he barked.

'Have I said I will?'

Could it be that he was blowing the whole thing up out of all proportion? Perhaps this Jake fellow meant nothing to her. Maybe it was a cost-effective arrangement. But he couldn't be sure and the thought of Megan sharing a bed with another man, the thought of her thrashing about with the same uninhibited responses, made his blood run cold.

'No, you haven't and you'd damn well better not,' he warned tersely. 'In fact, if he's there tonight I'll tell him myself. In fact I'll—'

'You don't have to worry,' she cut in. 'He's in Paris— with his fiancée.'

Luigi pulled the car into the side of the road and tugged on the handbrake. 'What did you say?'

'Jake's with Jenny in Paris for Christmas. Jenny's my housemate.'

'So why the hell didn't you tell me that in the beginning?' he roared, hating the idea that she'd made a fool of him.

'I found it amusing that you jumped to the wrong conclusion.'

'Well I don't find it amusing,' he retorted. 'I've suffered all sorts of horrors imaging you in bed with him.'

'There's nothing you could have done about it,' she pointed out. 'But do you really think I'd have agreed to move in with you if I was involved with someone else?'

He had thought he'd given her no choice; now he began to realise that Megan had had the upper hand all the time. 'I like to think that you would, for Charlotte's sake,' he told her grimly. He restarted the engine and drove fast and furious and silent until they reached their destination.

The house was freezing and he hadn't been as sensible as Megan and pulled on an overcoat. 'I hope your pipes haven't frozen,' he said testily, rubbing his hands together. 'You really shouldn't leave it unheated like this, you could have a burst.'

'And who'd pay the fuel bills?' she retorted smartly.

'So how's your friend going to manage?'

Megan shrugged. 'Maybe Jake will move in. What I do know is that she won't be very happy when she discovers that I've left without giving her notice.'

'Don't worry about that,' said Luigi offhandedly. 'I'll see that she's not out of pocket.'

'Here we go again,' she derided as she flung clothes into the suitcases she had brought back with her. 'Money solves all problems, that's your maxim, isn't it? Well, it's not mine, and I don't want you insulting Jenny by offering her money.'

Luigi was quite sure that her friend wouldn't be insulted. In fact he'd like to stake a bet that she'd be hugely grateful for any handout. What person wouldn't? But he didn't say this to Megan because he knew what sort of a response he would get. Instead he said, 'You know her best.' He fully intended, though, to see that the other girl didn't lose out because he had spirited her housemate away.

'When are your friends coming back?'

'I'm not sure. Tomorrow, I think,' she told him bluntly, reaching down a holdall from the top of her wardrobe and throwing in toiletries and other bits and pieces that he presumed she couldn't live without. Personally, he would rather she left them behind and he bought her a whole load of new stuff. But with the fuss she'd made about the Christmas presents he knew he dared not suggest it. Megan had become a highly independent lady.

Finally she wrote a note for Jenny and placed it on the kitchen table. 'OK, I'm ready,' she said. 'Let's go.'

He would have liked it better if she looked happy about it. Instead a scowl marred her lovely face. It wasn't going to be the happy union he'd hoped for. But given time... And a lot of persuasion on his part! And no working long hours! Though how he was going to achieve that he didn't know. There were always problems of one sort or another to be dealt with. Yes, he had managers, very good ones, but he liked to be kept informed at all levels. It was why he was so successful. Surely Megan could understand that?

'I wish you could be happy about this,' he said as they began their journey home.

Megan sighed and said nothing.

'If I'd known how unhappy you were before I would have done something about it. Why didn't you say?'

'Because it wouldn't have mattered, you'd have still gone your own way,' she retorted sharply. 'I couldn't stand living in an empty world any longer. And I pray I'm not making the same mistake again. I'm not sure that I'm doing the right thing even now, but I'll give it a try for Charlotte's sake.'

That night Megan wouldn't allow Luigi into her bed. Lord, she wanted to, she even ached for him, but the Serena issue prevented her. She didn't tell him it was because of his PA, but he guessed anyway.

'You're making a huge mistake,' he told her grimly, as they stood outside her bedroom door. Charlotte had been bathed earlier and they'd sat in his den with their now ritual night-time drink. 'Serena is not and never has been my bed partner.'

'But she'd like to be? And you've taken her out? There's more to it than a professional relationship?'

Luigi drew in a deeply pained breath. 'She'd like there to be,' he admitted.

'And you're strong enough to withstand the allure of a beautiful woman?'

'Serena, yes.'

Megan's eyes narrowed. 'So there have been others?' Her tone was deeply accusing.

'You can't blame me,' he rasped, his eyes dark and resentful. 'I'm a red-blooded male, full of sex hormones that need feeding now and then.'

'So that's what I was doing, feeding your hormones?' Megan's head began to spin. It was one way of putting it, she supposed. He'd always been highly sexed with a hot-blooded Latin male possessiveness that had at one time thrilled her, but now sent a sickening chill into the very heart of her soul. She fed his need; it was as simple as that. And she had compromised herself by agreeing to move in with him!

He had a lot to prove before she'd allow him into her bed again—and if he dared to let any other woman assuage his sexual urges then she'd be out of here quicker than he could say I'm sorry.

'You're different, Megan, you should know that. You're my wife, you're mine, and we need each other. Haven't we proved it?'

He stood close and she could smell the very maleness of him. It excited her beyond measure but she knew that she had to be strong. 'I need you like I'd need a boil on the end of my nose,' she spat. 'I've managed very well, thank you, for the last four years. The only reason I've agreed to stay is for Charlotte's benefit. But if you give me hell, like you're doing at this moment, then I'll run away again.'

'You'd be that selfish?' he blazed. 'You'd deprive my daughter of her father's guidance just because *you*—' he stabbed the word incisively '—can't handle the idea that while we've been parted I've had other girlfriends. God dammit, woman, I didn't think I was ever going to see you again.'

'So now I am here have you told Serena it's hands off time? Have you told her we're back together?'

'We had other more pressing issues to discuss.'

'So you haven't told her,' accused Megan, her eyes glinting. 'Damn you, Luigi, you'd better do it quickly, because if I take any more calls from her I'll fill her so full of home truths that she won't even want to work with you, never mind insinuating herself into your bed.'

Megan knew that she was getting too wound up for her own good but she couldn't help it. She was afraid that everything was going to go pear-shaped, and she'd end up being even more hurt than before. And this time Charlotte would be hurt too. This was her main concern.

'I can assure you, Megan,' he said in a low growl, 'that you are my number one priority. Serena never has nor ever will enter the equation.'

He looked as though he wanted to kiss her, actually bowing his head and inching closer. Pulses began to race and Megan knew that if she hesitated it would be too late. With speed born of panic she flung open the door. 'I wish I could believe you. Goodnight, Luigi.' And she slammed it behind her.

Her heart raced as though she'd run a hundred-yard sprint. It would be so easy to fall back into their old ways, to become Luigi's wife again in every sense of the word. But it was too soon. He had to prove himself first. She must take control of her feelings, not give the slightest hint that she wanted him like she never had before. It was going to be hard but she had to do it, for the sake of their future.

Sleep didn't come easily. What was easy was remembering Luigi in bed beside her. The space felt empty. She felt empty. If they had nothing else in common she couldn't deny that they made a spectacular couple in bed.

Frequently she wandered into Charlotte's room to check that she was OK. She looked so beautiful and so innocent with not a care in the world, happy to be in this house with her father, and for her sake Megan was glad that she'd agreed to stay on.

When she went down to breakfast the next morning Megan was surprised to see Luigi seated at the table, the morning paper spread out in front of him, a steaming cup of coffee in his hand. Luigi was very much a coffee man. He'd once told her that he'd had so much tea poured into him as a child that it had put him off it for life.

'Good morning.' He looked up with a warm smile. 'Did you sleep well?'

Should she lie and say yes, or tell the truth? Megan lied. 'Brilliantly well, thank you. And yourself?'

'Yes, I had a good night too.'

But she knew they were both politely lying. She was willing to bet that he'd tossed and turned the whole night as well, wishing they were together, reliving the magical moments they'd shared. Feeling stirred by them, feeling a hunger that was hard to dismiss.

Even as she'd walked into the room and their eyes met, Megan's senses had skidded out of control and she'd had to turn away quickly, making a big thing of helping Charlotte into her chair.

Charlotte chatted away to her father and Megan was able to take a firm hold of her dithering emotions. This was ridiculous. How could she live with Luigi and follow her own self-imposed rules feeling as she did? Why not share his bed? Because, came the severe answer, you'll be doubly hurt if it doesn't work. And that had to be the truth.

Not until Edwina had brought in their breakfast did Megan question Luigi. 'I thought you'd be at work. It's a quarter past eight. If I remember rightly you're normally at your desk by seven-thirty.'

'So you didn't believe me when I said I was going to change?' he asked with a mocking lift to an eyebrow.

His hair was neatly combed, his jaw clean-shaven and he smelt heavenly. For the life of her she couldn't remember the name of his cologne, but he had always used the same one for as long as she'd known him. To her it was an aphrodisiac and as she inhaled it she closed her eyes and dreamt of him making love to her.

'Is something wrong?' asked Luigi sharply.

'What? I'm sorry. No! Nothing! And, no, I didn't believe you. But I'm glad to see that you've kept your word.' He was wearing a white silk shirt, open at the throat, and she had an insane urge to touch his chest with her fingertips, to feel the strength of that muscular body, to—

'Megan?'

Again he brought her back to the present.

'Are you sure you've had enough sleep? You look as though you're in a trance. Shall I take the day off and look after Charlotte while—?'

'No!' she exclaimed strongly. 'There's nothing wrong with me. I was thinking about something, that's all. Mmm, this bacon smells good.'

As they ate she was aware of him watching her, and when Charlotte had finished and run away into the kitchen to 'help 'Wina' he said, 'Something's wrong, isn't it? I hope you're not having second thoughts, or should I say third? Because, make no bones about it, this is now your home.'

'I know,' Megan said quietly. 'You don't have to rub it in. I have no intention of leaving, not yet anyway.'

'By the way,' he said, as he poured himself yet another cup of coffee, Megan shaking her head when he offered her one, 'I've employed a nanny for Charlotte.'

'You've done what?' That really did wake her up and Megan bounced her hands off the table, her eyes flashing furiously. 'What have you done that for? I'm perfectly capable of looking after my own daughter.'

'Of course you are,' he said evenly. 'You've proved that, but wouldn't it be nice to have more time to yourself?'

'No, it wouldn't,' she slammed. 'You'd better ring her right now and tell her she's not wanted. You have no idea what a child needs. It's certainly not a stranger looking after her; her parents' time and love is far more important.' She was beside herself with rage. How could he do this without consulting her? Quite easily, came the answer. He was used to giving orders, used to organising. But she was not one of his employees and he wasn't going to tell her what to do.

'I happen to think that it's important for *us* to spend more time together,' he said, visibly containing his patience. 'We have a lot of catching up to do, Megan.'

'And how can we do that when you work all the hours God gave?' she snapped.

'Because I shall make time,' he retorted harshly, pushing himself to his feet and glaring down at her.

'Ha! That will be a first,' she thrust back. 'How long will it last, I wonder? One day? Two? A whole week at the most?' And she too sprang up from her chair.

'Things are different now I have a daughter,' he

rasped, dark eyes glittering. 'I'm a family man now and I intend to take care of my family.'

'And hiring a nanny is part of that care?' she yelled. 'What if Charlotte doesn't like her? What if—?'

'We'll give it a try,' he interjected tersely, his fingers clenching as he fought for control. 'And that's the end of it.'

Megan flounced out of the room. Arguing with Luigi when he was in this mood got her nowhere, but she was fiercely determined not to give in. When the nanny arrived she would tell her in no uncertain terms that she wasn't needed. Luigi could say what he liked; Charlotte did not need a nanny. Not when she was at home all day to look after her. If Luigi wanted to spend more time at home he would have to put up with Charlotte as well, he wasn't getting rid of her that easily.

Was that it, she wondered, for all his fine words he found an excitable, energetic daughter too daunting? He didn't like his routine upset. A nanny would solve the problem. Another case of using the power of his money to get what he wanted. Megan spat fire as she sought her daughter in the kitchen. How dared he dictate? How dared he try to take over her life?

It was evening before she saw him again and her anger hadn't subsided. As soon as Charlotte was in bed she began her attack. 'I hope you've cancelled the nanny?'

'Why would I do that?' A harsh frown dragged his thick brows together.

'You mean you didn't listen to a word I said?' Megan's eyes flashed her fury. In fact her whole body grew stiff with rage and she battered her fists against his chest. 'Just because *you* can't handle Charlotte it doesn't mean *I* need help.'

In response he pulled her hard against him, his arms

binding her so that she could no longer fight. 'I am doing this for *us*, not Charlotte.' His dark eyes pierced her own, sending a *frisson* of awareness through her despite the anger that she felt—or perhaps because of it! '*We* are the ones who need time,' he asserted strongly. 'We have a whole four years to catch up.'

'And you think that handing over *our* daughter to a complete stranger will help?' she questioned hotly. 'As far as I'm concerned there's nothing to talk about. I'm still convinced that I did the right thing.'

Luigi snorted his annoyance. 'If it were just you and me then I could perhaps understand. But I'll never be able to forgive you for depriving me of my daughter's first years.'

'I doubt you'd have seen much of her,' she scorned, struggling in vain to free herself. 'In case you've forgotten, your continual absence was the reason I walked out.'

'Dammit, Megan, why do you keep throwing that at me?' he charged, tightening his hold. 'What I want to know is why you never made me aware of it?'

'Oh, I did, believe me, many times,' she yelled into his face, her eyes flashing dramatically. 'You wouldn't listen, that was the problem. You were so wrapped up in your entrepreneurial world that nothing I said sank in. You assumed that making money was high on my list of priorities too. Well, let me tell you—' Her words were cut off by Luigi's mouth closing over hers. And in that moment Megan knew that she had lost.

CHAPTER SIX

LUIGI found it hard to accept that Megan was against him employing someone to look after Charlotte. It was the perfect solution. They needed to spend more time together, they needed to iron out the problems that had sent her fleeing; how could they do that with a three-year-old constantly demanding their attention?

He'd thought hard about their situation and had made up his mind that he would delegate more in order to give Megan his undivided attention. Admittedly he would like to be involved with the problems with the new software, and he'd like to keep his eye on the running of Gerards. But in truth he had staff who were more than capable of dealing with any situation.

He didn't pay good wages for nothing. He expected hard work and loyalty, and that was what he usually got. It was only his own desire to be involved in all aspects of his varied business interests that kept him going long hours. But now he was needed in another, more important, direction. Probably the most important one of his life. His whole future depended on it.

His arms became more possessive. Megan was his! She belonged to him for all time. He'd made mistakes but their future was transparently clear. The three of them were a family and nothing or no one was going to split them up. Employing a nanny was a necessity as far as he was concerned. He and Megan desperately needed time; they needed to renew their vows, to renew the love that had once bound them so firmly together.

On the day they met he'd fallen instantly in love and even if she hadn't let him drive her home with her dangerously overflowing bags of Christmas goodies he would have found some other way to get to know her. Maybe meeting her again at Christmas time was a good omen. The thought pleased him and he deepened his kiss, even more thrilled when Megan didn't resist.

She felt so good in his arms, her slender body moulding perfectly to his, and he silently prayed that she would let him back into her bed. He had tasted paradise and then been denied it. More than once in the endless dark hours he'd padded to her door, prepared to storm in and not take no for an answer. How he had turned around and returned to his room he didn't know. It had been sheer hell.

But thankfully she was weakening. The way she was kissing him now with complete abandonment, the way she moved her body suggestively against his, was all the encouragement he needed. He lifted her into his arms with the initial thought of carrying her up to bed, but then thought better of it and they ended up on the sofa instead.

'My beautiful Megan,' he whispered huskily into her ear. 'You've no idea how hard it's been having you in my house and not being allowed to touch you.'

'Don't talk,' she breathed, pulling his mouth down to hers and kissing him so passionately that he felt as though all his dreams were coming true. But suddenly Charlotte's scream cut through their pleasure.

They were both on their feet in an instant, Megan hurtling up the stairs in panic. He followed close behind. What had happened to his daughter? Had she fallen? Was she hurt? His heart thudded as he realised how deeply he had come to love this child in the few short days he'd known her.

Charlotte was sitting straight up in bed, her eyes wide and staring. 'She's asleep,' said Megan, slowing her hectic race. 'She's dreaming.'

'Does she often do this, dream with her eyes open?' asked Luigi in concern. It looked weird to him.

'Only when something's upset her. It's some kind of nightmare, I think. It's always the same.'

As they watched Charlotte's body relaxed, her eyes closed and she gave a half smile as she curled up beneath the bedcovers again.

Megan leaned over her and gave her a gentle kiss. 'I try not to wake her because then she doesn't remember.'

Luigi frowned. 'What could have upset her?'

Megan shrugged and straightened the quilt. 'Maybe she heard us arguing. She's a sensitive little soul and we didn't keep our voices very low, did we?'

Luigi shook his head. 'We were too far away.' But a shadow of guilt made him uneasy. He had a lot to learn about children. 'Will she be all right if we leave her?'

'I'm going to stay in my room just in case,' declared Megan. 'Alone!' she added warningly.

Luigi compressed his lips. 'We have unfinished business.'

'That was a mistake,' retorted Megan on a loud whisper.

'Like marrying me was a mistake?' He couldn't help himself. He'd been so confident that tonight was the night they'd both realise that they couldn't sleep apart, and to have it all snatched away from him because Charlotte had had a bad dream drove him crazy.

'Since you put it like that, yes.' Her eyes were cool

on his, her earlier passion gone, melting as quickly as the snowflakes outside.

'I think you're lying,' he snarled. 'You're afraid to admit it but you still care for me.'

'In your dreams, Mister,' she hissed.

'Then why, when I kiss you, do you melt in my arms? Why do you return my kiss with so much passion that it makes a lie of everything you're saying? Tell me that, dear wife of mine. Look me in the eye and tell me you have no feelings for me.'

Megan woke with a start. She'd been dreaming about Luigi and had the strangest feeling that he was standing beside her. But the room was empty. Even Charlotte hadn't yet stirred. She switched on the bedside lamp and looked at the clock. Almost half past seven! It was unusual for her daughter to still be asleep. Usually she crept into her bed at around six and they both dozed for another hour.

She rolled out of bed and padded across to the window. It was dark, and all was still and cold and eerily white outside from a further fall of snow. Then she crossed to the adjoining door and opened it wider. What she hadn't expected to see was Luigi sitting in a chair beside Charlotte's bed holding her hand. They were both asleep.

For at least two minutes Megan stood there watching and wondering. Had her instinct been right when she'd thought he was beside her bed? She didn't like the thought that he'd crept into her room in the middle of the night. He could have slipped in beside her and she wouldn't have known! Had that been his intention and then he'd had second thoughts and decided to sit with his daughter instead?

Last night she'd declared that she had no feelings for him, that he managed to arouse her sexually but that was all. She'd even looked him straight in the eye as she'd said it. Because it was the truth. She didn't love him any more. *She didn't!*

Suddenly she realised that Luigi had opened his eyes and was watching her. 'What are you doing?' she asked in a fierce whisper.

Gently he let his daughter's hand go and moved stiffly across the room towards her. Megan shut the adjoining door and glared at him as she waited for his answer.

'Charlotte cried out again,' he informed her.

Megan was horrified that she hadn't heard. In fact she found it hard to believe. 'Are you sure?'

'I wouldn't have been sitting there if I wasn't,' he informed her, stretching his arms above his head and yawning widely. His silk dressing gown fell open, revealing a pair of black boxer shorts and a tanned bare chest.

Megan's heartbeats quickened.

'She didn't wake but I thought she ought to have company and, as you looked so beautiful and comfortable in your sleep,' he growled, 'I didn't want to disturb you.'

'You should have woken me,' she tossed stormily. 'It's my place to be with her.'

'Not any longer,' he said with a warning light in his eyes. 'We share responsibility now.'

The days of sharing with Luigi had long since gone. Luigi was his own man, doing only what he wanted to do. And at this moment he thought that sitting holding Charlotte's hand made him look good. Would he be as quick to be at her side if she were throwing up? Somehow Megan doubted it.

'We *share*?' she echoed, 'and yet you've gone to the trouble of employing a nanny. How hypocritical is that?'

'It's different; it's a necessity.'

'So you keep saying. I don't happen to think so. I like looking after my daughter; perhaps you're not aware of that. I don't want a stranger doing it for me.'

'I've said all I'm saying on that matter,' he retorted sharply and headed for the door.

By the time he'd gone Charlotte had woken and when they went down to breakfast Luigi had left. 'He said he won't be more than a couple of hours,' informed William, who had been entrusted with the message. 'Something urgent cropped up.'

As it always did, thought Megan bitterly.

Amazingly, though, within the two hours he was back. Accompanying him was a smart young woman with long blonde hair. She was tall and slim and very good-looking. Serena, thought Megan, her hackles instantly rising. How dared he bring her here?

She and Charlotte were outside building yet another snowman and Luigi was all smiles as he approached them. 'Megan, let me introduce Kate Swift, Charlotte's nanny. Kate, my wife, Megan, and this is my daughter,' he added proudly.

Megan knew she must look stupid with her mouth falling open and it was with a great deal of reluctance that she took Kate's outstretched hand. 'I hadn't realised you were starting today,' she said, trying to smile, but unable to keep a terse note out of her voice.

'I thought it a good idea,' explained Luigi.

And Megan knew why. He didn't want Charlotte spoiling their lovemaking again. With a nanny on call twenty-four hours a day it would clear the way for him. The selfish swine! But if he thought she was going to

leave her precious daughter totally in the care of someone else he was gravely mistaken.

'And this is Charlotte?' Kate stooped down to the
child's level. 'Hello, Charlotte. What a grand snowman!
Have you built it?'

But Charlotte had her thumb stuck in her mouth and
clung to Megan's hand, looking curiously at the smiling
woman.

'She's always shy with strangers,' explained Megan,
a cool note still in her voice.

'I think we should go indoors and let Kate settle in,'
said Luigi cheerfully.

'Charlotte and I need to finish our snowman,' said
Megan. She was furious with Luigi. He had no right
bringing that woman here without telling her first. She
had thought, or at least hoped, that she'd convinced him
that she didn't want anyone else looking after Charlotte.
It was a crazy idea. What the hell was she supposed to
do all day while Kate took over?

'Who's that lady?' asked Charlotte as soon as they
had disappeared into the house.

Megan drew in a deep breath and paused a moment
before answering, 'She's come to help Mummy look after you, sweetheart.'

'I don't want her, I want you,' Charlotte said almost
on a shout. 'And Daddy,' she added after a moment's
thought.

'You'll still have us, don't worry, sweetheart. But
sometimes, if Daddy and I have to go out, then Kate will
look after you.' It was the best explanation she could
think of.

'Will she play with me?'

'Of course.'

'Will she build a snowman, and play snowballs?'

'I'm sure she will.'

'Will she read me bedtime stories?'

Megan's heart began to break. 'Sometimes, perhaps, but that's my job. That's the best, don't you think, when you're tucked up in bed and I read to you. That's our special time of day.'

Charlotte nodded her satisfaction and then began to play in the snow.

By the end of the day Charlotte had accepted Kate and Megan had to grudgingly admit that Kate was very good with her daughter. It didn't alter the fact, though, that she resented her presence, and she fully intended telling Luigi exactly what she thought.

Once Charlotte was in bed Kate retired. She'd made a fuss about Megan wanting to bathe Charlotte and put her to bed, declaring that it was part of her job, but Megan had been adamant.

Luigi had provided the new nanny with her own sitting room and bedroom, opposite Charlotte's room, so that she was on hand should she be needed quickly. This was something else Megan didn't approve of. Why should Kate need to be so near?

Megan was silent over dinner, her anger simmering away inside her, trying to decide how best to tackle him.

'Why don't you spit it out?' asked Luigi harshly. There was fire in his eyes too.

'You know I didn't want Charlotte to have a nanny. Was that why you presented me with a *fait accompli?*'

He shrugged laconically. 'Don't you like Kate?'

'That's nothing to do with it,' she shot back. 'You went behind my back. You knew how I felt and yet you didn't even have the decency to talk it over with me.'

'We'd already discussed it.'

'You mean you told me what you'd decided. My feelings didn't count. You're a rat, Luigi. I don't know what I ever saw in you. And I honestly don't know what I'm doing here. Second to marrying you it's the biggest mistake of my life.' She pushed her plate away and jumped up from the table. 'I can't even face eating with you.'

She heard Luigi's swift intake of disbelief before he was on his feet too, his hands on her shoulders, fingers merciless. 'You don't mean that.'

'Don't I?' she rasped, looking angrily into the hard darkness of his eyes.

'You know deep in your heart that it's for the best,' he thrust fiercely. 'We need this time together. In fact, once Charlotte's got used to Kate, it will do us good to go away for a few days.'

'And leave my daughter?' she screeched.

'Our daughter,' he corrected harshly. 'And don't think I'd dream of leaving her if I wasn't sure that she'd be in good hands. But we need time together, the two of us, alone, completely. We need to sort out our lives.'

'And you'll arrange that, without consulting me yet again?' she blazed. 'I think not. I think you're under a great big delusion. You think that now you've got me in your house you can do what the hell you like. It's not true. I'm tougher than you think. I've had to be. If you don't believe me just wait and see. If you carry on in this vein you might find one day that I've disappeared again.'

The grip on her shoulders tightened so much that a sharp pain seared through her bones. 'Do that at your peril,' he threatened menacingly. 'What I'm doing is for your good, for *our* good. How the hell are we supposed to get back on an even keel with a child at our heels all the time?'

'*A child?*' Megan screamed. 'Is that how you see

Charlotte? A mere child, a nuisance! How dare you? You make her sound like a stranger. She's your flesh and blood, Luigi. You should be delirious with pleasure. You should be glad to have her around. You should be getting to know her better.'

'And I think,' he grated harshly, 'that we should work on our own relationship before Charlotte's. Of course I love my daughter; she's brought life to the house. She's a beautiful, intelligent little girl and I'm proud of her. But we need to get our own lives in order.'

'That's rich, coming from you,' she riposted. 'You were the one who let our marriage down. And, to be perfectly honest, I can't see you changing. Your answer to everything is to pay someone to do your dirty work. Including looking after your daughter. How sad is that?' And finally, with strength born of desperation, she managed to tear free. But she didn't leave the room. Instead she stood a few feet away, glaring at Luigi like an enraged tigress.

His eyes narrowed, becoming two glittering slits that reflected the light from the lamps. And his whole body was tense with a rage he was doing his level best to control. Not that Megan cared whether he controlled it or not. She was past caring what Luigi felt. All she was concerned about was her darling daughter's welfare.

'I think,' he said fiercely, 'that you're blowing this thing up out of all proportion. It will do you good to have more time to yourself.'

'And there'll be lots of that,' she retorted hostilely, 'because you'll still be working all the hours God gave. You're all talk, Luigi. How could you possibly take time off? Everything would collapse if you weren't at the helm.'

Her sarcasm wasn't lost on him. She saw the muscles

clench in his jaw, the way his mouth went even straighter and grimmer, and it was a second or two before he answered. And when he did his voice was deadly calm. 'I've said I'll take you away, Megan, and that's exactly what I intend to do.'

'And if I don't want to come? Charlotte's never been parted from me. I wouldn't leave her if I thought she'd be upset.'

He brushed her doubts away. 'We'll give her time to get used to Kate. She comes with the highest recommendation; I don't think we have a problem.'

'And no doubt you're paying her the highest wage,' she retorted. 'I truly never expected that you'd turn out like this. Money, money, money, all the time. I must have been insane to marry you.'

'Is it a crime to want to better oneself?' he asked icily.

'Of course not, but there's a limit. You're taking things a step too far.'

'In your eyes, not mine.'

'So you're happy here in this mausoleum of a home? You enjoy having other people run around after you, pandering to your every whim? Is that the pleasure money brings? It doesn't seem like pleasure to me.'

'So tell me, Megan.' He cocked his head on one side and looked at her consideringly. 'What does pleasure you?'

Her cheeks flushed beneath that knowing stare, and her heart faltered as she realised that she had left herself wide open.

He moved purposefully towards her. 'Don't tell me,' he said on a low growl. 'Let me show you.'

Before she could even draw breath she was in his arms, her mouth opening of its own volition beneath the persuasive power of his. Megan knew that she ought to protest—loudly, volubly; she ought to push him away, show him that actions like this got him nowhere. But, fool that she was, she let her senses take over.

She enjoyed the thrill of his hard, sexy body against hers. She revelled in the feelings he aroused deep within her. She wanted more. She wanted all of him! The thought set off alarm bells in her head but she chose to ignore them. Luigi had talked about catching up on the years they'd spent apart, but it was their times in bed that she'd missed. Missed without really knowing it. Was it any wonder that she'd kept herself a man-free zone? No other man was good enough. No other man could possibly arouse her to this extent. They were soulmates as far as good sex was concerned.

Megan oughtn't to have taunted him. Kissing her at this moment in time was the worst thing he could possibly do—except that she was so damned gorgeous how could he resist? Which begged the question, why hadn't he made more of an effort to find her? Luigi knew that he could never come up with an answer. He'd been a fool. It was as simple as that. A blind fool, who thought that immersing himself in his work was the answer to everything.

And now he had a lot of making up to do. He was fully aware that it was going to be a long, hard slog and that he mustn't go too quickly—even if at times like this she actually seemed to welcome his advances. It was pure sex, she'd said, and although he didn't want to believe her he sometimes felt that she was right. And this was one of those occasions.

With reluctance he drew away. He stepped back a pace and felt virtuous that she looked surprised and a teeny bit disappointed. No, hugely disappointed. She was totally aroused, he could tell by her flushed cheeks and shining eyes, and if he had pushed his luck he could have taken her to bed. Which he wanted to! Very much so! His testosterone levels had risen to danger point. But it was good that he had stopped. It would show her that sex wasn't the only thing he wanted from their relationship.

'I think we ought to finish our dinner,' he said gruffly.

'I'm not hungry.'

Nor was he—except for this woman, his wife. He clamped his lips and nodded, only the slightest movement of his head. Megan didn't even notice. But that was what she was, his wife. She belonged to him. She could run but he would never divorce her. One day they would be a happy and contented couple again. With perhaps another child to keep Charlotte company. It was only a matter of time.

Megan went to bed with a heavy heart. Luigi was doing his best and she appreciated that, but in her eyes it wasn't good enough. And letting him make love to her was no answer either; it distorted her judgement, it reminded her of all that had been good in their marriage. It made her forget the long hours of neglect. So, although she had felt bereft when he backed away, she was now glad of it, and determined not to let herself be swayed into such a position again. Easy to say but difficult to do! Even the thought of kissing Luigi had her aching inside and she wasn't sure that she could be strong enough to deny him.

But she would give it a good try. Luigi needed to reform; he needed to put his wife and daughter before his business interests. And when he did that—then perhaps their marriage would stand a chance.

His idea of taking her away for a few days was a sound one in principle. In fact it would be heaven—if it weren't for Charlotte, and the fact that Megan knew unequivocally that once they were back he would revert to his old ways. Who was it who said that a leopard never changed its spots? Luigi would never change. Working was his way of life; his wife and now his child came second. They always would.

She was almost asleep when her door slowly opened. At first she thought she was dreaming when she saw Luigi's shadowy shape in the doorway, but as he began to make his way softly over to her bed she sat bolt upright. Her heart stampeded as her need for him rose like a phoenix from the ashes.

But fear overrode her desire. 'What the hell are you doing here?' Her voice was low but shrill and there was panic inside her. He was a danger to her system—and he probably knew it. He knew that relaxed in bed she would be at her lowest ebb, and it would be easy to take advantage.

'There's something I need to ask you.' He came to a halt at her side and looked fiercely down. And Megan didn't see desire, she didn't see a deep-seated need of her body, instead she saw something that sent a chill through her entire system.

CHAPTER SEVEN

'I'VE just discovered that you haven't been entirely truthful with me,' Luigi spat.

Megan frowned. 'What do you mean?' She had no idea what he was talking about. And she'd never seen him look at her so coldly or accusingly. It set her teeth on edge and made goose-bumps rise all over her body.

'The fact that you indulged in an affair with another man and lied to me about it,' he shot at her harshly.

'What?' she shrieked, jumping up from the bed. 'You're not making sense. Who, for pity's sake, am I supposed to have slept with?' She dragged her dressing gown on over her nightie and hugged it closely around her. 'Where did you conjure up that piece of fiction?'

'Straight from the horse's mouth, if you must know,' he thundered.

Megan shook her head. 'This is nonsense.'

'I knew you'd say that,' he scorned. 'I was expecting it.'

'So why don't you tell me who's made these accusations?' she asked him coldly, an icy shiver beginning to take over. It was all she could do to keep herself still.

'Your dear friend, Jake.'

'*Jake?*' Megan echoed dazedly. 'You have to be joking. In any case, when did you speak to him? Jenny hasn't rung to say they're back.'

'They are, I assure you. I phoned them myself.'

'Why?' she questioned loudly.

'I needed to make sure she wasn't out of pocket with you moving out so suddenly.'

'And you spoke to Jake, and he told you that he and I had had an affair, is that what you're saying?' Megan couldn't comprehend. Why would Jake make such a statement when it wasn't true?

'He hinted that you'd been friends before Jenny came on the scene, and the emphasis he put on the word "friends" made me realise what he was trying to tell me.'

'So he didn't put it in as many words?'

'He didn't need to. I got the message.'

It was true; she had known Jake before Jenny did. She had worked with him when she first came to London, and he'd sort of taken her under his wing. But she hadn't had any kind of relationship with him, even though he would have liked to. She hadn't felt ready to commit to any man. One day he'd gone back to the flat with her to borrow a book and she'd been delighted when he and Jenny struck up a close friendship.

'Why should it bother you that I might have seen other men during our separation?' she asked him coolly, at the same time thinking that this could work in her favour. Luigi had had other girls, she knew, but he seemed incensed when it came to her doing the same. This could be a way to keep him at a distance.

'Because you're my woman,' he snarled, practically bouncing on his feet. His dark eyes glittered in the light from the bedside lamp, and his face was angular and savage—and gorgeously handsome.

Megan shook the thought away. Luigi was her number one enemy. She must remember that. She must never see him as an expert lover, as a man who could melt her bones by a mere glance or a touch. He had never treated her fairly, not once in all the years of their marriage. He was self-centred and egotistical. She dismissed the fact that he was an excellent provider and an expert businessman. It was the unadulterated love of a good man that she desired. And love wasn't high on Luigi's list of priorities. In fact she doubted it even existed.

'I am not your woman,' she told him tersely. 'You gave up all rights to me when you chose work over your marriage.'

'I did it for *us!*' he exclaimed loudly.

'So you keep saying. But it wasn't what I wanted.'

'And did Jake Whatever-his-name-is give you what you wanted?' he demanded fiercely.

'That's my business.' She saw the angry glitter harden in his eyes and his body swayed dangerously towards her. But she stood her ground, her eyes fierce in their determination, even though there was a part of her that couldn't dismiss the sensations playing on her nerve-ends—excitement and hatred bundled into one.

'And I think it's my business now to remind you, in a very personal way, that I don't want any other man to touch you ever again.' They were so close that Megan could feel his breath on her face, feel the warmth of his body, and she could even smell the male sexiness that had at one time driven her insane. 'You *are* my woman,' he continued grimly. 'You can deny it all you like, but you belong to me for the rest of your life.'

If that wasn't a warning she didn't know what was. *For the rest of her life!* In her present frame of mind it sounded like a death sentence and she wanted to lash out, to pound her fists on his hard, muscular chest, to kick his shins, to let him know in no uncertain terms that he was mistaken.

But she was afraid to make too much noise in case

she woke Charlotte. So she maintained a reasonable decorum. 'Carry on like that and I really will divorce you,' she said quietly. 'Marriages aren't built on threats, nor on absentee husbands. And if you can't live with the fact that you *believe* I've had an affair with Jake then I'll willingly move out.'

'*No!*'

The boom of his voice sent her eyes fluttering towards Charlotte's door, fortunately closed. Sometimes she left it open, but tonight she'd been reading and was afraid the light might waken her daughter. She thanked her lucky stars now for her foresight.

'I've told you, I will never let you go.'

'Unless you change your ways you won't be able to hold me,' she declared vehemently. 'Threats won't work.'

'I'll threaten you all I like,' he snarled, 'since you don't seem to be prepared to even meet me halfway.'

'Meet you, when you are the one laying down the rules?' she questioned heatedly. 'You are the one who insisted I stay here. You are the one who insisted on employing a nanny for Charlotte. You are the one who's insisting we go away for a few days. My opinion has never counted.'

'Because I know what's good for you.'

Megan's anger boiled over. 'There you go again. When are you going to get it through your thick skull that a happy marriage means give and take? All you do is take, and I'm heartily fed up with it. Change that attitude and we might get somewhere.'

She watched as his mouth folded into a grim line and his eyes narrowed until she could see nothing through the slits of his lids. A quiver of unease tracked its way through her limbs. It looked as though she'd gone too far. Yet he deserved it. Why shouldn't she toss him a few home truths?

'I'd appreciate it if you'd meet me halfway, Megan.'

It was not the response she'd expected and although it was delivered in hard, terse tones she couldn't help feeling a twinge of guilt. She dismissed it immediately. Guilt had no place to play in this scenario. Not on her part anyway. Luigi was the one at fault—every inch of the way.

She had thought that meeting his daughter would soften him up, but that hadn't happened. He was no nearer to being a caring husband or father than he had been all those years ago. He was in charge and he expected everyone to jump at his command. Well, not this girl!

'Why should I?' she asked with a toss of her head. 'Why should I subject my daughter to a tyrant of a father?'

'Tyrant?' he exploded. 'Is that how you see me?'

'All the time.'

He closed his eyes and his fingers curled into tight fists, and Megan had the feeling that it was taking all his self-control not to lash out at her. She was tired of this confrontation. She wanted him to go. He had come here ready for a fight and because she hadn't caved in and eaten humble pie he was still spoiling for one.

She wouldn't give him that pleasure.

'Fortunately Charlotte doesn't see it that way,' she added. 'Perhaps because she hasn't been here long enough and you're on your best behaviour in front of her.'

Luigi snorted derisively. 'You have no idea what you're talking about. You're blinded by hatred. In fact you're the one with the problem. If you'd jump down off your high horse occasionally you'd see how much I've changed.'

Megan gave a tight, brittle laugh. 'Then I must be blind. Have we finished this conversation? I really would like to get some sleep.' Not that she expected to drop off now. She was far too uptight.

'Maybe it is finished, but not satisfactorily,' he barked, swinging on his heel and heading for the door.

'You mean that it hurt when I didn't deny having a fling with Jake?' she taunted. 'I wouldn't worry about it if I were you. I'm not worrying about the girls you bedded while I was busy bringing up your daughter. We were free agents at the time. Why drag up the past?'

Again his mouth thinned but to give him his due he didn't retaliate; he simply wrenched open the door and stepped smartly outside. She half-expected him to slam it, was thankful when he didn't. She didn't want Charlotte or even Kate wondering why he was storming out of her room.

The thought occurred to her that Kate might not know they slept in separate rooms. Had Luigi told her anything about their circumstances, or did she think they were a normal happily married couple? It could be embarrassing if she ever came in to see to Charlotte and saw that Megan slept alone.

Luigi had been spitting fire when he sought Megan out. He had phoned her friend on the spur of the moment, not really knowing whether she was back from France. Jake had answered. And when Luigi stated his business he had gone into a long tribute to Megan. So much so that Luigi had begun to gain the impression that more had gone on between them than Megan had ever admitted. He'd felt an indescribable jealousy. The very thought of another man touching his wife was sickeningly abhorrent and he'd been prepared to shake the truth out of Megan.

And now when he thought back on their conversation he realised that he hadn't won at all. Megan was tougher than he'd realised and she had fought back with admirable qualities. He still didn't know whether she'd actually slept with Jake and the thought drove him crazy.

So much so that he couldn't sleep. In the end he dragged on a tartan dressing gown over his boxer shorts, went downstairs to his den and sat at his computer. There was work that needed to be done but, dammit, he couldn't do that either. He kept seeing images of a fired-up Megan as she stood before him.

How he had fought the urge to pull her hard against him he didn't know. He'd wanted to forget everything Jake had told him and make love to her. With her hair tousled and her face flushed, and nothing on beneath her cotton nightdress, his virulent male hormones had sprung into life. He loved Megan so much that it tore him apart when she rejected him. Was he really as bad as she painted?

It was true that no one ever saw themselves as other people did, but a tyrant? Always taking, never giving? He wasn't like that. The presents he'd bought both her and Charlotte should have proved it. And she had this huge house to live in, no more worries about rent. He was prepared to give her anything she wanted. He'd even cut down on his working hours; hadn't she noticed that?

The more he thought about it the more confused he became. He picked up the whisky bottle and poured himself a generous measure, tossing it down his throat in one swallow before refilling it. This time he set it on the desk in front of him, fingering the cut-glass, twisting it absently round and round. But the more he thought about the situation the more he failed to understand it and fury rose once more inside him. He gulped down the rest of the whisky and in a fit of rage threw the glass at the fireplace, shattering it into a thousand tiny pieces.

The next moment his door was pushed open and there stood Megan, pale-faced and questioning, still in her nightdress and dressing gown. *With nothing on underneath!* This was the first thought that registered. The second was, what was she doing here? Why wasn't she in bed? And his third, perhaps she'd had a change of heart, realised that she'd been too hard on him, and had come to make amends.

His entire body throbbed in anticipation.

Megan looked from him to the fragments of glass in the hearth and then back again, a faint frown dragging her brows together. 'So you're still angry about Jake?'

Damn! She wasn't supposed to have said that. He felt his sudden hope draining away. 'What are you doing here?' he enquired gruffly.

'I was on my way to the kitchen to heat some milk.'

'Your conscience troubling you?' he sneered. He couldn't help himself. His optimism had been so miserably dashed.

'Not as much as yours, obviously,' she riposted, backing away from the doorway, ready to carry on her journey.

'Wait!' he said, though he didn't know why. He wanted her company and yet he knew it would be volatile. But better that than nothing.

She looked boldly and questioningly in his direction. 'For what? More of what you've just put me through? No, thank you.' And this time she walked away.

But Luigi wasn't prepared to let her go. He couldn't get through this night without her. 'Megan, please.'

She faltered and stopped.

'Come and talk to me.'

'Why should I?'

'It's silly us both being wide awake. We may as well keep each other company.'

'Not if you're going to pick another fight.' She half turned towards him but still looked prepared to flee.

He held up his hands. 'Truce.'

'How can I believe you? You already have me hung, drawn and quartered. Why should I escape more misery?'

'Because I don't feel like my own company at this moment.' He was exposing his feelings in a way he never had before. He always liked to give the image that he was in complete control—which he usually was. It was only Megan who managed to instil doubt into him—doubt and despair.

'You mean you might throw a few more glasses? Is it an image of me that you're throwing them at or disgust with yourself?'

He winced, but refused to give her the pleasure of seeing how accurate her second guess was. 'Perhaps it's a bad idea. I wasn't intending it to be a re-run of what happened upstairs. I simply thought we might both enjoy some company. But if it's too much for you...' He saw her hesitate, the doubt in her eyes, then the reluctant decision that he might be right.

'Very well,' she answered quietly, 'but I'd still like some hot milk. How about you?'

On top of whisky! But if it helped keep her at his side... 'I'd like that, shall I—?'

'Come and help? No thanks! I'll be back in a few minutes.'

He watched her walk along the corridor, her behind swaying seductively with each step that she took. She walked like a model, every inch of her alerting his senses to such a degree that he began to question the perverseness that had made him invite her into his sanctum. He wouldn't be able to touch her, he knew that, there was a mile-wide gap between them that would be difficult, if not impossible, to bridge. Not in a few minutes, or even hours. Days, weeks maybe, but he wasn't that patient.

To him it was simple. They resumed marital relations and the rest would follow. It was Megan who was making progress difficult, finding problems when there were none. He would never understand her.

In the five minutes it took her to heat milk and make their drinks he'd decided that they needed to have a real heart to heart. It was the only way they would be able to solve their problems. And probably now, in the middle of the night, was the very best time. No Charlotte to interrupt, no phone calls, nothing except the two of them—together.

Hunger for her crept through every one of his strong male veins. How he was going to sit there, knowing that she was as naked as the day she was born beneath her enchanting white nightie, laced from waist to throat with a Christmas-red ribbon, and do nothing about it he didn't know. It would be the worst form of torture.

She returned with their drinks on a tray, together with a plate of home-made biscuits which he knew would choke him if he attempted to eat one. What he wanted to do was suck one of Megan's nipples into his mouth. She always tasted so beautiful and reacted so wantonly.

He wanted to suck and bite and tease until she was putty in his hands. He wanted to feel her softly scented body close to him, he wanted to mould her with his palms, feel every curve and contour; he wanted to touch her most intimate places, feel her moistness, make her as ready for him as he was for her.

But he knew he couldn't.

She was out of bounds.

For the moment!

But soon…

Megan nibbled on a biscuit, sitting in the armchair opposite him where he couldn't possibly touch her, but he could look… It was warm in the room. He had stoked up the fire and it burned brightly in the grate. Her purple dressing gown was undone, the ribbon on her nightdress beckoning his fingers to untie the bow and unlace it. Lord, he wanted to look at her—she was his wife, after all. Instead she was covered up as primly as a nun.

He picked up his mug of malted milk and cradled it in his palms. It was absolutely no compensation for her temptingly full breasts. He felt compelled to close his eyes so that he needn't look at her.

'Are you tired now? Shall I go?'

Her question had his lids jerking open. 'Not at all. I was simply thinking.'

'About what? Us?'

He shrugged. 'Does it matter when you're determined that—?'

'I'm not determined about anything,' she forestalled him.

'I don't see any sign of you wishing to kiss and make up.'

'That's because a lot of water's gone under the bridge.

Before we kiss we talk. We have to resolve our differences. It's the only way.'

'I'm trying.'

Megan raised her beautifully shaped brows. 'You could have fooled me.'

Something red shot in front of his eyes and he was ready to blast. It was only with an extreme effort that he managed to exercise caution and say calmly, 'Perhaps you're not really looking. You have it so firmly fixed in your mind that I'm the baddie in all of this that you're missing the improvements.'

'Spell them out to me.'

He didn't want to do that. It wasn't the answer. 'If you can't see them then perhaps I'm wasting my time.'

'I have noticed,' she said with slow consideration, 'that you don't spend quite so much time at work. But I assumed it was because of the Christmas holidays. It doesn't really prove anything.'

His breath whistled thinly through his teeth. 'Did I ever take time off at Christmas?' He couldn't help the sharpness of his tone.

'The first year we were married you did. We had a wonderful Christmas together.' Her eyes lit up as she spoke and he saw a glimpse of the girl he had first met. The girl who had ensnared him in an invisible net that could never be broken. 'But after that,' she went on, 'you only took Christmas Day off. Even then you were a grouch.'

That was because his mind was always connected to whatever money-spinning idea he was working on. Looking back, he could see that perhaps he had been a little unfair on Megan—but not as much as she was making out. 'So surely you can see,' he pointed out, his tone strong and firm, 'that I'm doing my level best to spend more time with you.'

'And how long will it last?' she asked caustically.

'With your co-operation, if you don't constantly raise your hackles whenever I'm around, for ever.' He saw the way her brows rose ever so slightly, the disbelief in her perfectly shaped grey eyes. 'I'm serious. I want this to work, Megan. You are my whole life. Without you it has no meaning.'

Disbelief gave way to surprise, her eyes widening as they remained steadily on his. 'You've never said anything like that before.'

'I didn't feel I had to. I thought you knew.'

'I know nothing unless you tell me,' she insisted.

Not that he loved her? How could that be? He didn't find it easy to say the words, but surely she knew? Why else would he want her back? He took a long, slow drink from his mug, watching her over the rim as he did so. He could prove to her in bed exactly how much he loved her—if she would only let him. Dared he suggest it?

He didn't think so.

She was just as likely to slap him across the face. But even that contact would be better than the distance that separated them. It felt like a mile instead of a couple of feet.

Megan sipped her milk too, avoiding his eyes, staring absently into the flickering flames of the fire. She looked so beautiful sitting there, the glow from the coals warming her face, softening the shadows. He could imagine her in just such a position breast-feeding her baby. He had missed that! He had missed everything to do with Charlotte's birth and her first important years. He hadn't seen her learn to walk or talk, her first teeth coming through, her first word—which might have been 'Daddy' if he'd been there! Instead she'd never known what it was like to have a father.

Bitterness crept in and he began to wonder whether it had been such a good idea to invite Megan to sit with him. He didn't want a confrontation, but that was exactly how he felt. *So much he had missed!* And it was all her fault! He clattered his mug down on the table.

Megan followed suit. 'I'm feeling sleepy now,' she said, although he knew she was lying.

'I think I might go to bed too,' he declared. This wasn't how he had wanted it to end but it looked as though he had no choice.

'I'll leave you to make sure the fire's safe. Goodnight, Luigi.'

'Goodnight, Megan.'

So formal! No kiss, no touch, no sign that they meant anything to each other, and yet he would stake everything he owned that her body craved his just as much as his did hers.

Perhaps he should kiss her, a gentle peck on the forehead, nothing more, just enough to let her know that he cared. But already it was too late; she had left the room and he could hear her running lightly up the stairs.

When he followed later his footsteps were much slower and heavier.

CHAPTER EIGHT

WHEN Megan woke the day was bright and sunny—and Charlotte's room was empty! It took her a second or two to remember that there was now a nanny to attend to her daughter's needs. It didn't please her. She enjoyed cuddling her sleepy-headed daughter first thing in the morning, feeling the heat of her skin, ruffling her already tousled hair. It was a mother-child thing and she didn't like the experience being taken from her.

Something else that she hated Luigi for!

She showered and dressed in a red sweater and black ski pants and went downstairs to find her daughter. Instead she found Luigi—in the breakfast room, his empty plate in front of him and a cup of coffee in his hand. 'Good morning.' He gave her a smile that sent an electric tingle down her spine.

Careful, she warned, don't fall into his trap. He was expert at seducing her senses. She had felt it last night; she had wanted to stay with him in his den and let him make love to her in front of the fire. So much she had wanted it. His needs had been her needs. She hadn't lived with him without being able to tell when he desired her. And, despite all the harsh things that she'd said to him, she had wanted him too.

But it wasn't in her plan of things. Before anything like that happened again she needed to be convinced that he'd reformed. Not only fewer hours at work but he needed to love his daughter in the way a child needed to be loved. Armfuls of presents were not the answer.

She was still determined to take most of them back to the store, the ones he'd given her as well. She couldn't be bought; she wasn't a piece of baggage.

'What's going through that mind of yours? That frown's enough to frighten away the fiercest predator.' There was lazy amusement in his voice and it was good to see him looking so relaxed. Usually at this time of the morning he was eating a piece of toast while he fixed his tie—either that or he had already left. Perhaps he *was* turning over a new leaf.

'It is? Then I guess you're the predator as you're the only person in the room.'

'And you're my prey?' He looked pleased at the thought.

'I think not. Is the coffee still hot?' She was aware of his eyes on her breasts where they pushed against the thin wool of her sweater. His examination made them go taut with expectation, her nipples peaking, and the rest of her body filling with tingling warmth.

'Amy's going to bring you in some tea.'

'That's good of her.' She sat down quickly. This immediate reaction was unexpected. She even felt slightly breathless. It was madness. How could she keep up her campaign, feeling as she did?

'What would you like to eat?' Luigi pushed himself easily up from the table and strode to the heated tray on the sideboard, lifting lids on the silver dishes. 'Bacon? Sausage? Tomatoes? Mushrooms? Eggs? Some of each?'

He wore grey worsted trousers that fitted snugly over his hips, and a yellow cashmere sweater. It was a colour she'd never seen him in before. It suited his dark complexion. As she watched him peering into each dish in turn it occurred to her that she was studying him in exactly the same way as he had looked at her earlier, and she turned her head away. 'Toast and marmalade will be fine, thank you,' she announced primly.

'You're going to let this good food go to waste? Is that really all you want?'

'You know I never eat much in the morning. On the other hand, perhaps you don't. You were always in too much of a hurry to sit and have breakfast with me.' Her tone was deliberately sharp. It annoyed her that he was still able to arouse her without doing anything.

'I imagine that happens in most working families,' he said. 'But all that's changed. You no longer work. I don't have to go in so early. There's no reason in the world why we shouldn't sit and have breakfast together every morning.' He was back in his chair, pushing the toast rack and marmalade and butter dishes closer towards her.

'Pardon me,' she said, 'but I haven't given up my job yet. I'm still on Christmas leave.'

A brow rose. 'I forgot to tell you; I rang your firm and told them that you wouldn't be going back.'

'What?' Megan's eyes flashed outrage. He'd gone over her head again. 'You had no right. In any case, how did you know where I worked?'

'I made it my business to find out.' He didn't look in the least apologetic.

'Jenny told you—or Jake. Was it him?' She'd kill him when she next saw him.

'Does it matter who?'

It mattered to her. Very much! Where was her friends' sense of loyalty? She was trapped now, whether she wanted to be or not. She'd agreed to a few days. Now, without an income, she'd have to spend for ever with Luigi—or as long as it took for her to find another job and somewhere else to live! And the longer they stayed here the more settled Charlotte would become, and the harder it would be to move!

'I hate you, Luigi Costanzo.'

He smiled. 'You look beautiful when you're all fired up.'

At that moment Amy came in with a pot of freshly brewed tea, and the girl beamed when she heard Luigi tell Megan that she was beautiful. There was a skip to her step as she walked out.

'I think Amy approves of you,' he said, still with that aggravating smile.

'I don't care what she thinks,' Megan riposted. 'You had no right to do that. You're trying to make me your prisoner and I'm not.'

'Of course not, you're my wife,' he shot back at once. 'My very beautiful wife,' he added on a low growl. 'Red suits you; you should wear it more often. It makes your face come alive.'

'Flattery will get you nowhere,' she retorted coldly, her spine stiffening. She didn't want to be reminded of last night, when she had been uncomfortably aware of them both in their night clothes. It had brought back memories of the early weeks of their marriage when sometimes, at weekends, they hadn't bothered to get dressed at all.

Luigi used to say that he liked it when she was ready for him at any time, without the hindrance of top clothes with their buttons and zips and hooks. And she had to admit that she'd found it exciting too.

She poured herself a cup of tea, nibbled on a triangle of toast, and for once wished that he'd leave her and go to work. Contrarily, he showed no sign of moving. In fact, he gave the impression that he'd be happy sitting here all day.

'It's New Year's Eve tomorrow,' he reminded her.

Megan nodded. It was just another day as far as she was concerned. Another day in purgatory! Well, not quite, but that was how she preferred to think about it. She couldn't imagine living the rest of her life like this. If things were different between them, if he loved her, really loved her, and if he loved Charlotte the same way as she did, then perhaps there'd be hope. But not as things stood.

'I'm having a little get together.'

Megan frowned. 'You are?' She couldn't imagine Luigi celebrating New Year, not in his own home. Someone else's party, maybe, if it didn't interfere too much with his work. He'd probably network anyway. But a party here? There had to be some ulterior motive. 'Why?'

'It's time I brought this house alive. You've taught me that, Megan. Your reference to a mausoleum made me think. I'm going to open my doors to everyone I know.'

'Everyone? You said a little get together.'

'Perhaps not so little,' he agreed with a dangerous smile that revealed even white teeth.

He had beautiful teeth but they reminded her at that moment of the wolf in Little Red Riding Hood. Predatory! Here was the word again. 'So who are you inviting?'

'Business associates, colleagues, friends, neighbours. Anyone who cares to come.'

'And you didn't think to tell me?'

'I wanted it to be a surprise.'

'It's certainly that. Who's organising it?'

'Various people. Edwina and William are arranging everything here. Serena's seeing to the invitations—'

'Serena!' Megan slapped her toast down and glared at him. 'Why Serena? It should be my job.' She wished that she'd thrown the bread in his face; he deserved it. He was an out and out swine. Serena this, Serena that; she was always ingratiating herself into his favour. And how was she to know that he didn't share his PA's bed sometimes as well?

'Of course, my darling, but you know hardly anyone here yet. Next year you can write the list.'

'I doubt I'll be here next year,' she gritted through clenched teeth.

She wasn't looking at him but she heard his chair scrape back on the wooden floor and the next second he had hauled her to her feet and his big, strong hands were gripping her upper arms. 'You *will* be here,' he threatened. 'Haven't I made myself clear? I'm not letting you go again.'

'You won't be able to stop me,' she retorted. 'I won't have you flaunting Serena in my face. If you don't get rid of her, I go.'

Luigi's eyes narrowed damningly. 'You know I can't do that. She practically runs my business affairs for me.'

'That's no reason why she should run your private life as well. Unless she is part of that too! Is she?' She looked directly into his eyes and they didn't flicker.

'Megan, you are the only woman for me. You must believe that.'

She wanted to, but there were so many things that filled her with doubt and, just when she was beginning to learn to trust him, along came something else to threaten her tenuous hold. 'So you keep saying. I have little proof of it so far.'

His brows met, his eyes narrowed into dangerous slits. 'That's because you won't let me in.'

'With just cause. As you've this very second proved.'

'Serena is no threat to you.'

'She wants to be.'

'Maybe,' he admitted. 'But she's very well aware that you're now back in my life, a total part of it, and that there's no place for her. You have nothing to fear where she is concerned.'

'Really?' Megan doubted his conviction. And she noticed that he didn't say that Serena knew that he loved her. It was always missing. The one thing she most wanted to hear. *She was a total part of his life.* What the hell was that supposed to mean? Anyone could be a part of your life. Edwina the cook was a part of his life. As was Amy, and William, and now Kate.

'Truly. You'll see tomorrow. She'll probably be over early to oversee the final details. I—'

'*No!*'

Her sudden and savage exclamation brought his chin up with a jerk.

'I won't have that woman doing things that I should be doing. I'll see to everything—and I won't let you down,' she added caustically as she saw the beginnings of doubt creep across his face.

'You're jealous!' he accused with a swift smirk.

'Don't flatter yourself,' she tossed smartly. 'It's just that I don't think your business life and private one should intermingle. Serena can do what she likes in the office, but not here.'

He shrugged and his hands dropped from her shoulders. 'Very well, I'll leave it to you.'

'How many are you expecting?'

'About fifty.'

More than she'd thought. But there was a ballroom that would hold them all easily. She'd better go and see Edwina, check on the arrangements, see if there was anything she could do. 'Are you working today?' For once she wanted him out of the way.

'I thought I'd pop in for an hour or so.'

'Mummy, Mummy, we're having a party.' Charlotte charged into the room and threw herself at her mother.

Megan whirled her around and kissed her soundly. 'It's not for children, sweetheart.'

Her daughter's bottom lip began to drop.

'But if you're a very good girl, maybe Daddy and I will let you stay up for a little while. What do you say, Daddy?'

He lifted Charlotte into his arms, the first really natural gesture Megan had seen. 'For one hour, but that's all.'

'Are we having jelly and ice-cream?'

'It's not that sort of party, princess.'

Charlotte frowned. 'What sort then?'

'People drink and talk and dance, and at midnight everyone sings Auld Lang Syne and—'

'She won't understand any of that,' interrupted Megan. 'It's just a lot of grown ups, sweetheart, who do lots of boring things.'

'No children?'

'None at all.'

'I don't think I want to come then. Will you still read me a bedtime story, Mummy, or will you be too busy?'

'I'll never be too busy for you, my little darling.'

'And you, Daddy, will you read to me too?'

It was the first time she'd asked Luigi and Megan held her breath as she waited for his answer. She prayed he wouldn't reject her.

'Only if you tell me which story you want.'

'Yes, yes, the one about the little girl sliding down the rainbow.'

'Then I'll read it to you,' he said, 'but you'll have to help me because I'm not very good at reading to little girls.'

'Mummy's good at it. She'll help you.'

Megan smiled weakly. The thought of sitting side by side with Luigi reading to their daughter should have filled her with immense pleasure, but it didn't—because she knew he wouldn't have his heart and soul in it. He wasn't doing it because he wanted to, but because Charlotte had demanded it.

When Luigi finally left for the office Megan went in search of Edwina. William was already filling the ballroom with holly and mistletoe gathered from the estate, and Edwina was beside herself with excitement. 'It's been many a year since we had a party here, long before Mr Luigi took over. Oh, it's good to see the house being brought back to life again.'

Soon, Megan was immersing herself in the preparations. Even Charlotte helped, carefully watched over by a hovering Kate. Apparently Edwina had been baking and freezing for days and there was only the fresh food to be prepared as soon as it was delivered. The drinks arrived—enough cases of champagne and wine to last a lifetime, thought Megan, but she couldn't help getting caught up in the excitement of the occasion.

It was pandemonium at times, but with the gardener to help William, and both Amy and Megan helping Edwina, by the time Luigi came home all was ready. And there was even plenty of time for them to sit with Charlotte while she had a light tea. Afterwards Kate bathed her while Megan decided which of the dozen or so delectable dresses Luigi had given her for Christmas she was going to wear. Then they both sat at their daughter's bedside and took turns in reading to her until she fell asleep.

Megan was impressed by Luigi's rendition of The Rainbow Children. She had imagined a dull monologue; instead he'd put exactly the right inflection into his voice for each of the characters. She said as much to him.

'I imagined that if I'd ever had anyone read to me that's what I would have wanted.' There was a gruff grimness to his voice as he spoke, reminding her what an awful and loveless childhood he'd had. And it made her wonder whether she was being too hard on him.

But the moment they were out of Charlotte's room he spoilt it all by saying, 'Serena's going to be here early. She needs to check that—'

'Serena needs to check nothing,' Megan told him tersely. 'We've all worked like Trojans today and if there's something not quite right then it's too late to do anything about it. Phone and tell her.' She didn't want the other woman parading all over the place as though it was her rightful duty. Not while *she* was living in this house!

Megan took extra special care getting ready. She had a strong feeling that Serena would try to outdo her, that she would want to be the star of the evening. Of course, she might be wrong, but she couldn't forget the way the other woman had spoken to her. ''I think Luigi will be available if you tell him who I am.'' ''He's a fool not to have divorced her.'' If that didn't tell her that Serena had designs on him then nothing would.

She was glad now that Luigi had given her some beautiful dresses for Christmas. She'd decided on the red one, bearing in mind what he'd said about the colour suiting her. It was far more sophisticated and daring than anything she'd worn in the past, but as she slid the soft material over her head and smoothed the folds over her breasts and hips, she began to feel a different person. More elegant than ever before, full of confidence, totally in charge of her feelings. She could be whoever she wanted to be. And that person was Luigi's wife. In every respect!

Look out, Serena!

Their guests were arriving at eight. At a quarter to she was ready. Luigi tapped on her door and entered, and he took her breath away. His cream tuxedo and black trousers emphasised his fine physique and complemented his Latin colouring. She had never seen him so devastatingly handsome and crazily she wanted to rip off his clothes and make love to him.

'Megan, you look ravishing.'

Not half as ravishing as you, she thought, swallowing hard and moistening lips that had gone suddenly dry. In fact her whole mouth was dry. She needed a drink, a good stiff drink.

Luigi was looking at her as though he'd never seen her before, appraising every inch of her body, starting with the strappy, high-heeled silver sandals and her scarlet painted toenails. Over the long, softly flowing skirt which swirled about her ankles but clung lovingly to her slender hips, following it up to the deep vee which finished just below her breasts.

It was almost as though he was touching her. Wherever his eyes went she felt a burning sensation, and when he paused on the swell of her breasts she ached for him to touch her. It would have been so easy for him to cross the space that divided them and take what she was willing to give.

But he didn't move. He seemed transfixed. She wondered whether he had ever actually seen the dress before. Whether he had picked it personally or had his shop assistants pack half a dozen or so in her size. Probably so. But at this moment she didn't care.

It was doing things to both of them that should never be allowed. She was thankful for the light support built into the dress that hid her peaking nipples. She didn't want anyone but Luigi to know how aroused she was. But she wanted him to know it; she needed him to want no one but her this evening.

The back of the dress dipped low as well, though he couldn't see that yet. He would find out when they danced together, when his hands held her close, when she felt the strong beat of his heart against her own. When they declared to the whole world that they were man and wife and no one could put them asunder. Lord, she was running ahead of herself. Was she ready for this yet? Was Luigi ready? Or was she doing it simply to spite Serena?

The dress was sleeveless and ruched on the shoulders, and beaded with intricate embroidery. This one dress alone must have cost him a small fortune. But she loved it.

'We'd better go down before I rip that thing off you and carry you to my bed,' he said gruffly.

Megan couldn't even speak. She simply nodded and smiled—weakly, and as she walked towards him her heart pounded like a sledge-hammer within her breast. 'Thank you for the dress, Luigi,' she said in a faint whisper.

'Thank you for wearing it. You look sensational.

You'll knock everyone dead tonight, and I shall be so proud to introduce you as my wife.' He tucked her arm into his and together they walked along the landing and down the stairs.

Megan felt proud and she walked tall, and when the first person she set eyes on was Serena she grew another couple of inches.

At least she presumed it was Serena. Who else would be standing waiting at the bottom of the stairs? Their first guest to arrive, tall, slender and sophisticated with stunning flame-red hair and eyes only for Luigi.

Megan was able to study her and she didn't like what she saw. The woman was beautiful, and she knew it, and she had a poise that Megan had never possessed. Until she wore the red dress! It was a magic dress, as Charlotte would have said. It turned her into a different person.

Serena had green eyes, cat's eyes, which could spit fire if she so chose, and her dress was green too, a deep emerald taffeta, pinched in tight to emphasise her tiny waist, smooth over her stomach, but full at the back. And there was not an inch of bosom showing. It was a very clever dress. It moulded Serena's high, taut breasts to perfection. Tantalising but not revealing; making a man want to find out for himself what lay beneath.

Megan turned to see whether Luigi was as entranced as Serena obviously hoped he would be, and to her delight found that he was looking at her. He put his hand over hers where it lay on his arm and squeezed tightly. 'Serena,' he whispered below his breath.

'I guessed,' she replied in a husky voice.

'You have nothing to worry about.'

'I'm glad about that,' and she smiled lovingly into his face.

By this time they had reached his PA and Megan saw the swift coldness that entered her eyes.

'Megan, I'd like you to meet Serena, without whom my work would never flow freely. Serena, my wife.'

'The one who walked out of your life?' came the chilling response. Implying, thought Megan, that she had a nerve walking right back into it.

'The very same,' declared Megan cheerfully, 'but I'm here now—for good.' And she held out her hand.

The woman looked at her steadily for a few long seconds, as though trying to read her mind, wondering whether she was telling the truth, or whether it was all an act for her benefit. Truthfully, Megan wasn't sure either. They still had a lot of sorting out to do. And she couldn't help but wonder what Luigi had told her about his wife's return. Judging by Serena's careful scrutiny, Megan had a feeling he hadn't been entirely truthful.

But whatever, tonight Luigi was hers. Serena wasn't going to get a look in. Megan had never been the possessive type, but a woman had to draw the battle line somewhere.

Serena reluctantly shook her hand, but it was a very light, cool, impersonal touch, and she pulled quickly away. 'Luigi tells me that you've personally overseen arrangements here.' And she looked around her, as though hoping to find fault.

'Naturally,' answered Megan with forced exuberance. 'Come and look in the ballroom. I know you're going to love it.' In actual fact she knew nothing of the sort. It probably wasn't to Serena's taste, but there was no way she was going to give this other woman the opportunity to say so. 'And the food,' she continued, 'is perfect. Luigi has a treasure in Edwina. Between us we've provided a buffet that no one can fault.'

She very lightly touched Serena on the elbow and urged her in the direction of the ballroom. Over her shoulder she looked at Luigi and found him looking at her in stunned admiration. Round one to me, she thought.

And then the rest of the guests began to arrive, all of them curious to meet Luigi's wife. She was the centre of attention, much to Serena's chagrin. Megan saw her trying to be polite and friendly but constantly glancing in her and Luigi's direction. 'I think,' she said softly to her husband, 'that Serena's feeling her nose pushed out of joint.'

'Nonsense,' he declared, looking across at his assistant. 'Serena's in her element. She knows everyone here.'

He was so blind, thought Megan. Perhaps he *had* been speaking the truth when he said that there was nothing going on between them. But couldn't he see that the woman was in love with him? Weren't men's antennae alerted to that sort of thing? Didn't they take advantage? She wasn't sure that their relationship was purely the business one he would have her believe.

Luigi had hired a three-piece band and as the evening progressed Megan found herself whisked around the dance floor by several of Luigi's business colleagues and friends, all pumping her for information about their reconciliation. She was deliberately evasive. 'Delightfully so,' said one of her partners. 'I never even knew Luigi was married,' said another. 'Except to his work.' At which she was supposed to laugh. Unfortunately she didn't find it funny and gave a weak smile instead.

The buffet was an unmitigated success, although Serena only picked at it distastefully. Megan was talking to one of Luigi's business partners, keeping half an eye on what was going on around her, when she saw Serena dart over to her husband and take his arm. Luigi had only that second finished a conversation with someone else. Clearly the woman had been biding her time, had probably been doing so all evening. In fact Megan had made sure there was no opportunity for the two of them to get together, finding grim satisfaction in doing so.

Now she watched them closely and when she saw him lead Serena out of the room, his guiding hand lightly on her back, her heart felt as though it had turned to ice.

Megan wanted to follow but her companion of the moment was in the middle of what he clearly thought was an amusing story and she couldn't be rude enough to walk away. She watched the doorway, though, for their return, and long minute followed long minute. Ten minutes, twelve. Fifteen. What the hell were they doing?

Just as she knew that she could wait no longer they came back, Serena looking very smug, Luigi's eyes searching for hers. When he saw her he headed immediately in her direction, but Megan didn't want to speak to him, she didn't want to smell Serena's perfume on him, or see a smear of make-up on his collar, or lipstick on his cheek. She dashed smartly away, pretending not to have seen him, heading through one of the other doors and into a downstairs cloakroom.

A big mistake!

Serena followed.

CHAPTER NINE

MEGAN was checking her make-up in the mirror when the door opened and Serena entered, a confident smile playing about her lips and a light of triumph in her vivid green eyes. She looked like a cat who'd stolen the cream!

She sauntered over to Megan, but before she could say anything Megan blazed into attack. 'If you think that a five minute grope with my husband gives you any rights over him you're very much mistaken.' Immediately the words were out she regretted them. What had happened to her new-found poise? She oughtn't to have let Serena see that she was jealous.

Serena smiled, totally unperturbed. 'A five minute grope? I think I have slightly better taste than that. And so has Luigi, though perhaps you don't know him as well as you think. I bet he hasn't told you that he's still carrying on his affair with me. I don't mind being a kept woman. An illicit relationship is far more exciting, don't you think? Or perhaps you wouldn't know.'

Megan's stomach muscles clenched so tight that they hurt, as did her heart—it felt as though it had been crushed between two pieces of stone. 'Whatever you say, whatever Luigi promises you,' she retorted coldly. 'The truth is that I am the one he comes home to at night. I am the one he loves. I am the one who has given him a daughter. And I shall never let him go again. Never!'

She had hesitated over the word *loves*. Luigi didn't love her; he loved no one—not even Serena. Or did he?

Was this glamorous girl the reason he'd never pro-
claimed his love? She looked deep into Serena's eyes
and saw the supreme confidence. This woman was so
very, very sure of herself. Sure of Luigi's love! But
Megan refused to give in to her fears. She faced Serena
with her head held high, no doubt at all on her face that
she was the one Luigi loved.

'I think perhaps you're underestimating Luigi,' said
Serena, her voice low and sultry. 'He doesn't like to be
stifled, he doesn't like to be held down by a child. He's
a free spirit; he was happy in the years you were gone.
We were happy. He's changed since you came back.
You're a burden to him, Megan, I think you ought to
know that.'

For a brief moment Megan closed her eyes. Despite
all his denials, Luigi was still carrying on with Serena.
He had never stopped. He was a liar and a cheat—and
yet she still loved him. But enough to continue living
with him? That was the question she had to ask herself.

'I'll leave you now to brew on those facts,' said
Serena in a sugar-sweet voice. 'Perhaps they'll make you
think twice about nesting with Luigi for, believe me,
you're wasting your time; it will never last.'

Megan stood for several long moments after the red-
haired girl had gone. Luigi had done a good job convincing her that there was nothing going on between him
and his PA. And now Serena had made a mockery of
every word he'd said. He was a liar and a cheat and she
didn't know how she was going to get through the rest
of the evening without telling him so.

Luigi looked everywhere for Megan. One minute she
was in his sights, the next gone. It had annoyed him
when Serena took him to one side with an urgent dis-

cussion about work, something that couldn't wait, she'd said. Which was nonsense. At one time he might have thought it important, but his home life was becoming his top priority these days. Unfortunately Serena couldn't seem to see it.

He supposed it was his own fault because he'd always been the one to keep her working late. When there was a job to be done he'd seen no sense in leaving it in the middle, working until midnight if necessary. And Serena had always co-operated. It was why he'd repaid her by taking her out for a meal now and then, and even a weekend away after they'd been particularly busy. But he wished she'd understand that things were changing now that Megan was back on the scene and he was a father.

A whole new direction had begun in his life, one he had never foreseen but he liked very much. Where *was* Megan? There was Serena looking very pleased with herself. She liked to think that she was the linchpin in all of his dealings, and she'd been a teeny bit peeved when Megan insisted that she wanted to handle the arrangements for tonight. But she'd been pleasant enough to Megan when they met so he didn't have any worries on that score.

Then he saw Megan, talking to a neighbour's wife at the other end of the room. He began to weave his way towards her. In truth he couldn't wait for the party to end. She looked so ravishing that he found it difficult to take his eyes off her. His whole system had gone into overdrive the second he'd seen her in that slinky red dress, and all he'd wanted to do was tear it off her and make furious love. That feeling hadn't diminished.

If it hadn't been their own party they could have sneaked away for half an hour, but unfortunately they couldn't do that. He would have to be patient and wait, though the ache in his groin was almost unbearable. He couldn't remember ever wanting her as much as he did now, and the good part about it was that she wanted him too. He had seen it in her eyes.

'Megan, the dancing's started again.' He finally reached her and with a smile and an apology dragged her away from her companions. 'I can't wait for tonight to end,' he muttered in her ear as he held her close, his hand on the naked skin of her back. Lord, she felt so good, he thought, as they moved to the rhythm of the music, and he pressed her hard against him so that she could feel his raging desire.

He failed to notice that she wasn't looking at him quite so lovingly, or that her responses were fractionally cooler. It wasn't until the dance ended and she pulled away from him that he realised something had changed. 'Megan?' he asked with a frown. 'What's wrong?'

'Nothing.'

But it was too quick a response, and she hadn't quite met his eyes. 'Aren't you feeling well?'

'I'm all right,' she said quickly. Too quickly, he thought. Something was definitely going on in her mind. Was she regretting giving herself away earlier? Could that be it? If so he didn't care because he knew that once they were alone he would easily persuade her that she needed him as much as he needed her. He'd kept away for far too long.

He had thought he was doing the right thing, letting her come to him in her own time, but there was only so much a man could stand. And this abstinence was driving him crazy.

The music started up again, something slow and smoochy, and before she could move away he slid both arms around her and she had no option but to hold him too. He felt the faint, unsteady throb of her heart and he inhaled her sweet fragrance, but simply holding her was intoxicating his senses to such a degree that it was all he could do not to whisk her away up the stairs. 'You're the most beautiful woman in the room, did you know that?' he asked softly against her ear. 'Which makes me the luckiest man alive.'

She made some sort of response that he didn't quite catch, but which suggested that his compliment didn't altogether please her. And he couldn't understand why. 'Megan, are you sure there's nothing wrong?'

'Absolutely nothing,' she said, but he sensed it was false.

'I'm sorry if I haven't spent as much time with you as I'd have liked, but there are so many people who want to talk to me, and you, of course. You're quite the star of the evening. Everyone's telling me how beautiful you are, and how pleased they are that we're back together.'

'They have no idea,' she muttered, and he could feel acid dripping from her tongue.

Instantly he had dragged her away into the silence and privacy of another room. 'What's got into you, Megan?' he asked sharply, his fingers forcibly under her chin so that he could look into her eyes. Troubled eyes.

'Nothing,' she repeated stubbornly. 'And we oughtn't to shut ourselves away from our guests like this. They'll wonder what's going on.'

'*I* am wondering what's going on,' he retorted loudly. 'You can't suddenly change for no reason.'

'It's a woman's prerogative.'

'Rubbish! Someone's upset you. And, judging by the cold shoulder treatment, it would appear to be me. Am I right?'

Megan averted her eyes.

'Look at me, dammit.' He clenched her chin so tightly that he knew it must hurt but she didn't even flinch. 'I said look at me.'

Slowly she did as he asked, and what he saw sent his heart crashing into his shoes. Hostility, hatred, accusation! Everything he had hoped never to see again. 'OK, what's going on?.'

'Need you ask?' Her grey eyes were filled with raw hurt and he wished he knew why.

'If I knew, I wouldn't be questioning you, would I?' Then something suddenly clicked in his brain. 'It's Serena, isn't it?' And he laughed with relief. 'You saw us leave the ballroom? My dearest Megan, that was pure business. Serena lives and breathes it, the same as I used to. I tried to tell her it wasn't important, that it would wait until we were back in the office, but no, she needed to talk it over with me.'

'And that's all there was to it?' She looked as though she didn't believe him.

'I swear it.'

'If you say so.' But it was clear she didn't accept that he was telling the truth. 'Dammit, Megan, where has all this come from? I could have sworn earlier that you were as ready for me as I was for you. And now it's all gone.'

'And you can't guess why? But for your sake I'll behave exactly how you want me to—until our guests leave.'

And then she would shut him out! He let his breath whistle through his teeth. He would never understand her, not in a million years. She had nothing to fear where Serena was concerned; how was he going to convince her of that?

Suddenly the door was pushed open and the woman

who was the cause of their dissension poked her head inside. 'Ah, there you are.' At a glance she took in the fierce glare on Megan's face and Luigi's unhappiness, and her smile was wide.

'I wondered where you two lovebirds had got to. It's almost midnight; we need to charge our glasses. Coming, Luigi?'

Luigi looked at Megan and saw the green sparks of jealousy shooting from her eyes. 'We'll be out in a minute,' he told Serena. Part of him was glad that Megan was so deeply jealous, but the other half knew that it was not going to be easy winning her round.

What they needed to do was sit down and talk, get everything out into the open, lay all their cards on the table. Perhaps, with the start of a new year, they could do that. A new year, a new relationship. He couldn't go on like this, that was for sure. After their guests had gone he would insist that they have a heart to heart. For now he would have to accept that she was simply play-acting.

When Serena closed the door he took Megan's hands and their eyes met. She looked so miserably unhappy that he wanted to kiss her and promise that everything would be all right. But when he arched his head towards her she drew away.

'Let's get it over with,' she said abruptly.

And for the rest of the night she was the life and soul of the party, throwing herself wholeheartedly into singing 'Auld Lang Syne', singing the loudest, laughing the longest. She was too happy, brittly so, but no one knew it except himself.

And, of course, Serena, but he was unaware of that.

Megan didn't know how she managed to act as though nothing was wrong; it was hard when your heart was broken in two and you knew that it could never be repaired. Luigi was an out and out liar. Did he really think that she didn't know what he'd been up to? She had known, even without Serena telling her, but to have it confirmed so blatantly, so cheerfully, had frozen every vein and nerve inside her. Nor had she been able to hide her hurt from Luigi, no matter how much she'd wanted to. In fact she couldn't remember anything about the latter part of the evening. Except Serena's gloating smile every time their eyes met.

She had shaken hands and made the right platitudes, but when everyone had gone, when she and Luigi were alone at last, she stripped the façade away. She looked at him with hatred in her eyes. 'What a fiasco. I'm glad it's over. I'm going to bed, goodnight.'

But Luigi was having none of it. 'We're going to talk. *Now!*'

'It won't do any good,' she said bitterly. Was he blind or stupid or both? She'd felt happier today than she had in a long time—until Serena stuck the knife in. It still hurt, and it proved that her husband was a consummate liar, and why he never professed any love for her 'First thing in the morning I'm packing my bags.'

Luigi looked as though he'd been turned to stone. He didn't speak; he simply stood there looking at her, total incredulity in his eyes.

'I've given it a good try,' she added. 'We've had a good Christmas and New Year, and I thank you for that. Now it's time for me to go back to my old life—where I was happy and contented. And you'll be able to carry on as many love affairs as you like.'

Megan found that she was breathing hard by the time she'd finished. She couldn't look at Luigi now without seeing Serena at his side—a smiling, complacent Serena, confident in the knowledge that Luigi preferred her to his wife. There was a red blur in front of her eyes, red rage that matched the colour of her dress. Luigi became the devil with horns. The red turned to black—to nothing.

Megan was unaware that Luigi caught her in his arms as she began to fall to the floor in a dead faint.

When she came to, Megan was being carried up the stairs, Luigi's strong arms around her. She felt fear and alarm and began to struggle, unable to comprehend what was going on. How had she ended up here?

'Keep still!' he warned. 'You fainted. I'm taking you to your room. You need to lie down.'

She closed her eyes; she didn't want to see the look of love and tenderness on his face. It had never been there before. Why now? Was it a trick of the light? 'Fainted?' she echoed. 'I've never fainted in my life. If this is some ploy to—'

'It's nothing of the kind,' he assured her, the softness disappearing, making her realise that she must have imagined it. 'I think the evening proved too much for you. You were on your feet all day, and then...'

Megan stopped listening. She was remembering the real reason for her distress, and she began to struggle even more violently.

'Dammit, keep still,' warned Luigi, his arms tightening around her. 'Are you trying to get us both killed?'

They reached the top of the stairs, but he still didn't put her down, despite her continuing fight. He waited until he had kicked open the door and carried her across to her bed before he finally released her.

Megan immediately sprang up again, but was unprepared for the dizziness that overcame her, and was compelled to sit back down, a hand to her forehead and a dazed look in her eyes.

Luigi fetched her a glass of water. 'Sip that slowly until you feel better,' he commanded.

Suddenly subdued, Megan did as he asked. She had clearly worked herself up to such a pitch that everything had exploded inside her head. What she needed to do now was be calmly organised. She still intended to leave, but she would do it quietly one day while Luigi was at work. She wouldn't go back to the house she had shared with Jenny, but would find somewhere else where her husband would never find her.

'Are you feeling better?' To give him his due, Luigi looked genuinely concerned. It would be so easy to believe that she was the only woman in his life—if the image of a pair of gloating green eyes didn't continually haunt her!

She nodded. 'I'll be all right now.' Meaning, please leave. But he didn't take the hint.

'Let me help you get undressed and into bed.'

There was such tenderness and concern in his voice that it almost broke her in two. But she knew it was an act. He wanted the best of both worlds. A wife and daughter, *and a mistress on the side!* She sat bolt upright, slamming the glass down on the bedside table.

'I wouldn't let you help me if you were the last man on earth,' she yelled. 'Get out! *Get out now!*' So much for her plans to lull him into a false sense of security and then quietly disappear. How could she live for even a minute longer with a two-timing swine like him?

'If this is still about Serena—'

'You can bet it's about Serena,' she tore in furiously. 'You're welcome to her, and she to you.'

'But—'

'But nothing,' she thrust, pushing herself up from the bed and hastening across the room to open the door so that he could leave.

He made no attempt to move, simply following her with his eyes, sad eyes, she noticed. What a good actor he was. 'Serena means nothing to me.'

'So you keep saying.'

'It's the truth.'

She lifted her shoulders.

'But you don't believe me?'

'No.'

'Why? You have no proof that anything's going on. It's all in your suspicious little mind.' He took a step forward.

Megan froze. 'Maybe I do have proof, not that I intend to share it with you.'

Luigi frowned. 'How can there be proof when—'

'When you don't feel anything for her? Spare me the platitudes, Luigi. Just get the hell out of here.'

His lips thinned to a narrow, straight line and to her relief he marched determinedly towards the door. But when he reached it he came to an abrupt halt and turned to face her, his eyes mere inches away from hers. Megan's breathing quickened. Despite everything he could still melt her bones, still send her crazily into a state of readiness. Such was his power! It looked as though she was destined to love him for the rest of her life.

Which made her even angrier.

'I realise there's no point in me saying anything more tonight,' he said grimly, his eyes steely hard. 'Not while you're in this mood. Your over-active little mind is putting two and two together and making five. But I'll prove to you that you're wrong. Tomorrow I'll fetch Serena here and she can tell you herself that you're worrying for nothing.'

He didn't wait for her response. He swung away and she slammed the door behind him. Too late she thought of Charlotte and Kate, and prayed that she hadn't woken them.

What good would it do, Serena coming here? The woman would lie through her teeth, not for one nano-second wanting Luigi to hear of the conversation she'd had with his wife. Maybe she ought to pack now and disappear before he woke up in the morning. Unfortunately it was New Year's Day. Not an ideal time to find alternative accommodation.

She threw herself down on the bed and punched her frustration out on the pillow. Damn Luigi! Damn Serena! And she was still damning them to eternal hell when sleep overtook her.

Two hours later she woke, shivering. With desperate fingers she ripped off her dress, uncaring whether she tore it in the process, then pulled on her nightdress and curled up beneath the softly padded quilt. But sleep was far away now. Anger and hatred filled the rest of her night.

Daylight was beginning to steal through the sky when she finally dropped off and she dreamt that the green-eyed Serena, in her hateful green dress, was floating above her, a leering glitter in her eyes. And she was pleading with Serena to let her share Luigi. Serena laughed, a mocking laugh that echoed in Megan's ears as she awoke.

Charlotte and Kate were in Charlotte's room and her daughter was laughing helplessly. Megan climbed out of bed and opened the dividing door.

'I'm sorry if we woke you,' apologised Kate at once.

'It's all right,' said Megan as Charlotte hurled herself into her mother's arms. She held her daughter close, immediately expunging the bad memories. 'What were you laughing at, sweetheart?'

'Nanny was tickling me. Was it a good party, Mummy? I wanted to come down but Nanny said I mustn't because it was only for grown-ups.'

'That's right, and actually, my darling, it was a bit boring. I didn't know anyone except your daddy and Serena.'

'Who's Serena?'

'She works for Daddy.'

'Is she pretty?'

'Very pretty.'

'That's good, 'cos Daddy likes pretty things. He told me so. He told me I was pretty, and that he loved you 'cos you were pretty as well.'

Megan's veins stiffened as an electric shock ran through them. Luigi had said that? But the feeling quickly faded as she accepted that Luigi's declaration of love would have been a throwaway comment, something to please a little girl anxious for affection. The aftermath left her feeling more dispirited than ever.

'Will you come and have your breakfast with us?' asked Charlotte eagerly. She had been encouraged into the routine of eating her meals with her nanny in the newly furnished nursery.

'Of course I will, my precious.' Anything to avoid seeing Luigi.

She wondered whether he was still serious about fetching Serena. Maybe he would have realised after sleeping on it that it would do no good. But probably not! When Luigi had a bee in his bonnet he stuck with it. He was adamant about wanting to prove that Serena had no part to play in his private life. Of course he would prime the woman first; that would be his reason for picking her up. He wouldn't just phone and say, 'Come over.' They needed to consolidate their strategy.

She and Kate were laughing over something Charlotte had said when Luigi walked into the nursery. His frown was deep when he saw her. 'Why are you here?' he asked, and she could see that he was trying desperately, for his daughter's sake, not to sound cross.

'Charlotte invited me.'

'And it didn't matter that I was sitting downstairs waiting for you?'

Megan became aware of Kate's raised eyebrows. 'I'm sorry, I should have told you,' she said in a deliberately warm voice. 'Why don't you join us? I'll ask Amy to send—'

'I've already eaten,' he announced abruptly, 'but I'd appreciate it if you'd find time to join me for coffee.' And with that he turned abruptly on his heel and left.

'Oops!' said Kate.

'It's all right,' returned Megan, smiling. 'I'd forgotten there was something he wanted to talk about.'

'Then you should go now, not keep him waiting any longer.'

And, although Kate tried to pretend that everything was perfectly normal, Megan could see that she was besieged with curiosity.

Ten minutes went by before she finally joined Luigi. Ten minutes in which he'd had time to grow even angrier. 'Were you deliberately avoiding me?' he rasped.

'Actually, yes,' she answered calmly. 'I didn't like the tone of our conversation last night. I had no wish to carry it on.'

'Ah, you didn't like the tone.' His voice was heavily

condescending. 'And how do you think I felt when I was accused of doing something that I'm not guilty of?'

'So you say,' she retorted smartly.

'I am not a liar,' he slung back.

'And I'm not in the habit of making things up.'

'You see what you want to see.'

'I hear what I don't want to hear,' she thrust.

'And what is that supposed to mean?' The frown was harsh again, slicing his brow in two, eyes as hard as metal bullets.

'You work it out.'

'I'm aware,' he said slowly, 'that there's gossip about Serena and myself. Ugly rumours. It's natural in a workplace. So who's been speaking out of turn? Tell me and I'll damn well sack them.'

Megan found it hard to believe that he was still doing his utmost to deny a relationship with his good-looking PA. If his business colleagues were talking about it then it must be true. The maxim that there was no smoke without fire was almost always spot on.

'I have no wish to divulge my source of information,' she told him icily. 'I expect it will come out in time. These things always do. Meanwhile I don't wish to speak with Serena, or even see her again. I wouldn't believe her if she swore on the Bible.' Her heart was banging away in her chest like a kid bouncing a ball on the pavement. Thump, thump, thump. Thump, thump, thump. And everywhere else her body tingled and pulsed and resented every inch of this man standing in front of her.

He was wearing a black sweater this morning and black trousers and, added to his swarthy skin and raven-black hair, menace leaked from every pore in his body. At one time, when he dressed in black, she had thought it was sexy, turning her on like never before, but not this morning. In her eyes he was the devil incarnate.

Luigi's nostrils dilated as he strove for self-control. Something had gone radically wrong last night. Someone had said something out of school and Megan had believed them. The jealousy that he'd seen, and been pleased about, had turned into something ugly and dangerous and his whole future lay in the balance.

She had threatened to walk out on him again. Would she? His heart had stopped when she hadn't appeared at the breakfast table. He had feared the worst, racing up to her room to check on her wardrobe, his relief knowing no bounds when he'd discovered that her clothes were still there. Or were they simply the ones he had bought her? Another mind-stopping moment as he rifled through her drawers. Nothing had gone. He had checked Charlotte's room next, to make sure. He was safe. His daughter's clothes hung in the wardrobe.

He had been both relieved and angry when he'd found Megan in the nursery. There was no doubt in his mind that she was avoiding him and it had been hard for him not to drag her away. And now she stood before him as prickly as a hedgehog sensing danger, believing he was having an affair with Serena!

'How can I prove to you that you're wrong?' he asked, his arms spread wide, his palms open and towards her. His whole body was rigid, and he knew there was exasperation in his eyes; he couldn't help it. She was driving him insane.

'By sacking Serena. Banishing her from your life altogether.'

He stared at her with a mixture of horror and anger.

'I can't do that. She knows the business inside out. I'd be lost without her.'

'And would she be lost without you?' came Megan's caustic response.

She wasn't talking about work either. If only he knew who had put these suspicions into her mind he would have him hung, drawn and quartered without mercy. Or at the very least he would have him retract his statement in front of Megan. There was a very real danger here of him losing both his wife and his child because someone had stupidly repeated unfounded rumours.

No, not his child—he would *never* let Charlotte go. She was his flesh and blood. If all else failed and he couldn't persuade Megan to stay, then he would fight tooth and nail for custody of their daughter. She had added a very real meaning to his life, and he would never treat her the way he had been treated as a boy.

'You're seeing things that aren't there,' he said sharply. 'You shouldn't listen to gossip. But I'm not going to beg and ask to be given a chance to prove it. A woman of your integrity should know fact from fiction.' Lord, she was spectacularly beautiful this morning. Why was it that a woman aroused, whether in anger or in lust, always looked beautiful, whereas an angry man looked ugly?

'Last night you threatened to leave me. Are you still of that mind?'

She hesitated a moment before nodding.

His lips thinned. 'We seem to have had this conversation before,' he told her drily and not a little impatiently. 'But perhaps I'd better reiterate one point. Charlotte stays.'

Megan's chin jerked and her eyes hardened. 'We

came as a package, Charlotte and I, and that's how we'll leave.'

'Then you'd better think very hard about your decision. Because, believe me, wherever you go I'll find you.'

In answer Megan swung on her heel and walked away, leaving him with no idea what she intended to do.

CHAPTER TEN

MEGAN spent the whole morning considering her future. She had no doubt that Luigi meant every word. He *would* find them. No place would be safe. And he would take away his daughter. She would be left with an empty life. Merely the thought of Serena being a mother to Charlotte sent cold nervous shivers down her spine.

Serena thought of no one but herself; she would resent having a sometimes recalcitrant child under her feet. She would probably send her away to boarding school as soon as she was old enough and Charlotte would hate that. And so would Megan. Over her dead body would she allow him to take Charlotte away from her!

On the other hand, she couldn't stay here and ignore Luigi's affair. She had hoped desperately that he'd learn to love her as she loved him. She'd been jealous of Serena, yes, but had prayed that the woman meant nothing to her husband. She had tried so hard to believe him. To what avail?

It was lunchtime before she saw Luigi again. She'd heard him go out, and no prize money for guessing where he'd gone, but she hadn't realised that he was back. Amy had laid the table, coming to find her to tell her that lunch was ready. Rather than upset her by declaring that she'd share with Kate and Charlotte again, Megan had made her way into the dining room, coming to a sudden halt when she saw Luigi sitting there.

He smiled as though nothing was wrong. He had changed out of his black gear and instead wore a blue polo shirt and grey slacks. He looked far more relaxed than he had earlier, no doubt due to Serena's influence, thought Megan caustically. She slid into the chair opposite him.

'No work today?' she asked, in an attempt to make conversation.

He shook his head. 'New Year's Day's an official holiday.'

'And one you don't usually adhere to.'

'I'm reformed, or are you forgetting?' he asked with a winning smile.

Megan was confused. He was acting as though nothing had happened. Was this going to be his strategy? Was he hoping that he could win her round by ignoring their argument? Not a cat in hell's chance! But as she didn't want her daughter seeing them at loggerheads she'd go along with it for now.

There had been a further sprinkling of snow during the night and after lunch the four of them went outside to play snowballs. Charlotte was in her element, and Kate almost as bad. They had a riotous time—until Charlotte wandered too far away from the house in search of deeper snow.

Megan wasn't concerned, and she didn't give the lake a thought until Luigi gave a yell and raced frantically towards it. Fear gripped her then with icy fingers and she chased after him. 'Charlotte!' she screamed. *'Charlotte!'* How could she have fallen in with three adults to watch over her? What had they been doing? Snowballing each other, that was what, like big kids let out of school.

Luigi stripped off his jacket and shoes and jumped in and Megan's heart was in panic mode. She should have kept a closer eye on her daughter. The lake was deep in the centre but not around the edges, but even a few inches was enough for Charlotte to drown.

She could see her now, lying in the water, and big, wet tears mixed with her terror. 'Oh, my God, my baby!' She began to tear off her own jacket, her throat tight with fear, but Luigi had reached her and pulled a painfully still Charlotte up into his arms.

Megan thought she was dead—she was so white and still—but Luigi gave her a thump on the back and she coughed and spluttered and spilled out the water she'd swallowed. After that she started crying and asking for her mummy.

'I'll carry her into the house,' said Luigi roughly.

Megan ran at his side, constantly reassuring her daughter that everything was going to be all right. Charlotte was blue around the lips and shivering violently.

'I'll run a warm bath,' said Kate, who was as pale and shocked as the rest of them.

'Should we send for the doctor?' asked Luigi.

'Not unless she goes into a state of shock,' declared Kate, and they were both reassured by her confidence.

Megan stripped her daughter and gently helped her into the warm bath water, comforting her all the time, and gradually her colour returned to normal and she stopped crying and gave a weak smile.

Luigi had stood in the background watching. Now Megan turned to him and saw that he was shivering too. 'You fool,' she said. 'Go and take a hot shower or it'll be you we take to hospital.'

'Is she going to be all right?' There was a tremor in his voice and tears glistened in his eyes.

'I think so.'

'That damn lake; I'll get it filled in. Charlotte could so easily have drowned.'

'No, she couldn't,' assured Megan. 'We were all there, keeping our eye on her.'

'We didn't see her go in that direction. And one day she might be outside alone. I can't take the risk. I never thought. Oh, Megan, what if—'

She didn't wait to hear the rest. Instead, she wrapped her arms around him, wet as he was, and said, 'No what if's. She's all right, thanks to you. It's a beautiful lake, you can't do that.'

'Then I'll fence it. No parent should have to go through this.'

And Megan agreed with him.

It moved her, seeing him so upset. It proved how much he'd come to love his daughter. Even if he was unable to express himself openly, the feelings were there.

Charlotte appeared to suffer no ill effects from her dip in the icy water but for the rest of the day she wanted her mummy and daddy rather than Kate. Megan watched Luigi as he played with her, throwing himself whole-heartedly into whatever game she suggested. And he gave her spontaneous hugs and whispered words in her ear that Megan wasn't supposed to hear. But it sounded suspiciously as though he was telling her that he loved her.

It brought a lump to Megan's throat to see this man, whose business life had always meant so much more to him than anything else in the world, baring his soul to his daughter. It proved miracles did happen. And, even if he didn't love her, it meant a lot that he loved Charlotte. Once again she wondered whether it would be fair to take Charlotte away from him.

Simply looking at them together she could see the adoration in Charlotte's eyes. He was the epitome of all she'd ever wanted in a father. She had asked Santa Claus for him and he had provided the goods. Their daughter would be devastated if he was taken from her now. On the other hand, how could she live with a man who was carrying on an affair with another woman? She was in a catch-22 situation and there seemed to be no way out.

When it was bedtime Charlotte insisted that Luigi carry her up and tuck her in. Whether it was because he was the one who had rescued her, or because he'd given her more attention than ever before, Megan couldn't be sure, but whatever, she didn't want to let her father go.

He read her two stories before she fell asleep, her tiny hand clutched in his big one. Afterwards Luigi took Megan's hand and led her from the room. 'Let's go and sit in the den before dinner.' And in her mellowed mood Megan didn't demur.

The first thing he did was apologise again for what had happened.

'It's not your fault,' she assured him, 'though I have to admit I have had faint reservations about the lake.'

'You should have said,' he returned at once. 'I'd have done something about it.'

'If our situation had become permanent I would have.'

A shadow darkened his brow. 'I don't want you to leave, Megan. You and Charlotte mean so much to me.'

Her eyebrows lifted. '*I* do?'

'You're my wife. What do you think?'

Yes, that was right. She was his wife. And it was his duty to care about her. *But he didn't!* Or he wouldn't be carrying on with another woman. Not wanting to start another argument, she let it pass. Instead she said, 'I hope Charlotte doesn't suffer any after effects.'

'Is there a chance?' he asked with an instant frown. 'Should we have taken her to hospital?'

'I don't think so. We just need to keep an eye on her.'

'I'll sit with her all night if necessary.'

'There's no need for that,' she said gently. 'I'll hear her if she wakes.'

'You didn't hear her the other day,' reminded Luigi.

'Tonight I'll be listening.'

'We could listen together.'

Megan's whole sensory system stirred into life. Sitting here with him, a cosy log fire burning in the grate, the rich red curtains drawn against the cold winter's night, it was easy to forget everything else and remember only the good times they'd had. Amazingly, despite all that she'd gone through, she found herself still wanting him.

And, judging by the intensity in his eyes, he wanted her too.

Take what's on offer, she told herself. Easier said than done. How could she let him make love to her when the image of gloating green eyes would hover and disturb? Lord, she wanted him, but, hell, she couldn't have him! No, that was wrong. She *could* have him, but not on her own terms. Terms which would exclude Serena from his life for evermore.

'Megan.' His voice was soft and persuasive. 'I want this thing to work. I want you and Charlotte with me for all time.'

'I know,' she said on a husky whisper. 'But I can't—'

'Forget what you've heard?' he interjected with a slight edge to his voice. 'I wish I knew who had told you. It's lies, you know. All lies.'

'Can you prove that to me?'

'Only if you let Serena tell you herself.'

'No!' Megan shook her head quickly. 'The proof has to come from you.'

'You mean I have to cut her out of my life completely?' And when she gave a faint nod, 'I can't do that. It's impossible.'

She refused to break eye contact, hard though it was to see him struggling with his conscience. 'Then there's no future for us.'

Neither of them had raised their voices. It was a calm, civilised conversation and Megan congratulated herself on controlling her temper. Yelling at each other had got them nowhere.

'I happen to think that there could be,' he said, 'and for that reason I'm taking you away for a few days.'

Megan felt an instant surge of outrage. Not this again. It would be a pointless and futile exercise.

But before she could speak he went on swiftly, 'Not Charlotte; she's staying with Kate. Just you and me and I won't take no for an answer. More than ever we need this time to sort ourselves out. We're leaving straight after breakfast in the morning—providing Charlotte's OK, of course.'

'You can't do this,' she protested. 'It won't work. Nothing will.'

'I beg to differ.' His dark eyes were steady on hers, daring her to refuse him. 'It's what I've been trying to do ever since you came here. And I sorely wish now that we'd done it before your mind was poisoned.'

'As far as I can see,' she said, averting her gaze because he was causing another agonising dance of prickles over her skin, 'it wouldn't have made any difference. The truth would have come out in the end.'

'Yes, the truth!' he said with an edge of irony to his tone. 'I can assure you it *will* manifest itself. As you say, it always does. And on that day you and I will renew our wedding vows.'

He sounded so confident that Megan wanted to laugh. He was living a dream. There was no future between them, except as Charlotte's parents. For their daughter's sake they might keep up a pretence of normality—she was wavering as always, wondering whether she should leave or not, hating herself for being so weak-willed— but he would have Serena to satisfy his hormonal urges, while she would have no-one. Her life would be barren and empty and filled with pain. She wished with all her heart that she'd never gone into Gerards on that particular day.

'So where are you thinking of taking me?' Arguing seemed pointless. He would have his way no matter what so she might as well go along with his decision. Not that she could see any good coming out of it. And if he thought he was going to get her into bed then he would be sorely disappointed.

'That would be telling,' he said. 'But I know you'll approve.'

Luigi felt excitement such as he hadn't experienced in a long time. It had been easier than he'd expected persuading Megan to join him and now that she'd agreed he found his mind running on ahead. He would use the time to convince her that he wasn't the villain of the piece. He would use every skill he possessed to make her forget Serena and accept that he was the love of her life—as she was of his!

The fact that someone had thoughtlessly ruined what fragile hold they'd had on their relationship filled him with despair every time he thought about it. And one day he would get to the bottom of it, of that he was sure.

But for the moment he was determined to concentrate on the days that lay ahead. He'd thought hard and long where to take her and had found the perfect place.

When morning dawned and Charlotte was her usual bright and cheerful self he breathed a sigh of relief. There was nothing now to stop them—except Megan. Half expecting her to have had a change of heart and prepared to use his powers of persuasion all over again, he was pleasantly surprised at breakfast when she confessed that she was all packed and ready. She didn't look happy about it but for the moment he didn't care.

He loaded the car and straight after breakfast they left, Charlotte waving them off a little tearfully, but accepting that they'd be gone only a few days and that Kate would be there to look after her.

After a few minutes travelling in silence he looked across at her. 'Don't look so miserable, Megan. It's not the end of the world.'

'I've never left Charlotte before.'

It wasn't the answer he'd expected so he grinned warmly. 'I'm sure she'll survive. She loves Kate. They'll have a whale of a time together.'

'What if she resents me when I get back? What if she loves Kate more than me?'

'How can she do that?' There was warm reassurance in his eyes. 'You're everything to her. She'll be counting the days. I saw her and Kate making a calendar this morning.'

She looked better after that and began to take an interest in the scenery around her. It was unusual for them to have snow this far south during the Christmas and New Year period. Everything had a picture-book quality and she was as excited as her daughter would have been as they rounded each bend and saw something different. It enchanted him just looking at her.

'It seems a shame to be leaving all this behind,' she said.

'Who said anything about leaving it behind?'

Megan frowned. 'I assumed we were going abroad. A few days in the sun. I've brought my passport.'

'Why waste time on a plane? As I said before, Megan, you're going to love this place. Now, don't ask any more questions. Sit back and enjoy the drive.'

They travelled north on the motorway. There were parts of the landscape with no snow at all. Others had deep pockets where in the distance Megan could see children tobogganing and making the most of this early fall of snow. She began to relax, though she couldn't help thinking about Charlotte and how much she was missing her already.

They stopped for lunch at a motorway service area but they didn't linger as Luigi was anxious to push on. Megan began to relax. Their conversation was desultory, Luigi making no demands other than she enjoy herself. And she did her best to forget about Serena and her influence over him, concentrating on the present instead. It wasn't difficult, not with her dark Latin husband at her side, oozing sexuality from every pore.

She had no idea what lay ahead, what trials or tribulations, what pleasures or delights. She was going to take each day as it came.

Maybe—a thought suddenly struck her, a glaringly simple idea that should have occurred to her before. If she relented and slept with him, if she let him share both her bed and her body, and she freed every one of her inhibitions, he would forget about Serena. They'd always had a superb sex life, and had proved at Christmas that nothing had changed. It could even be better!

Would that be the answer?

Would it be her weapon against this other woman?

If she gave Luigi everything he wanted he would have no need to look elsewhere!

Lord, she'd been blind!

The answer to all her problems was staring her right in the face. Only one thing was missing. His declaration of love! But why let that worry her? It hadn't in the past. It was just a word. It was feelings that counted, feelings and emotions and a sense of *being* loved. Luigi could say as many times as he liked that he loved her, but it meant nothing unless he showed it in every little way possible. And already he'd begun to do that by taking more time off from his business affairs.

Suddenly she felt happier than she had in a long time.

'Why are you grinning?'

Megan hadn't realised that her devious strategy was showing and she turned to look at her husband. 'Was I?' As if she didn't know!

'You look beautiful.'

It was going to be so easy! Already her hormones were racing, vying for position, ready to act on her every whim.

Were they going to Scotland? she wondered, as he drove further and further north. It would be fantastic at this time of year, especially if they'd had snow too. But a little before then, as they reached Cumbria and the Lake District, he left the motorway.

'The Lakes!' she exclaimed, her excitement showing. 'I've always wanted to go.' So many people had told her how beautiful the area was, with its mountains and lakes. It was where William Wordsworth had lived, and

Beatrix Potter, and she'd always promised herself to come but had never made it.

'You look like Charlotte,' he said, 'when she first saw the snow.'

'I probably feel like her.' Megan couldn't hide her pleasure—not that it was all connected with where they were going! Her devious plan whirled round and round in her mind. If all went well she would get her husband back again—a reformed man who spent more time with his wife and child—and Serena would be left out in the cold. His PA might even decide that she could no longer work for him.

Megan wanted to throw her arms up into the air and whoop—except that explanations would be required! So she contented herself with a further inane grin.

It was dark when they reached their destination. They passed through a gateway guarded by tall iron gates into the grounds of a big house, lit up by floodlights that made it look like Buckingham Palace. For a moment Megan was disappointed. From one mansion without a heart to another!

But before she could say anything, Luigi veered off the main path and drove down a much narrower one overhung with the bare branches of trees. It ran for perhaps a third of a mile before their headlights picked out the shape of a log cabin huddling in the shadow of giant firs.

'We're staying here?'

He nodded. 'It belongs to a friend of mine who's in the Bahamas at the moment.'

'But he knows we're using it?'

'Of course.'

Megan got out of the car and ran over to the cabin. She could see smoke curling from the chimney and a light inside and she turned questioningly to Luigi, who was close on her heels.

'I gave instructions for it to be got ready. Open the door; it's not locked.'

Cautiously Megan did as he asked. Warmth greeted them. She stepped over the threshold. What a fantastic place! The central fireplace spilled its heat into the huge living area. There was plenty of comfortable seating and a dining table and chairs in one corner.

She explored further. One door led into a rustic kitchen, where a delicious smell of cooking assailed her nostrils, making her realise how hungry she was. Before she could ask questions, Luigi opened another door that led into a bathroom, and the third into a bedroom with two single beds. Mmm, that might prove difficult. Unless they shared, of course! Very cosy, but comfortable? Doubtful!

Then she spotted an open staircase going up from one corner and, catching Luigi's eye, he nodded, as if to say, Go on, go and have a look up there. At the top was a galleried landing overlooking the living area beneath, but, set back out of sight from anyone downstairs, was a huge bed covered in a magnificent red and gold woven quilt. Chunky wooden furniture accompanied it and through a stable type door, with the top half missing— her brows lifted at this—was a shower room. Not a bog-standard one, a huge one. You could hold a party in the shower basin, she thought, as her eyes roved over shelves filled with towels and toiletries. There was no window and the lighting was cleverly concealed. The whole effect, of both the bathroom and the bedroom, was stunningly erotic. There was no other word for it.

'You like?' asked Luigi.

Megan hadn't realised that he was standing quite so

close behind her. 'It's—er—different,' she agreed. It was too soon yet to begin her plan of action. Actually it was perfect. It was planned for seduction. Was this what Luigi had in mind too? For some reason she hadn't thought along those lines; she'd been so excited by her own vivid thoughts. But perhaps he had known what to expect. Perhaps he'd been here before. With Serena!

The thought made her feel violently sick.

'What's the matter?' asked Luigi at once, seeing the sudden change in her.

'Nothing.'

'Nothing, my foot. Are you not feeling well? Or are you hungry? You only pecked at your food at lunchtime. What was I thinking? Come, let's go and eat. I'll unload the car later.'

Downstairs, he insisted that she sit while he laid the table. He opened a bottle of wine, cut thick chunks of fresh crusty bread, and sat the steaming casserole dish in the centre. 'Let's get started,' he said. 'I'm ravenous too if the truth's known.'

By this time Megan had pulled herself together. Did it matter whether Serena had been here or not? She was fighting for her marriage. This was her best chance at expurgating the other woman from his mind and, hopefully, his life. And she had to grab it with both hands.

'Who did this?' she asked, indicating the excellent beef Stroganoff.

'Michael's housekeeper.'

'And Michael is?'

'My friend who owns the big house. We met through business.'

'We must thank his housekeeper; this is wonderful.'

'*If* we see her,' he said with a wry lift of an eyebrow.

'She's stocked the cupboards and freezer with enough food to last a fortnight.'

'Who did you tell your friend was accompanying you?'

He pretended to look shocked. 'Why, my wife, of course. Michael thought it was hilarious because he knew we were separated. I'm not sure whether he believed me. But one day I'll introduce you to him. He's half Italian like me.'

He was talking as though it was a given that she would stay with him. And yes, she would, but only on her terms. Little did he know that they didn't include a very vicious red head.

CHAPTER ELEVEN

DURING the meal Megan deliberately pushed all thoughts of Serena out of her mind, concentrating totally on Luigi. Not that it was difficult. In this cosy place, with its wooden walls and soft lighting, she felt that she was in a different world—a world where only the two of them existed. And she could do anything or be anybody she wanted.

'You're looking better.' His dark eyes, black in the low lighting, smiled into hers.

'I feel it,' she said. 'You were right about me being hungry. This Stroganoff is delicious.' She didn't really want to talk about food. It was what strangers talked about; food, the weather, particularly the weather. And Luigi was no stranger. Luigi was about to be seduced by his wife. The thought made her smile.

'And you certainly look happier.'

'It's strange there's no snow up here,' she said, not yet ready to let him know why she was feeling so happy.

'I'm glad because otherwise we mightn't have made it. There's been a heavy fall in Scotland, in the Aviemore area. Maybe we could go skiing while we're up here?'

'I've probably forgotten how to ski.' She hadn't done any since the early days of their marriage when Luigi had taken her to Norway.

'Nonsense, it's like riding a bicycle. Once you've learned you never forget.'

Like making love with him. She had never forgotten how good it was. She might have told herself that she hated him, had even shut him out of her life for years, but at this moment in time she could recall every pleasurable moment they'd ever spent. It warmed her thinking about them; it set her toes curling in her shoes and her thighs pressing close together to try and stem the delicious flow of sensation that invaded her.

'I don't really think I want to go,' she said.

He grinned. 'Good, because I don't either. All I want to do is spend time here with you. This is the best place I know for rest and recuperation.'

Megan gave an inward smile. He wasn't going to get much rest.

'And we both have a lot of catching up to do.'

That was right.

'Lots to talk about.'

Hopefully actions would prove better than words.

'I want this to be a place where we sort out our problems.'

His problems!

'Where we start a new life together.'

Here! Here!

'Have you nothing to say about that?' he asked when she remained silent.

Megan smiled, a slow smile that lit up her entire face, not that she was aware of it. 'I think that perhaps tonight I'm too travel weary to talk. Let's just clear this stuff away and sit and listen to some music.' Romantic music preferably, seduction guaranteed.

'It suits me,' he said, jumping up from his chair immediately. 'I'll do the honours here, you fix the music. There are plenty of CDs to choose from.'

It made a change seeing Luigi in domestic mode and Megan quite enjoyed it. And he looked as though he was enjoying himself too. So what on earth had made him buy such a huge stark place for a home? A status symbol? That was all it could be. When they were back together—in every sense of the word, when she had ousted Serena; she would insist that they move.

They could have a large house without it being coldly impersonal. She didn't want to rattle around with a butler and cook and a whole retinue of servants. They could still employ Kate, and maybe a part-time housekeeper— they might need her if they had more children! Her thoughts had never got this far before but the idea appealed, and Charlotte would enjoy having a brother or sister to keep her company.

'Hey, you're supposed to be choosing music, not going into a daydream.'

Luigi had finished in the kitchen and had come to join her, and here she was, not a single CD selected, sitting on her haunches, staring into space.

'At least it must have been something good you were thinking because it's put a beautiful smile on your face. I was worried that you might not like it here, that you might miss Charlotte too much. Speaking of which, would you like to phone her before we settle down? There's no phone here but I've brought my mobile.'

How kind! Why had she ever felt that he thought more about work than he did her? Or was he intent on making the right impression? Would it last? During the next few days she had to make sure that it did. Make him want her so much that he would find it difficult to drag himself away, even for the few necessary hours he had to spend at work.

To her consternation there was no signal in the cabin, not even when she went outside and turned the phone every which way. She looked at Luigi in real concern. 'What if Kate needs to reach us? What if Charlotte suffers after-effects? What if something else happens to her?'

'I'm sure it won't,' he said, putting his arm about her shoulders. 'But don't get into a panic. I've already given Kate Michael's telephone number. If there's an emergency she'll ring the house and the message will be passed on to us.'

He had thought of everything, this man of hers. *This man of hers!* She liked that, it sounded good. He didn't belong to Serena any more. Not that he knew it at this moment, but at the end of their stay here he wouldn't even want to cast a glance in the other woman's direction. She would make sure of that.

It felt weird, planning to seduce her husband. Not that he would need much persuading, but she had to make very, very sure that his thoughts would never turn again to his gorgeous red-headed secretary. Not in the context of bedding her, at least.

'Come on, let's go back indoors,' he said gently. 'I don't want you catching cold.'

Megan hadn't realised quite how chilly it was until they were met by the warmth in the log cabin. She gave a huge shiver and went towards the fire with her hands outstretched.

'Shall we finish the wine or do you want a hot drink?' he asked.

'A huge mug of hot chocolate, I think,' she said. Then, realising that it wasn't in the least bit romantic, she changed her mind. 'No, let's finish the wine. You choose the music.' She sat down in a deep, comfortable armchair to one side of the fire and Luigi threw on another couple of logs, put on some CDs, poured their drinks, and then flopped into the chair opposite.

'I can't remember the last time I got away from everything like this,' he said, his head back, his eyes closed.

'You should do it more often. It's good for the soul.' Whatever that meant! She was able to study him unobserved and saw tired lines round his eyes and mouth that she'd never noticed before. He took on too much, *this man of hers*. Lord knew how many companies he owned these days, and he liked to have his finger on the pulse of every one. She would have to teach him differently. He had a few grey hairs at the temple as well, though she had to admit that she found them very attractive.

Suddenly she realised that his eyes weren't properly shut. He was studying her too from beneath lowered lids, and her body grew warm. She took a sip of her wine for courage then went over and sat on the floor beside him. He didn't say anything but she felt his surprise, and he stroked her hair as she rested her head on his thigh.

'This is nice,' he said, as Sibelius's *Finlandia* washed over them.

'Mmm.' She began stroking his thigh, tiny movements at first but then growing bolder, reaching higher, making each stroke more intense than the last, until he jerked away.

'Good God, woman, what are you trying to do to me?'

Megan smiled, a dreamy smile. 'Pardon? I wasn't doing anything, just listening to the music and—'

'Sending me to merry hell, you little witch.'

'Was I?' she asked with a frown. 'I'm sorry.' And she stood up and went back to her chair.

'Are you honestly trying to tell me that you didn't know what you were doing?' he growled.

'What *was* I doing?' It was hard trying to keep a look of innocence on her face. She wanted to laugh—and she wanted to do it again. She wanted to touch him, to feel the full force of his feelings for her. But she would save that for later. For the moment she wanted to tease him, to make him want her but deny him. She was being the *femme fatale*. A role she had never played before but one that she knew she would enjoy.

His eyes narrowed. 'It felt very much as though you were trying to arouse me. Not that that would be the case, of course, considering you've kept me at arm's length since Boxing Day.'

'You didn't like me sitting there?' she asked softly. 'It reminded me of when I was a child and I'd sometimes sit by my father while he read his newspaper. He'd absentmindedly stroke my hair like you did.'

Dammit, he didn't want to be a father-figure. He wanted to be her husband, her lover, her heart's desire. He'd thought it was too good to be true when she came to sit by him. Megan wasn't in the habit of such arousing little gestures, not these days at any rate.

At one time, in the very early days of their marriage, she had loved to get him going. Sometimes coming up behind him and cupping her hands hard over his manhood, massaging expertly and sending him into instant readiness. Or she'd rub her breasts sensually against him, arching her body temptingly into his. She'd been everything a man could wish for—and he'd taken it all for granted!

Never again! If at the end of these few days he could manage to win her back he'd make sure he kept her for ever.

'Come here again,' he said softly. She did so but he thought it was reluctantly, and it saddened him. What had prompted her to sit by him in the first place? he wondered. Unless it was because she was worried about Charlotte? Maybe that was it, and she needed comfort.

This time she crossed her arms on his leg and resting her head on them, she stared into the flames licking up the chimney. 'It's so peaceful here,' she said.

'I'm glad you like it.'

'Why don't you buy a place like this?'

'If it will make you happy, then I will.'

'Not for me,' she said at once.

It felt like a rebuke. 'Why would I want such a retreat for myself?'

'I'm sure you could find someone to share it with.'

'There's no one I'd want except you.' He felt a sudden tension in her as he spoke. Perhaps now wasn't the time to insist. 'This is perfect, Megan. You and me. We can talk. We can relax. We can do whatever we like with no fear of interruptions. A far cry from my normal hectic schedule.'

'I can't believe you'd find this perfect,' she said. 'You thrive on being busy.'

It was true, he always had. It had taken the sudden jolt of finding out he had a daughter to bring him back to reality. And the discovery that he still loved his wife very much. He intended to do everything in his power to make sure she didn't run away again.

He hadn't liked threatening that he would take Charlotte away from her, and he wasn't even sure that he would have done, but at least it had done the trick. She was still here, and happy to be with him by the look of things. Unless, of course, she was simply humouring him? He prayed that she wasn't. He couldn't bear the thought of them spending three days together if she didn't really want to be here. He was hoping she would share his bed. If not tonight, then for the next two nights.

It might take all his powers of persuasion, but that would be half the fun.

'I'm actually finding it a pleasant change,' he admitted quietly.

'For how long?' she asked. 'How long before you'll be itching to get back to the hub of things?'

'Oddly, I have no desire to do so. All I want is to be here with you, repairing our marriage.' As he spoke he stroked her hair again. Such soft, sweet-smelling hair. He wanted to bury his face in it; he wanted to bury his face in *her*. It was hard holding himself in check, stilling the desires that rose and raged.

Suddenly Megan lifted her face and looked at him, and in the glow from the fire he imagined that he saw love in her eyes. He was mistaken, of course, but just for a fraction of time she'd been the girl he had first met—the girl who had adored him from the start, and whom he'd loved deeply in return.

Silently he urged her to her feet and then encouraged her to sit on his lap, all the time expecting her to refuse, gladdened and excited when she eased herself down. *Finlandia* had changed into Frank Sinatra and as Megan rested her head on his shoulder and the old crooner serenaded them he felt that he was another step further towards his dream.

Poor Luigi. He didn't know what was going to hit him, thought Megan. He hadn't a clue that she was planning a concerted attack on his senses. He thought he had the upper hand; he thought he was the one taking the lead. He had no idea that she was in full control.

She began by blowing gently in his ear. It was something that had always turned her on, so why not him? And then she nuzzled his ear, then nibbled it. He tasted good, and he smelled wonderful. His breathing grew a little erratic but he didn't speak, or move, just a faint satisfied grunt in the back of his throat. As though he was waiting to see what she would do next.

You'd better be ready for it, mister, she said beneath her breath, because this is a full-scale sex attack. Actually, though, she hadn't quite thought about doing anything this early. She ought to at least have waited until tomorrow. 'Gosh, I'm sorry,' she said, drawing back. 'I can't think what came over me. It's a bit like old times, I suppose, and I forgot. You must be tired with all that driving. I expect you want to go to bed?'

'You mean you're going to stop?' he muttered thickly. 'Just when it was getting interesting? Unless, of course, you were suggesting we *both* went to bed?'

'I'm tired as well,' she admitted. Liar! She was wide-awake, and so aroused that it would be many hours yet before she was able to sleep.

'Then let's go up the wooden hill.'

'I didn't mean together,' she said, with a flash of false outrage in her eyes, getting up from his lap and glaring down at him. 'I'll take one of the beds down here. You can sleep upstairs.'

Luigi stopped breathing. This wasn't what he'd expected. He'd been sure that she was prepared to sleep with him. Well, almost sure. She had given all the right signs. Then he remembered to breathe again and dragged in a deep unsteady breath and pushed himself to his feet.

He wanted to question her. In fact he wanted to insist that she share the big bed upstairs, but a voice inside his head told him it would do no good. He had to play things her way if he wanted to get anywhere. And since she wasn't being coldly indifferent he could afford to be patient. So long as she didn't suggest the same arrangements every night!

'Whatever you like,' he said pleasantly, and caught a flicker in her eyes which told him that she'd been expecting him to object. 'I shouldn't have jumped to conclusions.'

'No, you shouldn't,' she returned, but she was smiling again. 'Goodnight, Luigi.' And she leaned towards him and kissed him full on the lips.

Megan smiled to herself as she felt Luigi's surprise, not even objecting when his arms imprisoned her and he deepened the kiss. She still planned on sleeping alone but meanwhile this could be a very pleasant night-cap. Or a highly erotic one!

He was probably feeling completely bewildered. One moment she was teasing him, the next declaring she was sleeping alone. That really had stunned him but he'd hidden his feelings well. Perhaps he'd learned his lesson. Realised that laying down the law got him nowhere at all. And perhaps pigs might fly! Luigi wasn't a man to give in. He'd declared that they needed to resolve their differences by talking. And they would talk, but little did he know that her plan was to evict Serena from his mind once and for all.

'Thank you for bringing me here,' she purred, rubbing her body gently against his, and then, just as his arms were about to close even tighter, she slid away from his embrace. 'Night, night, Luigi. Sweet dreams. See you in the morning.'

It was the sort of thing she said to Charlotte and she could tell by his clamped lips that he was aware of it. But she put an innocent smile on her face and skipped in the direction of the bedroom. It wasn't until she'd closed the door behind her that she realised her case was upstairs. Luigi had carried them both up earlier, evidently expecting her to sleep with him from the onset. His confidence sent a niggle of annoyance through her brain. For once she wanted to be in charge and it was infuriating to find that she was not.

Then came a tap on her door and it gently opened. Luigi appeared with a smile on his face and her bag in his hand. 'You forgot something.'

The fact that he was being so cheerful and understanding incensed her even further. 'So I did. Thank you.' And she virtually snatched it from him.

'Is there anything else that you require?'

'No, thank you.'

'There's plenty of hot water if you want a shower, or there's—'

'I said I'm OK.'

'I'll say goodnight then.' And still he stood there with that irritating smile on his lips.

'Goodnight, Luigi,' she said pointedly.

'You won't change your mind? It could get cold in the night, you know.'

'If I'm cold I'll come and crawl into your bed.'

'I'll be waiting.'

And you'll wait all night, she thought, as he finally closed the door. She was playing this game her way, not his.

Amazingly, as soon as she curled up beneath the duvet Megan fell asleep and when she woke the next morning a weak sun filtered in through a crack in the curtains. For just a moment she wondered where she was, then she sprang out of bed and looked eagerly through the window.

It had been too dark last night to see anything and

now, to her delight, she saw that they were practically on the shore of a lake. Well, a hundred yards away, but that wasn't much. She spotted a path winding down to it—and there was Luigi making his way to the water's edge.

He had on a thick padded jacket pulled up to his ears and his hands were shoved deep into his pockets. Megan wanted to join him and wished he had woken her. She skipped through to the bathroom and then back to the bedroom and was soon dressed in her warmest clothes and running along the path he had taken.

Luigi turned and when she reached him he took her hands and looked deep into her eyes. 'I didn't expect you to be up this early. Did you sleep well?'

'Like a log. And you?' The hormones were buzzing again.

'Good,' he answered, but there were shadows beneath his eyes that hadn't been there last night.

'Why didn't you tell me we were this close to a lake?' she asked enthusiastically, turning away from him and taking everything in. With a backdrop of snow-capped mountains and a panorama of green fields and trees it was stunningly beautiful. Her eyes sparkled as she looked at him. 'It takes your breath away.'

'I knew you'd like it.'

'You *must* buy somewhere like this,' she said. 'I wish we'd brought Charlotte; she'd love it.'

'And you'd feel safe with her here with this vast expanse of open water? It makes my lake look like a puddle.'

'Perhaps you're right,' she agreed. But it was so incredibly lovely that it made her want to cry.

'Come on,' he said, with an arm around her shoulder.

'Let's get back indoors before we freeze to death. It looks as though we might have snow.'

There was an icy chill to the wind that she hadn't noticed till now, and the blue sky was already being taken over by ominous grey clouds.

Luigi kept his arm about her as they made their way to the cabin and it felt good. She even turned and gave him a peck on the cheek. Just that, nothing more, but his arm tightened and his brown eyes glowed like hot coals as he looked at her.

Indoors, Luigi cooked their breakfast while Megan laid the table. He must have lit the fire when he first got up, she decided, as flames and sparks shot spectacularly up the chimney. It was a perfect place to be; she couldn't have chosen anywhere better for her seduction of Luigi.

She sauntered through to the kitchen and stood in the doorway watching him deftly breaking eggs into the pan. 'You've become quite an expert,' she said lightly.

'It was either that after you left, or pile the weight on by eating out all the time.'

'I can't imagine you with even an ounce of extra fat,' she said, deliberately allowing her eyes to roam over the whole length of him. He wore a sky-blue polo shirt and close-fitting navy trousers that showed off his slim hips and taut behind, making her senses shudder into life. 'You've always had a superb body. And you certainly have none now. Did you stop exercising as well?' He'd been a gym fanatic at one time.

'I'm afraid so,' he admitted. 'Work took precedence. But—'

'But not any longer. I hope that's what you were going to say?' she suggested archly.

'Why would I want to work twenty-four seven when I have the most gorgeous wife in the world?'

Why would you want to bed another woman if that were true? Megan formed the question but didn't ask it. She had such faith in this holiday that it would break her heart if it didn't work. 'If you keep saying things like that, and meaning them, then I think that perhaps we might have a future.' She kept her eyes steady on his as she spoke, unaware that they were shiny bright and she was projecting an image of a woman falling in love again with her husband.

His smile was warm and all enveloping and Megan felt her breasts go taut beneath her lilac lambswool top, especially when his gaze dropped. It was one of her favourite sweaters and she had teamed it with a pair of wide-legged aubergine trousers. Luigi clearly approved because he couldn't take his eyes away from her, until the eggs gave a loud splutter and he turned just in time to rescue them.

'Perhaps I'd better move,' she said with a light laugh, 'or we'll be having burnt offerings for breakfast.'

'Perhaps I'd better kiss this ravishing wife of mine,' he said, moving the pan off the heat and closing the space between them. 'You look a million dollars this morning, did you know that? The fresh air has brought an extra glow to your cheeks. You look wonderful.'

The fact that he was taking the initiative when she had planned to do the leading every step of the way escaped Megan for the moment. She wanted this kiss, needed it like a person dying of thirst, and her lips parted of their own free will. Every pulse throbbed, blood coursed hotly through her veins and she couldn't stop herself leaning into him, feeling the same strident pounding inside Luigi as well.

'I think,' he said gruffly, 'that we should forget about breakfast.'

So did she, but it wasn't part of her agenda. Sanity had flickered briefly into her brain, telling her what she must do. She gave the smile of an angel and pushed her hands against his chest. The unsteady throb of his heart against her palm felt like his life-blood pulsing into her, but she bravely ignored it. 'Not on your life, I'm starving.' And she turned away from him.

She felt his shock and her lips twisted in amusement as she made her way towards the table. Not that she wasn't feeling deprived; that was an understatement. But she liked these little tasters of what was to come, and she prayed that Luigi liked them too.

There was silence in the kitchen for a few moments, before he spurred himself into action again. Megan sorely wanted to see his expression but knew that she dared not look round. Instead she sat down and poured them both a glass of orange juice, her back deliberately towards the door.

'Here we are.' He set down the coffee and teapots, a rack of toast, and finally her breakfast plate. It both looked and smelled delicious. Nicely crisp bacon, sausages, tomatoes, egg, fried bread. The perfect Full English Breakfast. It would be a miracle though if she ate it all.

She was hungry—she hadn't been lying when she said she was starving—but for one thing she didn't usually eat this much, and for another her hunger was turning into hunger for Luigi and not food. She was almost afraid to look at him now because she didn't want her feelings to be so blatantly obvious.

'I thought you were hungry,' he said, when she made no attempt to start.

'I am.' She eventually looked at him and saw not

desire, as she'd expected, and which she knew would trigger off her own rampant mood, but concern.

'Perhaps I should feed you.' He cut a slice off his sausage and, picking it up with his fingers, he offered it to her.

With her eyes on his, Megan leaned slightly forward and opened her mouth. When he popped it in she felt the warm rasp of his fingers against her lips and she had an urge to suck them into her mouth too. But already he had moved and was preparing another morsel.

A tiny square of toasted bread this time, topped with golden egg. He was enjoying the game, feeding himself a mouthful in between times, until Megan took the initiative and began to feed him her breakfast in exactly the same manner.

It was the most erotic game they'd ever played, especially when fingers and food became intermingled, or when his eyes darkened with desperate need as she ran the tip of her tongue over her lips to collect any remaining crumbs.

Quite how they managed to finish the whole meal without leaving the table and making mad passionate love on the hearth she didn't know. There was a goatskin rug there and she'd had her eye on it ever since she'd arrived. It was where she intended to perfect her seduction routine.

'That was some breakfast,' he said when he had drunk two cups of coffee and she had finished what was left in the teapot.

'Perfect,' she announced. 'But far too much. I think that as soon as we've cleared away we should walk it off.'

He looked through the window. 'It's beginning to snow.'

And so it was, but nothing more than a few flurries.

'I can think of a much better form of exercise.' His face was straight but Megan knew exactly what he was talking about. The trouble was, he was beginning to take her for granted and this wasn't part of the deal she'd made with herself. Nothing had to come easy for him. He had to work for it, realise that some things were worth a bit of effort.

Like holding on to a wife whom he had taken for granted all those years ago!

CHAPTER TWELVE

MEGAN remained insistent that she wanted to walk, but by the time they'd stacked everything into the dishwasher and put on their outdoor clothes the snow was falling heavily. 'Shall we risk it?' she asked as they stood in the doorway watching the white flakes settle. Already it had coated the ground. 'If this keeps up it'll be inches deep within a few hours.'

'I'm game if you're game.'

'Then let's go,' she said with a laugh.

They trudged towards the lake, leaving footprints, Megan laughing when she slipped and Luigi's strong arms saved her. He held on fast to her after that, and the cold outside air that turned their breath into white mist was a huge contrast to the heat that raged inside her body.

When she slipped again, her feet going right from under her, Megan landed on her back. Luigi had released her for just a moment to point out a duck that was sheltering beneath some overhanging dead grasses, and now he knelt instantly beside her, real concern on his face. 'Megan, are you hurt?'

'Only inside.'

A deep frown gouged his brow. 'What do you mean?'

'It's something that only you can make better.'

'You know I'll do anything I can.'

'I want you to make love to me, Luigi, right here.' The words seemed to come of their own volition; they had nothing to do with her. She wasn't saying these things, it was crazy to want to make love in these freezing conditions.

There was a great silence around them. It was as though they were in the House of God. And, although she knew He wouldn't approve of an open-air ritual, it was what her heart desired.

'Are you sure?' There was the beginning of a smile playing on the edges of his mouth, and she could see that the idea had begun to appeal to him too.

Megan nodded.

'You're a crazy woman, do you know that? And you never fail to amaze me.'

She amazed herself too, if the truth were known.

Half expecting her request to fail because of how cold it was, Megan was exhilarated when Luigi performed with as much panache and aggressive eagerness as he'd ever done. Naturally they couldn't get fully undressed because of the still falling snow, but it was an experience to surpass all experiences.

And when it was over, when they'd both had time to draw breath, they ran laughing into the house ready to begin all over again. First of all they showered together in the spacious upstairs bathroom, turning it into a sensual game, each soaping the other, exploring each other's bodies, touching and kissing every sensitive zone.

Until Luigi exclaimed, 'Enough!' He insisted she stand while he towelled her dry, a long task because there were so many parts of her that needed different attention. Megan was sizzling by the time he'd finished touching and stroking and teasing and kissing.

He carried her to the bed and, although she was desperate again for him to make love to her, he refused to hurry. 'We have all the time in the world,' he told her gruffly.

So much for her being in charge! At this moment she was putty in his hands and he knew it. And he was making the most of it. Every single inch of her body was responsive to his touch, and she wriggled uncontrollably as he drew her to such a crescendo that she knew she would climax any second—without him!

It was only then that he entered her, slowly, only just controlling himself, and when Megan wrapped her legs around him and thrust her hips urgently upwards, he groaned and cursed and between them the world exploded.

'You're truly an incredible woman,' he said, once they'd come back down to earth. The covers were pulled over them and they were huddled together like two bunnies in a burrow. 'I thought I knew everything about you and yet you continue to surprise me.'

'I do?' she asked with a crooked smile.

'Since when has making love in the snow been an ambition of yours?'

She grinned. 'Never. It makes me shiver just thinking about it.'

'And yet you begged me for it. It was the most erotic thing I've ever done. I love you, Megan.'

His admission stunned her into stillness. 'Pardon?' she asked in the quietest of voices.

'I love you.' It was a simple admission, his tone suggesting that it was something he had always done and he couldn't understand why she was questioning him.

'Do you mean that?'

A faint frown narrowed eyes that were still dark with emotion. 'Of course I mean it. I've always loved you.'

'But you've never told me.'

'I know,' he admitted wryly, 'and I'm sorry. It's not something I find easy to do.'

'Because of your upbringing?'

He nodded, a shadow on his face as memories returned.

'So why tell me now? What's different?'

'The difference is *us*! I'm finally beginning to realise what a swine I've been. I'm keeping my promise to cut down on my workload. I'm putting family first. And since we came here things have changed as well. *You* are more relaxed. And I am more relaxed in your company. I find it easier to say what's in my heart.'

Megan felt as though all her hopes and wishes had come true at the same time, but she also knew that she still needed to exercise caution. This could be emotion speaking. In the cold light of day, when their bodies weren't entwined, when their senses weren't so heightened, he might feel differently.

'I think we should talk about this again later,' she said.

He frowned. 'You mean you don't believe me?'

'I want to.'

'But you don't!' he claimed roughly, rolling out of bed and glaring down at her. 'Dammit, Megan, what does a guy have to do to repair his marriage? Get down on my knees and beg? Believe me, that will never happen. You take me as I am or not at all.'

OK, if he wanted to get heavy then she'd let him have it. 'I don't want a husband who comes with baggage.' Her grey eyes glittered angrily and she too got up. But she didn't stand there naked as he was doing; she grabbed his robe and hugged it around her.

'Baggage? What the hell are you talking about?'

'As if you didn't know!'

'You mean Serena? For heaven's sake, Megan, when are you going to accept that there's nothing going on there?'

'That's not what she told me.' She saw the way his breath caught in his throat, the way his eyes stilled with suspicion, and she waited.

His words were slow and deliberate. 'You mean *Serena* told you—that she and I—were lovers? On New Year's Eve?'

Megan nodded.

He shook his head, unable to accept that she was telling him the truth. 'Why would she?' And it was clear to see that he didn't want to believe it.

'Because she's jealous, you blind idiot. She's in love with you.'

He winced then, giving away the fact that he'd suspected it. 'But I'm not in love with her.'

'That only makes a woman scorned more eager. Don't you know that?'

He ignored her question. 'And she actually came right out with it? She tried to make trouble between us?'

'Yes,' whispered Megan, finding it hard to see Luigi coming to terms with the fact that his PA was not as perfect as he'd thought.

'I don't suppose you want to tell me the details?'

And hurt him more? Megan shook her head.

'I've never taken her to bed.'

It was said so simply and sincerely that Megan accepted he was telling her the truth. She wouldn't have done a few days ago, but now she did.

'And I shall have a word with her when I go back to work. This won't happen again. She can stay in the job and behave, or leave.'

Megan's heart began to sing. 'I think I believe you this time, Luigi.'

She could see the relief flooding out of him, his body

relaxing and a slow smile returning. 'I do love you, Megan, with all of my heart.'

'And I love you.'

'You'll stay with me for ever?'

She nodded.

He groaned and gathered her into his arms. 'I love you, I love you, I love you,' he claimed joyously. It was as though once he'd said the words, once he'd realised how easy it was to express his emotions, he couldn't stop.

'And I love you too. In fact I think we make a pretty good pair,' she added spontaneously.

'In bed and out of it,' he agreed, opening the robe she had folded protectively around her. When naked flesh met naked flesh their bodies set on fire, bed beckoned again and time lost all meaning.

Megan wasn't sure whether it was hours or days before they admitted hunger of a more prosaic kind. It seemed like for ever that they lay in bed pleasuring each other, sometimes reaching heights never before attained, sometimes dozing, their bodies still entwined. They had become one again in this peaceful place, and the next two days were filled with more of the same...

When it was eventually time for them to return home they were both sad. The car was packed, and they were taking a last look around to make sure they hadn't forgotten anything. 'I wish we could stay here for ever,' Megan said. 'Except that I'm missing Charlotte.' But not as much as she'd expected! Luigi had wiped everything from her mind. Her glorious husband.

'Me too, on both scores,' Luigi agreed firmly. 'I couldn't have wished for a finer wife or a lovelier daughter, and I hope that one day in the not too distant future we shall have a brother or sister for her to play with.'

'I think that might happen sooner than you think,' Megan told him with an amazingly shy smile considering their uninhibited behaviour.

Luigi took her face between his palms, his eyes shocked and questioning. 'What are you telling me?'

'That I've missed my period.'

His eyes widened, like Charlotte's when she saw something wonderful. 'Which means that you could have conceived on Christmas Day? Or even Boxing Day?'

She nodded. 'Of course it could be that my system's out of sync because of all the upset I've had lately. It's a little early to tell, but—'

'But nothing!' he insisted. 'I knew there was something different about you. You have a bloom that only a pregnant woman has.'

'And how would you know what a pregnant woman looks like?' she taunted, and then wished she hadn't because she had deprived him of that opportunity with Charlotte.

But he didn't seem to mind. 'I love you, Mrs Costanzo. And I'm never going to stop telling you. And I love our daughter too, more than you'll ever know. I'm going to be the world's finest father—to all of our children.'

A spread of pleasure flooded Megan's limbs. She believed now in his reformation. Entirely.

'Charlotte got her daddy for Christmas,' he mused, 'and we created a new baby at Christmas. Isn't that just perfect?'

'Absolutely,' she said. 'And there's one thing I must do.'

He grinned. 'And that is? I'm not sure we have time to make love again.'

'I think I can manage to wait until we get home—just,' she added with a provocative smile. 'But I need to tell my parents that we're back together. They thought the world of you, you know, and were really angry with me when I left. In fact, we haven't spoken since.'

'I know how they felt,' he agreed. 'I contacted them when I was trying to find you, and I promised I'd tell them if I ever did.'

'And did you?'

He nodded guiltily. 'They needed to know you were safe and well. I know I should have told you, but I still wasn't sure whether we'd make a go of things. You were so damn stubborn, so insistent that it was going to be a Christmas break and nothing more. I was terrified each time you threatened to leave.'

'What would you have done if I had gone?'

'Thought of a way to get you back. Believe me, my darling, I wasn't going to let you go again.'

'You won't have to worry now,' she said, secure in the knowledge that Luigi was going to be a perfect husband for all time. 'There's another couple of things, though.'

Luigi looked resigned. 'OK, spill them out. Let's not leave any skeletons in the cupboard.'

'It's nothing like that,' she assured him. 'Firstly, there never was anything going on between me and Jake. I let you think so to make you jealous. I'm sorry.'

'And you certainly did that,' he said. 'I hated the thought of any other man having you.'

'There's been no one but you,' she insisted.

He gave a pleased smile. 'So what's the other thing?'

Megan swallowed hard. 'Don't be hurt, but I don't like your house. Can we move?'

'Do you want to know the truth?' he asked with a

sheepish grin. 'I don't like it either. At least, not since you've been living there. It's not a home, is it? It's too soulless. It doesn't have a heart. We'll choose something together, my darling, though it will have to be big enough to house all the children we're going to have.'

'Of course,' said Megan demurely.

He patted her tummy. 'Did I ever tell you that there are twins in my family?'

'Spare me, please,' she said with a laugh.

But actually the idea of having lots of babies for Luigi to dote on really appealed to her.

CONFESSIONS OF A MILLIONAIRE'S MISTRESS

ROBYN GRADY

CHAPTER ONE

'TRY to stay calm, but Mr Terrific-in-a-tux over there is undressing you with his eyes.'

Celeste Prince quietly grabbed her friend's arm and forced her to look away too.

'For heaven's sake, Brooke,' Celeste hissed under her breath, 'don't encourage him.'

Yes, the sexy stranger who'd just arrived was beyond intriguing. Neat dark hair, strong shadowed jaw, beautiful big shoulders that left her feeling a little weak at the knees. Superior specimens like that didn't magically appear every day. But, damn it, tonight she didn't need the distraction.

Over a hundred guests, all shimmering and crisp in their after-five wear, had gathered at the behest of Australia's franchise genius, Rodney Prince, to celebrate his company's twentieth successful year. But this soirée meant far more to Celeste than just another party. Tonight her father planned to step down as head of Prince Landscape Maintenance and hand over the Sydney empire's reins to his only child.

After her mother's death fifteen years ago, her dad had withdrawn from everything but business and they'd drifted apart. How she'd waited for this moment—the chance to be visible in his world again and make both her parents proud. Nothing mattered more.

Not even meeting that tall, dark, delectable dream.

Buckling, Celeste dared one more glance from beneath her lashes.

The stranger was leaning against a French door jamb, this side of the mansion's manicured court-yard. As his hand slid into his pocket his left leg bent and the ledge of those shoulders, magnificent in a white dinner jacket, slanted into a casual but confident pose. He was handsome in a rugged yet refined way, a toned powerhouse cloaked in classic Armani. However, his eyes mesmerised her the most...seductive pools of vibrant blue light. Captivating.

Aware.

Smiling straight into hers.

A bevy of exquisite tingles raced over her skin and she spun away again. Still she felt his heated gaze caressing her back, stroking her arms, slipping the satin straps from her shoulders, easing the dress all the way down...

Brooke tipped closer. 'Who do you think he is?'

Celeste tossed back a mouthful of chilled champagne. Her throat was suddenly parched. 'I don't know,' she replied, 'and I don't care.'

She needed to concentrate on reciting her acceptance speech without her cheeks turning into torches and her tongue tying itself in knots. "Stuttering Celeste" rarely made an appearance these days. After years of torment in junior school, she'd learned to slow down, think ahead and ease her way through most situations—even something as overwhelming as tonight.

Brooke arched a brow. 'You don't care, huh?' With one arm crossed beneath her gown's scarlet bodice, she rested her champagne flute near her cheek. 'We went through high school together, backpacked Europe together. Never once have I seen you this cagey over a man.'

Celeste couldn't smother a grin. 'Let's face it... he's not just *any* man.'

Drawn again, she glanced over a hitched shoulder. Like a cool-headed hit man, now the stranger was perusing the room, checking out the territory, assessing his targets. Such a composed air of indifference, yet she had the eeriest feeling he had his thumb on everyone's pulse...particularly the one beating a mouth-watering rhythm right between her—

'Celeste, I need to see you in private.'

Heart leaping, Celeste pivoted around to see her father's serious suntanned face gazing down at her.

When she'd arrived this afternoon he'd talked

about the future of PLM, hinting again at his retirement and subtly sussing out her aspirations with regard to the company. Was she happy running the central Sydney handbag and accessory store she'd opened this year? Did she want to look at doing something more?

She'd replied that her profit margins were healthy. And, yes, she was definitely ready to do something new. No gushing or taking the words from his mouth, but clearly her father had wanted to confirm his decision before making the big announcement that had been coming for months. Soon the room would be toasting a new CEO.

Celeste Ann Prince.

Noticing that her stranger had disappeared into the crowd, she excused herself from Brooke and accompanied her father down a wide airy hall. As they passed the ethereal image of her mother's portrait, Celeste heard more clearly the crystals rustling around her evening gown's hem.

She'd considered wearing a smart black jacket and trousers ensemble, but had decided on the feminine look her mother had said suited her best. The peachy tone complemented her long Titian-blonde waves, and in no way challenged the last faint smattering of freckles that refused to leave her nose and shoulders. Anita Prince had said her daughter's sun kisses made her glow like an angel. She'd never understood that Celeste hadn't wanted to glow quite so much.

When they reached the study, her father shut the door on a room stacked with filing cabinets. He drew her towards his desk, then held her eyes with his. 'In ten minutes I'll make an announcement. I've given it a great deal of thought.'

Celeste gathered herself against rising excitement. 'I'm sure you have.'

'Prince Landscape Maintenance has grown into a huge enterprise...a swag of employees to oversee and organise. Master and subordinate franchises that need to be monitored. Its director should be involved at all levels, and can't be above driving a Bobcat or trimming a tree.'

Although Celeste nodded, her toes wriggled in their silver high heels. She didn't intend to be that hands-on; a great second-in-charge could handle any day-to-day grind. Rather she planned to invest her time in branching out to incorporate a chain of florists, which would accommodate only the biggest occasions, like celebrity weddings and gala events. She wanted the new section to be exclusive, celebrated, in demand by the elite. It would be her personal contribution to the further development of the company. Under her leadership, they would reach even greater heights.

Her father crossed his arms. 'Papers need to be signed, but I've invited Mr Scott to stay a few days to help ease him in.'

Celeste's smile wilted. 'Who's Mr Scott?'

A new accountant? Lately, whenever she visited

her father here at the office he ran from home, he'd been poring over the books, his face more lined than she could ever remember...and not merely from years spent in the sun. At sixty-five, he needed to relax and leave the toil to her.

'Mr Scott has enjoyed a meteoric financial rise these last five years,' her father went on. 'He's offered to buy Prince Landscape Maintenance. I thought you should meet him before I address our guests and share the news.'

The mahogany panelled walls warped and receded as her legs threatened to buckle and give way. She held her somersaulting stomach and forced the bitter-tasting words from her mouth.

'You want to sell our company to a *stranger*?'

She was hit by a frightening impulse to grab her father's tux lapels, shake him and shout, *Don't do this. You can't do this!* But she'd learned long ago that such displays of emotion got her nowhere. The last time she'd 'acted out', she'd been sent to boarding school. Thank heaven for Brooke.

Her father droned on about 'the generous offer' and 'everything working out well'. But Celeste could only think of how she'd always done what was expected of her. She'd excelled at school—even in reviled Maths—and had never attracted trouble while she'd waited in the wings.

How could he do this to her? More importantly, how could he do this to her mother?

She wouldn't hold her tongue. 'You knew I wanted to step in when you bowed out. We spoke about it just today.'

Her father's arms unravelled. 'Sweetheart, we talked about your handbag shop. I asked whether you'd thought about expanding.'

On the surface maybe. But the subtext had been there…hadn't it? Although she loved her shop, it was a placeholder business—somewhere to build on her university knowledge and practical skills until *this* happened. She constantly inquired about PLM, whether the franchises were growing, if there was anything at all she could do to help. Damn it, it had always been understood!

She grabbed at a likely buoy. 'You said no papers have been signed. Tell this Mr Scott you've changed your mind. That you're handing your daughter over the f-f-firm.'

While her cheeks caught fire, her father's brow lifted in surprise, then furrowed with mild disapproval at the stutter he hadn't heard in years.

He shook his head. 'This is best. It's a man's business, and, believe me, I've found the right man for the job.'

Celeste set her jaw. *She* was the only man…er, woman for the job. Besides robbing them of a chance to reconnect, selling PLM was tantamount to betraying her mother's memory. Anita had been yesterday's New-Age woman. She'd stayed so strong and had given so much, and she'd done it not only out of loyalty to her husband, but in the staunch belief that Celeste would benefit by taking over one day. Without her mother's sacrifices, frankly, the Prince franchise wouldn't exist.

A knock on the door echoed through the high-ceilinged room. Her father glanced over and raised his voice. 'Come in, Benton.'

Benton…? Benton Scott. Yes, the name rang a bell. Exceedingly wealthy, rather an enigma. Big on charity but stayed well clear of the press.

Her free hand fisted by her side while the other clenched her flute's stem. She didn't care if Scott was a monk. PLM was hers. Watch out anyone who stood in her way.

But when the enemy entered, the oxygen seeped from her lungs until there was no air left to breathe.

That jacket. Those eyes. *Oh, Lord.*

Her tall dark delectable hit man.

His eyes met hers and widened at the same time he stopped dead.

So he'd been just as clueless about her identity when he'd given her the once-over earlier. Well, if he was still interested, so was she…in getting rid of him as fast as she could.

She jumped in to take advantage of the awkward moment. 'Sorry to sound rude, but my father and I are in the middle of an important discussion. Perhaps we could talk later.'

Her father went to protest, but perceptive Benton Scott held up a hand. 'It's fine, Rodney. This doesn't appear to be the best time for introductions. And possibly tonight isn't the night for announcements either.'

Celeste shivered. Those exquisite tingles again, but this time at a voice that was as rich and tempting as it was dangerous, like a stream of darkest chocolate undulating over jagged rock.

'No, no.' Rodney Prince moved toward his guest, his five-ten stature minimised beside this other man's impressive height. 'Come through.' He flicked a glance at his daughter. 'We've finished here, haven't we, hon?'

Emotion thickened in her throat. Had he forgotten that much? Did her feelings matter so little?

Benton Scott spoke up. 'Actually, Rodney, I overheard a guest—Suzanne Simmons. She said she needed to find you to say goodbye. She'd already called for her car.'

Her father's moustache twitched and he cleared his throat. 'I should go. Ms Simmons is one of my most important clients.'

The younger man stepped aside. 'I understand.'

When her father clapped his guest on the back and left without a backward glance, Celeste braced herself against another twinge of hurt. But she didn't have time for self-pity. Savvy businesswomen didn't pout; they dealt the hand rather than merely played it. And, as much as it pained, Benton Scott could well be her trump card.

Outwardly cool, she concentrated on her words and indicated a leather tub chair. 'Please, take a seat.'

He smiled almost gently, then caught the door knob. 'As I said earlier, it's best we leave more thorough introductions for now. Goodnight, Miss Prince.'

No way. She had a plan and this man was her key. She needed to keep him here and talking.

She shot out the first ammunition that came to mind. 'Can't handle being alone with a woman?'

He stopped, then slowly turned. His grin was lopsided and shamelessly sexy. 'That's never been my problem.'

Inventing an easy shrug, she moved towards the wet bar. 'There's always a first time.'

He leant against the door, one long leg bent, his fingers gripping the rim near his head. 'You look like a nice lady—'

'I noticed you doing some looking earlier.'

While her heart pogo-jumped in her chest—where had she found the nerve?—his hand fell from the jamb and he straightened. 'I didn't know you were Rodney's daughter.'

'That would've made a difference?'

A muscle in the sharp angle of his jaw began to tic. 'Perhaps.'

Her hand barely shook as she refilled her glass from an opened bottle set in a shiny silver bucket.

She crunched the Bollinger back into its ice. 'Aside from being someone's daughter, I also have a double business degree. I run a successful concern of my own—Celestial Bags and Accessories,' she finished with a note of pride.

With what looked like a straight Scotch in his hand, he sauntered closer, a naturally languid and predatory gait. 'I'm suitably impressed.'

'Because I'm a woman?'

His eyes narrowed—amused or assessing? 'Because of your age.'

Good grief! She was tired of hearing about that too. Twenty-five was hardly a baby.

'I'm a determined person.' Gaining courage, she leant back against the polished oak bar. 'When I want something, I don't give in easily.'

He cocked a brow and Celeste relaxed a smidgeon more. Her bluff appeared to be working.

'And what is it that you want, Miss Prince?'

She took a breath. *Here goes.* 'I want to keep the family business in the family.'

After a considering moment, he squared his shoulders. 'We're being frank?'

'Of course.'

'Even if your father had thought to consider it, he wouldn't give you control.'

After the initial shock, she suppressed a growl. How dared he presume to know her family and their situation so well?

She placed her crystal flute on the bar ledge. 'It's not over till it's over, Mr Scott.'

His blue gaze turned steely. 'Your father's company is in financial straits.'

Her thoughts froze. That wasn't possible. They were one of the leading franchise businesses in the country. Had been for a long time. Her father hadn't had any financial problems since before her mother had died.

Benton Scott's voice penetrated the fog. 'Your father didn't want to worry you with it.'

I just bet he didn't.

She absently moved towards the open concertina doors as a wave of dread fell through her. But even if the company were in trouble, that wouldn't change her mind. A dip in profitability only meant that her innovative ideas were needed now more than ever.

But what did it mean to her hit man?

She rotated back. 'You're a successful investor. What do you want with a failing business?' Her stomach gripped as an answer dawned. 'Unless it's to sell off the assets.'

'I'm not a corporate raider. I see this company as a perfect opportunity to mix business with pleasure. Gambling on the stock market has been lucrative. But I want a business I can get involved with— pardon the pun—from the ground up.'

She studied him, from the top of his coal-black hair to the tips of his polished-Italian-leather shoes.

Was she getting this right? 'You want to mow lawns and drive trucks?'

'As a matter of fact, when time permits, yes, I do. This company needs tender loving care for it to survive.'

She sent a dry look. 'And you're an expert on TLC?'

'In the right circumstances—' his gaze licked her lips '—absolutely.'

The tips of her breasts tightened as if he'd brushed each bead with the pad of his thumb. What could he do with a graze of his mouth, or the tickling tip of his tongue?

She swallowed against another hot rush of arousal.

Rewind, Celeste. Not in the plan, remember.

She crossed out onto the cool patio. Gazing at the fairy-tale spread of city lights and majestic arch of Sydney's Harbour Bridge twinkling in the distance, she considered her next move. When he joined her, the scent of earlier rain and damp eucalyptus leaves faded beneath the proximity of another influence... spicy, expensive and achingly male.

Out the corner of her eye, she saw Benton lift the Scotch to his lips. 'We're not going to agree,' he said.

'I disagree.'

He chuckled and turned to her. 'You're one stubborn woman.'

'I prefer the word persistent.'

She flicked a glance at his left hand. Of course no gold ring. Did he have a girlfriend? More likely he had several, which was fine with her.

Fine, fine, fine.

His eyes, reflecting light from the low slung moon, trailed her jaw. 'I wish we'd met under different circumstances. It could've been—'

'Mutually beneficial?'

He swirled his drink. 'That's one way to put it.'

'How about memorable? Meaningful?'

A corner of his mouth curved up as his brows nudged together. 'Why, Miss Prince, are you hitting on me?'

When his eyes twinkled again, her nipples tightened more and an alarmingly vivid image of his white teeth tugging one tip, then the other, bloomed in her mind.

Battling the sparks firing low in her belly, she cleared the huskiness from her throat and explained. 'Actually I'm suggesting you do the honourable thing and step away from this buyout.'

Disappointment dragged down his smile and he faced the view. 'Whatever you might believe, your father is being cruel to be kind. So am I. If this business takes one more wrong turn, you could lose everything.'

Sorry? Did she have 'walking business disaster' hanging from a sign on her back?

She crossed her arms. 'Thanks for the confidence boost. When I'm as successful as you are now, I only hope I'm as modest.'

His jaw tensed. 'Sarcasm is so predictable. I prefer it when you flirt.'

She huffed and mumbled, 'Well, you are a man.'

'And you're a woman,' he drawled. 'A beautiful woman, who obviously likes to wear pretty clothes and keep her nails buffed.' While her brain registered 'beautiful', the strong planes of his face softened. 'Why don't you take your share of the cash and buy a couple of boutiques to go with your handbag store?'

Her mouth dropped open. 'I'm not sure whether it's the sexist nature of your suggestion that rankles most, or the fact you sincerely mean that to be sage advice?'

Maybe he was bigger, wealthier…hell, maybe he *was* smarter than her. That didn't mean she couldn't fight for what was hers. Anita Prince would be cheering her daughter on all the way.

He considered her for a long moment. Then the mask cracked. He groaned and tugged an ear lobe. 'What are you proposing?'

She faced him full on. 'Compassion. You can buy any business you like but PLM is personal to me. My parents lost blood, sweat and tears getting it started.' She remembered the highs and lows as if it were yesterday—the flying champagne corks as well as the fights. 'You say you have our best interests at heart. Prove it. I know this business backward. Give me three months to show my father I can get the company back on its feet.'

The tugging on his mouth told her he was chewing his inside lip. After another nerve-racking delay, he exhaled. 'One month.'

Snap!

She hid a smile. 'Two.'

'Six weeks and with one condition. I'll be here, working beside you the whole time.'

'I don't need to have my hand held.'

'Plenty of damage can be done in six weeks. I have no intention of cleaning up any more mess than I need to.'

Her smile was tight. 'If I had thinner skin, I'd be insulted.'

She had to think fast. To have Benton Scott around would be far too distracting. For more reasons than one she needed her mind set on accomplishing her goal, not watching her back. Perhaps a different tack would dissuade him...something to make his super-sized ego jump.

She feigned a sigh. 'When I first saw you tonight, I assumed you were a man who enjoyed a challenge. A man who took risks. Guess I was wrong.'

When she turned away, he caught her wrist and flames leapt up her arm, colourful and consuming enough to ignite her body like a Roman candle.

What was this guy's secret? Sex appeal pills with every meal?

Hoping the blistering effect didn't show on her face, she counted her heartbeats, then cautiously met his gaze.

While his eyes flashed, the grip on her arm eased. 'That's the deal. Take it or leave it. But something else needs to be out in the open.' He spoke to her lips. 'Six weeks is a long time. I'm not sure we can work that close for that long without…consequences.'

The innate heat radiating from his body toasted hypersensitive places Celeste hadn't realised she possessed—and had no intention of letting on she'd discovered.

She kept her words slow and even. 'You've come a long way since *this isn't the time for introductions.*'

'Don't get me wrong,' he continued as if she hadn't spoken. 'Consequences are fine. As long as you know I'm not after a *Mrs* Scott, no matter whose daughter I'm with. Or what that daughter wants.'

Celeste almost gasped. He was suggesting she'd try to manipulate him into marriage to keep the business! How many times had Benton Scott had his face slapped this week? 'Sorry to disappoint you, but listen carefully…*I am not interested.*'

'No?'

She coughed out a laugh. *'No.'*

He chewed his inside lip again. 'I'm not convinced. Being a thorough as well as cynical man, before we go any further, I'll need to have proof.'

He left her no time to think. With a single arm he brought her near and like an apple falling to Earth—as if it was always meant to be—his mouth dropped and landed on hers.

The first few seconds were a blackout—all brain function shut down and energy funnelled to a suspended point a notch below zero. Then, as if waking from a coma, one by one every erogenous cell in her system zoomed up and blinked on. A heartbeat later, a ground-shaking surge of heat zapped like a lightning bolt right the way through her. When the palm high on her back pressed her closer, the intensity grew—brighter, hotter—until the magnetic inferno he'd created inside threatened to burn her alive.

This wasn't a kiss.

It was an assassination.

With skilled reluctance, he drew away, but only until the tip of his nose rested on hers. Caught in the prisms of his half mast eyes, she tried to make sense of her surroundings while her chest rose and fell, her limbs hung like lead and her core compressed around a tight, glowing coil of raw physical want.

When his head slanted as if he might kiss her again, she held her breath. But then his mouth hooked up at one side and he released her. Thank God she didn't teeter.

'I'm staying the week,' he said. 'If you're still

interested—or was that *not* interested?—tomorrow we can talk more, perhaps over a drink.'

By some miracle she steadied her breathing and dredged up a smile.

'A drink sounds good. But just so we're clear, I'll take mine with plenty of ice.' She took his glass and pitched the warm Scotch over the rail. 'And so, Mr Scott, will you.'

CHAPTER TWO

EARLY the next morning, Ben Scott woke up face down on the sheets, hugging a comfortless pillow, painfully aware of a mean morning hard-on.

He cracked open one eye.

Strange room. No one beside him. Good Lord, he needed to roll over.

Taking the pillow with him, he groaned as spears of light spliced through the sheer blowing curtains. Then the night before flooded his mind, foremost his conversation with the irrepressible Miz Prince. Relaxing back, he closed his eyes and remembered their bombshell kiss and her clever parting remark.

He grinned. She wanted ice? More like she wanted gasoline poured on her fire. However, while he would very much like to help, common—and business—sense told him if he played too close to those flames, someone would likely get burned. He was here to take control of a high-profile business that needed an injection of funds and his undivided attention to bring it back from the edge. But if Rodney Prince viewed this takeover as a saving grace, so did Ben. He couldn't wait to plunge in.

Soft laughter drifted in through his bedroom's second-storey doors. Setting the pillow aside, Ben strolled out onto the balcony. Celeste Prince was in the yard, ruffling the heads of two mid-sized poodles. When she threw a ball, they raced off like chocolate-brown rabbits across the wide-open lawn.

Crouched in the shade of an enormous Morton Bay fig tree, golden tresses framing her face, she might've been a fairy from the garden. Then she pushed up onto shapely long legs, her rounded cleavage popped into view, and those innocent thoughts flew from his mind.

He combed back his hair and, fingers thatched behind his head, stretched his arms and spine. While he'd been wrong to take advantage and kiss her last night, he couldn't regret it. In fact, if he had less moral fibre he'd do it again.

He finished his stretch, then cupped his hands around his mouth. 'Ahoy down there!'

She glanced up, but her widening gaze stopped short of reaching his eyes. Rather it got stuck on his bare chest, which suddenly felt twice its usual size. His mouth twitched. What was that about moral fibre?

Lowering his hands and setting them apart on the rail, he deliberately leaned forward. Realising what he'd done—given her a better look—she stiffened, then quickly dropped her gaze. When she peered back up, although her smile was controlled, her green eyes were glistening, just as they'd glistened last night.

'You're up early,' she said.

He thought of his crotch. 'I'm an early riser. Mind if I join you?'

'I was hoping you would.'

His brow lifted. 'I take it you're ready to get down to business.'

'I've never been more ready in my life.' She wound her arms up under that delectable bust. 'Let's do it.'

Thirty seconds later, Ben was face up under a cold shower, getting a good grip on himself.

He'd had women before. He'd respected and enjoyed every one. But, from the moment their eyes had met across the room, there'd been something different about Celeste Prince. He should've guessed she was Rodney's daughter. Later, in her father's study, he should've known she was laying a trap, leading him into a plan that would hopefully see him surrender his bid on the company.

He stepped from the shower recess and, dripping, grabbed a towel.

Yes, his normally clear sights had been blurred where Celeste was concerned. But he had her number now. She was a lady on a mission. He was in her way. She'd knock him down and drag him out any way she could.

He rubbed his chest and grinned.

It'd be fun letting her try.

Halfway out the front door, the thin middle-aged housekeeper caught up with him to hand over a note.

Benton, an urgent personal matter has called me away. Deepest apologies. Celeste is aware and will make sure you're comfortable. Rodney Prince.

That bought Celeste a little time to think of a way to explain this situation to her father, Ben thought, pushing the note into his pocket and walking out onto the veranda. It was clear she believed filling Daddy's shoes would make him proud. Ben sympathised with her—even envied her a touch. He'd give anything to have known a real father. A mother, too.

But he'd got something at least from his foster-home days...a survival technique, which had later crossed over into business: the uncanny ability to quickly and accurately sum up people and situations. Case in point, he had no doubt this deal would go through; Rodney Prince would never entertain the idea of passing on his ailing business to his pretty young daughter.

And Celeste? She was all about deportment classes and new season fashion. She didn't want to accept it yet, but she was better off following her more feminine sway. He was rarely wrong and he sure wasn't wrong about that.

When he met Celeste in the yard, despite the cold shower, the sight of her fresh face—those cute freckles sprinkled over her nose—had his toes stiffening in his heavy-duty boots.

He bent to ruffle both dogs' ears, then fixed the Akubra hat on his head while she sauntered over, eyeing his khaki outfit. 'My, my, you're taking this seriously.'

'And while I like the frock,' he said, 'you don't look dressed for a day at work.'

Not a flinch. Only a measured reply. 'I thought we could go over the books. I can change into a suit if you prefer.'

Picturing her draped over a desk in a vest and tie and nothing else, he cleared his throat.

Focus, Scottie.

'*I* thought we should start by tackling the more practical side of things.' Eager to begin, he rubbed his hands together. 'Where's a mower?'

She smiled, a cheeky tilt of perfect plump lips. They'd tasted like cherries last night. The juiciest, ripest cherries he'd ever known.

'Are you going to give me a quiz?' she asked. 'You want me to name the parts?'

He copied her grin. 'Not quite. You said you could rescue this business. That you could prove you knew it all backwards. Why don't we start with something basic, like lopping an inch off this lawn?' He surveyed the grounds, patted his chest and inhaled. 'I can smell the petrol fumes and hot motor oil now.'

A dog came to sit either side of her as she stooped to slip an espadrille on each foot. 'If you're trying to deter me, save your breath. I was brought up on the aroma of fertiliser and grip of secateurs.'

He shrugged. 'Then you'll be able to show me a thing or two.'

'I didn't want to say it, but that's kind of my point.'

She strolled away, her derrière swaying a little too freely to be entirely unconscious. Ice, be damned. If her head was saying to concentrate on business, her body hadn't got the message yet.

She cast a look over one delicate shoulder. 'Are you sure you want to do this? You could always tell my father you needed more time to decide. I'll work around him and the situation, and when you check back in two months—'

'Six weeks.'

'Six weeks,' she conceded as he caught up, 'you'll see everything is going forward nicely and you can, in all good conscience, step away from the buy.'

'You mean do the *honourable* thing.'

She flashed him a toothpaste-ad smile. 'Precisely.'

He had his own ideas on how to approach Rodney with the subject of this 'trial'. But Celeste was right about one thing: she didn't give in easily. Pity for her, but he didn't give in at all. He wouldn't be fobbed off.

'Having me right alongside you was part of the deal, remember? Of course, if you'd like me to remind you again…'

Knowing full well what he alluded to—*the kiss*—she looked away, dropped her chin and quickened her pace.

He slipped his hands in his pockets. Interesting response. Was Celeste Prince a pussycat masquerading in vixen's clothing? Although that would make her easier to handle, he almost preferred it the other way. She'd been dead on when she'd said he liked a challenge—particularly one who kissed like she did.

She stopped before a large metal shed, then, putting her weight behind its sliding door, pushed until a row of lawnmowers was revealed. She waved a theatrical hand. 'Choose your poison.'

He let out a whistle. 'That's quite a selection.'

'Before my father started the franchise, he fixed mowers for a living. Now he collects them.'

'Like stamps, only bigger.'

She laughed. 'Something like that.'

Sauntering into the enclosure, which smelled of rags and dry lawn clippings, he fought the urge to kick a few tyres. 'This one should do the trick.'

Red and clearly well maintained, it reminded him of a model he'd used when he was a kid. He'd received a dollar whenever he'd tended the yard, but his foster dad's smile had been the best reward. He had only ever given praise, and had never raised his voice as some of the other 'dads' had. Six months into Ben's stay with his new family, that man had died of a heart attack. In his foster mother's red-rimmed eyes—in her overly kind voice—Ben had guessed his fate. Next house. Next family. Hell, by that time, he should've been used to it.

Celeste ran her hand over the metal handle. 'This one must be over twenty years old. Wouldn't you like a newer model?'

He wheeled it outside. 'This'll do fine.'

He stooped and ripped the cord. The engine whirred, but didn't kick over. Putting some back into it, he pulled again. Splutter, whir, then nothing. Seeing her dainty foot pegged out, but avoiding her eyes, he set his hat on the ground and yanked the cord almost out of its connection.

He smothered a wince and stood back. He would *not* rub his shoulder.

'It must be broken.'

Celeste sauntered forward and, with one perfectly manicured tip, flicked a small lever. Frowning, he looked closer.

The lever said 'Fuel'. How'd he miss that?

'Try it now,' she said.

He shifted his jaw, bent to rip the cord again and the motor roared to life.

With a solemn face, he nodded deeply. 'Good work,' he said over the noise.

Her eyes were laughing. 'Does that mean I pass the first test?'

He flexed a brow. 'I believe that was the *second* test.'

Her emerald eyes darkened but this time she didn't look away.

Pleased to have his vixen back, he settled his hands on the metal bar and remembered a vibration that shook all the way up to rattle his teeth. 'In your professional opinion, how long do you think this will take?'

'This model's not self-propelled, so the best part of the morning,' she called back.

He stepped away and indicated the mower. 'There you go.' Distaste dragging on her face, she stepped back too. 'What's wrong? You grew up with fertiliser and secateurs. You've mown a lawn before, surely.'

If he worked her hard enough, she'd be running off to her handbag shop by midweek. One day, she might even thank him.

She turned off the fuel. 'It's a large block. If you insist I do this, I'll use a ride-on.'

A few moments later, another engine was growling, a monster this time. A ride-on? This model was more like a tractor.

She found some gardening gloves and wriggled

her French tips into each slot while he plonked his Akubra on her head. 'You'll need this. It's getting hot.'

Her chin tilted and she peered at him from beneath the overly large brim. 'Thanks.' Her tone said she wasn't sure she meant it.

After she'd pulled herself up behind the wheel, he hauled up behind her.

She rotated around, then ducked as his leg swung over her head. 'What the hell are you doing?

He squeezed down behind her on the adequate seat, tandem style. Nice fit. Nice perfume too. Light and flowery with a hint of a bite. Suited Miz Prince to a sassy tee.

'I told you last night. If we're doing this, I'll need to be your shadow.'

As if he had rabies, she shunted closer to the steering wheel. 'Perhaps you need a drink first. How's ice tea?'

'I prefer something hot in the morning.'

She turned fully around and sent him a warning glare from way beneath that Akubra brim. 'You won't scare me off.'

Well, hopefully not *too* soon.

He waved his hand at the steering wheel. 'Then I suggest you drive.'

Determination filled her eyes. She released the handbrake and planted her foot. The machine lurched forward and her hat flew in his face. Then she yanked the wheel, the tractor arced to the left and Ben fell sideways, barely managing to stay on.

Righting himself, he jammed the hat back on her head and, setting his hands on her hips, drove her rump back hard against his inner leg seams. She'd given him reason to hang on and her backside was the quintessential grip.

She slammed on the brake and scrambled off. When she threw the hat on the ground, he saw her face was flushed. 'I'm not doing this.'

He shrugged. 'You set the agenda.'

Talking him into this crazy plan, choosing this tractor, then trying to tip him off.

'You—you—' She bit her lip. Averting her gaze, she got her breath and maybe counted to three before she pinned him down again. 'You're not playing fair.'

'This isn't about what's fair. I'm doing what I need to do to ensure the welfare of a future investment.' *And, in due course, set you on your merry way.*

Her gaze zigzagged over his face as if trying to find a way in, or out. Then, with her mouth set, she pulled herself up on the ride-on again.

For the next hour they rode that baby in a diagonal pattern back and forth over the massive square of lawn. The vibration worked up his legs, rippling through every bone in his body. It should've been entirely non-sexual, but for her sweet behind planted before him…shifting, shaking, rubbing, until he gripped the seat either side and prayed for the torture to end. By the time they returned to the shed and she dismounted, his pants were on fire.

She grabbed the brim of his hat, flung it like a frisbee and set her hands on her hips. 'Satisfied?'

He groaned. *Not quite.*

He edged off the opposite side and held off rearranging himself. 'Well done,' he croaked.

'So, what's next on your agenda?'

'How about a long cold drink?' He turned to face her.

She looked half pleased. 'Possibly something with ice?'

He frowned. 'A man is not a camel, Miss Prince.' Nor was he a block of wood…well, not literally. At this precise moment, he was a desperately aroused animal who was a second away from showing her just *how* aroused he was.

Forcing his testosterone-driven brain to visualise a bleak snowy landscape—no valleys, no peaks—he headed towards the house, sensing the dogs padding behind him. When he slowed down, she caught up, but he steered the conversation towards a safe topic.

'How long have you had the dogs?'

'Matilda and Clancy were from the same litter. We got them…' Her words faded before she finished the sentence. 'Dad got them about fifteen years ago.'

He calculated. 'You would've been—'

'Ten,' she said, keeping her eyes dead ahead. 'Same year my mother passed away.'

His chest tightened, but his step didn't falter. Although, of course, he was 'sorry for her loss', in his opinion, that kind of phrase rarely sounded sincere. In her place, he wouldn't want to hear it. They didn't know each other well enough to ask about the circumstances. Instead he clicked his fingers and both dogs pranced up. Smiling, he brushed a palm over one wet nose, then the other. 'They act like pups.'

She swept her hair back in a temporary ponytail off her neck. 'They'll go and sleep under a tree half the day now.'

'They've had breakfast, then.'

Getting his hint, she smiled. 'I bet Denise has whipped up a feast. You look like a bacon-and-eggs man.'

His brows lifted. Good guess. 'And you say that because…'

She dropped the ponytail. 'I have a crystal ball.'

'A crystal ball would come in handy. Have you asked it about our six-week trial?'

As a warm breeze blew back the ribbons of her hair, he thought he saw her brow pinch. 'What do you think it would say?'

He didn't need a crystal ball to predict what would happen here. But suddenly he wasn't feeling so hot about playing a game that could only end one way. Even if he did step aside, Rodney would find another buyer. If, indeed, he *could* attract another decent bid for a business on the brink. Celeste was in a no win situation. Should he convince Rodney to allow her to continue with this doomed plan until she chose to walk away herself? Or would it be kinder to call stumps now? He knew from experience that holding onto fantasy could be worse than facing the truth. The sooner a person accepted, the sooner they could start to hold it together and survive another way.

When they entered the house, those thoughts evaporated as he soaked up the aroma of warm toast and, he was betting, fresh muffins. Man, he was starved. He was about to excuse himself and wash up when a familiar voice drifted down the hall.

Celeste turned to him with a curious gaze. 'My father's back.'

A female voice tinkled down to them next. 'Sounds like he's brought company.'

They found Rodney and his guest standing in the middle of the Axminster-carpeted living room, beneath the shifting reflections of a sparkling chandelier. From the night before, Ben recognised the woman. He wasn't the least surprised that Rodney was kissing her. He'd had the strongest feel-ing...

Celeste's hands flew to her mouth, but a gasp escaped.

Startled, Rodney broke the kiss and stepped back from the beautiful widow, Suzanne Simmons.

His moustache drooping, Rodney cleared his throat then rubbed the back of his neck. 'Celeste, Benton, you both know Mrs Simmons.'

Ben anticipated Celeste's reaction. He stepped closer, surreptitiously steadying her before her legs gave way. Ben nodded a greeting at the couple. Celeste couldn't manage the same courtesy. Who could blame her? This must be a shock.

Her voice was threadbare. 'What's going on?'

With her eyes on Ben and Celeste, Suzanne Simmons touched her beau's arm. Reassuring her, Rodney patted her hand, then walked up to his dazed daughter. 'Suzanne and I are going to be married, Celeste. We're very happy. Really looking forward to kicking back and having a family.'

Celeste's long lashes fluttered several times as she took it in. 'Dad, you're *sixty-five*.'

His jowls pinked up. 'Suzanne's having a baby. She's a fair way along with your little brother or sister. She had a scare last night but we've been to the doctor and everything appears to be fine.' He looked back at his bride-to-be and sent a smile. 'Just fine.'

While Ben felt Celeste's disbelief to his bones, he did what was expected. He put out his hand. 'Congratulations, Rodney.' He finished shaking and nodded towards Suzanne. 'I'm sure you'll be very happy.'

Another empty phrase, but this time, no doubt, appreciated. Ben believed in love wholeheartedly. It was the *happily ever afters* a man could never count on.

Suzanne's expression was kind and concerned as she came forward and took both Celeste's hands in hers. 'I'm sorry. This must be a huge surprise. We wanted to tell you tonight over a quiet family dinner.' The widow's gaze dropped to her rounded belly, then found Celeste's eyes again. 'I hope we can be friends.'

Ben's heart went out to Celeste as her slender throat bobbed up and down. Then she seemed to find some inner strength and somehow smiled. 'I'm... very happy...for you both.'

Suzanne addressed Ben. 'This buyout has come at the right time. We want to enjoy each other and the baby without the worry of a big business hanging over our heads.' She spoke to Celeste. 'Your dad tells me you'd like to buy another shop. That's so exciting. Bet you can't wait to get out there and start looking.'

Celeste's eyes glistened with a different kind of emotion as she looked to her father, who only looked away.

The circumstances were hardly the same and yet Ben felt Celeste's pain as if it were his own. It was a similar stab in the gut he'd experienced at age ten when he'd stepped one way, fate had stepped another, and suddenly he hadn't had that home any more. Guess the hurt of being pared off was no different no matter your age or position. Today at least he could do something to help.

Ben moved forward. 'I didn't expect to see you so soon, Rodney. I've invited your daughter out for the day. We were about to head off to grab something to eat.'

Rodney's expression jostled. 'Denise has a banquet on its way out.'

'And with my appetite—' Suzanne's settling hand found her fiancé's arm again '—I'm sure I could eat at least half of it. You two run along,' she encouraged Ben and Celeste. 'We'll see you both back here later.'

Five minutes on, Ben and the still stunned Celeste were seated in his SLK Mercedes, heading into town. She didn't protest; he'd bet she could barely talk. Her last twelve hours had been one kick in the gut after another. Yet she'd been so strong.

He was definitely no expert in fixing family woes; today he was an outsider, as always. He shouldn't feel responsible. This wasn't his doing. And yet what would it cost him to see his vixen smile again?

He planted his foot.

He knew just where to start.

CHAPTER THREE

BEHIND her sunglasses, Celeste gazed blindly out at the endless stretch of gum trees as Benton Scott's high-powered sports car propelled them away from her father's house. She didn't know if she ever wanted to see it again.

Benton didn't try to talk, for which she was grateful. Rather, with the top down, they drove until the traffic skirting the city slowed their escape. It was enough. She'd had an hour and had reached a conclusion.

Things happened for a reason. Today's king-hit was meant to make her see that the dream she'd held onto all these years hadn't been real—had never really been *hers*, no matter what she remembered from the past. Now it was time to either be eaten up by a sense of betrayal or let go. Given that her heart had been cracked wide open and all hope had leaked out, the second choice was a shoe-in. She had no more to give.

The well had run dry.

A traffic light blinked to red and Benton rolled the Merc to a stop. Exhaling fully, Celeste removed her glasses and studied the driver, who, at the moment, seemed more like a godsend than an assassin. Either way, he was the hottest man she'd ever met. And, it seemed, a sensitive one.

She half smiled. 'Thanks for getting me out of there.'

Glancing over, Benton pulled his mirror lenses down an inch, lifted a brow, then pushed the frames back up his aquiline nose. 'No problem.'

He was bad-boy handsome, perhaps with a touch of Mediterranean blood. His skin was smooth and olive, hair dark as pitch and long enough, she realised now, to lick the collar of his khaki shirt. She couldn't see his eyes so she focused on his profile…on his lips…beautiful lips for a man…dusty pink, the bottom one full and soft. She remembered how soft. Remembered how he'd tasted too.

'We're almost into the city.' He slipped into gear. The car cruised off again and the magnificent steel arch of Sydney Harbour Bridge came into view. 'I'd like to see your shop.'

Celeste smiled, but shook her head. Now he was taking compassion too far. 'You're not the least bit interested in handbags and belts.'

'Doesn't mean I'm not interested in what you normally do with your day.'

Brooke helped manage Celestial Bags and Accessories and had taken this weekend shift. They'd been best friends for ten years, but Celeste couldn't face her today. Knowing the family history, Brooke would try to comfort her and Celeste would sooner forget today had ever happened. A long hot bath and a good thick book might be the best place to start.

When the Merc rolled up to another set of lights, she turned to him. 'Sorry, but I'd rather you just drop me home.'

His large hands slid down opposing arcs of the sports steering wheel. 'No can do.'

She frowned. 'I beg your pardon?'

'The day's too nice to spend moping around inside.'

'I won't be moping.' Her frown deepened. 'I'm all done moping.'

He removed his glasses. His look said, Yeah, right. Aloud he said, 'I'll make you a deal.'

She gazed out the window. *Please, not now.* 'I'm not in the mood.'

'Not that I'm keeping score, but you owe me one. In fact, you owe me two.'

Her mouth pulled to one side. Oh, hell. She really did—for going along with her six-week scheme, and then pulling her out of that awkward situation with her father and Suzanne Simmons.

She held back a weary sigh and faced him. 'What is it?'

'I'll drop you home, but only to grab a swimsuit.'

Her pulse rate picked up. That sounded ominous. 'What do you have planned?'

He drew a zip across his lips. 'Federal secret.'

She had a flash of him entertaining her in a bubbling spa tub on the balcony of some glamorous penthouse suite. But somehow that didn't gel. She wasn't getting a 'take advantage of the poor girl while she's down' feeling. Rather the opposite.

Oh, what was she agonising over anyway? She'd bought a new swimsuit last week. She was a couple of kilos past her ideal weight, which had gone directly to her saddle bags. But what the heck? Would it kill her to be impulsive for a change?

Decided, she gave him directions to her apartment building, and ten minutes after he'd pulled up she was back down with her swimsuit packed. With his hip propped against the bonnet, he disconnected his cell call and opened her door, then eased back into his side.

He fired up the engine. 'Feeling any better?'

'I'm not feeling anything.' She shrugged. 'I feel kind of numb.' Must be a defence mechanism; it had been one of the worst days of her life.

He adjusted the rear-view mirror. 'Let's fix that.'

Soon the Merc was swerving into the private car park of a marina. A middle-aged woman with white-blonde hair and shortie-shorts rushed out from the boathouse to greet them and hand Benton a large picnic hamper. After thanking the woman, he escorted Celeste—a guiding hand on her elbow—down a jetty. They stopped before an impressive white yacht.

Her gaze ran over the lines of the hull and stopped at the name written in red flowing letters—*Fortune*. 'I take it this is yours?'

When he removed the sunglasses, pride shone from his eyes, which sparkled with flickering light off the water. 'A beaut, isn't she?'

'Very nice, but I'd have imagined you with something bigger,' she teased.

He took her elbow again. 'Believe me, it's big enough.'

On board, they changed—she into her tangerine bikini and a sheer white beach shirt, Benton into chinos and a surf vest-top that emphasised the musculature of those shoulders and glorious breadth of his back. They stood side by side as he negotiated the passage out and into the harbour.

Enjoying the fresh salty air pushing against her face and the sun's warmth on her skin, she inhaled and took in the stretch of glassy blue sea. What a difference a day made. Last night this man had been her enemy.

Today?

Well, today she was a new woman with a range of possibilities, including Benton Scott.

While he talked on about boating, she watched his hair ripple with the breeze and admired the deep brackets that formed around his mouth whenever he laughed. Was Benton seeing anyone at the moment? If so, it couldn't be a serious relationship. He'd said he wasn't after marriage.

She pulled her hair from whipping around her face and studied him more closely as he spoke.

Was he avoiding a walk down the aisle because he was happy playing the field or for a different reason? Had anyone ever broken his heart? Somehow she didn't think so.

He steered into a tranquil cove and threw the anchor. The small stretch of deserted beach, which was enclosed by a curtain of rich green hillside, looked like a secret pocket in paradise.

After he dug out a picnic blanket and the hamper, he retrieved a bottle with an expensive label. 'Anyone for chilled champagne?'

She'd had enough bubbles last night. 'I'll stick to cola.'

He backed down the boarding stairs, then, extending a hand, helped her down too.

'Guess it's not a day for celebrating,' he said as they waded in knee-high water to the beach.

She thought it over.

'It is in a way. At least now I can start to move forward.'

They crossed to a shaded portion of sand and she helped him square out the rug.

'Do I get more than that abridged version?' he asked.

She flinched. 'It's a long, messy story.'

He rummaged in the hamper and handed over a cola. 'We've got all day.' He sat down, one arm resting on a raised knee, the other pegged out slightly behind him.

Celeste had kept the more sordid details of her past to herself, like a dog protecting a dirty bone. Brooke was her only confidante. But perhaps this was the ideal time to do a final purge and let it all out. But was it fitting to clear the air with the man who would soon own her parents' company?

Wrinkling her nose, she pressed the cool bottle against her chin. 'Are you sure you want to hear it all?' Was she sure she wanted to spill?

He examined the hamper's contents. 'We have sandwiches, cheese and fruit as well as chocolate hearts. Plenty of provisions to see us through till at least next Wednesday.'

She found a smile, but sobered again when she sat beside him and cast her mind back. *Here goes.*

'My father was a mechanic's son who'd become a mechanic himself, whereas my mother had come from money. You know that big house?'

He unscrewed a bottle of water. 'It's magnificent.'

'It was a wedding gift from my grandfather, who never thought Dad was good enough for his little girl. That put a lot of pressure on Dad, and when he began to gather more clients with his mower-repair service, my mother suggested he expand.'

She sat back, remembering snatches of those days like a favourite old movie. 'That time was the happiest I can remember. Dad was busy and productive and getting places, but he always had time for us.' She dug her cola bottle into the sand. 'Unfortunately his lack of business savvy got him into trouble with a partner who robbed him blind. He was devastated. That's when my mother got involved and pulled him out of the pit. She put together a business plan and asked for a loan from Grandpa, who wasn't at all pleased.' She drew up and hugged her knees. 'My father changed after that.'

Benton concentrated on her every word. 'Your father's pride was dented. When did you learn all this?'

'A child hears a lot when arguments are in full swing after bedtime. My father would want to do something with the business his way and my mother would warn against it. She usually won the toss. That is until the franchise was well established.' She hugged her legs tighter and peered out over the still water. 'I never heard my father acknowledge her efforts. In fact, I think some part of him resented it. Over time, the difference in background and lack of respect took its toll. All the love she'd had for him was gone by my tenth birthday.' She looked at Benton. 'You might not believe a child would know, but I could see it in her eyes.'

'No. I believe you.'

The deep understanding in his voice, the line

between his brows, told her that he did, which gave her the heart to go on.

'The day of my birthday, I'd had friends over for a party and my mother, as always, held it together well. My grandfather had died the week before,' she explained. 'But when my mother sat down to kiss me goodnight, it all came out. She was riddled with shame and guilt and hurt. Grandpa had left all his money to her older brother. They'd never paid Grandpa back, it seemed. Dad had put it off and put it off. My mother was placated by only one thought—one day her pains would count for something when PLM passed onto me. Not that I cared about it back then. I only wanted my parents to love each other again.'

'But after your mother passed away, she didn't have any say in what your father did with the company.'

Or if he remarried and had more children. Celeste thought of the widow Simmons and the baby she carried. Guess she would have a brother or sister soon; she'd always wanted one. But right now she couldn't view those circumstances as simply as that.

She sighed and lowered her knees. 'My mother died of a cerebral haemorrhage. I was so lonely, I physically ached. The longer I was without her, the more important it became that her prediction that night would come true. More to the point, I couldn't see any reason why it wouldn't. But after this morning, that part of my life is over.' Her jaw clenched and she lifted her chin. 'I hate to admit it, but I'm relieved.'

When Benton dropped his gaze, her heart squeezed. 'Do you think she'd be disappointed in me giving up?'

Celeste wondered again about Benton's background. What skeletons he had in his closet. He looked so polished. So squeaky clean.

'Not at all,' he said. 'Your cause was a noble one. But I agree. You need to put that away and think about you now.'

She fell back onto the sand, hands behind her head, and stared at the vacant blue sky. 'I'm just not sure what it is I really need. Or even who I am any more.'

He lay down beside her, up on one elbow, his head propped in his hand. 'You're a young, beautiful, smart-mouthed woman who looks as fabulous in a swimsuit as she does an Akubra.'

Her cheeks heated and she grinned. 'Must admit, you looked pretty cute in khaki.'

'Didn't stop you from trying to pitch me off that ride-on. Good thing I have a firm grip.'

As they smiled her gaze wandered down the thick column of his throat, past the beating pulse in its hollow to the loose neckline of his top. His bare chest would be as hard as granite, but hot and human. Hot and wonderfully male.

A wave of intense arousal washed through her

veins. Almost a reflex, she sat up quickly. The palm trees' shade had moved and the sun had crept up their legs. Heart pounding, she pushed to her feet. 'It's hot. I need to cool down.'

After shucking off her shirt, she waded into the water. But why had she run? Benton wasn't her enemy any more. The truth was she *wanted* him to touch her. Wanted it very much. She knew from the gleam in his eyes that he wanted that too.

When the water lapped her waist, she turned around. He'd taken off his chinos and, arms crossed, was pulling the shirt up over his head. Her breath caught. His bronzed athletic body, rippling with muscle, was a work of art in brief black swimmers. She'd seen that superb chest before, this morning on the balcony. But here, now, the extent of his masculinity almost overwhelmed her.

When he'd waded in to his thighs, he plunged under and, a few seconds later, surfaced inches away. He combed back his hair, leant forward and said, 'Boo.'

His biceps flexed as he dropped his arms and a thrill of anticipation gripped low in her tummy. His presence was so compelling it was nothing short of dangerous.

Should she play it safe—try to ignore their sizzling chemistry—or take a chance and lean forward too? She'd had a shock this morning. Was she in any frame of mind to accept and handle the consequences?

Still torn, she held her breath and dived away.

He was right behind her, holding her ankle and pulling her back so he could shoot ahead. Enjoying the endorphin rush and cool silk of the water on her skin, she dived on top of his back and pushed him under. When they came up for air, they were laughing. His hands were cupping her waist and, after the exercise, cords of golden brown sinew roped down the lengths of his arms.

Their smiles faded as the air between them sparked with awareness—charged with sexual promise. Simmering with sensual need.

This time she didn't move away.

'Did you really think I'd try to seduce you to retain my father's firm?' she asked, finding her breath.

His hands slid down over her hips. 'I didn't know what to think, which is odd. I usually have no trouble reading people.'

She gingerly laid her palms on his pecs. Yes, indeed…hot human granite. 'Is reading people your special talent?'

His eyes darkened as his fingers combed down over her behind and his chest flexed beneath her hands. 'One of them.'

Her pulse rate picked up a notch. 'I'll admit it now. I liked your kiss.'

He grinned. 'I guessed.' He took her right hand and grazed his lips over the delicate underside of her wrist. 'You might be interested to know that my kissing abilities aren't limited to mouth to mouth.'

The buzz from that intimate contact was still humming through her blood when she found her voice, which had gone curiously thick. 'Give me an example.'

Feigning affront, he tipped his chin at her wrist. 'That's not proof enough?'

She gave a teasing shrug. 'Might've been a fluke.'

His thumb pressed into her palm, opening her fingers. 'Then let's try the mouth-to-fingertip technique.' He concentrated on each finger, placing his lips on their tips, sucking the last one into his mouth just a little.

Her core smouldered and sparked. Although she pretended indifference, she was breathing faster now. 'Hmm. Not bad.'

His sexy smile was knowing. 'Here's a personal favourite…lips trailing the curve of the neck.'

He came forward and her head rocked back as he nuzzled skin that was connected to invisible strings that made her nipples tingle and jump.

As he slowly pulled away she stifled a syrupy sigh but offered only a half-hearted nod. 'Quite nice, Mr Scott. But hardly inventive.'

His eyes narrowed playfully. 'You want new and exciting?'

'Are my expectations too high?'

'I don't know. Are they?'

She knew what he was asking. He wasn't into commitment. God knew, after today's kick in the pants, neither was she.

She coiled her arms around his neck. 'The last fifteen years of my life I've spent limiting myself. Never letting my eye roam from the target. Today hurt, but you're right. I need to put that behind me and do what's best for me now.' Her fingers threaded up through the strong wet hair at his nape. 'Are *you* what I need now?'

He brought her hips forward. 'I know you're what *I* need.' Beneath the water, she felt just how much.

Giving herself over to the delicious pulsing ache deep inside, she rested her lips against his. 'I think I'm ready to try mouth to mouth again.'

His eyes smiled. 'I'll see what I can do about new and exciting.'

CHAPTER FOUR

CELESTE let go any remaining inhibitions and met Benton's kiss, head-on. A jet of colour-filled emotions swirled through her, just as they had when his mouth had claimed hers to such devastating effect last night. But this time the thrill and desire felt sharper—went deeper. She trembled, thinking of what was to come.

Beneath the water line, those large masculine hands on her hips gently rotated her against his swell.

His arms wrapped around her more, then he brought her down with him until they were kissing underwater—all sound cut off, daylight flicking faraway patterns over their heads. When they ran out of air and surfaced, her bikini top was in his hand.

Gobsmacked, she gaped down. Yep, she was naked from the hips up.

With a testing grin, he dangled the top. 'Not sure how *that* happened. Hope you're not shy.'

Normally she was. She was a keep-the-lights-off kind of girl. And she hadn't been with anyone for a good while. But no one had ever attracted her like this man. She could go on kissing him for ever. But since that wasn't possible, she'd gladly take every moment she had with him today.

So, after a small stab of embarrassment and a deep breath, she smiled. 'I'm feeling reckless.'

His blue eyes sparkled. 'Way better than feeling numb.'

He was about to kiss her again when she pulled back and threw a nervous glance over her shoulder. 'There's no one around, though, is there?'

His finger skimmed up her arm, then down to circle one tight nipple. '*Reckless*, remember.' He gently rolled the peak.

Melting at his touch, she couldn't find any words, particularly when he left her to stand alone as he sank beneath the water again. Feeling exposed, but resisting the urge to cover her bare breasts, she coughed out a laugh as she felt her bikini bottoms slipping down. A second later she quivered; she guessed it was his mouth that had brushed at the juncture of her thighs.

Benton emerged slowly…the top of his head, his eyes and nose, then his wicked smile. Standing before her like an eternal mountain, he dangled the bottoms. 'Still feeling brave.'

Yes. *No.*

Her stomach gripped. 'I've never done this before.'

His expression froze. 'You're a virgin?'

'I mean I've never slept with someone I've known less than a day.'

His hand combed over her crown, ending by tugging her hair, and head, gently back. He kissed her with a penetrating, calculated skill that curled her toes and left the tips of her breasts burning as they rubbed against his crisp chest hair.

His lips gradually left hers. 'Then I consider myself a very lucky man.' He took her hand and cupped it over his erection.

She felt her eyes bulge. 'Am I supposed to say I'm lucky, too?'

He growled. 'Right now, you're not supposed to say too much at all.'

He kissed her again, one hand on the small of her back pushing her against him as well as their hands sandwiched between. Then his hand turned and scooped between her thighs. His touch slid up her centre and down again, stoking the fire before honing in on that critical burning bead.

She groaned against his mouth. 'Can I just say that feels fabulous?'

'On one condition.' She felt the naked length of him jump and slide across her belly. 'I get to say the same.'

He bent so that his knees bracketed hers and

lowered enough to guide his hot velvet tip over and around *that* spot.

His warm breath murmured at her ear, reducing her to compliant putty. 'Are you protected?'

She faded back up.

Protection? *Oh, damn!*

She bit her lip. 'Sorry.'

His knees straightened as he dropped soft lingering kisses on her cheek and brow. 'I have condoms on board.'

She quelled a pang of hurt. So he'd brought other women here, or at least had had women on his boat. How many? Two? Twenty?

Inside, she forced a shrug.

So they were both experienced—he a good deal more than she, no doubt—but what did she expect? More so, what did it matter when her body had caught light and real time had twirled off into another dimension?

He handed over her bikini, swung her up into the mighty bands of his arms and waded to the boarding steps. Then he gazed down at her, his mouth pressed together. 'Don't think I can manage the steps with you in my arms.'

Well, of course not. But she wasn't climbing up first. At least he still had his swimmers on.

'Put me down. I'll follow on behind.'

'I have a better idea.'

With a single fluid movement, he manoeuvred

her body and flung her over the sturdy ledge of his shoulder, sack-of-potatoes style. Her naked butt was pointing in the air—*oh, God*—right next to his face. Clinging to the hard muscle of his sides—taking in the upside-down sight of his tight buns—she felt her cheeks burn unbearably hot.

'I'm not comfortable about this,' she cried out.

She felt his chest and back expand on a satisfied breath. 'I must confess I have an overwhelming urge to slap your tail.'

She threw one hand behind her. 'Don't you dare!'

His hearty chuckle reverberated all the way through her.

One arm pinned around her legs, he negotiated the stairs, then carried her to the front of the boat. But he detoured to a small bathroom and didn't set her down until he flicked on the tap. He kicked off his swimmers and, her heartbeat knocking against her ribs, her gaze slid down.

Oh, Lord!

But before she had time to think any longer on it, he ushered her into the shower recess, soaped up his hands and began to rub her all over. It was true. She'd died and gone to heaven.

She reached for the soap. 'Mind if I play?'

His touch slid lower. 'Join in any time.'

She pumped creamy liquid soap and while he lathered her tummy she palmed the gorgeous mounds of his shoulders. Her fingers wove down the middle of his chest, over his washboard abs, lower until…

She hesitated and he growled. 'Don't stop there.'

So she didn't.

The more she stroked and rubbed, the longer his eyes remained shut and the further his neck arced back. She was really getting the hang of it when, with a burst of energy, he seemed to come to. He smacked his hands on the glass either side of her head, the cords running down his neck strained.

His voice was a husky deep groan. 'I think you'd better stop now.'

They rinsed off, towelled off, then sped off to the bed, which wasn't king-sized but, in this case, size didn't matter.

He ripped back the covers and she crawled towards the middle. He pulled a blind on the oval window and the sky was shut out.

Way past eager, she flipped onto her back and he slid down over the length of her body until his lips grazed her left breast. He lovingly looped his tongue around the tip, then raked his teeth over the sensitive flesh until she was almost out of her skin.

Sizzling inside and out, she arched beneath him. 'I'll explode if you do that again.'

'What? You mean this?' He moved to her other breast and repeated the performance.

She pulled him up by his hair. 'Where. Are. The condoms?'

Soon he was sheathed and hovering above her again. When he eased in, her blood turned to fire and her bones liquefied to happy mush. As her nails skimmed his sides her hips bucked to meet his next thrust. The strength of him, the sheer power, felt so darn good…

'I think I might faint.'

Grinning, he pushed again. 'A few moments more.'

A few moments during which she discovered where she belonged. In this incredible man's arms. In his bed. She wrapped her legs around his and clung onto sheer bliss. 'I know we're not finished, but can we do it again?'

She knew he would've laughed if he could spare the energy. From the hot look in his eyes as he gazed into hers, he was utilising every ounce of strength to hold back the tide. *Her* tide had already built to a shimmering, soul-lifting arc.

He pushed in deliciously deep, hit the right place with the right mind-tingling amount of pressure, and the rolling tidal wave crashed over her. Her centre contracted and the intensity erupted with the booming power of a bomb blast.

Flashing stars shot from her core, the pleasure-filled rhythm gripping and radiating out again and again. The sensations—the knowledge—felt almost *too* wonderful. She never wanted to let this feeling go.

Then it got better.

He drove in again. Every hardwired muscle in his

body seemed to lock and tremble. The sound he made was almost one of pain that morphed into a throaty sigh as he plunged once more. Her fingers trailed up his arms as, eyes closed, she hummed out a dreamy smile that felt perfect on her face. Where had he been all her life?

She stilled at a flicker of regret.

Where would he be for the rest of it?

For the longest time afterwards, they lay in each other's arms, Benton holding her close against his hard body, her index finger weaving aimless patterns over his chest.

They seemed to fit…as if they'd once been physically joined and now both sides had been reunited. But that was her romantic imagination taking flight. Just as it was nonsense to believe she'd known his scent far longer than a day—clean and male. Real and intoxicating.

Later, when Benton suggested a swim, still feeling brave, Celeste followed his lead and skinny dipped in the cool revitalising ocean. They ate sandwiches and milk chocolate hearts on the beach, then made love again, this time leisurely, making the pleasure last, holding back the reward as long as possible…and the reward was twice as incredible second time round.

Benton's brand of bedroom skill was entirely inherent; the knowledge was as astute as the hands strumming the sweetest chords over her body. His pleasure in giving and receiving was sincere. Today she was the lucky one.

When the sun was a fiery ball sinking into the sea, they emerged from their boat bedroom cocoon. He'd whipped on his chinos. She was dressed in her white beach shirt and nothing else. She'd never been so casual with a man and yet today—with Benton—it felt only natural.

They each reclined back in a low slung canvas deckchair, their arms hanging in between—fingers laced—and gazed up at the rapidly darkening sky, its horizon feathered with rose.

She laid her free hand behind her head. 'The stars are coming out.'

Had they always looked so beautiful? Tiny twinkling jewels that spoke to her. *Everything will be fine now,* they seemed to say.

'How do you feel?' he asked.

'Alive!'

His fingers squeezed hers. 'Good.'

'And also that this is a little uneven.'

He looked at her. 'Uneven how?'

'You know so much about me and I know nothing about you.'

She wanted to know *everything*, starting with when he'd learned to tie his shoes, right up to his plans for tomorrow. Had he ever had a long term relationship? Did he ever want to fall in love? But didn't everyone? That was what kept the human race going. Attraction, desire, a sense of belonging that culminated in two individuals becoming a couple. She'd seen the movies, read the books. But she'd never experienced the possibility of falling in love herself more clearly than this minute. He was indeed a hit man and she'd been slugged hard and fast.

'There's nothing much to know about me.'

As if. She turned more towards him. 'Try me.'

His laugh was short. 'There's not much of interest to tell.'

'You're being modest.'

He grinned. 'Why don't you use that crystal ball of yours?'

She searched his eyes before he looked back up at the sky and her stomach clenched. He wasn't being modest, not even mysterious. What was in his past that he was so reluctant to share? But if he didn't want to talk, it wasn't fair to push.

'I'm sorry,' she murmured. 'I didn't mean to pry.'

He found her gaze again, raked a hand through his hair, then scratched his head as if to stimulate the memories.

'Okay. Uninteresting fact number one. I grew up in foster care. Fact number two. When I was sixteen I got a job, finished my education at night school, then put myself through college. Fact three. At twenty-four I discovered the stock market. A year later I'd earned my first million. The rest, as they say, is history.'

A little dazed, Celeste tried to soak it all in. His childhood background was so not what she'd expected. She'd imagined a home something similar to her own, regular vacations, two parents who cared.

'Your mother?' she ventured.

'Died a few days after giving birth. No need to say you're sorry,' he said sincerely. 'It's not as if I knew her.'

And her heart went out to him for precisely that reason.

'What about your father?'

'Good question.'

'Your mother wasn't married?'

'She was. And divorced. Scott's my father's name.'

Celeste tried to keep up. 'You haven't tracked him down?' If she were him, she'd be eager to discover that connection—to know a link to her past. Maybe he got his looks from his father, his intelligence from his mother. Perhaps he had half-brothers or -sisters. What about grandparents? Didn't he want some answers?

'As a matter of fact, I've had a private investigator looking these past weeks. He's come up a blank. I thought about trying a different agency, but if my biological father didn't care back then, it's unlikely he'd care now.' He gazed at the sky and crossed his ankles. 'Sometimes people don't want to be found.'

His expression was meant to be light but his furrowed brow told her he was a little more than ir- ritated. She understood, particularly if the PI's inability to track down his father was indeed a matter of the older Mr Scott not wishing to be found.

She studied his controlled face…the harder than usual line of his mouth.

Had Benton programmed himself not to care so the prospect of hope wouldn't eat him alive? Maybe that was why he'd been so sympathetic about her situation today. She'd held onto hope too. It hurt to let go, but she'd discovered that it would hurt more to cling on.

She searched for something supportive to say. 'I bet your father would be proud of you.'

His gaze still on the sky, he only offered a wry grin. Then his face broke into a genuine smile. 'Quick! Look there.'

She followed the line of his arm. A bullet shot across the blue-black sky, its silver tail trailing and fading behind.

Her hand went to her heart, which had leapt to her throat. 'A falling star! I've never seen one.'

She'd always wanted to.

'I've seen dozens. I used to watch out my bedroom windows, waiting.' He stopped as if he'd said too much, then he sat straighter. 'You're supposed to make a wish.'

Picturing a lonely little boy peering up at the stars, she squeezed her eyes closed and made a dual wish, for him and for her. As she opened her eyes he pushed out of his chair.

His eyes twinkled, reflecting the cabin's light. 'I know what you wished for.'

Perhaps half of it. But she wouldn't admit to anything. She didn't want him to know she was already close to addicted. To his smile. To his touch.

She lifted her chin. 'Let's hear it.'

He held up a finger—*just a minute*—and disappeared inside. Soon soft music filtered out. When he reappeared, a breathtaking masculine silhouette challenging the darkest blue sky, he helped her out of her chair.

Then he drew her towards him and began a slow dance, his chin resting lightly on her crown. 'You wished for a dance.'

She leant her cheek against his chest and bit her lip as emotion stung her nose. She'd never felt so special.

But was she? Was this 'just one night' or dared she hope for—*wish* for—more?

His deep voice rumbled through her. 'I'm glad we met.'

'Me, too.' Huge understatement.

'I promise I'll look after PLM.'

She closed her eyes at a sharp twinge but smothered it quickly. *Put it behind you.*

'I'm sure you will.'

He waltzed her around as the song's verse segued into the chorus.

'I'd like to keep in touch?'

Her heartbeat thumped so hard she was certain he

could feel it jackhammering against her ribs. Difficult, but she kept her voice level. 'That would be nice.'

'Every quarter or so I can let you know how it's doing.'

Every three months? What was he talking about? Her pulse rate took a dive.

Of course, he was talking about her father's firm. Soon to be *his* firm. Not about keeping in touch with her on a personal level.

She set her jaw.

Get with the programme, Celeste. Benton Scott wasn't a man after a relationship. A little afternoon delight wouldn't change that. Certainly not a shooting star. And, after needing to give up PLM, she wasn't supposed to be in the mood for commitment either.

He rocked her around and pressed a kiss to the top of her head while the music played on. 'Would you like to stay the night?'

An honest answer? More than all the stardust in the universe!

But if she spent any more time in his arms—in his bed—it would be harder to leave, and it was already hard enough. This might have been casual, but the emotions he evoked were anything but blasé. Safer to go now and save her heart.

She filled her lungs. 'This was exactly what I needed. Thank you, Benton—'

'Call me Ben.'

She smiled. *Ben* suited him far better. 'I think I'll go home.'

Was it imagination, but she thought he held her a little tighter.

He grazed his chin near her temple and murmured, 'Let's finish this dance first.'

By the time the song ended, the words of the chorus were buried in her mind and heart for ever.

Yes. She had a feeling time would go by very slowly. But now it was time to move on.

CHAPTER FIVE

NEW YEAR'S EVE?

Bah Humbug.

Celeste sank into a chair at Sydney Airport's domestic terminal and set her chin in her hand. Moments ago, she'd said bon voyage to Brooke, who'd boarded a plane destined for romantic Hamilton Island on the Great Barrier Reef. Brooke had swung a great deal with a travel-agent friend; they'd both begged Celeste to come too. Luxury accommodation. Parties every night.

Celeste heaved a sigh.

She didn't have the energy. She would love to be waltzing around, totally fine with the world, but her rose-coloured glasses were smeared with grey. Though she wished she were stronger, she was still coming to terms with the ka-thunk of losing PLM. And then there was her other problem...

Sitting opposite, a middle aged man, wearing shorts, brown fuzzy socks and black sneakers, blew his bulbous nose into a chequered handker-chief.

Celeste cringed and shifted her gaze to a vending machine.

Her jetting off with Brooke and Pip would only bring their tone down. They deserved to have a good time, and if they happened to find someone nice who took them in his arms at midnight…

A skinny man with a concave chest and long hairy arms passed Celeste's line of vision and she flinched.

Well, good luck to *anyone* who got lucky tonight. But she didn't want to be put in that situation—a spritzer in one hand and some half-sozzled Neanderthal trying to get up close and personal on the other.

A rush of regret, wrapped in longing, spiralled through her tummy.

Celeste, you've screwed it for yourself.

Six weeks on from saying goodbye, every man she looked at left her feeling either ill or ambivalent. No one could even half measure up to Benton Scott.

Her nape tingled with a strange awareness, as if a warm breeze had brushed by her back. A second later she tingled at a murmur at her ear.

'Boo.'

Heart catapulting to her throat, she spun around in her seat. Every millilitre of blood dropped to her toes, then surged back up, leaving her slightly giddy. The lump in her throat was so big she could barely get the word out.

'Benton?'

As he rounded the row of seats to join her she battled the impulse to run over and throw her arms around his big beautiful neck. Instead she stood up, then almost had to sit back down again. He looked too good…

The pale blue jeans, which rode his lean hips, dressed those long muscular legs well enough to make her mouth water. His shirt sleeves were rolled halfway up powerful bronzed forearms, and the open collar revealed a tantalising vee of crisp dark hair. She imagined the plates of rock waiting beneath the white silk blend and memories of his scent filled her mind.

She'd thought she would never see him again! Yet here he was, stopping a mere foot away, his dazzling smile so broad and sexy, she worried her lips might not work if she tried to speak.

He pressed a kiss, which was way too brief, high on her cheek. 'I told you to call me Ben, remember?' he said, tipping back.

Oh, how she'd missed that dark-chocolate voice. 'Ben. Yes.' *I remember.*

'What are you doing here?' they said together.

Then, 'You first,' at the same time.

He laughed. 'After you.'

She gathered her thoughts and sucked down a settling breath. 'I've just seen Brooke off.'

'Brooke…your friend who helps manage the shop?'

She nodded. When he'd driven her home that

night they'd talked about boarding school and Brooke, and how they were still best friends. He'd seemed interested but hadn't offered any more information about his past and she hadn't pushed, although her more curious side would've liked to.

'Brooke and another friend are on a week's vacation on Hamilton Island,' she explained.

He set his briefcase down. 'Should be one helluva party going off there tonight.' A frown pinched his brow. 'Why didn't you go?'

Slipping her hands behind her back, she crossed her fingers. 'I'll be busy with the shop—' she shrugged '—and things.'

'That's a shame. I imagine you could've done with the break.'

But if she'd boarded that plane, she'd have missed seeing him now. She'd daydreamed about just this sort of meeting, never believing it would ever come true.

She almost reached to stroke his hand, the hand that knew every responsive inch of her body. 'Where have you flown in from?'

Or, where was he flying out to?

What was the bet he was running late for his plane and had to rush off?

'I just got in from Perth.'

Excellent! But her smile dimmed. 'You must be exhausted.' Sydney was a six-hour flight from Perth, Australia's west coast capital city.

His gaze dipped to her lips before finding her eyes again. 'I've been in Perth since before Christmas.'

'Business?'

'Mixed with pleasure. A friend of mine wanted my opinion on some—' But he stopped. 'I must be holding you up. It's New Year's Eve. You'd have a party to go to.'

She'd had several offers but had declined every one. Same reason as Hamilton Island. She'd be about as much fun as a pregnant goldfish. But what excuse for being a sad sack could she pluck out of the air?

'I was going to have an early one, being so busy with work and all.'

His eyes narrowed. 'So you're tired?'

Backtrack, Celeste.

'Not *overly.*'

'It's just I've been invited to a party...' He waved a hand. 'Forget it.' He collected his briefcase. 'I'll get out of your hair.'

'You're not in my hair,' she piped up. 'I've got it up.' She flicked her ponytail. 'See?'

He laughed—that deep, rumbling, infectious sound—and she melted all over again. 'The party's in my building. Do you need to change?'

She assessed her black jersey dress and silver sequined flip-flops. 'I don't know. Do I?'

He caught her arm and a high-voltage sizzle shot over her skin. 'You look gorgeous.'

He only had to say it aloud and it was true. As they

walked from the terminal she felt like the most beautiful woman alive. A woman whose day was suddenly painted in sunshine.

'So, you're Cindy?'

Celeste shook her head and called out her name again.

Reece, the man Ben had just introduced her to, cupped his hand to his ear and shouted again over the head-pounding music. 'Was that Sheryl?'

Ben replied just as loudly. *'Celeste.'*

Reece raised his beer. 'Welcome, Celeste. Any friend of Ben's is a friend of mine. Help yourself to a drink.' He gyrated like Elvis. 'Have a dance.'

Celeste nodded but thought of the dance they'd shared on the deck of Ben's yacht. She was grateful for the invitation to the party…still, how she wished they were on that yacht now—alone, quiet, coming apart in each other's arms. Their unplanned meeting tonight was obviously meant to be.

But what did Fate have planned for tomorrow?

She thanked Reece and moved with Ben through the crowd to the small self-serve bar.

'Are all these people your friends?' she called out. They were packed like sardines.

He searched the room, then tipped forward. 'No.'

He withdrew a bottle from a sink full of ice, poured champagne, handed a glass to her, then raised his own. 'Here's to us.'

She smiled. 'To us.'

Whatever that meant. And she wouldn't find out here, with the music blaring louder than any nightclub she'd visited and people crushing all around. But at least *he* was here and they were close and when the party was over—

A tall, lean man elbowed through and slapped Ben on the back. 'Benton, mate.'

Ben swung around and, with a shout of greeting, shook the marginally shorter man's hand. 'Didn't know if we'd see you tonight.' Ben turned to Celeste. 'Malcolm, this is Celeste Prince.'

Malcolm affected a half bow. 'Pleased to make your acquaintance. I'll be even more pleased if you let me win some of my money back from your boyfriend. How about it, Ben? I'll let you break.'

While Celeste tried to get her mind around being thought of as Ben's girlfriend, her date shook his head. 'No pool tonight.'

Desperate, Malcolm clasped his hands beneath his goatee. 'One game. Just one.'

Ben was shaking his head when he saw Celeste nodding hers. 'I don't mind,' she called out. 'I like pool.'

Malcolm beamed and looped his arm through hers. 'Ben, your taste in women just keeps getting better.'

Malcolm meant it as a compliment, but Celeste remembered the supply of condoms on the boat. The circumstances surrounding that day six weeks ago had been unusual—feeling both freed from her past and somewhat lost about her future, she'd needed some TLC. She'd accepted his invitation, but had she been a fool to believe that the decision to make love had been her choice? Was it more realistic to admit that she'd been seduced by Ben's charm like, no doubt, many women before her?

Malcolm was already drawing Celeste away, calling over his shoulder to Ben, 'One hundred smackeroos down.'

Ben caught up. His gorgeous blue eyes quizzed hers. 'You sure? Watching eight ball isn't the kind of thing a woman wants to do in the hours leading up to New Year.'

She might have laughed. Ben could be a sweetheart, but he sure had his blinkers fixed when it came to stereotypical gender roles. Women weren't all about facials and pretty shoes and sexual conquest. At least she wasn't.

The noise halved when they entered and shut the door on a back room. A mid-sized pool table took up a large portion of the space.

Malcolm pulled a cue from the wall and chalked up. 'Balls are racked.' He waved a hand at the colourful triangle one end of the green felt. 'Your break, mate.'

Ben chose a cue and winked at Celeste. 'Malcolm and I have an understanding.'

Malcolm stroked his goatee. 'We play. He wins.

But not this time.' He stabbed the air. 'This time you're toast.'

Celeste made herself comfortable on a stool and applauded when either man sank a ball. It was a good game but a quick game, with Ben the victor.

Malcolm propped his cue against the table and drove his hands through his thick red hair. 'One more,' he pleaded as he sped off around the table. Balls clicked as he hurriedly lifted them from their nets.

After popping his cue back in the wall rack, Ben rubbed his neck. 'Not tonight.'

Malcolm grabbed the triangle and set the balls up. 'Double or nothing. Celeste's a good sport. She won't mind.'

Having eased off the stool, Celeste appropriated Malcolm's cue. She lowered her back over the stick, closed one eye, took aim, and the balls smashed. Number ten flew into the right back pocket. She scuffed more chalk on the cue tip and blew. 'No, I won't mind. I like pool.'

Ben's wide gaze narrowed. Then he crossed his arms. 'Lucky break.'

She dropped another ball into the left back corner. 'If you say so.' She lined up and number nine slid into a middle pocket.

Ben coughed out a laugh. 'You can *play*?'

She visibly shuddered. 'Shocking, isn't it?'

Grinning, Malcolm backed up and dropped his hip over that stool. 'This is gonna be good.'

With a confident smirk, Ben racked the balls again. 'I'll let you break, Eddie Charlton.'

'I don't want to take an unfair advantage.'

Smiling, he squeezed her ribs as he passed. 'Just break, will you?'

She'd sunk six of her balls before Ben got a look in. At first he was confident, then he got anxious, now his mouth was a tight line of determination.

When she finally missed, he all but elbowed her out the way. 'My turn.'

Celeste rested her cheek against the upright stick. She was enjoying this way too much.

By the time Ben dropped all seven of his balls, a sheen had broken out on his hairline. Lying over the cue, he closed one eye, sharpened his aim against the vee of his guiding hand, then, with a skilled gliding movement, connected the felt tip with the white ball. Celeste held her breath as white clicked on black, which rolled further away and closer to the far left pocket. A hair's breadth from plonking in, it stopped.

Ben straightened and blinked hard.

Far too tactful to punch the air—well, not just yet— Celeste put away her seventh ball, and took aim at the black while Ben knocked down the rest of his drink.

The sliding glass door, which led out to the balcony, whizzed open. A man, laughing and clearly inebriated, stumbled back into the room, thumped the table and the black rolled in.

Celeste swore, Ben smiled and Malcolm jumped off the stool.

'I'll rack up,' Malcolm said. 'My money's on Celeste.'

'We're done here, Malcolm,' Ben said, taking Celeste by the arm.

Ben guided Celeste out and the music hit them like a wall. He cringed, then leant near her ear. 'Do you want to stay?'

Not really, but she didn't want to go home either.

'What's the alternative?' she asked. He spoke, but over the music she couldn't hear. 'What?' He said something about fireworks. She shook her head and indicated her ear. 'Too loud.'

His mouth thinned into that determined line again and he looped his arm through hers. They nodded goodbye to Reece as they headed out.

In the much quieter corridor, Ben thumbed the lift button and shucked back his shoulders. 'We can watch the fireworks from my balcony. Unless you'd rather go someplace else?'

His balcony? Meaning his apartment?

She wanted to *so* much. Her heartbeat was tripping out at the prospect of being entirely alone with him again, particularly after that competitive game of pool. Their adrenaline levels had spiked to a point where she felt as if they were ready to pounce on each other, which, on the surface, sounded divine.

But what about Ben's bad-boy charm? Had he

thought about her these past six weeks even half as much as she'd thought about him, or had he pursued and enjoyed other women? The possibility of knowing Ben intimately again was as enthralling as it was dangerous, like leaping off a cliff blindfolded believing that she would be caught. But what if the reality was she didn't mean much more to him than a good lay?

Did she honestly want another one-night stand?

On the other hand, Ben had asked her to stay that night on his yacht; she'd been the one to decline and bid a convincing farewell. Maybe he would've phoned her otherwise.

Either way, couldn't she quit her over-thinking and simply enjoy this incredible man until she had to decide—if, in fact, it came to that?

She held herself tight and nodded. 'Your balcony sounds good.'

Two minutes later they entered a penthouse suite and she moved through into a living room that was tastefully decorated in light timber, black leather and arty stainless steel. She nodded. 'I'm impressed.'

While he hung his keys, she drifted towards floor-to-ceiling windows. In an hour, the bridge and harbour sky would fill with amazing explosions of colour. Each New Year the spectacle seemed to grow larger and last longer. This year was meant to be the biggest yet.

She sighed. 'The view from up here will be un-believable.'

The heat of his body closed in behind her, then he growled at her ear. 'Where did you learn to play eight ball like that?'

She grinned. That didn't take long.

She turned and tried not to sway when she found him so close, towering over her. His gaze was curious and amused. His mouth, lifted at one corner, looked way too tempting.

'My father taught me to play when I was young,' she said. 'I practised every afternoon for a year. There was a games room at the boarding school too.'

His eyebrows opened up. 'A *girls'* boarding school?'

She half laughed, half huffed. 'What is it with you?' She skirted around him. 'A woman's talents aren't limited to having babies and applying make-up, you know.'

He did know that...right?

'Are you saying you didn't expect me to be surprised when you sank those balls as easy as licking an ice cream?'

She almost buffed her nails. 'I hoped you would be.'

His eyes challenged hers as he sauntered over. 'What other surprises do you have in store?'

She couldn't think of any.

But she waved a hand. 'They wouldn't be surprises if I told you.'

'Tell me anyway.'

She cocked a brow. 'Can you handle it?'

'I can handle you.'

A spiral of delicious desire coiled around her core and squeezed. Talk about irresistible—as well as arrogant.

Smirking, she crossed her arms. 'Oh, you can, can you?'

His grin was so hot, it singed.

If she'd wondered before, she needn't now: he'd made his intentions clear. He wanted to pick up where they'd left off. And, in truth, she wanted him to wrap those strong arms around her, sweep her off her feet and kiss her until she didn't know what day it was. She'd thought often about being in Ben's bed again, but did she want to give him the satisfaction of handing herself over so easily? Which, it seemed, was precisely what he expected.

I can handle you.

He'd said it playfully, but he'd meant it just the same.

When he stepped towards her with that gleam in his eye, she ducked and moved out onto the balcony. By the time he joined her, she'd taken several calming breaths.

If she slept with Ben tonight, how much would it hurt if he didn't follow up their time together with a call? Of course, she could be honest and simply ask if he intended to see her again, but that presented a problem.

His response to 'are you going to call?' could

leave her looking like a first-class fool. *You're great in bed, Celeste, but let's not get ahead of ourselves.* She would die!

He sidled up against her, his arm brushing hers, but she moved an inch away. She needed more time to sort out what she wanted out of tonight. Which meant veering her thoughts, as well as his, away from the possibility of sex. They needed another topic of conversation. Something safe, if not totally settled.

'I've been looking at starting plans for an exclusive florist service. It was something I wanted to combine with PLM, but...' She fought back the doubt and put on a brave face. 'I've had time to think, now I'm sure that's where I want to head.'

He gave her a congratulatory nudge. 'Hey, that's great. Have you told your dad?'

'I'm not ready. He offered to put up the money to buy another handbag store. But I didn't take it.'

Leaning one elbow on the railing, he studied her. 'Why not?'

It was difficult to explain without sounding ungrateful. 'For a start, expanding that way was his idea. And if my father gave me the money for the store, I'd feel as if it was his, not mine. Whatever I do, I want to go forward without anyone's influence weighting my decisions.' Whichever way she went, however she got there, the future would be hers—decisions, mistakes as well as rewards.

His voice was a comforting warm blanket. 'Your mother would be proud.'

She'd said the same to Ben, but about his father, when they'd spoken on his yacht that night. What must it be like never to have known either parent? Perhaps like missing out on knowing a piece of yourself. She couldn't imagine feeling that...*displaced*. And yet it hadn't stopped him from succeeding. Speaking of which...

Now was the time to bring it out in the open.

She put on a smile. 'How's the landscape maintenance going?'

The breeze picked up, bobbing a black curl on his forehead. 'It's going very well. The debt's all clear, I've spoken with all the franchisees, mowed a few lawns. Yeah, I'm happy.' His smile faded. 'How are you coping with it now?'

She pushed back her shoulders. 'I'm fine with it being sold.' Liar. But hopefully one day soon. 'I'm glad Dad got a good deal.'

He searched her eyes. 'What about Rodney being a dad again?'

She sighed. 'That's still a little weird. I know I'll be happy when the baby comes. It'll be nice not to be an only child.' She shrugged. 'Better late than never.'

Pushing off the rail, he straightened to his full height and changed the subject. 'Do you want a drink?'

She changed it back. 'Have you ever wondered if you have brothers and sisters out there? Ever think of trying to contact them? Who knows? You might be an uncle by now.'

His smile was set. 'I'd rather not go there right now.' He clapped his hands on the rail. 'Want to help me throw together some salad? The housekeeper came in today to restock the fridge, and I've got a couple of steaks in the freezer I can defrost. I just realised, I'm starved.'

When he moved off, Celeste hung back. Ben knew nothing about his blood relations. Yet that hadn't stopped him from having a strong sense of self. On the other hand, she'd always clung to her familial totem pole. Now that pillar had, to a large degree, been taken away, she felt a little adrift. Tonight, her unsettled feelings for Ben hadn't helped. Could this go somewhere? If so, what did that mean for her future? A future that had seemed so clear-cut until six weeks ago, but now seemed up in the air.

She moved inside and made a place beside him behind the tiger-striped granite bench. They stayed clear of talk about family while she sliced lettuce, tomato, shallots and Ben did his thing with rib fillet on a hot-plate grill.

He seemed to know his way around a kitchen pretty darn well.

'You cook for yourself often?'

'Most nights, sure. Pass the pepper.' He seasoned the meat, then flipped. Watching the steak—having the tasty aroma fill her lungs—she wondered if he did his own sauces. Something creamy. Maybe something spicy.

When her eyes lifted from the grill to Ben's mouth, her knife slipped.

'Ouch!' She jumped back and squeezed her finger.

Ben rushed over to inspect the wound. 'It's not deep.'

He guided her over to the sink and put her finger under gently running water. Still holding her hand, he retrieved a fresh towel from a bottom drawer. He patted the small cut, then found a first-aid kit and applied antiseptic with a cotton ball. A Band-Aid on top of that, then the best part.

His head lowered, his soft lips touched the spot and her breasts tingled to life. So small a gesture and yet it set her insides alight with an intensely pleasant heat. Was he aware of even half his effect on her? Smart answer was, of course.

He lowered her hand and slipped the steaks off the grill. 'They're overdone.'

'They'll be delicious.' Recovering, she tonged up the shallots and placed them in the bowl with the other salad. Then she wiggled her bandaged finger. 'Thanks for this.'

He flashed a teasing grin. 'Maybe I should cut your meat for you?'

'Do you want to feed me, too?'

It was a joke. Well, mostly. Still, she couldn't get out of her head the image of feeding each other, but not finishing their meal because the overwhelming sexual pull had them devouring each other instead.

He didn't answer but merely smiled that smile, collected their plates, and she followed him out onto the balcony with water and salad.

The meal was way better than anything she'd cooked lately. Leaving little on her plate, she fell back in her seat and dabbed her mouth with the linen napkin. 'You can cook for me any night.'

He refilled her water. 'Glad you enjoyed it.' Sipping from his own glass, he checked his watch and shifted back his chair. 'Almost midnight.'

She tried to swallow the nervy flutter in her throat with a mouthful of water. Of course he would kiss her—maybe lightly at first, but no doubt deepening until she was floating. But what would happen next? Would she give him the signal to advance? What if he didn't acknowledge it?

Oh, God, what if he did?

Escalating noise mushroomed all around. Whistles blowing, bells ringing, crowds hooting and singing. Sydneyites loved New Year's Eve and this year their sparkling city had turned out in force. The tension on this balcony was just as combustible.

Her fingernails digging into her palms, she followed him to the railing. He checked his watch again, then studied the Harbour Bridge, which was set to ignite with transfixing kaleidoscopes of light at any moment.

Amidst the building excitement, he spoke, low

and almost grave. 'In case you're wondering, I am going to kiss you.'

Her bones turned to jelly.

But she lifted a shoulder, let it drop. If he could tease so shamelessly, she could outright lie. 'I hadn't wondered at all.'

From way below, distant and near, the countdown drifted up.

Ten, nine, eight...

His fingers laced with hers as his face, dramatically cut in the moving light and shadow, came close. His next admission poured over her, hot and drugging. 'I've wanted to do this all night.'

Five, four, three...

How to react? What to say? She wanted his kiss, but how much, or little, did he want from her?

As she searched his eyes a roar of 'HAPPY NEW YEAR' went up and the sky erupted with loud bursts of colour-filled stars. While magical showers rained and thunderous cracks exploded all around, his hand, joined with hers, wound around her back and tugged her in.

He spoke close to her lips, his breath warm and inviting. 'Stars are shooting, Celeste. Make a wish.'

His physical presence was so strong—so close to hypnotic—she could barely catch her breath, let alone think. Her voice was tellingly husky. '*You* make a wish.'

His hand on the small of her back urged her closer. He was already hard. 'I wish you'd stay the night.'

Her skin was on fire. Her legs were loose rubber bands. What did she want? Where would this lead?

She groaned. 'I—I…I'm not sure.'

He smiled. 'Guess I'll have to convince you.' His lips tasted hers, tender and coaxing. *'Happy…'* another, longer taste *'…New…'*

Cupping her jaw, he kissed her slow and deep, with a scorching knowledge and soul-filled necessity that she'd dreamed of every night for weeks. When their mouths gently parted, he didn't say *Year*.

Instead, she sighed and said, *'Yes.'*

CHAPTER SIX

CELESTE didn't care if *yes* was the right decision. Lord knew it was the right decision for *now*. With fireworks whistling, bursting and collapsing all around, Ben smiled and led her from the balcony into his large shadowy bedroom. She followed, only knowing she was walking on moonbeams.

The smell of spent gunpowder drifted in through a giant open window. That, mingled with his masculine scent and indistinct shapes shifting over the walls, made the moment seem almost surreal. With flashes working over the strong planes and angles of his face, Ben kept his eyes on hers and effortlessly peeled the dress up over her head.

As he heeled off his shoes his gaze dipped and he smiled. She knew why.

Black underwear—a delicate crop top and scant panties. She could kiss Fate smack on the lips for guiding her hand in her drawer this afternoon when she'd dressed for her trek to the airport. She'd dreamed of standing before Ben Scott wearing her best French lace—but her fantasy hadn't gone this far…Ben corralling her back onto his bed, that devilish glint in his eyes, two minutes past the stroke of midnight.

As she reversed on all fours towards the middle of the mattress, he followed, unbuttoning his white collared shirt as he walked on his knees. When he reached her, he cupped her face and decimated her with a perfect-in-every-way, penetrating kiss. The stars falling outside had nothing on the wonderland going off in her mind and through her body. The only spectacle worth experiencing tonight was happening right here in this room.

When their mouths parted, he took warm, slow kisses from the line of her jaw. 'I've thought about you a lot, Celeste.'

Her insides jumped. One checkmark. Should she be so honest?

She combed her fingers over his shoulders. 'Me, too.'

She'd said those words before, on his yacht when they'd danced. He'd said he was glad that they'd met—*Me, too*—then he'd gone on to say he would take care of PLM. Soon after, they'd said goodbye. As days had grown into weeks it had seemed the farewell was final. Then tonight's miracle had landed in her lap.

His skilled mouth trailed down her neck and those memories floated off as a hot haze of desire built within her then condensed. She wouldn't think about anything other than the sensations she enjoyed this minute. Plenty of time later to dissect right from wrong. Not now. Not now…

She grabbed a corner of his shirt and coaxed the fabric from his shoulders. Her palms fanned over the human granite she adored, hotter and more vital than she'd remembered. In reply, he slid a thin, forgiving strap off her shoulder, then brought her close to adoringly taste the slope. 'I'm going to hold you to your promise.'

She fell into the heady splendour of his teeth grazing her neck. 'Hmm…what promise?'

'That you stay the night. *All* night.'

Fiery fingertips found the bottom edge of her top and, like the dress before, lifted it over her head. One arm bracing their weight, he eased her down, back onto the cool silky quilt. His touch was beyond exquisite. The way his fingers played her—over her hair, down her limbs—was a symphony fit for angels. When his mouth suctioned over one tight, pleading nipple, her lit fuse almost burst into a bonfire.

Her fingers knotted in his strong dark hair and she held him close. How on earth would she last?

'I like you best naked,' he murmured.

No one had ever spoken to her in that manner before—so sultry and commanding. And there wasn't a moment's doubt that she'd comply. Her breathing shallow, she lifted her legs and, quivering, closed her eyes. He caught a corner of her panties, and the black lace slipped up and over her pointed toes. She bit her lip against a whimper of pleasure as the edge of his hand sliced down…between her calves, lower to part her thighs, at last coming to rest at that pulsating hot divide.

She gripped the quilt as his expert touch wove in and around, driving the fire higher, compacting her passion to a finite beating force before—at the crucial moment—he broke contact and moved away. Breath rushing out, she snapped her eyes open and found his colossal silhouette kneeling before her.

Gripping her hips, he dragged until her legs draped over the thick steel of his thighs. Then he leant to scoop her up so they were positioned front to front with her sitting on his folded lap, her legs wrapped low around his hips, his length throbbing against her own burning need. His palms ironed up her sides before curling down her back, ultimately manoeuvring her behind until his shaft found an exquisite, heart-stopping way in. As his mouth claimed hers he began to move. She threaded her arms around his neck and trembled as the thrill and passion spiralled closer to out of control.

She'd been mad to think she might not want this. Tomorrow she'd survive whatever came. This minute she couldn't contemplate not having Ben Scott at least one more time.

* * *

Celeste drifted off to sleep around dawn and awoke to the rich aroma of freshly brewed coffee. Before she opened her eyes, she ran through her mental projector the sublime hours she'd spent in this bed. With *that* man.

Ben *Super Sexy* Scott.

She stretched and smiled.

Life certainly was wonderful.

'About time.'

At the cheerful greeting, her eyes sprang open. Wearing jeans and a white T-shirt, Ben strolled in holding a tray with coffee and something smelling of melted butter on the side.

She pulled herself up, feeling a little odd about bringing the sheet with her. He'd seen everything, *done* everything. There was nothing left to hide. And yet when he looked at her, all hot and expectant as he slid the breakfast tray onto a table, her cheeks burned. She felt freer with him than anyone she'd ever known. At the same time she'd never felt more vulnerable.

Last night was over. Tomorrow had begun. Where to now?

He held up a white ceramic coffee pot. 'Milk? Sugar? It's freshly brewed. Can't stand the instant stuff.'

Feeling like a princess, she told him how she liked it—hot and strong. When he joined her with two mugs and perched himself on the edge of the mattress, she had to fiddle to navigate a sip without her sheet falling.

He tasted from his mug then his index finger snaked out. 'What's this?' The tip of his finger curled around the top of the sheet and tugged.

Her respiratory rate jumped ten rungs, but she didn't retrieve her cover. Rather, she held her breath, as she'd done that day in the ocean, and let the sheet fall in soft folds to her lap.

He looked deeply into her eyes. 'It's not about feeling reckless. It's about feeling comfortable knowing that you're beautiful. This morning, you're glowing.' He bent close, dotted a kiss on each breast, then found her lips and kissed her with more meaning than she'd ever known possible.

When he drew away, she wanted to drag him back. He affected her in a sense that defied words. It was as if she'd always known him and this was like coming home, sweet home. Was it the same for him?

Getting herself together, she nodded at the table. 'What's on the tray?'

He swallowed a long sip. 'English muffins. Your choice of honey, jam or Vegemite.'

She laughed. 'Now you're trying to spoil me.'

He twirled an imaginary moustache. 'All to serve my wicked purpose. We're going to eat in bed.'

'You're not afraid of crumbs?'

His grin was dry. 'I'll suffer it.'

He crossed the room and returned with the tray.

When he was propped up beside her, long legs out, bare feet crossed, she plied more butter onto her muffin, poured honey till it was drowning, then sank her teeth in and savoured the sweet taste. She'd never enjoyed breakfast so much.

In between bites, they talked. Ben ate two halves to her one, then pushed the rest aside. 'I could eat more but I thought we might go for a walk and find somewhere nice for lunch, seeing it's after eleven.'

She choked on her food. 'Eleven o'clock!'

She'd been so preoccupied, chatting about the party and poor Malcolm and snatching glances at the musculature evident beneath Ben's T, she hadn't bothered to check her watch, or his.

'I've had a swim, pressed some weights, done some work.' His smile was curious. 'You looked too peaceful to wake.'

'I've usually done heaps by this time of day.'

'It was a pretty big night.'

She quivered to her toes. Big was right.

He trailed a finger around her cheek and kissed her with just the right amount of tenderness. 'Happy New Year, Celeste. I'd rip off my clothes and dive under there with you, but you probably need a break from my attentions.'

Uh, no. But that wasn't the right answer. She shouldn't sound overly eager after crumbling so easily and falling into bed with him last night.

Maybe a touch of the truth. 'I could use a shower.' She wanted to add, *After that I'm yours.*

But was she? This morning she was twice as keen on him as she'd been yesterday. She wanted to see him again. If she was unsure about some things in her life, she was certain about that. But if this was going nowhere—if last night had been a bit of fun on the side for Ben, nothing more—well, she would rather know now.

As if reading her thoughts, he quickly downed the rest of his coffee. 'There's fresh linen in the bathroom,' he said, nodding at the attached room. 'I'm afraid I can't offer you a fresh change of clothes.'

She brightened. Better than having a wardrobe full of dresses left behind by past lovers.

When he left, she dived from the bed under the shower. She felt revived and formidable when she emerged half an hour later. Ten minutes after that, she felt empowered strolling down an inner city street, her arm looped through his. Everyone seemed to smile as they passed. The grey had all gone away.

They found a Turkish café at The Rocks open for lunch and Celeste relaxed more over pide bread, zucchini puffs and home-made hummus. Ben was in great form and only stopped talking to listen with interest when she had something to say, which was often. When he told a story about dressing as Santa for his friend's children in Perth, and how his impromptu rendition of 'Jingle Bell Rock' on the front lawn had attracted every child and howling dog in the neighbourhood, she laughed so much her sides ached.

Afterwards they strolled again and window-shopped. It was getting late when Ben stopped and turned towards an interesting window. The bold black and gold letters said 'Magicians' Haven'. She was secretly admiring his sexy sandpaper jaw when he tipped his chin at a mysterious-looking orb on the lowest shelf.

'Is that yours?'

She looked down and laughed. 'My crystal ball?'

The ball's glass was clear yet somehow misty, flicked with colour that seemed to spark, then die away. The depths almost reminded her of her future—what once had seemed unclouded was now evolving, shifting, including what would happen next with Ben.

'It looks pretty authentic, doesn't it?' She half meant it.

He sucked in air between his teeth. 'Sorry. It doesn't convince me.'

'You think you could spot a fake from the real deal?'

'If there's any such thing.'

She had to ask. 'Do you think there *is* a real deal, Ben?'

He chuckled and squeezed her hand. 'I guess all those gypsies can't be wrong.'

This was it. He might yet ask to see her again, but nothing had been mentioned at lunch. Not, *How about a movie next week? Or, Are you doing anything next Friday night?* Wasn't that usually what happened when a 'date' was going well?

But times had changed. Women proposed to men. Females occupied top positions in business and politics. Wearing a skirt didn't equate to being considered a delicate flower any more. She wanted to know. If his answer was 'no' or 'let's see', she would deal with it.

'I didn't think we were talking about crystal balls any more,' she offered.

His brow knitted. 'What were we talking about?' But she could see in his eyes that he knew.

'Guess what I'm asking is…' *Say it. Say it.* 'Are we real, Ben?'

He didn't hesitate. 'What we shared last night was one-hundred-per-cent real.'

'And today?'

'If you're asking if I want to see you again, you bet I do. If you're asking if I want long term…' He paused, then shook his head. 'That won't change.'

She took his answer in and on one level was pleased. He wanted to see her again—that was comforting. But what did his statement say pared down? He liked being with her, sleeping with her, but if she was looking for more, he wasn't it—subject closed.

She brushed a wave from her brow and tried to smile, but her lips were trembling so much, she looked away instead. 'I see,' was all she got out.

They began to walk again and he blew out a breath. 'Look, you deserve an explanation—'

She held up a hand. *No need.* 'Point is we can see each other again, have a few laughs, play some pool...' Jump in the sack. 'Or not.'

She hadn't wanted to be left in the dark. It would've hurt far more to enjoy a few more dates, *then* learn they could never be anything more than 'casual'. Now more than ever she knew she liked Ben way too much to be little more than sleeping partners.

Her throat tightened.

How many others did he have?

Ben scratched his temple. 'The simple truth is, I'm not prepared to pick up a bow, take aim and see if I luck out and hit the bullseye with a happily ever after.'

She forced a laugh. 'Am I the bow or the bullseye?' She sure wasn't the happily ever after.

'I don't try to fool anyone into thinking I'm anything more than I am.' His jaw clenched and he seemed to think it through. 'Long term usually comes hand in hand with kids.'

Had she mentioned kids? Sure, like the rest of humankind, one day she planned on having one or two. But motherhood seemed a good while away yet. She had lots to accomplish.

'I wasn't planning on falling pregnant, Ben.'

His voice deepened. 'Of course not. No one should even consider bringing children into this world unless they're sure. And certain today isn't necessarily certain tomorrow.'

She shook her head. Talk about damaged.

She knew she shouldn't, but her concern and hurt slipped out anyway. 'You'll never get over growing up in foster care, will you?'

His smile was jaded. 'I don't mean to sound harsh, but you really had to be there.'

Celeste weathered the sting. She couldn't imagine having her earliest memories include dejection over feeling alone and largely unwanted. The father Ben had never known had abandoned him. But should he always let that regret dominate a big part of his life?

She might be disappointed in how their relationship had turned out, but she'd gone into it with her eyes wide open and, regardless, she still thought enough of Ben to hope that he'd find happiness eventually. However, it was pretty obvious that if he didn't move on, he would end up a lonely old man one day.

The cogs in her mind continued to turn as they walked on.

'Have you had any luck with that PI who was tracking down your father?' she asked artlessly.

Ben blinked twice at her, then lowered his chin. 'No. Nothing.'

She shrugged one shoulder. 'Maybe you should try that other agency you were talking about.'

He frowned as if she'd read his mind. 'I've been thinking about it. The first guy was a younger brother of a friend. Might be time for a professional.'

She hoped he'd be able to track down his father—his family—and try to make peace, if not with them, then with himself. She could easily hate her own father for so many reasons, but then she'd risk being filled with hatred herself; no one needed that. Both she and Ben needed to move on from yesterday and rob their pasts of the power to make choices for them—commitment issues included.

She stopped at the taxi rank. When she craned up on tiptoe to kiss his raspy cheek, tears swelled to prickle the backs of her eyes.

She forced herself to smile. 'Good luck.'

She moved to open the taxi door, but he caught her hand. His face was set. 'Don't go.'

Her heart cracked straight down the middle. 'Ben, I have to.'

A pulse jumped in his jaw as he searched her eyes.

'I'll call.'

She shook her head. 'Please don't.'

On the brink of falling in love with a man who couldn't commit wasn't where she needed to be. Poor Brooke had been in a similar situation last year. At least Ben had been up-front.

She slid into the back seat and gave the driver instructions. She wouldn't look back. Not once. Not a peek. But as the taxi turned the corner she jolted around and peered out the rear window. Ben was standing there, just the way she'd imagined.

Incredibly sexy and all alone.

CHAPTER SEVEN

BEN ignored everyone else standing in the room and moved up behind Celeste. Fighting the urge to wrap his arms around her slender waist, he leaned around her shoulder, brushing a kiss upon her soft warm cheek. She jumped, her back straightened, then she edged around.

As her gaze caught his, Ben's chest stirred at the telltale glow in her eyes…the familiar intoxicating scent of her skin. After a month apart, the magnetic pull was still there—stronger than before—heating his blood from the moment she'd walked into his packed boardroom thirty minutes earlier.

Despite the electricity arcing between them now, she slid one foot back and away from him. He understood her motivation. She thought it was over.

She was wrong.

Celeste swallowed and found her voice. 'Hello, Ben.'

He tipped his head. 'Glad you could make it.'

As their gazes lingered the current intensified and the sexual pull cranked a notch higher, until Rodney, standing nearby, ended his conversation with a PLM franchisee from the southern district and rotated toward the couple.

Beaming, the former head of the company extended a hand. 'Benton, I appreciate today's invitation, though it wasn't necessary.'

Ben forced his attention away from Celeste's cherry-sweet mouth and shook Rodney's hand. 'I called today's meeting to bring all my franchise holders up to date, but I thought you'd enjoy being part of it and hearing about my initial push to expand.'

'Into Western Australia *and* New Zealand.' Rodney clapped Ben's arm. 'Well done, son.'

Ben sensed more than saw Celeste flinch.

So she still carried a flame for PLM. Last time they'd spoken, she'd had plans aside from her handbag shop—a florist venture. He'd hoped that would help her deal with PLM's change of hands, although, to be fair, it couldn't be easy.

Striking an interested pose, Rodney crossed his arms over his suit jacket. 'So, what's next for PLM?'

'It's early days yet,' Ben replied. 'But I have other development strategies I hope to incorporate while having some fun with this first expansion.'

Another flinch from Celeste.

Ben slipped a hand into a trouser pocket. They

needed to talk. Alone. He had plenty to communicate and none of it involved business.

Rodney called out a greeting and waved to someone across the broad expanse of the room. 'Will you excuse me? James Miller looks like he's about to leave. He was my first franchisee to come on board. Lots of history there.'

Ben happily stepped aside. 'Be my guest.'

As Rodney moved off Ben wasted no time claiming Celeste's elbow.

Taken aback, she examined his hold on her arm as he walked her towards a set of double oak doors.

'Did I agree to go somewhere?'

He opened the door and ushered her inside his adjoining penthouse office. 'We need some privacy.'

'You didn't call this meeting to speak with me.'

Not entirely. 'I've spoken to everyone I need to.'

Now it was time for *them*. He'd delayed this reunion long enough.

He shut the door and turned the lock while she tugged down the hem of her classic black jacket. The matching skirt was a little long. The blouse buttoned too high. In fact, he'd just as soon pry every article of clothing from her body—lingerie included—but they needed to talk before they could move on to rekindling more intimate contact.

He crossed to his desk. Thumbing on the intercom, he spoke to his secretary. 'Lin, if anyone asks, I have an urgent matter to attend to.'

Celeste raised her brows. 'I'm the urgent matter.'

Sauntering back, he nodded.

As she perhaps understood more clearly his intent, her eyes widened. 'My father…he'll wonder where I've got to.'

'Your father is in his element. He won't miss you for the moment.' Halfway to his target, he removed his jacket, tossing it on the leather settee as he passed.

Her eyes rounded more, but she held her ground. 'In case you have the wrong idea, I didn't intend to accept your invitation. I'm here only because Suzanne wasn't feeling well and asked if I'd keep my father company.'

He stopped inches away, deliberately looking down as she peered up. She was petite, yet luscious and entirely feminine. The perfect fit for his arms.

'You weren't the least bit curious to see me again.'

She looked away. 'That's irrelevant.'

Not in his book.

Two fingers trailed her cheek, crooking under her chin and lifting it high. His gaze drank in her lips. 'I haven't stopped thinking about you since you left me standing on that street corner.'

Had she done it to torment him? To tame him? Either way, today he intended to break the dead-lock wide open.

His voice lowered to a growl. 'I missed you.'

She visibly shivered and bit her lip the way she

had New Year's Eve when his tongue had trailed down between her breasts, around her navel and lower until she'd clung to his head and begged him not to stop.

'Ben, please…don't play games.'

He smiled. 'You like our games.'

On a groan she wound away and towards the door. 'I need to go.'

'Don't you want to hear my news?'

Her hand found the lock and twisted. 'I've heard enough.'

'I found my father.'

She froze. After a moment, she faced him.

'He's a retired teacher,' he explained, 'married with seven kids. I knocked on his front door, he opened it in a faded football jersey. A boy, about five, was standing behind him.'

'A grandson?'

'They were about to go out and kick a ball. He didn't know about me. His dentures almost fell out his mouth when I told him who I was.'

She drifted nearer. 'Didn't know about you? I don't understand.'

He strolled forward, closing the gap. 'Apparently he hadn't known my mother was pregnant. He wasn't in the country when I was born. They must have tried to track him down but gave up. Guess it didn't help that he took on his new wife's surname and became Bartley-Scott.' Although, knowing the system, he wouldn't hand out any gold stars that they'd tried too hard.

The crease between her brows eased. 'And you like him? He likes you?'

'Pretty much instantly.' He scratched his temple. 'Although his wife and their eldest let me know they weren't sure about a stranger turning up on their doorstep claiming to be a long-lost son and brother.'

She winced. 'That must've been hard.'

Years ago, whenever he'd been dumped at a new 'home' or had started at yet another school with shoes two sizes too big, he'd only ever imagined a reunion with his 'family' involving open arms. He should've known reality wouldn't be all rainbows and sunshine.

'The second eldest is tying the knot this weekend,' he went on. 'Christopher is marrying Marie, a lovely girl who, five-year-old Zack tells me, can whistle through her nose.' Celeste laughed. 'Despite two dis-approving glares directed my way across the dining-room table, Gerard, my father, and Chris invited me along. The invitation's for two.'

The penny dropped and her jaw unhinged. 'You want me to go? Isn't there someone else you'd rather take?'

His frown was teasing. 'Don't tell me you don't like weddings.'

'You know that's not it.'

'It'll be an excuse to buy a new dress.'

She hesitated, then shook her head.

His arm snaked around her hip. She stiffened, but didn't move away. Good, because he wasn't in a mood to take no for an answer.

He moved closer. 'Celeste, I want to dance with you again.' *Be with you again.* This tug was maddening. Hadn't she been in hell too? His mouth dropped lower. 'Say yes.'

Despite her stand four weeks ago, this charge zapping between them proved it: they didn't need to go their separate ways. They were both adults. Why not continue to enjoy each other for as long as it lasted? There was no harm in that—only advantages.

Her face pinched. 'Ben, I can't.'

He searched her eyes. Time to reveal his ace. 'I've told my family about you. They want to meet you.'

Celeste held her breath. Had she heard correctly? 'You told them about *me*?'

His sexy heavy-lidded gaze roamed her face, raking the coals already burning deep and low inside. 'I sure did.'

Her throat bobbed on an involuntary swallow. 'You want me to meet your *family*?'

He cocked a speculative brow. 'Is that a yes?'

Celeste pressed her lips together.

Had a night passed when she hadn't dreamed about this man? Or woken remembering how alive she'd felt whenever she'd been with him? In his car, in his boat, in his bed. But she'd stayed strong, refusing to call him, blocking from her mind the reckless hope that *he* might call *her*. Then last week, she—along with her father and Suzanne—had received an invite to today's meeting. She'd been determined not to come. She needed to forget about PLM—about Ben—and get on with her life.

But how could she when she'd been a week late and had begun to worry? Yesterday made two weeks.

This morning, she'd bought a home pregnancy kit.

'Celeste?'

At his questioning gaze, a spear of anxiety sailed through her centre. She'd chickened out performing the test. But if she were pregnant she couldn't ignore it—or keep it a secret—not that she'd want to. She'd have to tell him. Given Ben's concrete view on bringing children into the world—that both parties should be irrevocably committed—he wouldn't be pleased.

She chewed her lip.

But he *had* asked her to this wedding—and not just any wedding, but his newly found brother's. Despite her ambivalence about seeing him again, she wanted that experience to be memorable for him. Feeling connected was what Ben needed most, even if he wasn't fully aware of it yet. If he'd made this contact with his father, if he wanted her to be part of a family celebration, wasn't that a good sign? Wasn't there a chance…a chance they could talk, if nothing else?

Finally she let go a breath and nodded. 'What time should I expect you?'

A slow smile lit his eyes. 'Wedding's on Saturday at three. I'll collect you at two.'

It was done.

'I'll be ready.' She moved to leave. 'Now I really should be going—'

'There's one more thing.'

A strong arm coiled around her waist and tugged her back. Caught unawares with her defences down, she accepted his kiss like long-parched earth welcomed life-giving rain. She soaked up the texture and taste of him and with every passing moment only wanted more.

When their lips parted, she felt giddy. Worse, she knew her heart would be there in her eyes.

Damn the man.

Although her voice was thick, she managed to sound vaguely disapproving. 'I didn't say you could kiss me.'

'You must know by now—' he flicked the button at her waist and eased the jacket off her shoulders '—I don't ask.'

Her heart jumped to her throat. What was he doing? '*Ben*, you have a room full of people out there.'

His smouldering gaze hesitated, then lifted from the curve of her throat to her eyes. With a guttural sound, he replaced his hungry look with a frown and straightened. He slipped the jacket back up onto her shoulders and, jaw tight, led her to the door. 'Go join your father. I'll grab my jacket and be out in a minute.'

She smothered the sting of disappointment. It was goodbye again—for now.

'Then I'll see you later in the week.' When his frown deepened, she explained. 'I have to leave now to inspect my new shop fittings.'

His brows lifted. 'Sounds like fun.'

Well, she thought so. 'I need to give the okay on the cabinets and electrical—' She stopped. He'd gone to collect and shuck back into his jacket.

'Is it nearby, or will we drive?' he asked.

She coughed out a laugh. 'You can't come. You have work to do.' People to entertain.

Joining her, he lifted his chin and straightened the knot in his tie. 'I'm the boss. I get to punch my own clock.' He opened the door and waved her through.

It was on the tip of her tongue to say he wasn't invited. Yet how could she? He'd just invited her to accompany him on what promised to be a huge day in his life when hopefully Ben would be publicly accepted into his family—as long as that suspicious stepmother and her eldest behaved. If Ben had been pushy today…well, she could forgive him.

Truth to tell, she craved his company…as long as companionship didn't transgress into more heated waters. For a whole pile of reasons, sleeping together was on *big time indefinite delay*.

Back in the oversized boardroom, Ben tapped a glass with a spoon and addressed his audience. 'I have to leave for another appointment, but please stay and enjoy the refreshments. Thank you all for coming and sharing in the good news.'

After a burst of applause and raised glasses, the men went back to their conversations.

Ben returned to her side. 'If you want to say goodbye to your father I'll meet you in the lobby. Might save questions.'

She smiled. He'd read her mind.

Minutes later they met and walked to her shop, which was only a block and a half through Sydney's CBD bustle.

'This new shop,' he said over the growling engine of a passing bus, 'it's for your flower business?'

Her brows knitted. 'A florist. And not just any florist. I have plans of becoming *the* place on the east coast for gift baskets and all floral requirements if your name happens to be Kidman or Murdoch.'

He nodded. 'Big plans.'

Was that a patronising quality to his tone? Sure, it was a big dream, but the only way to achieve big was to dream big. He of all people must understand that.

At the address, she unlocked the glass door, which led into a smallish space that was three parts fitted out in the same colours as her handbag store—pastel pink and vibrant blue with splashes of silver.

'Smaller orders will be done through here,' she told him with a gesture that encompassed the room. 'When we expand, I want to build or hire space at a more industrial-located estate.'

'To save costs on rental.'

She wove around the partition to check out the shelves and central working table out the back. 'The money and glamour needs to be where it can do its best work—in the arrangements. Working out an advertising schedule is next. Word of mouth in any industry is important too, so whatever comes out of here must be superior, unique and eye-catching without being gaudy...' She gave a crooked smile. 'Unless that's what the customer wants.'

She felt his eyes on her as she wandered around, checking electrical fittings, running a hand over the surfaces, ever vigilant of scratches or marks. When she'd given everything a mental tick, he smiled over at her. 'All set?'

'I'm happy.'

He took her hands and hot tingles sizzled up both arms. 'Good. Now we both have business out of the way, how about we go somewhere for a drink?'

She arched a wry brow. 'Like your place?'

He grinned. 'It is handy.'

Handy or fatal?

She wound her hands away from his. 'I think it's safer to see each other on Saturday.'

That would give her time to do the pregnancy

test. See a doctor if she needed it confirmed. Figure out how to tell Ben he was going to be a father as well as how to duck the shrapnel after that.

He stepped into the space dividing them. 'Safe?' He frowned playfully. 'Come on. What happened to reckless?'

As he tipped forward she tipped back. 'Reckless has been packed up and sent on summer vacation.'

Reckless was what had got her into this mess. From the start she'd known he was dangerous. Dangerous for her heart.

'Pity. On Sunday I'd hoped we could take the boat out again.'

She recalled that day when he'd lavished her with his own spectacular style of attention and her stomach pitched. 'Let's get Saturday out of the way first.'

He narrowed one eye. 'Odd, but I don't get the sense you really want mc to leave.'

She was burning up with longing, but, 'I can spell it for you?'

'And if I kiss you again?'

She backed up. He followed and her tail hit the counter. She swung an anxious look around his frame. 'You're aware there are streams of people filing by.'

'Suppose there weren't?'

She tried to steady her breathing. 'I'd still ask you to leave.'

He loomed nearer and her nipples tightened. His eyes crinkled above a smile. 'You would, huh?'

She tried to look unimpressed while covering the evidence by crossing her arms. 'What? So you're irresistible now?'

He lifted a brow. 'You tell me.'

Her arms unravelled as he came close enough for her to feel the heat radiating from his jacket... through the fabric of his trousers. Digging into her last reserves of determination, she composed her expression and shrugged.

'Ben Scott, you are absolutely *resistible.*'

His face lowered close to hers. Spice and musk filled her lungs, burrowed beneath her skin, throbbed through her veins. When his lips parted a hair's breadth from hers, a wonderful drugging pulse kicked off at her core. Lord, she was melting from the inside out.

'Do you remember that last time we were together?' he murmured, tilting his head so his warm breath mingled with hers. She quivered. Another millimetre and she could taste him again.

'Do you remember what you said?' he asked.

Her cheeks flamed. She remembered her words. She remembered how he hadn't hesitated to grant her wish. More than anything she remembered how it had felt every time he'd invented a new way to make her fly. Lord above, she was taking off only thinking about it, which was, no doubt, his plan.

His fingertip slid up and down the centre front of her skirt. 'Say it for me now.'

Her heart belted a mesmerising rhythm against her ribs. He was frying her brain. Crushing her strength.

'Ben,' she begged, 'people can see.'

'Just my back.'

Think, think!

'I heard a rumour you were a gentleman.'

That finger traced up as he nipped her bottom lip. 'Only if you want me to be.'

'Yes...' Her breath hitched. 'Please.'

His eyes drifted open and held hers for a heart-pounding moment. Slowly he eased back. Her legs almost buckled. A rag doll had more strength to stand.

He looked over his shoulder at the street, scrubbed his jaw and exhaled.

'You okay to lock up?' he finally asked.

She let out a breath and managed a convincing nod.

'You sure?' he insisted, and she nodded harder. 'Then I'll see you two o'clock Saturday.'

The self-assured look he sent as he left said today had been practice. Come Saturday he'd bring out his big guns.

CHAPTER EIGHT

APPLAUDING along with the rest of the wedding reception guests, Ben leaned towards Celeste, who looked breathtakingly elegant seated beside him.

'This should be the last of the speeches,' he let her know. 'Then we get to dance.'

Her big green eyes fixed on his and she gave a soft but slightly hesitant smile.

After leaving her in that shop on Monday, the hours until today had crawled by. It had been worth the wait. He hadn't had a more enjoyable day...being included in this special occasion, joining in a couple of professional family shots—not that Rhyll, his stepmother, or Paul, her eldest son, had approved.

He wouldn't let their loaded looks mar his pleasure, least of all being with Celeste again. Gorgeous in a shimmering lemon-coloured gown, she'd been the focus of his day. While she might still have reservations about *them*, she would also be the focus of his night.

All night.

At the bridal table, his brother Chris stood. Decked out in a black tie and dress shirt, his tux jacket draped over the back of his chair, he told a few stories, thanked his guests and kissed his blushing bride after announcing he would always remember how beautiful she looked today.

The applause died and Chris continued. 'Finally, 'I'd like to officially welcome another new member into our family. We had no idea our brother Ben was out there. I'm so happy you found us, mate.'

As Chris raised his glass Ben swallowed against the swell in his throat. Damn. He hadn't expected that, but he sure appreciated it.

Following etiquette, he half rose from his chair, bowed acknowledgement at Chris, then his father, who was seated at a nearby round table. Gerard's glass was raised, his blue eyes sparkling in the candelabra light. Ben returned the warm smile, then his gaze hooked on Rhyll. Setting her napkin on the table, she pushed to her feet and made a statement by walking calmly from the room.

Celeste's hand on Ben's sleeve helped him lower the rest of the way back into his seat.

While Chris cleared his throat and finished up, Ben tried to see his way clear to finding a solution to such an unfamiliar problem. He had no personal experience to draw upon, other than his long-established habit of reading the motivations of those around him. Rhyll was perhaps jealous of her husband's former love, Ben's mother, and anxious over how the appearance of a stranger-cum-son would impact upon her family, her marriage included. Paul felt his place as eldest son threatened and had let it be known that Ben was trespassing on his turf.

Ben had figured he could ignore the hostility, assume his usual place on the peripheral of a family dynamic and observe, but his gut told him that wasn't the answer this time.

Celeste laid a warm hand over his. 'I think they're playing our song.'

Brought back, he blinked across at her and the tune registered—the same song he'd played on the boat that night. He pushed back his chair. He'd never needed Celeste in his arms more than now, and, from the look in her eyes, she understood.

He led her out onto the timber floor and gathered her wonderful curves close. As their feet began to move in sync he gazed down into her eyes. 'Have I told you how incredible you look?'

Her lips twitched. 'Once or twice.'

'Not enough.' He twirled a finger around a golden lock. 'Is that glitter in your hair?'

'Just a sprinkle.'

He breathed in. 'And a new scent.' He arched a brow. 'You're definitely trying to drive me wild.'

Her brow creased. 'You're definitely trying to charm me.'

His mouth grazed her temple. 'Is it working?'

'And if I say no?'

'I'll be forced to show no mercy.'

He dipped her, Fred Astaire style. She shrieked out a laugh and he whirled her back up.

Her hair was a tassled mess. He loved it!

She blew out a breath, pushed back her hair, then tried to scowl. 'If you do that again, I'm sitting down.'

Two fingers ironed down the length of her spine, ending at the curve of her behind. Although she endeavoured to hide it, he felt her body respond, heating and coming alive against him.

He grinned. 'I have more subtle moves you might prefer.'

She sent a dry look. 'Is that supposed to be a surprise?'

'It's an invitation.'

She looked away and sighed. 'I know about your invitations.'

'That doesn't sound like a complaint.'

Her eyes challenged his. 'What do you want me to say? We're good in bed?' Her shoulders went up and down. 'All right. We're good in bed.'

The middle-aged couple dancing nearby sent them a curious look. Embarrassed, Celeste tucked herself against him.

Ben rolled back one shoulder. 'Well, now that's settled—'

'Nothing's settled.' She mumbled, 'Not yet.'

He caught her chin and lifted it. 'Running from each other won't fix things.' What they needed was to be together as they had been on his boat, and that amazing evening in his bed when the fireworks had gone off all night. 'You said it—we're good together.'

Her eyes glistened. 'Are we?'

He wanted to laugh—what a question! But he couldn't pretend to misunderstand her deeper meaning.

He danced her over to a quiet corner of the floor, then escorted her out onto a balcony. They stopped beside a giant trickling fountain of a marble cupid drawing his bow. When he kissed her fingertips and saw her nipples hardened beneath her bodice's sheer fabric, his tongue tingled in his mouth.

'We don't have to stay till the end,' he said. 'The formalities are over.'

'You don't want to stay for the party?'

'It was great being included in the day's events, but it might be wiser to leave this final hour or two to the Bartley-Scotts to enjoy free from the impostor.'

She squeezed his hand. 'Oh, Ben, I'm sure it will work itself out.'

He moved closer. 'Right now, all I'm worried about is you.' *Touching you. Kissing you. Making love with you.*

All. Night. Long.

Unable to hold off a moment more, his mouth

took hers. When Celeste relented and dissolved against him, Ben cupped her nape and gave himself over to the intoxicating heavy thrum of his blood beating through all the parts of his body. Five weeks had been way too long. If he didn't take her soon, God save him, he might explode.

Their embrace was interrupted by a distant call.

'Two more love birds, I see.'

Recognising Gerard's voice, Ben reluctantly released Celeste. After shaking herself awake to her surroundings, she smoothed down the sides of her gown. Gerard was sauntering out into the brisk evening air, looking dapper, if not quite comfortable, in a full morning suit.

Getting his thoughts together, Ben inhaled deeply. 'It's been a great day, sir. Thanks for inviting us.'

Gerard stopped, a frown creasing the brow. 'I'm not a *sir*.' He clapped Ben's arm heartily. 'I'm your dad.' He gazed fondly at Celeste. 'You make a fine-looking couple.'

Ben smiled across. She was a fine-looking lady.

Gerard's expression turned solemn and he rubbed the back of his neck. 'Ben, son, I want to say I'm not unaware of my wife's and Paul's...*reluctance*.'

Ben waved a hand. He didn't want Gerard to feel bad. To be fair, it had been a shock for everyone involved.

'They'll come around,' Gerard assured him.

'There's no need to worry. You're part of my family now, no matter what.'

Ben nodded. That sounded good.

Maybe too good to be true.

Looking back at the reception doors, Gerard seemed to gather himself. 'Marie'll make our Chris a wonderful wife.'

Celeste agreed. 'She's lovely.'

Gerard tipped forward. 'She's the best cook. Italian, you know. Do you cook, Celeste?'

'Only when I have to.' Celeste laughed. So did Ben. Gerard took a moment, then joined them.

He nudged Ben. 'She's got a sense of humour. You need that in a relationship.'

While Celeste lowered her gaze, Ben froze. They weren't in a 'relationship'. Ben wasn't after a 'relationship'. They'd only seen each other a handful of times. They were in a…well, an 'understanding'. Or would be when he got Celeste back to his place and they could reinstate what she'd said earlier. They were 'good in bed'.

Stop the press. They were *great* in bed. Better than great.

The music drifting out from inside changed and Gerard exclaimed, 'I had the DJ play this song for Rhyll. We danced to it the first night we met.' He sighed. 'It goes so quickly. She has her ways, but I can't imagine my life without her.'

As Gerard left his words echoed in Ben's mind.

She has her ways. Sounded as if there was a lot of give and take in their marriage. Had to be, he supposed, with bringing up seven children. He might be worth millions, control the salaries of scores of people, but Ben couldn't imagine the responsibility that went with having a clutch of kids. The responsibility of having even one, for that matter. He couldn't think of a thing that scared him…other than the infinite obligations associated with being a father.

A left-field thought struck.

Would he remember his and Celeste's song in thirty years' time?

Celeste began to move off too. 'Perhaps we should get back inside.'

He followed. 'Only to say goodbye.'

'And then?'

'I'm taking you home.'

She stopped and shook her head at the ground. 'I…I don't know.'

His hands sloped down her bare arms. 'I think you do.'

She searched his eyes for a long moment. 'You know what I really think? I think we need to talk.'

He held her eyes with his and nodded, then walked her inside. Certainly they could talk, as much as she wanted.

Over breakfast.

CHAPTER NINE

AS THE lift glided up each floor to his apartment Celeste shrank a little more inside. Ben stood beside her, his big warm hand folded over hers. Every so often rocking back on his heels, he concentrated on the lift light, working its way higher.

Shaking inside, Celeste closed her eyes and tried to find her calm centre.

On the way home, she and Ben had kept the chatter light. But all the while she'd wondered, *Should I tell him? What will he say? We can't possibly make love. Will he even want to touch me when he knows?*

The lift pinged and he escorted her into the corridor. A moment later they were in his penthouse suite and all the memories of that New Year's night came rushing back—vivid, tingling. Dangerously, exquisitely hot.

He tossed his jacket over a chair back and moved to the bar. 'Can I get you a drink?'

'Water.' She trembled out a smile. 'Thanks.'

When he returned, she sipped while his chest breathed in and out mere inches from her hand. As her heartbeat boomed in her ears she fought the urge to swipe the cool glass against her feverish brow.

Who was she kidding? He hadn't brought her here to talk. His agenda was seduction and she'd walked straight into his lair. What must he think other than the obvious? And, yes, she *did* want him to kiss her, just as she wanted his skilled hands all over her, threading through her hair, roaming over her naked limbs.

But she'd be better off running. They could 'talk' another day.

Decided, she thrust the glass towards him to take. 'I'm sorry. I've made a mistake.'

As his hand caught over hers on the glass his head angled and his brow creased with concern. 'Celeste? You're shaking.'

His jaw tight, he drew her over to the couch and, weak all over, she sank down alongside him.

'What's wrong?' he asked. 'This is more than nerves.'

When his finger carefully scooped hair from her brow behind her ear, she shivered at the contact.

Ben was an extraordinary specimen. Prime-time male in every way. Did that explain it—this gripping, uncontrollable thirst? But how could she allow herself to drink when she'd still be parched long after he'd grown tired of 'short term' and had moved on? If he'd known what she'd gone through...wondering if she'd conceived, buying that pregnancy kit, discovering the results—

His arm looped around her and he brought her close, obviously wanting to comfort her. His clean, musky scent worked its way into her lungs, through her system and, right or wrong, needing some kind of support, she leant more against him. As his palm lightly grazed her arm she dared to look up.

The golden light from the bar shone dimly. She could make out the strong planes of his face, the gleam of his eyes gazing down at her. How her fingers itched to trail along his shadowed jaw. Sample the soft bow of his lip...

He smiled softly. 'I know what you need.'

She knew too. A shrink.

He said, 'A relaxing massage.'

Tempting, but...

She let out a breath. 'I don't think that's it.'

He reached across and his right index finger and thumb scooped between her left ear and shoulder. Then he began to rub. Instantly a fleet of endorphins sailed out from the spot and waved a stream of soothing white flags.

Eyes drifting shut, she moaned as his touch gently rocked her.

Heaven.

She had to ask, 'Why have you never done this before?'

His lips brushed her brow as he spoke. 'I was saving it for a rainy day. Is that good?'

'You know it is,' she growled, but she only sounded satisfied.

'I can do better.'

He worked the area more fully until her bones melted away and her limbs began to float. She'd never had a professional massage; she'd doubted anything could measure up to even this tiny taste of Ben's manipulations.

Several drugging moments later, he turned more towards her, dotting soft, lingering kisses against her temple, then jaw. When his tongue grazed the seam of her lips, the sparking kindling deep inside her began to smoulder.

With great care, he tipped his body weight against hers. As her back met the couch cushions his fingers continued working her shoulder, but his mouth descended, tasting a provocative line down her décolletage.

With her eyes still closed, she told her brain to function through the blinding haze of passion. It refused. When he tugged her bodice down and his warm, wet mouth suctioned over the aching tip of her breast, brain function shut down completely. It was over.

She didn't want to resist.

As if sensing the precise moment of surrender, his hand left her shoulder and skied over her waist and hip, all the way down her leg until it caught her hem and dragged the fabric of her dress way up. His fingers hooked under her panties and slipped between her legs. As his fingertip delved between and gently rode her, and the stiff tip of his tongue twirled languidly around her nipple, her neck arced back and hips rose off the cushions. When his hand withdrew, in the far reaches of her mind she heard his fly unzip.

Felt the hot tip of him prod her thigh.

No!

Drunk with desire, she managed to push against his chest and drag herself to her senses. Summoning all her strength, she propelled herself upright and tried to steady her ragged breathing.

'*I can't do this.*'

His warm breath was at her ear. 'Celeste, honey, relax—'

'I won't relax. Ben, I said I wanted to *talk.*'

He straightened more and shovelled back dark hair flopped over his brow. He studied her, then he came closer. 'I'm sure that if—'

'I thought I was pregnant,' she rushed out, and felt better and worse for having admitted it.

His mouth dropped open. She thought she saw the blood drain from his face.

'You're...*pregnant*?'

She shook her head. 'I *thought* I was pregnant. Ended up...I wasn't.'

He simply stared at her. 'So you're not…having a baby?'

She hugged herself. 'Seems not.'

He slouched forward and his hands caught his head. 'Thank you, God.'

She flinched. Although she understood his relief, after her recent roller coaster of emotional highs and lows, his reaction was a slap in the face. 'Well, it's great to see you're so happy about it.'

He stared as if her skin had turned purple. 'What's not to be relieved about?'

She held her chin firm. 'You have no empathy at all, do you?'

He frowned, genuinely puzzled. 'Empathy over what?'

Did she truly expect him to understand? To anyone who hadn't been in her place, it mightn't sound like much— *A bit late? Get over it.* But as Ben had once said…

'Guess you had to be there.'

His study of her cut her to the quick. 'Oh, I've been there. I was the product of an unplanned pregnancy, remember?'

Yes, she remembered, and she sympathised. But that was his experience. This had been hers.

She turned more towards him, needing to get it off her chest and for him to understand even a little.

'When I realised I was late, I was terrified. Then, as more days passed and the more I thought it over,

I grew used to the idea and…' Remembered warmth filtered through her. She confessed, 'Well, I got excited. At the same time I felt this enormous crush of responsibility land on my shoulders. I bought a home pregnancy kit. Half of me wanted to know for sure, the other half simply didn't believe it.'

'The test was negative?' Her nod brought another groan of relief. 'Then that was it.'

She quashed her irritation. 'No, that wasn't it, because by that time I'd visualised the baby. The colour of his hair. How healthy she'd be. And I started to think about names, furniture—even schools. Once all those questions had done a few cycles, I was already committed to something that was physically half the size of a pea but that would grow into a baby.' *Her* baby.

She understood so well now.

When a woman had a child, that little person became their mother's number one priority. Women sacrificed. It was called 'maternal instinct'. Men didn't have it. They had 'slay and drag home the dinosaur' instinct; the human race was biologically designed that way for the survival of the species. He hunted, she nursed.

Her own mother had sacrificed. Anita had done what was needed in order to keep the family intact, which had meant rescuing her husband and his crumpling business, borrowing money that had never been repaid, then stepping away when Rodney had been able to capably take over. Her mother had never been thanked or acknowledged for any of it. In fact, as director of PLM, Rodney had had control over the funds, not Anita.

Even if Ben had been displeased at the 'baby situation', she'd known he would provide for them; she wouldn't *need* financial independence. But Celeste wanted it.

In these past days it had become crystal-clear how impotent her mother had felt the night she'd cried at Celeste's bedside. Powerless, defeated, committed to a man who might have respected her as a wife and mother, was happy to take money when she offered it, but resented his clever wife's threat to his masculinity. When Anita had died, she'd left her daughter that legacy.

Celeste never wanted to be 'looked after'.

She chewed her nail.

Ironic that Ben should have control of PLM now. His voice deepened. 'Celeste, just so we're straight, I may not be ready for fatherhood, but there's no question that I would acknowledge my own child.'

She nodded. 'I know.'

He blinked at the floor and after a moment reached to hold her hand. 'I'm sorry.'

Her heart squeezed. She'd needed that.

She half shrugged. 'You didn't know.'

'But I was still responsible.'

Taking in his troubled face, she worried that she

should have kept the false alarm to herself, but a bigger part of her was glad she hadn't. More often than not, a man didn't get to hear or appreciate the fear and doubt, or perhaps happiness and sense of purpose that followed a missed period; if Ben held such strong beliefs about parenthood he'd needed to hear it as much as she'd needed to share.

He kissed her hand. 'Feeling better about it now?'

She nodded, then thought more. 'Although, you'll probably think I'm silly, but the idea of going to Suzanne's baby shower next weekend has been driving me mad.'

'You're not looking forward to it?'

'She's a nice lady. I'm happy for her. The day's just going to be...awkward.' Because of how raw she felt over her own pregnancy misdiagnosis. Because the day would underpin the sense that she and Anita had been superseded.

'Would it help if I came along?'

She let his words sink in and brightened. 'You'd do that?'

He offered a crooked grin. 'As long as I don't have to diaper any dolls.'

She laughed. 'I'm sure we won't rope you in.'

His smile slowly faded. 'You want me to drive you home now?'

She considered it. Then, feeling stronger than she had in weeks, she leaned back against the bracket of his arm available behind her and said, 'Maybe soon.'

CHAPTER TEN

AS THEY drove to her father's house the following Saturday Celeste drank in Ben's classic profile. Straight nose, strong bristled jaw, black hair and open white collar rumpling against the late summer breeze. Enthralled, she watched his tanned hands negotiate the sports wheel with such effortless precision.

Those hands worked magic.

However, after his massage and their discussion last weekend, she and Ben hadn't made love. He'd remained remarkably well behaved. They'd talked some more, then he'd driven her home. She'd thought constantly about him since. Although he'd started off commitment-phobic-minded when she'd confided in him about her *almost pregnant* dilemma, ultimately he seemed to appreciate at least some of what she'd gone through.

Better yet, he'd called every day this week, but hadn't hounded her. Because her story had scared him into holding back or because he'd discovered a new respect for her and their relationship, she couldn't be certain. Perhaps the shock idea of father-hood had planted a positive and patient seed in his mind. Heck, he was here with her now, helping her to face this awkward day, wasn't he? Dared she hope?

Could Ben Scott be her Mr Right after all?

Discovering her study of him, he reached to clasp her hand. 'It'll be good to catch up with Rodney and give him an update on that meeting a couple of weeks back. I was on location yesterday. Helped dig a few post holes.' He smiled to himself. 'I still get a kick out of getting my hands dirty.'

Celeste clenched her teeth.

There it was…the stab she felt whenever he mentioned her family—

Sorry. What *had been* her family's company.

She looked away. 'I'm sure he'll be interested.'

Ben held her hand tighter as if he'd realised and regretted that, under the circumstances, his comment might have bit.

Facing her father today—with PLM sold and celebrating the baby's imminent arrival—seemed to sweep the past even farther behind them. Sometimes it was as if her mother—and that life—had never existed. She didn't blame Suzanne and she didn't want to blame her father, but sometimes… Well, sometimes it just plain hurt.

'You look all tight.' With one hand on the wheel, he massaged the sensitive sweep of her nearest shoulder. He grunted. 'Big knot right there.' His therapeutic yet sensual rub travelled up the back of her neck. 'How's that feel?'

She closed her eyes. 'Like I want you to do that to the rest of me.'

Her eyes sprang open.

Had she said that aloud?

'Careful,' he growled. 'I might pull over.'

Her skin grew hot at the thought. She was playing with fire. But maybe if she was very lucky she wouldn't end up being burned. Maybe this time instead of saying goodbye, she would finally find in Ben a wonderful warmth as well as a blistering passion.

His hand returned to the wheel as he turned into her father's street. 'If this is too hard, we don't have to go.'

She sat straighter. Suzanne had invited them for dinner, but Celeste knew it was wise not to push herself. People under stress sometimes said and did things they lived to regret. 'I said I'd go to the baby shower. We can say we have tickets to a play tonight.'

He didn't look convinced. 'Give me the nod when you're ready to leave.'

He pulled the Merc into the long driveway and Clancy and Matilda belted out from around the house. When Ben opened her car door, both dogs dropped their tennis balls at her feet.

Laughing, she ruffled their heads and picked up Clancy's ball. 'Wanna play, boy?'

The brown poodle wagged his tail so hard, he almost fell over.

She cast back, threw the ball and Clancy raced off. Matilda pranced around. When Celeste threw the second ball, it sailed through the air and lodged atop a bushy grevillea.

While Celeste cursed under her breath, Ben jogged off. 'I'll get it.'

Celeste waited for either her father to appear from the house or Ben to reappear from behind the bush. When neither showed up, she strolled off to see if she could help with the ball. Two pairs of eyes were better than one.

Ben was on his knees, searching under the bush. Matilda was sniffing and searching beside him.

Celeste examined the surrounding ground. 'Need any help?'

Ben's arms swept under the leaves. 'The ball's not stuck up the top. I figure it must have dropped.'

Her gaze lifted to the bush. Reaching into a branch, she pulled out the ball. 'Had your eyes tested lately?'

He peered up, frowned and grunted. 'Lucky find.'

She laughed. 'If you say so.'

His eyes flashed, then he caught her around the calves. She shrieked as she fell. Like a star foot-baller, he dived, rolled and somehow saved her from hitting the ground. With her lying on top of him—

his arms locked around her trunk—he rolled again until she was pinned beneath him. He playfully manacled her hands either side of her head.

'Anything you want to say now, Miss Wise Guy?'

She found her breath. 'I hear horn-rimmed glasses are back.'

He chuckled. 'My eyes are just fine.' He squeezed her wrists. 'And they like what they see.'

She counted her heartbeats. 'What do they see?'

'Someone very special.' His gaze deepened. 'Someone I can't get out of my mind.'

Someone he'd want to marry?

His gaze narrowed as if he'd read her thoughts. Then he pushed up and helped her to her feet. 'We're expected. You'd better brush the grass off your skirt or tongues will wag.'

As they dusted off and walked back to the house Celeste couldn't help but wonder if she was a fool for setting herself up so easily for Ben's games. Or was she right in believing that since last weekend they'd finally made a real connection? That they were closer than they'd ever been to understanding each other?

Rodney descended the wide porch steps and greeted them. Her father brushed a kiss against her cheek, then took in her simple apricot to-the-ankles dress, her flowing hair.

'You look great, sweetheart.' He acknowledged Ben; Celeste had said he'd be joining her. 'Good to see you again, son.'

Ben took her father's hand. 'Rodney.'

'Hope you're taking care of my daughter as well as you're taking care of my business.'

Celeste cringed. Lord, she felt like a chattel. If ghosts existed—if her mother could hear this conversation—

Her father's next words broke her train of thought. 'Suzanne's inside with her friends, unwrapping gifts and talking baby talk.' His gaze softened. 'She's pleased you came today.'

Celeste couldn't seem to fall over either side of the fence. Being here under these circumstances was like selling out her mother's memory, and yet the child Suzanne carried deserved a sister, just as Celeste deserved a sibling. No matter how much days like this hurt, she couldn't turn her back on that relationship.

Inside, hellos were exchanged between Celeste, Ben and half a dozen ogling women, who were clearly enamoured with his masculine looks and physique. When Suzanne enquired, Celeste replied that her handbag store was doing a roaring trade and her florist concern—Star Arrangements—was a week away from opening its doors. When a lady in a pink silk lounge suit suggested she bring out the food, Celeste offered instead. Rodney had taken a phone call, so Ben said he would help.

In the kitchen, he collected a silver tray of ribbon sandwiches.

An image bloomed in her mind and, grinning, Celeste leant against the counter. 'What's the bet those women would love to see you serve them minus your shirt.'

He looked surprised, then gave her a devilish grin. 'I'm only available for private shows.'

As she remembered the blood-pumping feel of his bare, hot chest against her flesh her heart began to race. She fought the impulse to gravitate towards him and shook her head instead. 'Not today.'

'How about tonight?'

She wouldn't lie to herself and say she wasn't interested. And whether it was emotional suicide or not, she couldn't help but have some fun with his quip.

As he sauntered nearer she made an observation. 'You look hungry. Here. Have some dip.' She shoved a cracker in his mouth.

The surprise faded from his face as he chewed and mumbled, 'Thank you. Delicious.' He set down his tray. 'Now perhaps I could tempt you with something tasty. Do you prefer spicy—' he indicated fatty Mexican meatballs '—or sweet?' Scones and cream.

Smothering a grin, she turned to collect her own tray. 'I like a healthy diet.'

He caught her waist. 'I like you.'

As his mouth hovered close to hers the air hummed and throbbed between them. It was all she could do not to succumb to temptation and allow herself to be kissed. Every particle of her screamed out to give in.

But it wasn't the time or the place.

More than that…was it wise?

Summoning her will power, she ducked under his arm and scooped up her tray. 'Suzanne would like to start her shower.'

After delivering his tray, Ben bowed off and joined Rodney in his study. Gathering herself after their steamy interlude in the kitchen, Celeste sat next to a chatty lady on the twin couch and watched Suzanne fawn over beautifully crafted matinee jackets, cot mobiles, rattles, baby's first fine bone china…

When Suzanne unwrapped Celeste's gift, her eyes filled. Overcome, she moved closer. Celeste stood so she could accept her stepmother's hug and kiss.

'It's a perfect gift,' Suzanne, smelling of 'Joy', murmured at her ear. 'Thank you.'

Pleased that she liked it, Celeste showed her the bag's many compartments. 'It might look like a big teddy bear but it's very practical. The head fits all your bottle needs, the tummy is for diapers. Its back pouch is for lotions and such. The front pouch for food.'

'Where did you get it?' Miss Chatty with the black bob asked over her Royal Doulton cup.

'I designed it and had a seamstress do the work.' She indicated the bear's tummy. 'See. *Celeste's.*' Then a trademark silver star.

As the women spoke up, each desperate to make an order, without warning, Celeste's throat constricted. She'd thought of this design during *that* week.

The test had shown she wasn't pregnant. It was silly to be upset. It was only this environment—clucky women, some of them pregnant—that had brought all those empty emotions back home.

Suzanne held the teddy baby bag to her belly. 'It's a wonderful gift. I'd always wanted children. I'm so happy it's happened now and she'll have such a special sister.'

Suzanne was being genuinely kind, but right now Celeste felt as if she might suffocate.

Mrs Perfectly Poised with the blonde chignon bit into a jam and cream scone and licked her thumb. 'Did you bake this, Suzanne? Your scones are always lighter than air.'

'It's all in the oven temperature.' Suzanne crossed to retrieve her cup from a polished timber trolley. She exercised her back and her pregnant tummy stuck out more. 'It needs to be *very* hot.'

Celeste raised her brows. Her mother had taught her nothing about cooking. Instead she'd passed on her love for watercolours and horse riding. Celeste remembered her father being cross one morning when he'd needed to iron his own shirt. Had that been after Anita had acquired that loan from Grandpa, or a night when she'd been up until three stringing together strategies to pull PLM out of the hole her husband had dug?

Suzanne wouldn't need to iron any shirts. Those struggles were over, fought and won by another.

Brushing back her hair, Celeste tried to breathe. She needed air. Or, more simply, she needed to get out of here.

Ben materialised at the right moment, looking darkly attractive and capable as ever. She begged him with her eyes.

He checked the time and commented to Rodney, who was a step behind, 'We must be going. Tickets to the theatre.'

He mentioned the name of the play and all the women swooned. They said goodbye on the porch and everyone, including Miss Chatty and Mrs Poise, waved them off.

When they were a mile down the road, Ben pulled over. He ratcheted up the handbrake, cupped his palm around her nape and dragged her close. His kiss had the detonating accuracy of a precision missile. It left her completely shattered and buzzing with a high-powered sexual need as well as a promise of what was yet to come…*if* she were brave or stupid enough to accept.

Too soon, his lips left hers. He growled in his throat. 'I've been dying to do that all day.'

She wouldn't admit that she'd been just as desperate. Her body felt alight with sizzling want and need. What would happen when they reached home? Probably not much talking. But the same question haunted her. As an affirmed bachelor, would Ben ever want more from her than casual companionship and sex?

Ben released her and, after checking the rear view mirror, pulled back out onto the deserted road. After a few moments he asked, 'Did you have a nice time?'

She conceded, 'It wasn't all bad.'

'Suzanne looked very pregnant today.'

'She hasn't got long to go.'

'She seemed happy. Rodney too.'

'Most couples do in the beginning.' She cringed. 'That wasn't nice.'

'It'll take time to get used to seeing your dad with someone else. Don't feel bad.'

'Suzanne's so friendly and sincere. She doesn't deserve snarky comments like that.'

'She's just the kind of woman Rodney needs in his later years.'

She blinked over at him. 'What kind of woman is that?'

She could make out his expression. *Foot in mouth.* 'That wasn't meant to be a slur against your mother.'

She tried to smile. 'That's all right. What kind of woman did you mean? Attractive? Thoughtful? A woman who'll be content to stay home and look after the baby while he plays nine holes?'

He scratched his temple. 'I didn't say that.'

'Suzanne is lovely—' she made that clear again '—but not everyone wants to stay home and look after babies. Nothing against those who do, coz I hear it's the hardest job in the world as well as the most rewarding.' She thought of her mother and herself. 'But some of us want to explore our options and keep them open alongside marriage and motherhood. It's not a crime.'

Or not in most countries.

'I'm not suggesting women shouldn't have careers. But you must admit it's logical that if a couple choose to have a family, given that women are the main care givers, they need to put things on hold. That's what the paid maternity leave ruckus is about, isn't it?'

Celeste pulled on her seat-belt sash.

Ruckus?

She turned more towards him. 'Why does a woman have to be the one to step down?'

He seemed amused. 'Not step down. Delay.'

'Because the family might suffer if she's not home to mash the spuds?'

She remembered how pleased Gerard had been that Chris's new bride was a ten in the kitchen, and how her own father had subtly criticised her mother's cooking. Celeste had thought her mother's failed attempts at sponge cake were good fun. They got covered in flour and she was always allowed to lick the spoon. And if ever Anita burned the roast, it simply meant more dessert. Who could complain?

'Celeste, you know I can cook.'

'Very well. But you're avoiding the question.'

He lifted a brow. 'You *are* after an argument.'

She almost laughed. 'Because I want to discuss equality of the sexes.'

His face hardened. 'It's not about equality. It's simply the way the world works.'

Her chest burned with indignation. 'Your world or mine?'

He clenched his jaw—a warning to drop it—but she couldn't let it rest there.

'These days there are men who stay at home to look after the baby while a mother works.'

While she high-fived that initiative if it suited the couple concerned, Celeste didn't feel that was her answer. She dearly wanted to nurse and care for her own baby when it was time. She simply didn't want to relinquish her individual power as a consequence. Wasn't that fair enough?

She turned the tables. 'Would you be prepared to delay your goals and be dependent on another person?'

'I was dependent enough on others the first sixteen years of my life.'

As she thought of the sad little boy he once must have been her heart dropped. However. 'I wasn't responsible for your past. Right now I'm concerned with the future.'

'I've pretty much accomplished my goals.'

'Like being boss of a company like PLM?'

He turned at her tone. 'You knew how I felt about PLM from the start. I can't change my story now.'

'And I can't change mine.'

Her mother had sacrificed everything and someone called Benton Scott—the man who had become her lover—had ended up with the prize. Sometimes she couldn't believe that twist of fate. It wasn't Ben's fault, but, truth was, it still stuck in her craw.

His expression softened. 'You're much better off with your florist concern. It'll be huge, and you know I'll help anyway I can.'

Another brick went up. Why did he think he could decide what was best for her? 'I don't want your help.'

She didn't want *anyone's* help—not her father's any more, and not Ben's. She wanted to do it her way, just as Ben had done for himself, and would continue to do.

His mouth hooked up at one side but she saw the muscle jump in his jaw. 'You could make a guy think his help isn't good enough.'

Her chin pulled in. 'That's not it.'

He kept his gaze on the road as if she might read too much from his eyes.

'Are you sure?' he asked. 'You were born with a silver spoon in your mouth. I'm the penniless orphan with no pedigree who clawed his way up from the gutter.'

What? 'Why would you say something like that?'

'Because your father wasn't good enough for your mother.'

She blinked several times. 'What's that supposed to mean?'

'If he had been, she wouldn't have tried to make him into something he wasn't. Hell, maybe the guy was sincerely happy fixing mowers. Maybe she should've let him be the man he wanted to be and—'

Stunned, she waited. 'And what?'

He changed gears. 'And nothing.'

She said it for him. 'And their marriage would've been more of a success? Rodney didn't have to take my grandfather's money, you know.'

Ben coughed out a humourless laugh. '*Didn't he?* I can feel the pressure on him now and it happened twenty years ago. You said it yourself. Your mother usually won the toss and your father grew to resent it.'

Her mouth dropped open. 'So a woman should hide her intelligence? Never aspire to achieve?'

But somewhere deep inside a young girl whispered, *I just want Mummy and Daddy to love each other again.*

Which meant what? Mummy had to sell her soul to keep the peace?

Ben scrubbed his jaw and spoke more calmly. 'You should never need to worry like your mother did. While we're together, you'll always have the best. I don't want you to be concerned over money matters.'

While they were together? And how long would that be?

She felt torn for another reason. 'That sounds sweet on the surface, but it equates to being kept in the dark. Would you take me seriously if I suggested that to you?'

He looked at her as if she might be coming down with something.

Darn it, she wanted answers. But were there any?

She couldn't run from it any longer. She'd fallen in love with the very man who had exploded into her life three months earlier and had unwittingly taken what had amounted to her right to see her mother's memory, and last wish, honoured. Ben sympathised over how the deal had worked out. But could he ever appreciate how she felt—not only about that specific issue, but also the broader issues?

She'd wanted to put the past behind her, but maybe she shouldn't because she was loath to repeat her mother's mistakes and Ben's attitude set off alarms. Clearly he thought a woman's—or at least a mother's—place was primarily in the home, and a man should be allowed 'to do what a man needed to do'. She, on the other hand, advocated individuality and equality between the sexes in all things. He had trouble seeing her point; she had to wonder, given his childhood of wishing for a textbook family, if he was even capable.

'You know what's wrong with this discussion?' she finally asked. 'That you should want to come off sounding like such an expert on a subject you otherwise avoid like the plague.' Marriage.

'I'm entitled to my opinion.'

'Based on what? You cling to these idealised notions of how a family should work.' The man as head of the house, the woman happily keeping her place in the bedroom and kitchen. 'You want to preach about the way a couple should be content and stick together as a family, yet you don't have the guts to go for it yourself.'

He edged over a patronising look. 'Celeste, we only met three months ago.'

'Are you telling me that in the future you'd consider long term? That you'd no longer view *us* as a romp, or me as someone you won't commit to beyond the bedroom?'

His face hardened and hands tightened on the wheel.

Her chest ached. She crossed her arms and looked out the window. 'I didn't think so.' So full of wisdom, but not prepared to put his own heart on the line.

Must be high time she withdrew her own heart as well.

He swerved into a park outside her apartment building. She opened her door at the same time his door unlatched.

His leg was already out the door. 'I'm coming up.'

She spun on him. 'No, Ben, you're not. This ends now. Maybe happy families isn't a matter of waving a magic wand or wishing on a star. I know that as well as you do. But one day I hope to find the man I'm meant to spend the rest of my life with. Though I would've liked it to be you, for so many reasons it's obviously not. Aside from sexual attraction, we started off miles apart and I can't ever see that rift closing.'

He reached for her hand, but she pulled away as her throat clogged with emotion. She bit her lip, then lifted her chin. 'I don't want to do this any more. Don't call. You have the company, you have my heart, but I'll get over it. I'll get over you—if you have the decency to stay away.'

She needed to get on with her life—find her place—and this was only delaying it.

She shut the car door behind her—made it all the way up to her apartment. Then reality hit, pain overwhelmed her and stinging tears began to flow.

CHAPTER ELEVEN

COULD things get any worse?

Gerard's voice on the phone this morning had suggested the family matter was urgent. But after the disastrous end to his outing with Celeste, Ben felt more like donning his track shoes and running out his frustrations till he dropped than attending a Bartley-Scott family meeting.

He wasn't good at collaborating with others on family politics. Hadn't Celeste slammed home that point so well before she'd strode away yesterday? But today Ben felt stuck. After the way his father had welcomed him into his fold, Ben didn't want to refuse Gerard's invitation to his home—although Ben sensed he alone was the reason for the gathering.

As Ben walked into the Bartley-Scott kitchen his misgivings seemed to be confirmed when two pair of eyes out of a dozen glared up at his arrival. Ben's irritation, as well as another emotion he wouldn't name, spiked into the red. Hell, you'd think he'd killed someone.

Gerard indicated a chair. 'Take a seat, Ben. You're the last to arrive.'

Ben shucked back his shoulders. 'I prefer to stand, thank you.'

Since his earliest memories, he'd dreamed of finding his family, being accepted. But the cold facts of reality weren't that shiny or clear, and, like nothing else could, it made him want to run.

Maybe Celeste was right. All his life he'd relied on no one but himself. Maybe he would always come up short when it came to taking that final leap—being able to commit totally. Trust wasn't easy to come by.

Zack, Paul's young son, scooted up and tugged Ben's trouser leg. 'Where's C'leste? She was at the wedding.'

Ben ignored the emotional kick in his gut. 'She couldn't come today.'

Gerard patted Zack's shoulder. 'Can you go out the back to play for a few minutes? Grandpa needs to talk to the adults.'

'Will Ben be here when I get back?' Zack spoke under his breath, 'Daddy doesn't like him so much.'

Paul shot up from his chair. 'Zack!'

Ben suppressed a groan. Nothing could be worth this. He'd felt like the whipping boy for the first half of his life; what the hell was he doing here feeling uncomfortable when he could go back to feeling…

Nothing.

Gerard ruffled his grandson's hair. 'Run along. Daddy'll go fetch you when we're done.'

After the back screen door closed, Gerard moved to stand at the head of the table. His seven children—eight including Ben—waited for his next words. Rhyll sat by a window, head down, busy darning a sock.

Gerard called her over. 'Rhyll, put down that needle and thread and come stand beside me.'

Reluctantly she set down her work and joined her husband.

Gerard leant forward, his two palms on the table. 'It's sometimes difficult to know how to handle family situations. They come along a lot—disagreements, discipline issues, agreeing on whose turn it is to take out the garbage.'

Ben crossed his arms. He hoped that wasn't a subtle reference.

Gerard continued. 'No one's missed the vibes generated toward Ben. Most are welcoming, but some...' His face twisted and he pulled up tall. 'Well, some are disappointing if, perhaps, understandable. I'd initially thought I should let the waters calm by themselves, but Ben deserves more than that. And so...' He turned to his wife.

Before he could speak, Rhyll's face coloured and she stepped back. 'I don't think there's a need to talk in front of the—'

Gerard held up a hand. 'There's a *big* need.' He took both her hands in his. 'Yes, I was married before, but I assure you that I didn't see Ben's mother again after that final night when Ben was obviously conceived. I have never been unfaithful to you. Never will. You are my wife and will be till the day I die. My family is the most important thing in the world to me. I know this uncertainty is partly my fault. I should remind you of my feelings more often.'

While Ben blinked at Gerard's unadorned honesty, Rhyll seemed to hold her breath, then her shoulders came down and she smiled.

Gerard pressed a loving kiss to her cheek and turned to Paul, who sat up straighter. 'You are my firstborn. The baby boy I held in my arms and was so proud of. Still am. But I've been given a gift most men could never hope for. *Another* firstborn, and I won't turn my back on him for anything, just as you will never turn your back on Zack. Paul, I spoke to you constantly about Ben when I first found out, about how successful he was, how he'd built himself up from nothing. I didn't mean to make you feel uncertain of your place in my heart. You could never be replaced, but just as you hope that Zack will one day have a brother or sister, you need to understand that we, as a family, have been blessed in the same wonderful way.' His next words addressed the whole room. 'Life's never long enough. Let's all spend it making up for lost time, starting now.'

Everyone's eyes fell to Paul. Paul's jaw flexed, then his gaze drifted towards the screen door, to the backyard where his son played. His young wife touched his hand. He nodded, pushed out his chair and walked over to Ben. Nodding, he stuck out his hand.

His throat aching, Ben exhaled and accepted his younger brother's olive branch.

Paul grinned. 'Guess the last couple of weeks make up for all the spats we missed out on growing up. A little late but—' Paul brought Ben close for a brotherly hug '—sorry for being an idiot. Welcome to the family.'

Her face contrite, Rhyll came forward. 'Can I get you a cup of tea, Ben? I baked some banana bread this morning. It's always been the kids' favourite.'

Melissa, Dana and Belinda, Ben's three half-sisters, chirped up to agree. Paul's wife, Chris and Marie moved over towards Ben too, while Michael and Terrance, Ben's youngest siblings, swiped some banana bread off the table.

Gerard waved a beckoning hand. 'Ben, when you're ready, will you join me on the back porch?'

Ben's mind was spinning. He'd witnessed foster dads address their families, however—other than that one time when he'd briefly felt included—he'd hovered on the outside. He'd never felt connected.

Or loved.

Until now.

He and Gerard moved out onto the back porch and

sat on the back steps side by side, watching Zack ride his bike minus trainer wheels.

Ben spoke first. 'Thank you.' Simple words, but heartfelt.

Gerard smiled. 'I hope you'll come by often. With seven...sorry, *eight* children, the fun never ends, even when they're all grown up. But you'll know about that one day yourself.'

Ben watched Zack and his bike weave around.

Would he know one day? Three months ago becoming a father had been the farthermost thing from his mind. Celeste's pregnancy alarm the other week had been an eye-opener. But he'd still baulked at seeing himself in what he'd perceived as a scary role. Marriage. Kids.

Ben frowned. He needed to know. 'What was my mother like?'

Gerard inhaled deeply. 'She was a good woman, who felt strongly about her independence and opinions. Not a thing wrong with that. I admired her courage.' He shrugged. 'We just weren't meant to be.'

Ben read between the lines.

'You didn't see eye to eye.' Like Celeste and himself at times.

'Ben, your mother and I thought we were in love. We made a mistake. But even Rhyll and I—in fact, in any marriage a husband and wife aren't going to agree on everything. It's simply not possible. It's how you deal with those issues that will help make a family solid and endure.'

Ben had witnessed that sound advice in action first-hand today. Being a good father wasn't easy. It was a responsibility to be handled with great care and deep consideration. It meant bridging disagreements as well as admitting to your own mistakes. Admitting to your feelings. Having the guts to say I love you to the people—the person—who mattered most…

And doing it before it was too late.

CHAPTER TWELVE

CELESTE glanced up from her Star Arrangements counter and felt her heart leap from her chest. Her pen clattered to the floor as she tried to catch her stolen breath.

'Ben…what are you doing here?'

He sauntered up, his gaze dark and penetrating as if he'd walked a thousand miles and nothing could shake his resolve. 'I need to speak with you.'

She came out from behind the counter. 'I told you two days ago…' Her stomach muscles gripped but she said it anyway. 'I need you to stay away.'

His voice lowered. 'I can't, and I don't think you want me to either.'

The conviction in his eyes…the temptation of his suggestion…

She found the strength to turn away. She couldn't survive another round battling Ben's magnetism.

'What I *want* doesn't count. I'm concerned with

what I need.' What was *best*, which was to put their affair from her mind and down to experience.

She couldn't regret the time she'd spent with Ben; what woman could? But on Saturday he'd made it clear: their relationship was going nowhere. If she relented now, she was as good as telling him she was prepared to be his mistress. It was an old-fashioned term, but well suited the situation he obviously preferred. No ties. No hassles. Just good times, including very good sex. But, she'd learned, sometimes good sex had big consequences.

His hands cupped her shoulders. A tingling moment later, his warm breath stirred her hair. 'I spent some soul-searching time with my family yesterday and I've come to a decision. You need me, Celeste. And I need you.'

Soul-searching?

She set her teeth and shrugged away to face him. 'Here's a newsflash, Ben. Sex isn't everything.'

'I'm not talking about sex.' He ran a hand through his hair. 'Well, not *only* sex.'

She huffed. Nothing had changed.

She lifted her chin at the door. 'Please leave. I'm opening the store next week and I'm busy tying up loose ends.'

She needed to concentrate her efforts here—on her business and building her own niche in the world, not wasting time vacillating over a silver-tongued playboy who had all the answers but wasn't interested in putting his heart where his mouth was.

'Celeste, I've thought a lot about us. I've had no sleep these past days, going over every aspect of our relationship.'

Her hands curled at her sides. 'We don't have a relationship.'

He ignored that. 'And I kept coming back with the same answer. I want long term. I want to marry you.' He shrugged and smiled. 'It's that simple.'

The cogs in Celeste's brain seized as every element of time seemed to screech to a halt. She waited for the brackets to form around that oh-so-kissable mouth. But he didn't grin.

This wasn't a joke?

But a proposal from a man who two days ago had shuddered at the prospect of settling down, even while dictating how it should be done? It didn't fit.

Unless…

The chain mail went back up around her emotions. She shook her head. 'It won't work.'

He frowned. 'What won't work?'

'A fake engagement that's designed to get me back beneath your sheets.'

His brow creased more. He was a good actor—good enough to appear as if her suggestion had stung. 'That's not it.'

Wasn't it? When had he said that he loved her? She'd have thought those words would play an important role when a man asked a woman to spend the rest of her life with him. If he'd thought so hard about this, where was the ring? This was clearly a scam, Benton Scott digging extra deep to work his ticket into her bedroom. Well, sorry, but that train had left the station.

She crossed her arms over the empty ache expanding beneath her ribs and arched a brow. 'So you've had some kind of revelation?'

His head cocked. 'If you want to call it that.'

She called *it* something else.

Seduction.

She wouldn't go there again. 'Sorry, but I'm not convinced.'

He moved towards her, his arms out. 'Celeste—'

She shot her arms out too, but warning him away. 'I asked you to leave me alone.' Her voice cracked. 'Can't you respect me that much?' He was breaking her heart all over again. She'd had her hopes raised before. She didn't need to have them crushed still more.

He held her gaze for a heart-rending moment, then he pushed out a breath. 'I need to admit you were right. I had this vision of what a family should be, but I was too much of a coward to test the theory. And part of the reason was that I knew I would never find my perfect *home-sweet-home* package. But yesterday I learned that I don't need perfection. I need to work every day on what means more to me than anything.'

He was referring to her?

She wound her arms tighter. She would not be swayed by his entrancing blue eyes and deadly brand of charm. 'I can think of at least one thing that means more to you than me.'

'PLM?' She nodded. He handed over a large envelope he'd been carrying.

She flipped it over. 'What's this?'

'Documents to release the proprietorship of PLM into your name.'

Her eyes narrowed. 'Is this some kind of joke?'

'I won't pretend it wasn't great fun…to own that company…to be a boy but be in charge. But PLM will always be far more than that to you.'

Her heart pounded high in her throat.

He couldn't be serious.

This wasn't right.

She shoved the envelope back. 'I can't accept this.'

He shook his head slowly. 'Take it, even if you eventually find you want to sell it again.'

She swallowed hard, trying to make sense of it all. 'But this must be worth…well, at least the debt you paid.'

'Money isn't the issue.'

He'd told her he wanted to marry her. Now he was handing back something that had meant so much to both of them: to her because it had encompassed where she'd come from and who she'd thought she needed to be, and to Ben because when a person hadn't been given love, they naturally sought out some other source of power. More than anything, PLM had represented power over his lost childhood. Now he was giving that power up.

For her.

Her tongue was still tied when he dropped a kiss on her brow. 'Take it,' he murmured. 'It was never mine.'

As he turned to leave her cell phone rang and he turned back. 'You should get that. Could be your first big Star Arrangements client.'

Right now—with her mind in turmoil—she didn't care if it was.

He concentrated on her, then on the phone ringing on the counter. He moved to collect it and handed it over.

Her rubber lips worked enough to say hello. When she hung up a few seconds later, the world seemed to have tilted. She dropped the envelope as her legs threatened to collapse beneath her. She heard Ben's voice, though distantly.

'Celeste? What's wrong?'

She touched her clammy forehead. 'Suzanne had the baby but she's haemorrhaging. I've never heard Dad sound like that before.' Thick with unshed tears. But she *had* heard him like that—when her mother had passed away.

Ben secured her cold hands in his. 'Which hospital?'

She dug through the fog and came up with a name. He grabbed her purse off the counter and ushered her out the door, through the busy city pedestrian traffic and into his building's underground car park.

By the time they were in the car and on their way, Celeste had settled enough to explain. 'The baby's fine but Suzanne's in a bad way. The doctor's examined her. She's on medication to help stem the bleeding. But her vital signs are far from stable. If it doesn't stop, she'll need a transfusion.'

And surgery if the situation didn't improve. Celeste didn't want to think beyond that and yet she couldn't help but worry about that new tiny baby—her own little sister—growing up without her mum as she had done from the age of ten. As she held her knotting stomach another thought struck. She fixed her eyes on Ben, whose face was more set than she'd ever seen.

He was here for her; he obviously wanted Suzanne well, but surely he was pondering the fact that he'd lost his mother in similar circumstances.

He reached for her hand and shot her a determined smile. 'She'll be fine.'

Her chest grew warm. She'd never felt closer to him than at this moment. He was a man anyone could rely on in an emergency to keep his head and get everyone through. She knew that as well as she knew her own name. And he'd said he wanted to marry her and had proven it the best way he knew how. By giving her back her past.

But what of their future?

Her free hand gripped in her lap as she took in his strong profile.

Was he sexist? Was she too much the feminist? Was theirs a volatile and ultimately toxic combination? Or could there be a compromise on their thinking?

When they entered the hospital ward, a nurse at the station let them know which room.

They fast-tracked it down the corridor and into the private maternity suite. Suzanne lay asleep—or unconscious—in a crisply made bed, a drip in her arm. Rodney sat in a chair beside her, holding close a small wrapped bundle.

He looked up as they entered and his suntanned face beamed. 'Sweetheart, you're here.'

She felt Ben's arm steadying her, but she didn't dare speak. Was Suzanne any better? Had she had a transfusion? Gazing down again at his new little daughter, her father appeared relaxed.

Suzanne's heavy eyes opened. She wet her lips and attempted a smile. 'Here's big sister.'

Her heart belting against her ribs, Celeste moved closer. 'I thought... Dad, you said...'

Her father groaned on a nod. 'I shouldn't have phoned when I did. It was a scary time. I'm sorry now that I worried you. Suzanne was wheeled back in ten minutes ago. The doctor's happy with how she's responded to the medication.'

Her face pale but content, Suzanne took in her family—husband and child. 'I wasn't worried. We have the best obstetrician in Sydney. And the baby's healthy. She cried almost the second she was delivered.'

Celeste smiled, then felt a flicker of disloyalty that she was happy this woman was alive when her own mother was dead. But that, she realised fully, wasn't the way it should be. She had wonderful memories of her mother. And now she had a thoughtful stepmother, who wanted them all to be a family. She also had a father who had his faults, but loved her nonetheless and deserved a second chance as much as anyone.

And what about this new addition?

Celeste drifted towards the bundle in her father's arms. She gazed down and her heart brimmed with immediate unconditional love.

She swallowed against rising emotion. 'She's so tiny. And *beautiful*.' Delicate rosebud mouth…jet-black hair and lashes…bunched above the wrap, fingers that were so small and perfect, each and every one was a miracle.

Rodney nodded. 'I think she looks a little like you.'

'Same nose,' Suzanne offered.

Celeste remembered the week when she'd wondered if she was pregnant. She laid a hand atop this sleeping baby's head and knew when the time was right, it would happen.

'We named her Tiegan,' her father said. 'It means little princess.'

Ben's low voice rumbled behind Celeste. 'Every girl deserves to be a princess. Congratulations.'

Celeste looked over her shoulder and let her gaze roam Ben's face—his genuine smile as well as the faint line drawn between the dark slashes of his brows. Seeming to convey some message with his eyes, he reached to take her hands and press his lips to each one.

'Want a hold?'

Her father's offer brought Celeste back. Nodding, she positioned herself in a comfortable chair. Her father stood and carefully placed the baby in her arms.

A rush of wonderment had Celeste muffling a laugh. The baby was so real and warm and somehow heavier than she'd expected. 'I thought she'd be lighter.'

'Like the dolls you used to carry around.'

She studied her father. 'You remember?'

Chuckling, he sat on the bed and laid his hand over his wife's. 'You were doll crazy. Every Christmas, every birthday, you only wanted to add to your collection. Your mother and I would joke you'd have twelve children some day.'

Suzanne smiled. 'There's still time.'

Twelve children! Celeste wanted to hoot, but the moment was too special…the kind of moment a person remembered and treasured for ever. Then she knew.

She didn't need to be visible or prove herself in

her father's, or anyone's, world any more. She simply wanted to share and be a part of it. Of this.

'Does this mean we have a babysitter?' Rodney asked.

Tiegan yawned and Celeste's heart melted more. 'Whenever you need me, I'll be there.'

It might've been all the emotion in the room, but didn't it follow that if she'd found her way here—to a place where she could wholeheartedly accept this new phase in her life—maybe she could accept a little more? Should she give Ben the benefit of the doubt just one more time? Would it be foolhardy, or her own chance to find lasting happiness?

She looked up from the baby's peaceful face, searched the room, then frowned. 'Where's Ben?'

Her father threw a glance around; Suzanne opened her eyes and blinked into the corners too.

'He's probably popped out for some air,' Rodney decided.

Without saying a word?

Celeste swallowed the dread creeping up her throat.

She had another theory. Having understood that everything was squared away here—including her relationship with the baby, Suzanne and her father—Ben had ducked out quietly without putting her through yet another goodbye.

Should she go after him?

She blew out a breath. 'Dad, can you take Tiegan?'

'Sure, sweetheart.'

He scooped the baby up and Celeste headed for the door. 'I'm sorry. I have to go.'

'Go where?'

She was halfway out. 'Hopefully home.'

While her father looked at her oddly, Suzanne's smile said she understood.

Celeste passed the unattended station, then came across a nurse checking a chart. 'Did you see a very tall, very good looking man pass by here?'

The nurse grinned. 'Did I ever.' She pointed her Bic at the lifts. 'He went down.'

When Celeste jumped out of the lift a few moments later and made her way outside, the air had turned unseasonably cool. The nippy air wrapped around her shoulders and inched up her skirt. She hunched, then rubbed her hands. She wished she'd brought a jacket. She'd always kept one in Ben's car—

Her focus honed in on the car park. His Mercedes was zooming off down the road.

Her hand shot up as she called out, 'Ben!'

Celeste's hand slowly lowered.

He was gone. But should she have expected anything more? He'd told her that he wanted to marry her and she'd said she didn't believe him. And yet he'd still acted to get her here in record time. Without making a scene, he'd kissed her hands and had said a final goodbye. Should she leave it at that? Would she only be opening a tin of worms to want to see him again?

With a thousand questions buzzing through her brain and her heart thudding low in her chest, she dragged herself around to face the hospital entrance. But Suzanne must need rest, and her father would want time on his own with baby Tiegan—it was only natural.

So…where to now?

Hugging her chilled arms, she walked aimlessly down the path, along a back street and eventually came across a field, set up with a lively long weekend carnival. A slow spinning Ferris wheel, enthralled children on merry-go-rounds, a juggling clown with baggy striped pants riding a unicycle and tooting a horn…

She wandered in, waving off a man who offered five balls to knock down the cans and win a giant doll. She couldn't throw for peanuts. But she wouldn't tell Ben that.

Her eyes misted over.

She'd missed him so much. Now she felt that sense of loneliness like a hot lance through her heart. What should she do?

'Approach and have your fortune told.'

Celeste edged around. An old woman, fitted out in green and purple classic gypsy garb, crooked a gnarled finger, beckoning her near.

'You're lost,' the gypsy predicted above the carnival din, 'but you'll soon find your way.'

Celeste grinned. Of course she looked lost, wandering around, her chin on the ground. Still…

Spotting the crystal ball—much larger and more impressive than the one in the window that day—Celeste drifted over. 'What else do you see?'

The woman's dark eyes gleamed. She dramatically cast age-worn hands over the globe once—twice.

'I see warmth…then cold and hard walls of ice.' Still looking into the glass, her grave expression eased. 'Now I see great warmth return. You think it will burn, but don't be afraid of the new and exciting.' Her eyes slid up to meet Celeste's and she whispered, 'Listen to friendly ghosts.'

Fixed to the spot, Celeste shivered at the same moment the breeze picked up, blowing the hair over her face. When she threw her hair back and turned into the wind rather than against it, Ben was standing there.

He leaned forward.

'*Boo.*'

Celeste jumped out of her skin.

Listen to friendly ghosts?

She spun around. The gypsy straightened her fake wart nose before collecting a rag from under the table to polish her ball. She smiled. 'I do teacup readings too. Otherwise that's two-fifty, hon.'

Feeling like Alice in Wonderland, Celeste rotated back. Gingerly she touched Ben's black crewneck sweater and sighed her relief. He was real.

'Where did you get to?' she croaked, setting a hand against her racing heart.

'I went out to find a café that made a decent coffee. Have you ever tasted hospital instant?' He visibly shuddered. 'I asked the nurse at the station to tell you if I was missed.'

The tension locking Celeste's muscles eased a fraction. He'd left a message but she'd obviously seen a different nurse—the one with the chart.

'When I pulled back into the car park,' he went on, 'you were wandering off down this way. I left the coffees in the car and followed.'

Absorbing each detail, she stroked the sweater he hadn't worn earlier. 'You've changed.'

'I heard on the radio a cold snap's set in. I brought your jacket with me.' He presented it, then walked around to help her into the sleeves. He gave her shoulders a rub and the chill left her bones.

When he stood before her again, they looked into each other's eyes and said together, 'There's something I need to—'

He grinned. 'Ladies first.'

She told the nerves to quit jumping rope in her stomach, then tried to put her feelings into words.

'I've been thinking…about you wanting to return my parents' company…about you racing to bring me here today…about how we might be able to work *us* out.'

Something flared in his eyes, then faded. 'I'll be honest. I don't want my children brought up by anyone but their parents. It's important that a child knows and trusts his mother *and* his father without reserve every day of his life.'

'I agree. As long as it's a joint effort and everyone's happy with the arrangements, including the child.'

He nodded—*good*. 'And, let me say, I have no intention of being a "bring my slippers", "where's my dinner?" type of husband—not next year, not in fifty. You stimulate me—my mind, my body, even my beliefs. I don't want to ever hold you back or hide you away.'

Tears thickened in her throat. He'd touched her more deeply than she'd thought possible. But she had to voice the obvious. 'I bet our parents thought much the same when they agreed to marry.'

'That was their lives and our past.' His expression said he was done with it. 'If we work together—if we *both* want to make this work—we won't regret our decision. I've never loved anyone before. Do you think I'd do anything to lose you?'

Soaking up the raw emotion in his words, she smiled and those tears blurred her vision.

'You love me?'

His chest expanded. 'Completely and for ever. I want to be there for you in everything, whether we have a family or not. You helped open my eyes to so much, most importantly the fact that I can belong. That we belong together.'

Her brow pinched. 'But you do want a family of your own?'

His expression melted. 'Very much. But only with you.'

With curious people milling around, he pulled a jewellery box from his trouser pocket. When the clasp sprang open, the sun hit the rock and threw back a halo of shifting coloured light.

Oh. My.

'I should've thought to present this when I asked you the first time,' he said as he took her hand. 'But now I'm asking again.' His eyes searched hers. 'Celeste, will you marry me?'

She took a breath.

She'd wanted to know what her future held, but the future was constantly unfolding. All she knew for certain was that she loved this man with everything she was and would ever be. He was right. It was up to them both—two halves of the whole—to move forward together and make certain *they* worked.

She cupped his strong jaw and committed her heart. 'I'd love to marry you. I love you, Ben.' So very much.

Beaming, he slipped the ring on her finger. He gathered her near, but before they sealed her acceptance with a kiss she needed to say—

'I'd like to have a garden ceremony. Is that okay with you?'

He smiled. 'That's fine.' He brought her close again.

'And I think we should make a pact not to work on weekends. All work and no play…'

'A couple needs time together.' He nodded. 'Done.'

Hugging her extra tight, he slanted his mouth over hers. Her hand shot up, blocking his lips from capturing hers.

'Ben, there's one more thing…'

He caught her hand and smiled a sexy smile that made everything but him, and his obvious love for her, fade away. 'Honey, now would be a good time to let me kiss you so we can get on with our happily ever after.'

She smiled. He was right.

So she did.

EPILOGUE

Three years later.

SITTING at her home-office desk, Celeste clicked open the appropriate spreadsheet and typed the long-time client's name in the 'special order' header.

She collected the handpiece and set it to her ear again. 'So, you'd like lilies and freesias on the tables. No, I think that will work beautifully for a birthday celebration. Special bouquets for the mums? I love it. I have their favourites on file—'

A soft cry caught her ear and Celeste stilled.

'Nicole, sorry, can I call you back?' She laughed. 'Yes, it's the baby. I knew you'd understand. I'll email a price first thing in the morning.'

After disconnecting, Celeste rolled back her chair and headed for the adjoining room.

Star Arrangements was going ahead in leaps and bounds. Awards, international orders, A-list clients, as well as a number of charities she regularly helped with special events and sponsorships. All her goals regarding business had been achieved. But she'd fulfilled another, even more amazing dream.

She eased back the gliding doors and hurried through the semi darkness to her gorgeous one-year-old daughter. Standing in her cot, holding a rung with one tiny hand, rubbing a sleepy eye with the other, Ava Krystal yawned and grumbled. But when she saw her visitor, her face lit up.

'Mum-mum.'

Heart so full it sometimes ached, Celeste collected her baby at the same time the second set of adjoining doors slid open.

Ben strode in, surveyed the shadowed room, then smiled seeing mother with child.

He joined them and tickled Ava's chin. 'Hey, sweetie. You're supposed to be asleep.' He kissed his wife on the lips, his mouth lingering before he drew reluctantly away. 'You finish what you're doing. I can put her back to sleep.'

Still tingling from his kiss, Celeste caught the time on the unicorn clock on the dresser. Ten past eight. That late!

Ava stretched, reaching one hand out towards Daddy while holding onto her mummy's hair with the other. Celeste kissed her baby's chubby cheek. 'It's fine. I'm well and truly done for the day.'

She was glad tomorrow was Friday; she would work an hour in the morning, then it was family time right through until Tuesday. With Ben's chock-a-block investment portfolio, he mostly worked from home as well, organising his hours largely around family needs. Saturday they planned to go to the zoo—a first for little Ava. A first for Ben, too.

She finger-combed Ava's blonde curls. Knowing the game, with some indecipherable word, Ava tried to catch her mother's hand. Laughing, Celeste softly bopped her baby's nose.

Wanting to join in, Ben had put out his arms at the same time his cell phone rang. He checked the screen, then thumbed a button and clipped the phone back on his belt.

'You can see to that.' Celeste cuddled Ava, who cuddled back. 'I'll read Munchkin her favourite book.'

Ben's broad-shouldered silhouette crossed to the bookshelf. 'New York can wait. We'll both read to Ava.'

Liking the idea, Celeste moved to the comfy twin couch in the corner. Ben joined them and ten minutes after reading about fairies and magic mice, Ava was sleeping again.

Gazing down at his daughter, Ben looped an arm around Celeste's shoulder and absently twirled a wave with his finger. 'I can't wait till she's old enough to throw a ball,' he whispered.

She let her head rock back and his fingers strummed more of her hair, then settled on her shoulder. So nice.

'I'll leave that to you,' she whispered back. 'I've got my hand up for painting lessons.'

'I'm a whiz at stick figures, if that's any help.'

She looked over. 'It's not.'

His eyes turned hot and he grinned. 'You know what else I'm a whiz at?'

She shrugged, playing dumb. He moved close to nuzzle her ear and delicious longing kicked off through her veins, sweeping like a storm through her body.

She closed her eyes and sighed. 'Oh, yes, I remember now.'

His lips trailed her neck. 'Let's put the baby to bed.'

Carefully they moved together to the cot. Celeste lay Ava down, Ben tucked her in. So strong yet caring beside her, he looped an arm around her waist and drew her near.

'I love being a dad.'

Smiling, Celeste leant into him, forever thankful they'd believed in their love and had become engaged then married. They worked everything out together and it worked very well. Gerard, Rhyll and Ben's siblings were regular visitors to their home, just as Rodney, Suzanne and dear little Tiegan were. In fact, Tiegan stayed over at least one night a month. She'd asked to stay the whole weekend next time, and everyone, including Ava, had cheered.

Past the cot, the curtains were drawn apart. Beyond the wall-to-wall window, the night sky twinkled unbelievably bright.

'Any falling stars?' he asked.

For some reason Celeste thought of PLM, which she'd sold not long before they'd been married. The proceeds were in a bank account, ready for Ava when she reached twenty-one. Anita would have approved.

She sighed and burrowed into her husband's strong arm and chest. 'I don't need falling stars. There's nothing more I could wish for.'

He turned her into his embrace and, angling her chin, kissed her with all the emotion she also felt burning inside—passion, deepest longing, made stronger by trust and respect.

When his mouth gradually left hers, he searched her eyes. 'I love you.'

She smiled. 'I love you, too.'

It was that simple. And tonight, tomorrow—for the rest of their lives—nothing would matter more.

THE ITALIAN'S
NEW-YEAR
MARRIAGE WISH

SARAH MORGAN

CHAPTER ONE

'I want a divorce, I want a divorce, I want a divorce...'

Amy recited the words in her head as the taxi wound its way along the small country roads that led towards the North Cornish coast. The snow that had fallen overnight had dusted fields, trees and bushes with a wintry layer of white that now glistened and sparkled under the bright early morning sunshine. It promised to be a perfect day—perfect for people who weren't about to end their marriage.

She felt sicker than she'd ever felt in her life and the brief glimpse of the sea in the distance increased the tension in her stomach until it felt as though she'd swallowed a loop of knotted rope. No amount of logical reasoning or deep breathing produced the desired feeling of calm and suddenly Amy wished she hadn't chosen to come in person. But what else could she have done when he'd refused to respond to her letters or phone calls?

He'd left her no choice.

Staring out of the window at the familiar landmarks, she admitted to herself that his protracted silence had surprised her. It was so unlike him. He was Italian after all, and she'd braced herself for an ongoing display of simmering, volcanic passion.

Marco was single-minded and determined. A man who knew what he wanted from life and took it.

Which just went to prove that he clearly hadn't wanted her.

Amy felt her throat close and she swallowed hard, controlling the tears, aware that she was being completely illogical. It wasn't as if she'd *wanted* him to put up a fight. It would have made it so much harder to do what had to be done.

Amy curled her hands tightly over the edge of her seat. She wanted to tell the taxi driver to turn round and take her back to the station but she knew that she couldn't give in to that impulse. If she didn't do this now then she'd only have to do it later and she'd already put it off as long as possible.

It was time to finally end their marriage.

She was so lost in thought that it took a moment for her to realise that the taxi driver was speaking to her. 'I'm sorry? Did you say something?'

The taxi driver glanced in his mirror. 'Just wondering if you live in Penhally.'

Amy managed a polite smile. 'No.' She consciously relaxed her hands. 'Not any more. I used to, before…' *Before her entire life had fallen apart.* 'I lived here for a while.'

'So…' He drove carefully down a road still white with snow. 'I expect you're home to celebrate New Year with your family? Are you staying long?'

No family. No celebrations.

'It's just a short visit,' she said huskily. 'I'm here until this evening. My train is at eight o'clock.'

Which left her just enough time to confront her husband and say, 'I want a divorce.' And then she would never see Penhally again.

'Well, keep an eye on the weather. Can you believe that it snowed again last night? I mean, when did we last have snow like this on the coast? When was it last this cold?' He shook his head. 'Global warming, that's what it is. Our entire climate has gone bonkers. And there are severe storms forecast. Leave plenty of time or you'll find yourself stranded and miss that train.'

Barely listening, Amy glanced out of the window. She'd be leaving Penhally that evening even if it meant walking.

As the taxi turned into the main street, her heart rate doubled, as if her body was instinctively bracing itself for conflict.

She slid down slightly in her seat and then frowned with exasperation and sat up again. *What was she doing?* She was behaving like a fugitive, not a thirty-five-year-old doctor with a responsible career!

But the thought of actually seeing Marco again shredded her self-control, confidence and dignity into tiny pieces. For the past two years she'd dreamed about him, thought about him and cried about him. No matter what she'd been doing, he'd dominated her thoughts, but she'd spared herself the torture of actually bumping into him by taking herself as far away as possible.

Unable to trust herself not to weaken, she hadn't just left the village or the country—she'd left the continent.

'Stop here.' Suddenly anxious that she might bump into Marco before she was ready to see him, she leaned forward. 'Thank you, this is perfect. I can walk from here.' She fumbled in her bag for her purse, paid the taxi driver and slid out of the back of the car, clutching her small bag.

She waited for the taxi to pull away and stood for a moment, staring down the main street of Penhally. It was still too early for the shops to open but Christmas lights twinkled in the windows and decorations glittered and winked. The addition of snow produced a scene that could have been taken straight from a Dickens novel and Amy gave a tiny smile, suddenly feeling more Christmassy than she had over Christmas itself. Memories slid into her head: memories of walking hand in hand with her grandmother, choosing decorations for the Christmas tree; collecting the turkey from the butcher.

She'd always thought that Penhally was a magical place.

Her few happy childhood memories were centred on this Cornish fishing village.

She'd wanted her own children to grow up here.

'Amy? Amy Avanti?'

The voice came from directly behind her and she turned, her palms damp with sweat and her heart pounding frantically against her chest. It was as if she'd been caught shoplifting instead of just returning home unannounced.

'Tony…' She managed a smile even though she was secretly wishing that the landlord of the Smugglers' Inn hadn't chosen this particular moment to walk up the street. 'You're up early.'

'Busy time of year.' The collar of his coat was turned up against the winter chill as he studied her face, a question in his eyes. 'So that's it? I haven't seen you for ages and all you can say is, "You're up early"?'

'Sorry.' Feeling suddenly awkward, Amy huddled deeper into her coat. 'I suppose I don't really know what to say…'

'You always were a woman who listened more than you spoke…' Tony grinned '…which makes a pleasant change. Does Marco know you're home?'

'No.' *She hadn't wanted him forewarned.* Her only hope was to catch him off guard. She was banking on the fact that he'd be so shocked to see her that he wouldn't say much. *Wouldn't make things difficult.* 'It was an impulse thing. We have things to discuss.'

'Well, I heard the Maserati roaring down the street earlier so he's probably already at the surgery. They're busy over there.'

His words brought a disturbingly vivid memory to life. A memory of a hot summer's day two and a half years before when she and Marco had just arrived in Penhally, newly married and full of plans. *Full of hope and optimism.* Marco had taken her for a ride in his beloved Maserati, a car that perfectly matched his testosterone-driven approach to life. He'd driven the car along the coast road, one hand on the wheel, the other laid possessively over the back of her seat, and Amy had been so madly and crazily in love with him that she'd spent the entire trip gazing in disbelief at his profile.

And he'd guessed how she'd felt, of course, because he was a man who knew women and his cool sophistication and greater life experience had just increased her own, deep-seated insecurity.

Why was he with her?

How many times had she asked herself that question? Amy swallowed hard and pushed the thought away. He *wasn't* with her. Not any more. And although it had been her decision, she knew that by leaving she'd simply hastened the inevitable. 'I'm surprised he's driving the Maserati. It always hated cold weather.'

'It still hates cold weather. Last week it died by the side of the road and your husband was gesticulating and letting out a stream of Italian. The entire village was in the bookshop looking up words in the Italian dictionary but we all know that when it comes to his precious car, Marco doesn't always use words that are in the dictionary.' Tony scratched his head. 'I suggested he buy a traditional English car designed to cope with traditional English weather, but he treated that suggestion with the contempt that it probably deserved.'

'I can imagine he wasn't enthusiastic.'

'It's good to see you back, Amy. We were surprised when you went.'

'Yes.' She had no doubt that she'd left the entire village reeling with shock. Marco Avanti just wasn't a man that women left, especially not a plain, ordinary woman like her, who should have been grateful to have attracted the attention of anyone, let alone an Italian heartthrob.

And she hadn't offered an explanation.

How could she? It had all been too personal, too private. *Too devastating.*

'Well, it's good to see you home, even if it's only for a short time. If you hurry, you'll catch Marco before he starts surgery. He's pretty busy. I expect you heard about Lucy? She had her baby early and so now they're a doctor down.'

Were they?

She hadn't had news of Penhally for a year, not since that one, solitary letter she'd received from Kate Althorp, the practice manager, who had once been her friend.

'They must be busy.' Which made it better for her. Marco wouldn't have time to argue or make things difficult. She was going to walk into the surgery, say what needed to be said and then leave before he had time to compose arguments. Hopefully he'd be too wrapped up in the needs of his patients to be particularly bothered about an almost ex-wife.

Amy shivered slightly, her breath leaving clouds in the freezing air. 'I'll see you later, Tony.'

'Make sure you do. Pop into the Smugglers' for a drink before you leave.'

'Yes.' She smiled, knowing that she wouldn't. What was the point of exposing herself to gossip for the sake of one drink when the entire liquid contents of the pub wouldn't be enough to dull the pain of seeing Marco Avanti again?

At the other end of the village in the state-of-the-art GP surgery that served the local community, Marco Avanti lounged in his chair, staring with brooding concentration at the computer screen on his desk. 'Kate?' he called through the open door. 'Didn't you say that the blood results for Lily Baxter had come through?'

'We haven't had time to enter them on the system yet.' Kate walked into the room, carrying a mug of coffee. 'With Lucy going on early maternity leave, we've been concentrating on finding a locum. Being one doctor down over the Christmas period just doesn't work. I found four more grey hairs when I woke up this morning.' She moved a stack of journals and put the coffee on his desk. 'Here, drink this. You're going to need it. It's going to take you until this evening to get through the amount of patients booked in today.'

The pungent, seductive aroma of fresh coffee filled the air and Marco gave an appreciative groan. 'You made that for me? Truly, you're an angel, *amore*.' He curled long, strong fingers around the mug and lifted it, the smell penetrating the clouds of tiredness that threatened to fog his brain. '*Tutto bene*? Everything OK? Tell me the worst. The village has been consumed by an attack of cholera? Plague? Everyone is queuing to see me, no?'

'Don't even joke about it. And as for the queue…' Kate smiled wearily. 'You don't want to know. Just take them one at a time and if you're still here tonight, I'll bring you a sleeping bag.'

'Just make sure the sleeping bag contains a warm, willing woman,' he drawled, and Kate smiled.

'You're incorrigible.' She moved towards the door and Marco put the mug on his desk.

'Did you find time to call the garage about the Maserati?'

'Yes. They're coming in a minute to see to it. Give me the keys and then I won't have to disturb you.'

Grateful that there was one less thing that he had to manage, Marco reached into the pockets of the coat that he'd thrown over the back of the chair and tossed her the keys. 'Here. *Grazie*, Kate. Not only are you *molto belissima*, you are also efficient.'

'It's called time management. If I sort out your car, then you spend more time with patients. It's a solution that works for everyone, so you don't need to waste your Italian charm on me.'

'Why is it a waste?' Enjoying the brief distraction of mean-ingless banter, Marco leaned back and gave her a slow smile. 'Run away with me, Kate. We could both leave this cold, windy place and live in sin in my beautiful Italy. I own a *palazzo* in Venice, right on the edge of the canal.' He watched as a shadow flickered across her eyes.

Then she noticed his gaze and blushed slightly, smiling quickly as if she didn't want him to know that she was unhappy.

'Maybe I will leave,' she said softly. 'Maybe it is time I did something different. But not with you. I'm not that stupid. My New Year's resolution is never to get involved with a man who is still in love with another woman and you fall into that category.'

Marco felt every muscle in his body tense but carefully controlled his facial expression. 'The only woman I love,' he purred softly, 'is currently parked outside this surgery with an engine problem. *She* is my baby.' He kept his tone neutral but Kate gave a faint smile and shook her head slowly.

'You don't fool me, Marco. Whenever Amy's name is mentioned, you always appear so cool and in control, but I know that you're not. What's happening under that cloak you put between yourself and the world?'

Nothing that he had any intention of sharing.

'You want to know what's under my cloak? This isn't the time or the place, *tesoro*.' How had they suddenly shifted from talking about her problems to talking about his? He teased her gently, swiftly and skilfully manoeuvring the conversation back to safer ground. 'I have surgery starting in less than five minutes and that won't be enough to do justice to your beauty. When I make love to a woman, I need at least twenty-four hours.'

'Stop it or I'll have to throw a bucket of water over you!' Kate gave a reluctant laugh. 'It's bad enough that all the women in the village are in love with you. They're all waiting for your broken heart to heal so that they can pounce.'

'My heart isn't broken.' Marco reached forward and checked something on his computer. 'In fact, all my organs are intact and in perfect working order.'

'Well, don't tell anyone that! There'll be a stampede and we're busy enough here.' Kate's smile faded. 'I wish I was more like you. How do you do it? You and Amy were so in love—'

Taken aback by her frank, personal comment, Marco uttered a sharp expletive in Italian but then noticed the haunting sadness in Kate's eyes. With ruthless determination he pushed aside dark, swirling thoughts of his wife and focused his attention on his colleague. 'Kate...' With an effort, he kept his voice gentle. 'This is not about me, is it? It's about you. About you and Nick. Perhaps you should just tell him that you love him. Be honest.'

'What? I don't...' Flustered and embarrassed, Kate lifted a hand to her chest and shook her head in swift denial. 'What makes you say that? Marco, for goodness' sake...'

'Nick is the senior partner and my colleague,' Marco drawled softly, wondering why relationships were so incredibly complicated. 'You are also my colleague. It is hard to miss the tension between the two of you. Often I am in the middle of it.'

'Nick and I have known each other a long time.'

'Sì, I know that.' Marco sighed. 'You're in love with him. Tell him.'

'Even if you were right, which you're not,' Kate added quickly, her shoulders stiffening, 'you think I should just knock on the door of his consulting room and say, "I love you"?'

'Why not? It's the truth. Speaking as a man, I can tell you that we prefer a direct approach. Feminine games arc an exhausting optional extra. If a woman wants to tell me that she loves me...' he shrugged expressively and lounged deeper in his chair '...why would I stop her?'

Kate laughed in disbelief. 'Sorry, but I'm just trying to picture Nick's face if I were to follow your advice.'

Marco watched her for a moment, noting the dark shadows under her eyes. 'Your problem is that you have fallen in love with an Englishman and English men know nothing about love. They are closed up, cold, unemotional. Give them twenty-four hours to make love to a woman and they would spend twenty-three of those hours watching football on the television.' As he'd planned, his words made her smile.

'Perhaps you're right.' She straightened her shoulders, suddenly looking less like a vulnerable woman and more like an efficient practice manager. 'You're a good friend. And for a man, you're very emotionally advanced. It would have been much simpler if I could have fallen for a hot Italian instead of a cold Englishman.'

Marco thought of his own disastrous marriage. 'Hot Italians can get it wrong, too,' he said wearily. *Badly wrong.* 'And Nick isn't really cold, just badly hurt. He carries a lot of guilt. A lot of pain. This has been a bad time in his life.'

A bad time in both their lives.

Given the events of the last few years, it was amazing that he and his partner were still managing to run a GP practice.

Reaching for his coffee, he cleared his mind of the dark thoughts that threatened to cloud the day.

Not now.

He wasn't going to think about that now.

It was the festive period and he had a punishing workload ahead of him.

There was going to be no time to brood or even think.

Which was exactly the way he wanted it.

Amy paused outside the surgery. The fresh sea air stung her cheeks and from above came the forlorn shriek of a seagull.

She had ten minutes before Marco was due to start seeing patients and she lost her chance to speak to him.

Ten minutes to finally end a marriage.

It would be more than enough time to say what had to be

said. And he wouldn't be able to prolong the meeting because he would have patients waiting to see him.

Without giving herself time to change her mind, she pushed open the door and walked into Reception. The sudden warmth hit her and she walked up to the desk and saw Kate Althorp in conversation with the receptionist.

Once, they'd been friends even though the other woman was at least ten years her senior. Had that friendship ended with her sudden departure? Amy had no doubt that everyone in Penhally would have judged her harshly and she could hardly blame them for that. She'd given them no reason not to.

'Do you have an appointment?' Crisp, efficient and obviously busy despite the time of day, Kate glanced up and her eyes widened in recognition. '*Amy!* Oh, my goodness.' Abandoning her conversation, she walked round the desk towards Amy, clearly at a loss to know what to say. 'You're *home*? I thought you were still in Africa with that medical charity!'

'Not any more. Hello, Kate.'

Kate hesitated and then stepped forward and gave her a warm hug. 'It's good to see you, Amy. Really. Does Marco know you're here? Why didn't you call?'

'I was hoping— Marco doesn't know I'm here but I'd like to see him for a moment.' Amy cringed as she listened to herself. She hadn't seen her husband for two years and she was making it sound as though she'd just popped in to ask whether he'd be home in time for dinner.

Doubt flickered across Kate's face as she glanced in the direction of the consulting rooms. 'He's about to start surgery and we've been incredibly busy because—'

'I know about Lucy and it's just for a moment,' Amy urged, unable to keep the note of desperation out of her voice. If Kate refused to let her see Marco that would mean waiting, and Amy wasn't sure that her courage would survive any sort of wait. She had to do this now. *Right now.* 'Please, Kate.' Unaccustomed to asking for help from another person, she stumbled over the words and the older woman looked at her for a moment, her responsibilities as practice manager clearly conflicting with her desire to help a friend so obviously in need.

After a moment of hesitation, Kate walked back round the desk and reached for the phone, her eyes still on Amy's face. 'I'll phone through to him and tell him that you're—'

'No!' Amy was already walking towards Marco's consulting room. 'I'll just go straight in.' Quickly, before she had time to change her mind.

Her heart pounding rhythmically against her chest, Amy tapped on his door.

'*Sì*, come in.'

The sound of his smooth, confident voice made her stomach lurch and she closed her eyes briefly. Despite his enviable fluency in English, no one could ever have mistaken Marco Avanti for anything other than an Italian and his voice stroked her nerve endings like a caress.

Her palm was damp with nerves as she clutched the door-handle and turned it.

He was just a man like any other.

She wasn't going to go weak at the knees. She wasn't going to notice anything about him. She was past all that. She was just going to say what needed to be said and then leave.

Ten minutes, she reminded herself. She just had to survive ten minutes and not back down. And then she'd be on the train back to London.

She opened the door and stepped into the room. 'Hello, Marco.' Her heart fluttered like the wings of a captive butterfly as she forced herself to look at him. 'I wanted to have a quick word before you start surgery.'

His dark eyes met hers and heat erupted through her body, swift and deadly as a forest fire. From throat to pelvis she burned, her reaction to him as powerful as ever. Helplessly, she dug her fingers into her palms.

A man like any other? Had she really believed that, even for a moment? Marco was nothing like any other man.

She'd had two years to prepare herself for this moment, so why did the sight of him drive the last of her breath from her body? What was it about him? Yes, he was handsome but other men were handsome and she barely noticed them. Marco was different. Marco was the embodiment of everything it was to be male. He was strong, confident and unashamedly macho and no woman with a pulse could look at him and not want him.

And for a while he'd been hers.

She looked at him now, unable to think of anything but the hungry, all-consuming passion that had devoured them both.

His powerful body was ominously still, but he said nothing. He simply leaned slowly back in his chair and watched her in brooding silence, his long fingers toying with the pen that he'd been using when she'd entered the room.

Desperately unsettled, Amy sensed the slow simmer of emotion that lay beneath his neutral expression.

What wouldn't she have given to possess even a tiny fraction of his cool?

'We need to talk to each other.' She stayed in the doorway, her hands clasped nervously in front of her, a shiver passing through her body as the atmosphere in the room suddenly turned icy cold.

Finally he spoke. 'You have chosen an odd time of day for a reunion.'

'This isn't a reunion. We have things to discuss, you know we do.'

His gaze didn't flicker. 'And I have thirty sick patients to see before lunchtime. You shouldn't need to ask where my priorities lie.'

No, she didn't need to ask. His skill and dedication as a doctor was one of the qualities that had attracted her to him in the first place.

His handsome face was hard and unforgiving and she felt her insides sink with misery.

What had she expected?

He was hardly going to greet her warmly, was he? Not after the way she'd treated him. *Not after the things she'd let him think about her.* 'I didn't have any choice but to come and see you, Marco. You didn't answer my letters.'

'I didn't like the subject matter.' There was no missing the hard edge to his tone. 'Write about something that interests me and I'll consider replying. And now you need to leave because my first patient is waiting.'

'No.' Panic slid through her and she took a little step forward. 'We need to do this. I know you're upset, but—'

'Upset?' One dark eyebrow rose in sardonic appraisal. 'Why would you possibly think that?'

Her breathing was rapid. 'Please, don't play games—it isn't going to help either of us. Yes, I left, but it was the right thing to do, Marco. It was the right thing for both of us. I'm sure you can understand that now that some time has passed.'

'I understand that you walked out on our marriage. You think "upset"…' his accent thickened as he lingered on the word. 'You think "upset" is an accurate description of my feelings on this subject?'

Amy felt the colour touch her cheeks. The truth was that she had absolutely no insight into his feelings. She'd never really known what he had truly been feeling at any point in their relationship and she hadn't been around to witness his reaction to her departure. If he had been upset then she assumed that it would have been because she'd exposed him to the gossip of a small community, or possibly because he'd had a life plan and she'd ruined it. Not because he'd loved her, because she knew that had never been the case. How could he have loved her? What had she ever been able to offer a man like Marco Avanti?

Especially not once she'd discovered—

Unable to cope with that particular thought at the moment, Amy lifted her chin and ploughed on. 'I can see that you're angry and I don't blame you, but I didn't come here to argue. We can make this easy or we can make it difficult.'

'And I'm sure you're choosing easy.' The contempt in his tone stung like vinegar on an open wound. 'You chose to walk away rather than sort out a problem. Isn't that what you're good at?'

'Not every problem has a solution, Marco!' Frustrated and realising that if she wasn't careful she risked revealing more than she wanted to reveal, she moved closer to the desk. 'You have every right to be upset, but what we need now is to sort out the future. I just need you to agree to the divorce. Then you'll be free to…' *Marry another woman?* The words stuck in her throat.

'*Accidenti*, am I right in understanding that you have interrupted my morning surgery to *ask me for a divorce*?' He rose to his feet, his temper bubbling to the surface, a dangerous glint in his molten dark eyes. 'It is bad enough that I am expected to diagnose a multitude of potentially serious illnesses in a five-minute consultation, but now my wife decides that that in that same ridiculous time frame we are going to end our relationship. This is your idea of a joke, no?'

She'd forgotten how tall he was, how imposing. He topped six feet two and his shoulders were broad and powerful. Looking at him now, she had to force herself not to retreat to the safety of Reception. 'It's not a joke and if I'm interrupting your surgery, it's your fault. You wouldn't answer my letters. I had no other way of getting in touch with you. And this needn't take long.'

He gripped the edge of the desk and his knuckles whitened.

'Do you really think you can leave without explanation and then walk back in here and end our marriage with a five-minute conversation?' His eyes blazed with anger and his voice rose. *'Is that what you think?'*

Startled by his unexpected loss of control, Amy flinched. *She hadn't thought he'd cared so much.* Or was he angry because she'd chosen to confront him in his place of work? 'Don't shout—there are patients in Reception. They'll gossip.'

'Gossip? It's a little late to be worrying about gossip.' But he dropped back into his seat, threw her a dark, smouldering glance and then raked both hands through his glossy, dark hair. Several strands immediately flopped back over his fore-head and she felt her breath catch.

The yearning to touch him was so powerful that she had to clasp her hands behind her back to prevent herself from reaching out and sliding her hands into his hair.

As if sensing her inner struggle, his gaze caught hers and held for a moment, his eyes darkening in a way that was ach-ingly familiar. The atmosphere in the room shifted danger-ously and awareness throbbed between them, drawing them into a tense, silent communication that said far more than words ever could.

Amy felt the instant response of her body. She felt her stomach quiver and her limbs warm.

It was still there, that inexplicable attraction that had pulled them together with magnetic force from the moment they'd met.

Which meant that she had to get this over with. Quickly. Trying to ignore the insidious curl of feminine awareness deep in her pelvis, Amy gritted her teeth and backed towards the door.

This was why she'd gone so far away. She'd known that only by putting an ocean between them would she be able to resist the unbelievably powerful chemistry that knotted them together.

She had to leave.
Fast.

'Marco—it's all history, now. Let's not make this more painful than it has to be.'

'You're the one who made the whole thing painful, Amy.' His voice was suddenly dangerously quiet, but before he could say any more the door opened and Kate flew in.

'Marco, you have to see little Michelle right now! I've explained to your first patient that they're going to have to wait. I'm sorry.' She threw an apologetic look towards Amy. 'Is there any chance that you can grab a cup of coffee upstairs in the staffroom or something?'

Amy watched as Marco straightened his shoulders and wrenched back control. But his mind obviously wasn't on his work because for the briefest of moments his expression was blank. 'Michelle?' He said the name as if he'd never heard it before and Kate looked momentarily startled, as if detailed explanations were uncommon in their working relationship.

'Yes, Michelle! What's the matter with you?' Then she glanced at Amy and blushed slightly, as if she'd just realised what might be the matter. 'Michelle *Watson*. Carol said that she was off colour last night but she's suddenly gone downhill. She called an ambulance but they said that they'd be twenty minutes because they're stuck behind a gritting lorry. Honestly, Europe can have feet of snow and manage fine, but if we have so much as a dusting the entire country grinds to a halt. I'm tempted to go and organise them myself.'

'Michelle Watson. Of course. Michelle.' Marco uncoiled his lean, powerful body and rose to his feet again but there were lines of strain around his eyes. 'Bring her in.'

'Watson?' Amy remembered that Carol Watson had just delivered when she'd left and she glanced at Marco as Kate hurried out of the room. 'Carol's baby girl?'

'She isn't a baby any more.' His tone was flat and he didn't glance in her direction as if he was trying to get his mind firmly on the job. 'You've been gone two years and I don't have time to brief you on everything that has been happening in the village during your long absence.' He moved across the consulting room. 'You left, Amy. You made your choice.'

'Yes, but—' She broke off, wrestling against an instinctive desire to defend herself. What would he say if she told him the truth? Told him that she'd *had* to leave. *That she'd done it for him.* But she knew that she couldn't. She could never, ever tell him the truth because if he knew the truth then everything would become even more complicated. 'That's right.' She felt horrible. *Just horrible.* There was so much she wanted to say but she couldn't say any of it. 'I left.' Her voice shook but his swift glance was unsympathetic.

'Go and get a cup of coffee. Or just leave. It's what you're good at.'

'I can't leave until we've talked.'

He yanked open a cupboard and removed a pulse oximeter. 'Then you're going to have to wait until I have time to see you,' he growled. 'I think the current waiting time for an appointment with me is a week. Ask the girls at Reception. They just might be able to fit you in.'

CHAPTER TWO

THE door flew open and Kate hurried back into the room with Carol, who was carrying the toddler wrapped in a soft, pink blanket. A sulky-looking teenager followed them, her pretty face half hidden by a thick layer of make-up.

Amy was on the point of leaving the room and then she looked at the toddler and saw at a glance that Kate had been right to interrupt them. The child was fighting for each breath.

'Oh, Dr Avanti.' There was panic in Carol's voice. 'Thank goodness you're here. She's had this cold and I was up in the night with her and then this morning she just seemed so much worse. Her little chest was heaving so I panicked and called the ambulance but they're stuck on the coast road and you always know what to do so I just thought I'd come and take a chance in case—'

'*Calma*. Try and be calm, Carol.' Marco's voice was gentle and reassuring as his gaze rested on the child, his eyes sharp and observant. 'You did the right thing to come.'

Amy stepped forward, her own problems momentarily forgotten. 'Let me help. What do you want me to do, Marco?'

He glanced at her and then gave a brief nod. 'Let's give her some oxygen straight away.'

Amy located the oxygen and mask. 'Do you want me to set up a nebuliser?'

'To begin with I'll give her a beta 2 agonist via a spacer. It is better at this age than a nebuliser.' He turned back to the child and stroked his hand over the child's neck, palpating the neck muscles with gentle fingers. 'Michelle, what have you been doing, *angelo mia*? Are you worrying your poor mother?'

No one would have guessed that only moments earlier he'd been braced for a fight. All the hardness had gone from his tone and there was no trace of the anger that had been simmering inside him. Instead, he was kind and approachable, his smooth, confident movements removing the panic from the situation.

He'd always been amazing with children, Amy thought numbly as she handed him the oxygen mask. They found his strength reassuring and responded to his gentleness. *Strength and gentleness*. A killer combination. When she'd first met him he'd been working as a paediatrician and his skills in that field were very much in evidence as he assessed the little girl.

To someone who didn't know better it might have looked as though he was simply comforting the child and putting her at ease, but Amy watched the movement of his fingers and the direction of his gaze and knew that in that short space of time he'd checked the little girl's respirations, her pulse rate and the degree of wheezing.

Carol cuddled the child and looked at him helplessly. 'She ate a tiny bit of breakfast and then she was sick everywhere. After that she was just too breathless to eat. I've never seen her this bad.'

The teenager slumped against the wall and rolled her eyes. 'For goodness' sake Mum, stop panicking.' She broke off and coughed a few times. 'You make everything into such a drama.'

'Don't you tell me to stop panicking, Lizzie,' Carol snapped angrily. 'You were giving her breakfast! You should have noticed sooner that she wasn't breathing properly!'

'Well, I'm not a bloody doctor, am I?!' The tone was moody and defiant, but Amy saw the worry in the teenager's eyes and remembered that this was Carol's second marriage. Presumably Lizzie was her child from her previous marriage.

Clearly things weren't altogether harmonious in the household.

'She is here now and that is what is important.' Swiftly but calmly, Marco reached for the hand-held pulse oximeter, attached the probe to the child's finger. 'I want her as quiet as possible so that I can examine her properly. You will have a nice cuddle with your mama, Michelle. I'm going to help you with your breathing, *tesoro*.'

Tesoro.

Trying not to remember that he'd called her the same thing in happier times, Amy looked at the pulse oximeter.

'That's a neat device.' It was typical of Marco to have all the latest technology to hand, she mused silently. Oxygen, spacer, pulse oximeter. He may have chosen to move from paediatrics to general practice but he still insisted on having all the latest equipment.

'It's a very fast and reliable method of obtaining a reading.' He glanced at Carol, immediately offering an explanation. 'It tells me how much oxygen is in her blood. I'd like the level to be higher than it is. I'm going to give her something that will help her breathing.'

Carol's face was white and strained. 'Is it her asthma again?'

'*Sì*, it seems that way. She has had a virus and that can sometimes be a trigger.' He connected a face mask to the mouthpiece of a spacer.

'Michelle, I'm going to put this mask over your nose and mouth and I want you to just breathe normally.' He settled the mask gently over the child's face and actuated the inhaler. 'Just breathe for me now. Good girl. We'll start with this and see if this improves things.'

Michelle stared up at him in terror, her breath coming in rapid, rasping gasps.

Equally terrified, Carol rubbed her back gently. 'It's all right, darling. Dr Avanti is going to make you better. He always does, you know he does.'

The little girl clawed at her face, trying to remove the mask, and Marco gently took her hand and squatted down so that he was level with the child. 'Don't pull it off, *cucciola mia*.' His voice was deep and soothing. 'This mask is going to help you breathe and I want you to try and relax and forget it is there. You're going to listen to me instead of thinking of the mask. The mask is doing magic.' Still stroking the child's fingers with his own, he lifted his head and looked at Carol. 'What's her favourite story?'

'Story? I—I don't know...'

'"Sleeping Beauty",' Lizzie muttered, and Amy glanced towards her, surprised.

So she wasn't as indifferent as she seemed, then.

Assessing Michelle and sensing that Marco was going to choose to put a line in, Amy turned away and prepared an IV tray and then reached into the cupboard for hydrocortisone, which she was sure he was going to need.

'Ah, "Sleeping Beauty". That is my favourite, too.' Marco gave a smile that would have captivated the most cynical princess and stroked the little girl's blonde curls away from her face, his eyes flicking to her chest as he watched her breathing. 'So now I will tell you my version of the story. Once upon a time there was a beautiful princess called Michelle who lived in a wonderful castle by the sea— Amy?' His voice lowered. 'Can you get me a 24-gauge needle and fifty milligrams of hydrocortisone? Normally I would try oral medication but if she's vomiting, we'll go straight to IV.'

Their differences momentarily forgotten, Amy handed him the tray that she'd already prepared and he took it from her, still telling the story. 'Princess Michelle was very loved by her mummy and daddy and they decided to give her a big party for her birthday. Everyone was invited.' He was a natural storyteller, his Italian accent curling around the words as he calmed the child. She looked at him, clearly listening as he spoke, and Marco stroked the back of the little girl's hand, searching for a vein. Then he gave a nod and looked at Amy. 'Can you squeeze for me? Michelle, I'm just going to put a little tube into the back of your hand so that I can give you some extra medicine to make you feel better. More magic.'

Amy stared at Michelle's plump, tiny hand and was suddenly relieved that she wasn't the one searching for a vein.

Carol looked the other way, her teeth clamped on her lower lip. 'There isn't another doctor in the world I'd allow to do this,' she muttered, screwing up her face in trepidation. 'It's only because you used to be a kids' doctor and I know you've done it before. Her hands are so small, let alone her veins. I can't even think about it.'

Amy was inclined to agree.

She never could have chosen paediatrics as a speciality.

But Marco's expression didn't flicker and it was obvious that he wasn't concerned. This was where he excelled—where he was most comfortable. 'And Princess Michelle invited all her friends to her party and her big sister Princess Lizzie, who she loved very much.' He lifted his head briefly and flashed a smile at Lizzie, who blushed furiously under his warm, approving gaze.

'Michelle, you might feel a little scratch now.' The movement of his fingers was deliberate and confident as he slid the tiny needle through the child's skin and checked that he was in the vein. The child barely whimpered and Marco picked up the syringe of hydrocortisone, swiftly checked the ampoule and injected it into the child, barely pausing in his rendition of the story. 'And it was the biggest and the best party that anyone had ever been to. Everyone was in pretty dresses and there was dancing and Princess Lizzie met a handsome prince.'

'Not likely in boring old Penhally,' Lizzie muttered, and then started to cough again.

Marco dropped the empty syringe back onto the tray and lifted his gaze to the teenager. 'The prince was in disguise, passing through on his way home to his castle.' His eyes were amused and Amy watched as Lizzie gave a reluctant smile.

It was impossible not to respond to him, Amy thought helplessly. He charmed everyone, whatever their age. And he did it all while managing a potentially serious asthma attack.

Anyone who said that men were incapable of multi-tasking had never seen Marco dealing with an emergency. Perhaps that was one of the advantages of having spent so long in hospital medicine. Or perhaps he was just the sort of man who coped well under pressure.

Carol was still watching him anxiously. 'Will she have to go to hospital? My husband is waiting at the house to tell the ambulance where we are. Lizzie can run back and tell him what's going on.'

'Why me? Use the phone, Mum!' Lizzie's momentary good humour vanished and her tone was impatient. 'It's freezing out there!'

'Why can't you ever just *help*?' Clearly at the end of her tether, Carol snapped, and then pressed her lips together. 'All you ever think about is yourself!'

'Well someone has to because you obviously don't give a damn about me!'

Carol gasped. 'Elizabeth!!'

'Oh, get off my back!' Coughing again, Lizzie turned and stamped out of the consulting room, slamming the door behind her.

Carol flinched, her face scarlet with embarrassment and anger. 'As if I haven't got enough on my plate,' she said in a shaky voice. 'I'm very sorry about that. I just don't know what's happening to Lizzie. She's undergone a complete personality change over the past few months. She used to be so sweet and loving. And she just adored Michelle. Now it's like living with a hand grenade.'

'She is a teenager,' Amy said quietly, aware that Marco was writing a letter to the hospital and needed to concentrate.

'She explodes at the slightest thing, she's out all hours and I never know where she is. She used to be top of her class and her marks have plummeted.' Carol cuddled Michelle closer. 'And she's been mixing with those awful Lovelace children and everyone knows what *they're* like. I see them on a Saturday night, just hanging around on the streets. I wouldn't be surprised if they're taking drugs...'

Reminded of the complexities of working in a community practice, Amy lifted a hand to her aching head and wondered how Marco managed to stay so relaxed.

He tapped a key on the computer and glanced at Carol. 'Have you spoken to the school about Lizzie?'

'Twice. They just gave me a standard lecture about handling teenage girls.'

The printer whirred into action. 'How bad are her mood swings?'

'Very.'

'I noticed she was coughing.' He took the letter from the printer and signed it. 'How long has she had that?'

'Coughing?' Carol looked a little startled. 'I don't know, really. A while, I think, now you mention it. Just an irritated sort of cough. I even asked her if she was smoking but she just gave me one of her looks and stomped out of the room.'

Marco put the letter in an envelope and handed it to her. 'Lizzie is reaching a difficult age, that's true,' he said softly. 'Not quite a woman but no longer a child. Unsure of who she is. A little rebellion is natural and good.'

'You think that's all it is?' The faith in Carol's eyes surprised Amy. It was quite obvious that the woman was ready to believe anything Marco told her.

'I think we should talk about it properly when there is more time.' He slipped his pen back into his pocket. 'For now your priority is Michelle. She has not improved as much as I would have liked so I want her to go to the hospital. In all probability she will be fine and we could monitor her here, but if we send her home, you will be worried.' He gave an expressive shrug that betrayed his Latin heritage. 'And you have already had enough worry for one day. So, we will send her to the hospital and then they can do the worrying. That will leave you free to give some attention to Lizzie.'

'I don't know what attention to give her,' Carol said flatly. 'It's like communicating with a firework. One minute she's inanimate, the next she's exploding in my face. I find it easier coping with toddlers than teenagers.'

Marco listened and then gave a lopsided smile. 'Being a mother is the hardest job in the world because your skills have to change all the time. You are a good mother and good mothers always find a way—remember that.'

Amy saw the gratitude on Carol's face and turned away for a moment, struggling with a painful lump in her throat. Why couldn't Marco have been careless and unfeeling? Even in a crisis he could see the bigger picture. He didn't just deal with the small child—he also handled the teenager and the worried mother.

She'd needed him to be unskilled and insensitive.

It would have made everything so much easier.

As it was, just ten minutes in his company had confirmed her biggest dread. That two years of self-enforced absence had made no difference to her feelings. She would love Marco Avanti until she took her dying breath.

Marco picked up the phone and spoke to the paediatrician at the hospital, keeping one eye on Michelle. He was concerned that her breathing didn't seem to be improving as much as he would have liked.

Had he missed something?

Was there something else he should have done?

He didn't usually have reason to question his medical skills but neither was he usually expected to handle an emergency while dealing with the unexpected appearance of his wife. Or was she now an ex-wife? It was obvious that she considered their relationship dead. And so had he. Until she'd walked into the room and asked for a divorce.

Seriously unsettled for the first time in his adult life, he ground his teeth, under no illusions that his concentration had been severely tested by Amy's sudden and unannounced arrival. Given that she clearly had no intention of leaving until she'd said what she'd come to say, he needed to somehow forget that she was there.

Forcing his mind back to Michelle, he ended the phone call and then mentally ran through the algorithm for handling an acute asthma attack in a toddler and assured himself that he'd done everything that should be done.

The child needed to be in hospital. And his wife was watching him, waiting for the right moment to ask him for a divorce.

Why now? Why did she have to pick what must be the busiest week of the year? And not only that, but they were a doctor down. He didn't have the time to argue with her. Their relationship was in its death throes and he didn't have the time to try and save it.

Which had presumably been her intention. Why else would she have picked this particular moment out of all the moments that might have presented themselves over the past two years? Was she hoping that the pressures of work would make him easier on her?

Was she hoping that he'd just sign on the dotted line and sever all ties? Kill everything they'd ever shared?

The door opened and Kate bustled in. 'Carol, your husband redirected the ambulance and he's holding on right now on the phone. I have a paramedic in Reception, wanting to know if they're still needed. Are you planning to send Michelle to the hospital, Dr Avanti?'

Carol looked at Marco. 'You really think she should go in?'

Pushing aside his own problems, Marco gave a decisive nod. 'Definitely. I called the paediatrician and she's expecting Michelle. They'll admit her overnight, monitor her breathing and then assess her in the morning. We might need to change her medication. I'll speak to her once she's had a chance to examine Michelle.'

Carol closed her eyes briefly. 'It's so hard,' she whispered. 'She's so tiny and it's so, so scary. Worry, worry, worry, that's all I seem to do. I just want her to live a normal life and be like any other toddler. What's going to happen when she goes to school?'

'Carol, I know that you're worried but you have to take it one step at a time—isn't that the phrase you English use?' He placed a hand on her shoulder, his touch gentle. 'I will discuss her management with the hospital and you and I will watch her and see how she goes as winter progresses. And if, from time to time, she has a few problems then we will deal with those problems together. We are a team. If you have a worry, you make an appointment to see me and we sort it out. And soon we will find time to talk about your Lizzie.'

Carol's eyes filled and she bit her lip. 'Don't be kind because you'll make me cry.' She pressed a hand to her mouth. 'Sorry. You must think I'm such an idiot.'

'I think you're a loving mother who is tired and worried,' Marco said quietly, his gaze flicking to Michelle. An uneasy feeling stirred inside him. The little girl was pale and her respiratory rate was more rapid than he would have liked. Making a swift decision, he looked at Kate. 'I want to go in the ambulance with her.'

The practice manager didn't manage to hide her dismay. 'You're leaving in the middle of your surgery?'

Aware that Carol was listening, Marco tried humour. 'Not in the middle,' he drawled, reaching for his bag. 'I haven't actually started yet.'

Kate shook her head, despair in her voice. 'Marco, we have patients queuing halfway back to the next county. Dr Tremayne and Dr Lovak are already seeing patients and with Lucy gone—'

'We have a sick child here who needs my care,' Marco reminded her softly, dropping a bronchodilator into his bag.

Kate gave him a desperate look and then sighed. 'Of course. Go with Michelle. That has to be the priority. We'll manage here. Somehow.'

Carol glanced between them, her expression guilty. 'I'm *really* sorry.'

'You have no reason to be sorry,' Marco said swiftly. 'In this practice each patient gets the attention they need when they most need it. The patients will not mind because they know that next time it could be them.'

Judging from the expression on Kate's face she wasn't convinced and Marco thought for a moment, aware that he was leaving her and the receptionists to cope alone with the flak from the patients. His gaze settled on Amy, who stood in the corner of his consulting room, looking awkward and out of place. 'Amy can take the rest of my surgery. That will save Nick and Dragan having to see extra patients.'

Judging from her shocked expression he might as well have suggested that she run naked along the harbour wall.

'I— *Me*?'

'Yes, you. You're a qualified GP.' He added a few more bits to his bag. 'You happen to have arrived when we're in crisis. I'm sure you won't mind helping out.'

'But—'

'What a brilliant idea! That would be fantastic,' Kate enthused, her relief evident as she ushered Carol towards the door, catching the pink blanket before it slid to the floor. 'I'll help Carol and Michelle into the ambulance while you pack what you need, Marco. Join us when you're ready. Then I'll come back and brief you, Amy. You can use Lucy's consulting room.'

Amy's expression was close to panic. 'But I'm not staying—' The door closed behind Kate and Amy flinched and turned to Marco, her hands spread in a silent plea. 'Marco, this is ridiculous. I just need to talk to you for five minutes, that's all.'

'As you can clearly see, I don't have five minutes. I don't have one minute. I can't talk to you until the patients have been seen.' Strengthened by the prospect of a brief respite before the inevitable confrontation, Marco snapped his bag shut with a force that threatened the lock. 'If you want to talk to me, help with surgery. Then perhaps I'll find time to talk to you.'

'But—'

He lifted the bag. 'That's my price for a conversation.'

'We *have* to talk, you know we do.' She wrapped her arms around her waist and then let them drop to her sides and gave a sigh. 'You don't leave me with much choice.'

'About as much choice as you gave me when you walked away from our relationship.' He glanced out of the window, remembered the snow and reached for his coat. Suddenly he couldn't wait to put distance between them. He was angry with her. *And angry with himself for still caring so much after two years.* He needed space. Needed perspective. He needed to work out what he was going to do. 'It's non-negotiable, Amy. If you want to talk to me, stay and do the surgery. When the patients have been seen, I might find time to listen to you.'

'If you can't find anything, just let me know.' Kate threw open a few more cupboards and waved a hand vaguely. 'Everything you're likely to need should be here. And if you need any inside information on the patients, Nick should be able to help. Press 2 on your phone and you're straight through to him.'

Nick Tremayne, the senior partner. Although he was a good friend of Marco's, Amy had always found him more than a little intimidating.

What would he think of her being there? Just after she'd left Marco, Nick himself had suffered tragedy when his wife, Annabel, had died suddenly.

'How is Nick? I was so shocked when I received your letter telling me the news.'

'Yes.' Kate slipped a pile of blank prescriptions into the printer, her face expressionless. 'We were all shocked. I thought you ought to know, although finding an address for you was a nightmare. Even the medical charity you were working for didn't seem able to guarantee that they could get it to you.'

'I was moving around. It took about six months to catch up with me.' Amy sank into the chair, remembering how awful she'd felt when she'd read the news. 'I wrote to him. Just a card. Is he—is he doing all right?'

Kate reached for a pen from the holder on the desk. 'I suppose so. He just carries on. Doesn't give much away. Lucy's baby will help, I suppose. They've called her Annabel.'

'Oh, that's lovely,' Amy said softly. 'I bumped into Tony earlier. He said the baby was premature?'

'Yes, she was born a few weeks early but she's doing fine by all accounts. Still in Special Care but once they're happy with her feeding, she should be home.'

'And Nick—has he met anyone else?'

The pen that Kate was holding slipped to the floor. 'He dates plenty of people.' She stooped and picked up the pen, her voice slightly muffled. 'But I don't think any of them are serious. Are you ready? I'll send in your first patient.'

Amy slid a hand over the desk and looked at the computer, feeling as though she was on a runaway train. She'd come to talk to Marco and here she was sitting in a consulting room, preparing to take a surgery. What had happened to her ability to say no? 'How many patients?'

'You don't want to know but let's just say that Marco is a very, very popular doctor around here. If Dragan Lovak gets any cancellations, I'll send a few his way.' Kate smiled. 'This is so kind of you, Amy. We really appreciate it. I've been trying unsuccessfully to find locum cover for the past few weeks but no one wants to spend Christmas and New Year in freezing Cornwall at short notice. You're a lifesaver.'

A lifesaver? Amy bit back a hysterical laugh. She didn't feel like a lifesaver. She felt like the one who was drowning. 'I'm not sure how much use I'll be. I won't know any of the patients.' She felt a brief flutter of anxiety. During her time in Africa, her focus had been on tropical diseases. Was she capable of running a busy surgery?

'You're a qualified doctor. That makes you of use.' Kate leaned across and flicked on the computer on her desk. 'Hit this key to get everything up on the computer. You'll be fine. You've been working in deepest Africa for the past two years so the problems of a little Cornish town should seem like a walk in the park by comparison.'

Suddenly she craved Africa. *Craved distance from Marco.* Amy closed her eyes briefly and tried not to think about what was going to happen when he returned. It was clear that there was no way the conversation was going to be easy. 'Kate, how do I call the patients?'

'There's a buzzer right there.' Kate moved a pile of papers. 'List of hospital consultants in your top drawer, just in case you need to refer anyone.'

Amy watched her go and then reached out and pressed the buzzer before she could change her mind. She squashed down a flicker of anxiety and smiled as her first patient was walking into the room.

'Hello, Mrs...' Amy checked the screen quickly '...Duncan.

Dr Avanti has had an emergency trip to the hospital with a child so I'm covering his surgery. How can I help you?'

'I've been feeling rotten for a couple of days. Since Christmas Day, I suppose.' Paula Duncan sank onto the chair and let her handbag slip to the floor. 'I assumed it was the flu or something—there's so much of it around. I wasn't even going to bother making an appointment but this morning my head started hurting and I've had this numbness and tingling around my right eye.'

Amy stood up, her attention caught. 'How long have you had that rash on your nose?'

'I woke up with it. Lovely, isn't it?' Mrs Duncan lifted a hand to her face and gave a weary laugh. 'On top of everything else, I have to look like a clown. I can throw away the dress I bought for the New Year's Eve party, that's for sure. Unless the Penhally Arms decide to turn it into a masked ball.'

Amy examined the rash carefully and remembered seeing a patient with a similar rash in one of her clinics in Africa. 'It started this morning?'

'Yes. Just when you think life can't get any worse, it gets worse.'

Thinking of her own situation, Amy gave a faint smile. 'I know what you mean.'

'If I wasn't in so much pain I'd be really embarrassed to be seen out but I don't even care any more. I just hope there's something you can do. I have no idea where the rash has come from. I spent Christmas on my own so I can't imagine that I'vc caught anything.'

Amy washed her hands and sat back down at her desk. 'The rash suggests to me that you have ophthalmic shingles, Mrs Duncan. I'm going to send you up to the hospital to see the ophthalmologist—an eye doctor.'

'Shingles?' The woman stared at her. 'That's like chickenpox, isn't it? And in my eye? Surely that isn't possible.'

'I'm afraid it's entirely possible.' Amy opened the drawer

and pulled out the list of consultants that Kate had mentioned. She'd had no idea that she'd be using it so soon. 'It's caused by the same virus.'

'So I *must* have been in contact with someone with chickenpox? But who? I don't even know any small children!'

Amy shook her head. 'It doesn't work like that. There's no evidence that you can catch shingles from chickenpox, although it can occasionally happen the other way round if a person isn't immune. But once you've had chickenpox, the virus lies dormant and then flares up again at some point.'

'Can we let it go on its own? Why do I need to see an eye doctor?'

'The rash on your nose means that it's likely that your eye is affected. The ophthalmologist will give you a full examination and follow-up. But I'm going to give you a prescription that I want you to take.'

'Drugs?'

'Yes. Aciclovir.' Amy selected the drug she wanted on the computer screen and the printer next to her purred softly. 'I don't always prescribe it, but if it's within seventy-two hours of the symptoms starting then there's a good chance that it can lower the risk of you developing post-herpatic pain. Hopefully, in your case, it will help. Take it with you to the consultant in case he wants to give you something different.'

Mrs Duncan tucked the prescription into her bag. 'So I have to go there now?'

'Go straight to the eye ward. I'll call them so that they're expecting you.'

Mrs Duncan rose to her feet. 'Thank you.' She looked stunned. 'I don't know what I was expecting but it wasn't that.'

'If you have any questions you can always come back and talk to me.'

And then Amy realised that she wasn't going to be here. In a few hours she'd be gone. She glanced at her watch and wondered how long Marco was going to be. Was Michelle all right? It felt strange to be back in England, taking a surgery.

She saw a seemingly endless stream of patients and then Nick Tremayne walked into the room.

'Nick.' Flustered, Amy rose to her feet. 'I— It's good to see you.'

'It's good to see you, too.' His gaze was quizzical. 'And surprising.'

'Yes. I— Marco and I had things to talk about and then things became very busy and so I said I'd help out.' She sank back into her chair and he gave a faint smile.

'We're glad you're helping out. How are you?'

'Good,' she lied. 'And you? I hear that Lucy's made you a grandfather! Congratulations. Although I must say you look far too young to be anyone's grandfather.'

'That's what happens when you have your own children young,' Nick said drily. 'So how was Africa?'

'Interesting.' *Miserable.* She hesitated, unsure what to say but knowing that she had to say something about the sudden death of his wife. 'I was so sorry to hear about Annabel, Nick.'

'I was grateful for your card.' He was cool and matter-of-fact, revealing nothing of his emotions. 'So what are your plans, Amy?'

Divorce. 'I'm not sure, yet. Marco and I need to talk.'

Nick nodded. 'Well, if you have any problems with the rest of his surgery, just call through to me or Dragan.'

'Thanks.' Amy watched him leave and moments later Kate appeared with a cup of coffee. 'Is that for me?'

'You've earned it. I can see the floor in the waiting room now, so that's a good sign.'

'Is Marco back?'

'Yes, but he had to go straight out again. Man from the brewery developed chest pains while he was making a delivery at the Penhally Arms. Probably the weight of the alcohol we're all going to drink on New Year's Eve.' Kate put the coffee on the desk. 'Black, no sugar. Is that right?'

Amy glanced at her in surprise. 'Yes. Thank you.'

'Tip from Marco. He said that you're useless in the morning unless you've had your coffee.'

Memories of long, lazy mornings lounging in bed with Marco filled her brain and Amy felt the colour flood into her cheeks. She reached out a hand and buzzed for the next patient. 'Right, well, thanks, Kate. I suppose I'd better get on. Is it always like this?'

Kate laughed. 'No, sometimes it's busy.'

Thinking of the number of patients she'd seen so far, Amy suddenly realised that Marco probably hadn't been playing games when he'd said he didn't have time for conversation.

'Dr Avanti?' A man hesitated in the doorway and Amy smiled, recognising him immediately. *A face from her childhood.*

'Rob! How are you?' She blushed and waved an apologetic hand. 'Sorry. Obviously you're not that great or you wouldn't be spending your morning in the doctor's surgery. How can I help you?' It felt weird, sitting here, talking to someone that she'd known as a child. Rob, a trawlerman, was part of her childhood. How many hours had she spent watching him bring in the boat and haul in the catch?

And how did he see her? As someone who was still a child?

Or as someone who was capable of handling his medical problems?

'My hand is agony.' Without hesitation, he sat down and took off his coat. 'Been like this for a few days. I thought it might settle but it's getting worse and the rash is going up my arm.'

Amy leaned forward and took a closer look at his hand, noticing the inflammation and the discolouration spreading up his arm. Her mind went blank and she knew a moment of panic. *What was it?* 'Have you been bitten? Scratched?' She lifted his hand, noticing that Rob flinched at her touch. 'That's tender?'

'Very.' He frowned thoughtfully down at his hand. 'I don't think I've scratched myself but you know what it's like, handling fish. It's pretty easy to get a cut from a fish spine or the bones. Then there's the broken ends of warps—to be honest, we're too busy to be checking for minor injuries all the time. Aches and pains and cuts are all just part of the job.'

Fish. Of course. Amy studied his hand again, noticing the raised purple margin around the reddened area and the pus. *Erysipeloid.* For a moment she forgot Marco and the real reason that she was sitting in the surgery. She forgot all her own problems in her fascination of practising medicine. 'I think that's probably what has happened, Rob. You must have scratched yourself without knowing and that's allowed an infection to get hold. Bacteria are easily carried into the wound from fish slime and guts.' She ran her fingers gently over his arm, taking a closer look. 'I'll give you some antibiotics. Are you allergic to penicillin?'

'Not to my knowledge. So you've seen this before, then?'

'Actually, no, but I've read about it.' Amy turned back to the computer, hit a few keys and then scrolled down to find the drug she wanted. 'Fishermen are particularly prone to infections of the hands and fingers because of the work they do. This particular infection is called erysipeloid. I'll give you an antibiotic and that should do the trick, but prevention is better than cure, Rob. You should be spraying disinfectant over the surfaces where you work and using a hand wash after handling fish. Something like chlorhexidine gluconate would do the trick.'

Rob pulled down his sleeve. 'It's there, but we don't always use it. When you're hauling in nets and fighting the wind and the waves, it doesn't seem like a high priority.'

Amy signed the prescription. 'Take these, but if it gets worse, come back.'

Rob stood up, his eyes curious. 'Little Amy. I remember you when you were knee high.' His voice gruff, he slipped the prescription into his pocket. 'Every summer you visited your grandmother and stayed in that tiny cottage by the shore. Always on your own, you were. You never joined in with any of the local kids. You used to stand on the harbour wall and watch us bring in the catch. You were all solemn-eyed and serious, as if you were wondering whether to run away to sea.'

Amy stared at him, unable to breathe.

She *had* been wondering whether to run away to sea. Every morning she'd scurried down to the harbour and watched the boats sail away, all the time wishing that she could go with the tide and find an entirely new life. A better life.

Happiness doesn't just land in your lap, Amy, you have to chase it.

Rob frowned. 'You all right? You're a bit white.'

Tripped up by the memories of her grandmother, Amy somehow managed to smile. 'That's right. I loved staying here.'

'She was a good woman, your grandmother. And she was so proud of you.'

Feeling her poise and professionalism unravel like a ball of wool in the paws of a kitten, Amy swallowed. 'She always wanted me to be a doctor.'

'And didn't we know it.' Rob grinned. 'Couldn't walk past her in the village without hearing the latest story about her clever granddaughter.' His smile became nostalgic. 'She's missed is Eleanor. But that young couple you sold the cottage to are very happy. The Dodds. They've got two children now.'

'Good.' Desperate to end the conversation, Amy rose to

her feet and walked towards the door. 'Come back to one of the doctors if you have problems with your hand, Rob.'

He didn't move, as if he sensed some of the turmoil inside her. 'She wanted to see you married with children—would have loved to see you together, you and Dr Avanti. It's good that you're back. And it's great for the practice. I know how much they're struggling with Lucy going into labour so suddenly.'

Back? 'I'm not exactly— I mean, that isn't why—' She broke off and gave a weak smile. 'It's lovely to see you, Rob.' There was no point in explaining that she wasn't staying—that she should already have been back at the train station. They'd find out soon enough that her visit had been fleeting and she wouldn't need to give explanations because she wouldn't be here.

Feeling a twinge of guilt that she was going to be leaving Marco to deal with still more gossip, Amy showed Rob out of the consulting room and then returned to her desk and sank onto her chair with her head in her hands, the lump building in her throat as memories swirled around her exhausted mind.

'So—judging from the expression on your face, delivering patient care in Penhally isn't any easier than it was in Africa.' Marco's smooth, accented tones cut through her misery and she jumped and let her hands fall into her lap.

Even though she'd been longing to have the conversation with him, now the moment had arrived she wasn't entirely sure she could cope with it.

CHAPTER THREE

'MARCO. I—I didn't hear you come in.'

'Presumably because you were miles away.' He pushed the door shut with the flat of his hand and strolled into the room, his cool control in direct contrast to her own nervous agitation. 'You look pale. What's the matter?'

That was twice in five minutes she'd been told that she looked pale. Making a mental note to dig out a pot of blusher and use it, Amy gave a humourless laugh. 'I would have thought it was obvious.'

'Not to me. Any woman who finds it that easy to walk away from a marriage can't possibly be daunted by the prospect of spending a few hours wandering down memory lane.'

He had no idea.

And that was her fault, of course, because she hadn't wanted him to know the truth. She'd wanted to spare him a difficult decision. Wanted to spare them both the slow, inevitable destruction of their marriage. So she'd made the decision for both of them and gone for a quick, sudden end. She'd thought it would make it less painful in the long term.

Now she wasn't so sure. *Could the pain have been worse?*

'It wasn't easy for me, Marco.' She didn't want him thinking that and she looked at him, almost hating him for his insensitivity but at the same time relieved, because she knew that his anger made him blind. Anger would prevent him from delving deeper into her reasons for leaving. *And she didn't want him delving.* 'I did what was right for both of us.'

'No, you did what was right for you. I wasn't involved in the decision.' He prowled across the consulting room to the desk where she was seated. 'One minute we were planning a future, the next you decided that you were going to spend the future on your own. There was no discussion. You gave me no choice.'

In a way, that was true, and yet she knew that the decision she'd made had been the right one.

'Do you want to talk about this now?' Strangely enough, even though she was the one who'd pushed, she just didn't feel prepared to say what had to be said. In Africa she'd thought she'd resigned herself to the reality of her life, but one look at Marco had unravelled her resolve.

'That was the reason you came, wasn't it?'

Feeling vulnerable next to his superior height, she rose to her feet and their eyes locked. 'All right, let's have this discussion and then we can both get on with our lives. I ended our marriage, yes, that's true.'

'You left without talking it through with me.'

'I *did* talk to you!'

'When?'

'I told you I was unhappy. We should never have moved back to Penhally. It was a mistake.' She sank back into her chair because her legs just wouldn't hold her any longer. 'I didn't feel the way I thought I was going to feel.'

'You underwent a complete personality transformation!' Anger shimmered in his eyes. 'One moment you were lying in my bed, planning our future, and the next thing you were packing your bag so quickly you almost bruised yourself running through the front door. It didn't make sense.'

It would have made perfect sense if he'd known what she'd discovered.

'I didn't have a personality transformation,' she said stiffly.

'I just changed my mind about what I wanted. People do it every day of their lives and it's sad, but it's just one of those things. The reason you're angry is because you felt that you weren't part of the decision and you always have to be in control.'

'*Control?*' He lifted an eyebrow in cool appraisal. 'You saw our relationship as a power struggle, *amore*?'

Unsettled by the look in his eyes and the sheer impact of his physical presence, she left her chair and walked to the window, keeping her back to him. 'It's time to be honest about this. We made a mistake, Marco. We never should have married. I mean, it was all far, far too quick! Three months! Three months is nothing!' She fixed her gaze on a point in the distance and recited the words she'd rehearsed so many times. 'How can anyone know each other in three months? Yes, there was chemistry, I'm not denying that. But chemistry alone isn't enough to bind a couple together for a lifetime.'

There was an ominous silence and when he finally spoke his voice was clipped. 'You're describing hormonal teenagers. We were both adults and we knew what we wanted.'

'Adult or not, the chemistry was still there. The relationship was fine, but marriage—that was a stupid impulse.' *A fleeting dream that had been cruelly snatched away.* She could feel his gaze burning a hole between her shoulder blades and this time it took him almost a full minute to reply.

'At least have the courtesy to look at me when you reduce our relationship to nothing but a sordid affair.' There was a dangerous note in his voice and she took a deep breath and turned slowly, struggling to display the calm and neutrality that she knew she needed in order to be convincing.

'Not sordid, Marco,' she said quietly, hoping that her voice was going to hold out. 'It was amazing, we both know that. But it was never going to last. We shouldn't have tried to hold onto it or make it into something that it wasn't. We wanted different things.'

He watched her for a moment, his eyes intent on her face as if her mind were a book and he were leafing through every single page, searching for clues. 'Until we returned to Penhally, I wasn't aware that we wanted different things. We'd made plans for the future. I was going to work with Nick in the practice and you were going to stay at home and have our babies until you decided to return to work. It was the reason we chose the house.'

She inhaled sharply, unable to stifle the reaction. *She couldn't even bear to think about the house.* 'I'm sorry I didn't keep my end of the bargain. I'm sorry I decided that I wanted a career instead of a family.'

He looked at her as if she were a complete stranger and then he muttered something in Italian that she didn't understand and Amy looked at him helplessly.

'If this conversation is going to have any hope of working then you at least have to speak English so that I can understand you.'

'*You* are speaking English and I don't understand you at all! The complexities of this situation appear to transcend the language barrier.' He raked long bronzed fingers through his glossy dark hair. 'You talk about wanting a career, and yet when we first met you talked about nothing but family and children. You were soft, gentle, giving. Then we moved to Penhally and suddenly, whoosh...' He waved a hand expressively. 'You underwent this transformation. Soft, affectionate Amy became hard, distant Amy. And distant Amy suddenly became career Amy. It was as if the woman I was with suddenly reinvented herself. What happened? *What happened to change everything?*'

She stared at him blankly, teetering on the edge of confession. It would have been so easy. So easy to tell him exactly what had happened.

But that would have made things so much more complicated and they were already more complicated than she could comfortably handle.

The truth created a bad taste in her mouth and for a moment she just stood there, trapped by the secrets and lies that she'd used to protect him. 'I suppose it was several things.' With an effort, she kept her tone careless. 'Penhally isn't exactly the centre of the universe. There wasn't enough to keep me occupied. I was bored. I missed medicine. I missed the patients.' It was true, she consoled herself, she *had* missed the patients.

'If that was the case, you should have said so and we could have found you work, if not in Penhally then at another surgery.' Marco turned and paced across the surgery, as if he found the confined space intolerable.

'It's all history now,' Amy murmured. 'Going over it again is going to achieve nothing. It's time to move on, Marco. Let's just have the discussion that we need to have and then I'll leave you in peace.'

'Peace?' He turned, his eyes glinting dangerously, his lean, handsome face taut. 'Is that what you think leaving will give me when you walk out again? Peace? I haven't known a moment's peace since you left.'

He hadn't?

Her heart gave a little lift and then crashed down again as she realised that his feelings made absolutely no difference to what she had to do. And anyway his feelings had more to do with injured pride and inconvenience than anything deeper. Marco Avanti was a man who knew what he wanted out of life and she'd temporarily derailed his plans—that was all.

'I'm sorry,' she said softly, telling the truth for the first time since she'd walked into Penhally. 'Truly I'm sorry for any hurt I've caused.'

He watched her, his eyes sharp on her face. 'But you're still asking me for a divorce?'

For the space of a heartbeat she paused. 'Yes,' she croaked. 'I am. It's the only course of action.'

'*Not* the only course.' He strolled towards her and then stopped. 'I never thought of you as a quitter, Amy, and yet you haven't once mentioned trying again. Instead of abandoning our marriage, you could try and fix it.'

She froze as he dangled temptation in front of her and her heart stumbled in her chest. Like an addict she gazed at him and then she remembered how far she'd come, how much she'd already suffered to get to this point, and shook her head. 'It isn't fixable.'

'You don't know that because you haven't tried. And this time we'd be trying together. Talk to me, Amy, and we can fix it.'

'You can't fix something when the two halves don't match. We want different things. You want a family, Marco. You made that clear on many occasions. Women have been chasing you for years, but you never settled down with any of them because you weren't ready to have children. But then suddenly that changed.'

'It changed when I met you. The first thing I thought when I laid eyes on you was that you were the sexiest woman I'd ever seen.' His voice was a soft, seductive purr. 'You were wearing that little navy suit with a pair of high heels and your legs came close to being the eighth wonder of the world. You were serious and studious and didn't stop asking me questions.'

She felt the colour rush into her cheeks. 'You just happened to be lecturing on an aspect of paediatrics that interested me.'

'Then, when I stopped looking at your legs and your beautiful brown eyes, I realised how intelligent you were and how warm and kind. I knew immediately that you were the woman I wanted to be the mother of my children. I knew it in a moment.'

The mother of his children.

There was a long, tortured silence. Knowing that some response was required, Amy tried to speak but her voice just refused to work. Instead, she stooped, picked up her bag and yanked her coat from the back of the chair. Only once she'd slipped her arms into the sleeves and belted the waist did she find her voice.

'I'm sorry I ruined your plans, but I can't be the mother of your children, so it's time you started searching for another candidate. And now I have to go.' *Before she collapsed in front of him.*

'I thought you wanted to talk to me?'

'It's not— I can't…' Needing fresh air and space, she stumbled over the words. 'You're just too busy. I shouldn't have come, I see that now. I'll leave you to see your patients and I'll write to you again and perhaps this time you'll reply. It's the best thing for both of us.' She moved towards the door but he caught her arm, his strong fingers biting through the wool of her coat as he pulled her inexorably towards him.

'You came all this way to talk.' He held her firmly. 'And we haven't finished. Last time you just walked out and you wouldn't listen to me. You're not doing that again, Amy.'

Why had she ever thought that seeing him face to face was a good idea?

'You still have patients waiting.'

'I'll see my patients. Then I'll buy you lunch at the Smugglers' Inn. We can talk then.'

He couldn't have picked a place more public. 'You want to be the subject of gossip?'

'Gossip doesn't worry me and never will. Kate will make you a cup of coffee and find you somewhere to sit. Then I'll give you a lift.'

She gave a faint smile. 'The Maserati has learned to cope with snow?'

'She is moody and unpredictable, that's true, but it is just a question of handling her correctly.' His eyes held hers and she wondered briefly whether he was talking about the car or her.

'You don't need to give me a lift. I'll wander around the village for an hour or so and then meet you up there. The walk up the coast road will do me good. But I'm going back to London tonight.'

His eyes narrowed slightly and his expression was unreadable. 'So that means that you have plenty of time for lunch. Twelve-thirty. Be there or this time I'll come looking for you.'

The Smugglers' Inn was perched near the edge of the cliff on the coast road, a short drive out of Penhally.

The Maserati gave a throaty growl as Marco turned into the car park. He turned off the engine and sat for a moment, breathing in the scent of leather. Usually the car calmed him but today he felt nothing, his body too tense after his encounter with Amy.

With a soft curse he locked the car and walked towards the pub, distracted for a moment by the wild crash of the waves on the rocks below. The temperature had dropped and Marco stood for a moment, trying to formulate a plan, but his normally sharp brain refused to co-operate and he suddenly realised that he had no idea what he was going to do or say.

The irony of the situation didn't escape him. Of all the women who'd wanted to settle down with him over the years, he'd finally picked one who was wedded to her career and wasn't interested in having children.

He frowned. Except that she *had* been interested in having children. More than interested. At the time, he'd assumed that her longing for a family stemmed from the disappointing relationship that she'd apparently had with her own mother. Perhaps he'd been wrong about that. Perhaps he'd been wrong about all of it.

It was true that people changed their minds, but still...

He should give her a divorce, he told himself grimly, because that was clearly what she wanted and, anyway, she'd been gone for two years. What was there to salvage?

Anger exploded inside him once again and he took a deep breath of cold, calming air before turning towards the pub. With only a slight hesitation he pushed open the heavy door and walked inside.

Warmth, laughter and the steady buzz of conversation wrapped itself around him and drew him in. Immediately his eyes scanned the bar, searching for Amy.

Would she be there or had she run? Was she now shivering on the station platform, waiting for the train that would take her away from him?

How badly did she want the divorce?

And then he saw her, a slight figure, huddled on her own by the blazing fire, still wearing her coat and scarf as if all the heat in the world wouldn't warm her. She looked out of place and vulnerable. Her dark hair had been smoothed behind one ear and Marco felt something stir inside him as he remembered all the times he'd kissed her slender neck, *the tempting hollow of her throat...*

He dragged his eyes from her neckline, frustrated by the unexpectedly powerful surge of lust that gripped him.

So, people were wrong about some things, he thought bitterly. *Time didn't always heal.* In his case, time hadn't healed at all. Despite everything, Amy still affected him more than any woman he'd ever met.

His jaw clenched and he stood for a moment, feeling the now familiar tension knot inside him. Why? Was it because she was the only woman who had walked away from him? Was this all about his ego?

Was he really that shallow?

And then the lust was replaced by anger and he didn't even try and subdue it because over the past two years he'd learned that anger was the easiest emotion to deal with. Anger was so much better than pain and disillusionment.

Back in control, he strolled across the room and nodded to the man behind the bar. 'Tony. Give me something long and cold that isn't going to dull my senses.'

The landlord's gaze flickered towards Amy, who was still staring blankly into the fire. 'Looks to me as though you might need something stronger.'

'Don't tempt me. I've always found that my diagnostic abilities are better when I'm sober, and I'm on call. Has she ordered?' No point in pretending that his ex-wife hadn't just appeared out of nowhere with no warning. The locals had eyes and he had no doubt that they'd be using them.

Tony reached for a glass and snapped the cap off a couple of bottles. 'Arrived ten minutes ago. Paid for a grapefruit juice, made polite conversation for about three seconds and then slunk into the corner like a wounded animal. Hasn't touched her drink. If you want my opinion, she's not a happy woman. You might want to use your famous doctoring skills to find out what's bothering her.'

Marco's long fingers drummed a steady rhythm on the bar. *He knew exactly what was bothering her.* She wanted a quick and easy divorce and he wasn't playing ball.

The landlord poured the contents of the bottles into the glass. 'Here you go. One doctor-on-duty fruit cocktail. Full of vitamins, totally devoid of alcohol. No charge. If you want to eat, let me know. Cornish pasties came out of the oven five minutes ago and the fish and chips are good, but I'm guessing you don't want to feast on cholesterol in front of your patients.'

Marco gave a faint smile, took the drink and strolled across to the fire. 'Sorry I've kept you waiting.' He put his glass down on the table and shrugged off his coat. 'Our patients haven't quite got the hang of developing ailments that can be seen easily within the allotted time.'

'It doesn't matter.' She looked across at him, the flickering fire sending red lights through her dark hair. Away from the pressure of the surgery he noticed that her face was paler than ever and there were dark shadows under her eyes. And she'd definitely lost weight since he'd last seen her.

He studied her thoughtfully.

For a woman following her chosen path of career over motherhood, she didn't appear either settled or happy.

Was something wrong with her? Something other than the prospect of a divorce? Had she picked up some tropical disease while she'd been working in Africa?

'So…' he lifted his drink '…tell me about your work. Is it hard?' Was that why she was so pale? Did her work explain the weight loss? Had she been ill?

'Sorry?' She glanced at him, her expression blank, as if she hadn't heard him.

'Your work. The thing you care most about, remember, *tesoro*?' It was hard not to keep the irony out of his voice. 'How is this amazing career that was so much more important to you than marriage and children?'

'My career?' She gave a little start, as though she'd forgotten that she even had a career. Then she straightened her shoulders, her gaze returning to the fire. 'Yes. I was running a malaria project.'

'And that was interesting? Fulfilling?' *Why wouldn't she look at him?*

'Yes.'

Marco felt the anger surge again and struggled against the temptation to slide his hand around the back of her neck and force her to meet his gaze. 'Worth sacrificing our marriage for?'

Her breathing quickened and her eyes slid to his. 'Our marriage was something separate.'

'No.' He growled the word and noticed a few heads turn towards them. *Why had he decided to have this discussion in a pub?* 'It wasn't separate, Amy. You ended our marriage because you chose a career over family. It's that simple.'

'There was nothing simple about it. Keep your voice down. People are looking at us, Marco.' She reached for her drink and her hair slid forward, framing her cheek. 'You chose to do this in a public place so can we at least try and keep this civilised?'

'Civilised?' Heat exploded inside him, the flame of his anger fuelled by her unreasonable calm. 'You ripped our marriage to shreds with your bare hands. Forgive me, *amore*, if I don't feel completely civilised. I feel—' He broke off, his fluency in English momentarily stunted by emotion, but before he could find the words to express his feelings she half rose to her feet.

'This conversation is pointless. I shouldn't have come.'

Grimly determined not to let her leave, Marco reached out a hand and caught her arm. 'Sit down. You're the one who wanted this conversation.'

'This isn't conversation, Marco, this is confrontation.' She was breathing quickly. 'You're losing your temper and I simply wanted us to discuss the facts.'

'I'm *not* losing my temper.' He drew in a breath, struggling to keep his tone level. 'I have a question.'

She sank back onto her chair, her beautiful eyes wary. 'What?'

'Do you think about us? About what we had? Have you forgotten what we shared?'

Her swift intake of breath and the brief flash of awareness in her eyes was sufficient answer. 'Marco—'

The phone in his pocket rang and he cursed fluently in Italian and slid it out of his pocket, wishing at that moment that he had chosen a different career path. One that would have permitted him five minutes' free time with the guarantee of no disturbance. He checked the number and sighed. 'That's Kate. She wouldn't ring unless it was important.'

'It's fine. Take the call.'

Frustrated that he'd been interrupted in what had to have been the most important part of the conversation, Marco hit the button and spoke to the practice manager, aware of Amy's eyes on his face.

Never before had he so badly wanted his work to go away.

And then Kate spoke and immediately she had his attention.

By the time he ended the call, Amy was no longer his priority.

She looked at him expectantly. 'Something bad?'

'The Knight boys have gone missing.' He rose to his feet. 'Eddie is only five years old.' He reached for his coat just as the door to the pub flew open and a little boy stood there, breathing hard.

'Dr Avanti! You have to come *now*! Alfie and I went to play on the rocks and Eddie followed because he always tags along and then he slipped and now we can't wake him up and he's bleeding everywhere and—' He broke off, his breath hitching as he spoke. 'We think he's dead, Dr Avanti. *He's dead!*'

CHAPTER FOUR

'*Calma*. Calm down, Sam.' Marco squeezed the boy's shoulder and squatted down so that he was level with him. 'Tell me where they are. Slowly.'

'We were playing pirates. Mum said we weren't to go near the rocks but we went anyway and Eddie followed and now...' Sam's face crumpled. 'He's dead. There's blood everywhere.'

Marco put an arm around the boy and spoke softly to him.

Amy couldn't hear what he said but it had a positive effect on Sam, who straightened his shoulders and stopped crying, his gaze trusting as he looked up at Marco. 'You mean that? Really?'

Marco nodded and let go of the boy. 'And now I want you to show me where they are.' He rose to his feet and noticed Amy. 'Stay here. Promise me you won't leave until we've finished this conversation.'

'I'm coming with you.'

Already on his way to the door with Sam, Marco frowned at her. 'I can't have a conversation while I'm administering first aid.'

'I'm coming to help you,' she said calmly. 'I'm a doctor, too, remember?'

Marco's jaw tensed. 'I thought you couldn't wait to leave

this place?' His tone was rough and his eyes scanned her briefly. 'You're not dressed to scramble down cliffs.'

'I'm fine. We're wasting time, Marco.'

'Hurry up or they'll have no blood left!' Sam was still in the doorway, his eyes huge and worried. 'I'll show you where they are.'

Marco glanced towards the bar. 'Tony—call the coastguard and let them know what's happening. If it's serious we might need the helicopter to lift them off the rocks.'

Sam sprinted from the pub to the steep, narrow path that led down to the rocky cove below. 'Come on! Come on!' he urged them.

Amy didn't hear Marco's reply because she was too busy trying to keep her balance on the path. The wind had risen and now whipped her hair across her face, obscuring her vision. She knew just how steep the path was because it had been a favourite of hers as a child. The cove below was rocky and dangerous and held just the right amount of wicked appeal for an adventurous child.

Ahead of her, Marco covered the distance with sure, confident strides, drawing away from her, leaving her only the occasional reassuring glimpse of his broad shoulders.

She couldn't decide whether she was relieved or sorry that their conversation had been interrupted yet again.

It was obvious that Marco was equally frustrated by the interruptions. The question was whether he was frustrated enough to just agree to the divorce and let her walk out of Penhally before nightfall.

Did he believe her claim that she'd chosen a career over marriage and children?

Resisting the temptation to hurry because haste might result in her crashing onto the beach and becoming another casualty, Amy followed more slowly and finally clambered over the huge boulders that guarded the entrance to the cove. In the summer it was a favourite place for tourists who came with their nets and their buckets to explore the rock pools. In winter it was a wild and dangerous place and the sudden drop in the temperature had made the rocky beach particularly deadly.

Jagged rocks glistened black with sea spray and Amy glanced across and saw the boys. One lay still, the other sitting beside him, his face covered in blood.

Sam and Marco were already there and Amy picked her way across the rocks to join them.

'We didn't mean him to die. We didn't mean him to die. Do something, Dr Avanti,' Alfie whispered, his whole body shaking and juddering as he fixed his terrified stare on the inert form of his little brother. 'We didn't know he'd followed us and then I tried to take him back but he slipped and banged his head really hard. And when I tried to get to him, I slipped and hit my head, too. Then he stopped talking. I couldn't get him to answer me.' He started to sob pitifully and Sam started to cry, too. He caught Marco's eyes and took a shuddering breath.

'It will be all right, Alfie,' he said in a wobbly voice. 'We've got to be strong and try and help. What do you want us to do, Dr Avanti?'

Marco was on his knees beside the still body of the little boy. 'Just sit there for a moment, Sam. He isn't dead, Alfie. I can tell you for sure that he isn't dead.'

Amy knelt down beside Marco, wincing slightly as the sharp rocks took a bite out of her knees. 'Is he conscious?'

'No.' Marco was checking the child's scalp, nose and ears, searching for injury. And then the child gave a little moan and his eyes drifted open. 'All right. Well, that's good. He's drowsy. Obviously knocked out, from the boys' description.' His fingers probed gently. 'He's got a nasty haematoma on the back of his skull. I can't be sure that he doesn't have neck injuries.'

'Is he going to die?' Alfie's voice shook and Marco lifted his head and looked at him.

'No. He's not going to die.' His voice was firm and confident. 'You did the right thing to send Sam up to the pub. Good boy. Well done.'

Alfie looked at him, clearly doubtful that he'd done anything worthy of praise, and Amy noticed fresh blood oozing from the cut on his scalp.

'I'll ring the coastguard and then look at Alfie.' Amy started to dig for her phone but Marco shook his head.

'There's no signal on this beach. We can't carry him back up that path without possibly making things worse. Sam.' Marco's gaze slid to the other boy who was huddled next to Alfie, a look of terror in his eyes. 'I want you to go back up to the pub and tell Tony that we need a helicopter. Do you understand me?'

Sam shot to his feet and nodded, his face white and terrified. 'Helicopter. I can do that. I can do that, Dr Avanti.'

'Good boy. Go. And be careful on the rocks. We've had enough casualties here for one day.' Marco turned back to the child. 'Eddie? Can you hear me? He's cold, Amy. Wet from the sea and freezing in this weather. If we're not careful it's going to be hypothermia that is our biggest problem.' He cursed softly. 'I have no equipment. Nothing.'

Next to them, Alfie started to sob again, the tears mingling with the blood that already stained his cheeks. 'He's going to die. I know he's going to die. He chose me a really great Christmas present. I don't want him to die. This is all my fault. We're not supposed to be down on this beach anyway.'

Concerned about the amount of blood on Alfie's head, Amy made a soothing noise and examined his scalp. As she balanced on the slippery rocks, searching for the source of the bleeding, she suddenly developed a new admiration for paramedics. Then she saw blood blossom under her fingers and pulled off her gloves and took the scarf from her neck.

'I'm going to press on this for a minute, Alfie, and that should stop the bleeding. They can have a better look at it at the hospital.'

'I don't want to go to hospital. I want my mum—*Ow!*' Alfie winced. 'That really hurts.'

'You've cut yourself,' Amy murmured. 'I'm just going to put some pressure on it.'

'I don't care about me.' Alfie's eyes were fixed on his brother. 'If we'd stayed in the house it never would have happened. I wish we'd done that. I'm *never* playing on the beach again. I'm just going to stick to computers.' He sobbed and sobbed and Amy tightened the scarf and then slid her arms round him, cuddling him against her.

'It was just an accident, sweetheart,' she said softly. 'Accidents happen. Eddie's going to be all right, I know he is.'

Having examined Eddie as best he could, Marco removed his coat and pulled his jumper over his head. Then he wrapped the boy in the layers, giving him as much protection from the elements as possible. Then he glanced at Alfie and winked at him. 'Do you know how many accidents can happen sitting indoors, playing on the computer?'

Alfie sniffed, still clinging to Amy. 'Now you're kidding me.'

'You can have an accident without ever moving from your chair at home. The ceiling can drop onto your head. You can develop muscle strain and eye strain from too much gaming. Heart disease from lack of exercise. At least you were having fun outdoors.'

'But Eddie wouldn't have been here if it hadn't been for me. I chose the smugglers game. He loves dressing up as a pirate.'

'So—you're a fun brother to have and pirates sounds like a good game,' Marco said easily. 'You'll have to tell me more about it someday soon.' He glanced at Amy and gave a faint smile of approval as he saw her first-aid measures. 'Very inventive.'

'You learn to be inventive in Africa.' She pressed hard on the wound. 'They're not exactly flush with equipment over there.'

Something flickered in his eyes and then he turned his attention back to his little patient.

'Do we have to go to hospital?' Alfie's voice wobbled and he sounded very young. 'Our mum is going to go mad.'

'She'll just be relieved you're safe. Now, sit down here for a moment.' Amy helped him sit down on a flat piece of rock. 'Don't move. It's very slippery and I don't want you to fall again and I want to help Dr Avanti with your brother.'

Shivering without the protection of her scarf, she moved across to Marco and knelt down beside him. 'You must be frozen. You gave all your layers to Eddie.'

'I have more body fat than he does.'

Amy's eyes slid to his powerful, male frame. Not an inch of fat was visible. Just lean muscle under a thin T-shirt that clung to the impressive width of his shoulders. But she knew there was no point in pointing out that he was getting cold. Marco would do everything within his power to save a child. She'd always known that about him.

A hiss and a crash reminded her that the sea in winter was hungry and unforgiving and frighteningly close. 'That was a big wave, Marco.'

'Yes.' Marco's tone was matter-of-fact. 'If the helicopter doesn't arrive in the next few minutes, we might have to move him. I don't want to but it's the lesser of two evils.'

Amy glanced up at the sky, willing it to arrive.

Eddie gave a little whimper and Marco murmured something reassuring and tucked the layers more tightly around the child. 'He's in and out of consciousness. I should have asked Sam to bring blankets down from the pub.'

'The helicopter will be here before Sam gets back,' Amy

said optimistically. 'I can give him one of my layers.' She started to take off her coat but he reached out and caught her arm.

'No.' This time his voice was harsh. 'Keep your coat on. You need it.'

'But—'

'Don't argue with me, Amy. You don't exactly have an excess of body fat to keep you warm. Didn't they feed you in Africa?'

She swallowed but was spared the trouble of thinking up an answer by the noise of the approaching helicopter.

'Good.' Marco watched with visible relief as the helicopter appeared in the sky like a giant insect. In a matter of minutes it was overhead and Amy could see the winchman in the doorway of the helicopter.

With precise, accurate flying and slick teamwork, the winchman was lowered onto the rocks next to them.

He unclipped the harness and moved across to them. 'How many casualties, Marco?'

Amy was wondering how they knew each other and then remembered that the RAF winchmen were trained paramedics who often practised their skills alongside local doctors.

'Two. One of them serious. According to his brother, he lost consciousness when he fell. GCS was 13 when we arrived on the scene...' Marco gave a swift, comprehensive summary of the situation and together they prepared Eddie for his transfer to hospital. Finally, strapped to a backboard, the child was winched into the helicopter.

Shivering like a wet puppy, Alfie watched. 'Wow!' His voice was awed, concern for his little brother momentarily forgotten. 'That's so cool!'

Marco pulled on his jumper. 'It's definitely cool,' he murmured, helping the boy to his feet as the paramedic returned, ready to take his second patient.

'I'm going up there, too? Just wait until they hear about this at school.'

'Maybe he would have been safer on the computer,' Marco murmured, watching as the second child was safely winched into the helicopter. Then he lifted his hand in acknowledgement and the helicopter soared away on the short journey to hospital.

Around them the sea thrashed and boiled like a wild beast, angered that its prey had been snatched from its jaws.

Amy was shivering uncontrollably. 'Let's get moving,' she muttered, and was suddenly enveloped in warmth as Marco wrapped his coat around her.

'Wear this.'

'You can't give me your coat!' Protesting, she tried to shrug her way out of it but he was stronger than her and more determined.

'Put it on.' His voice rough, he fastened the coat as if she were a child and then gave a faint smile. 'It swamps you.'

'Well, you're bigger than me.'

His eyes darkened and she flushed and turned away, picking her way across the rocks back towards the path. She knew that he was bigger than her. She'd always been aware of his physical strength. It was one of the things that drew women to him.

At the top of the path a little crowd was waiting, including the boys' mother, Mary.

'I sent them to play in the garden because they've been on those wretched game machines all holiday and then when I went to call them for lunch, there was no sign of them.' She covered her mouth with her hand but the sobs still came. 'I guessed they'd gone to the beach and that Eddie had followed them. Everyone's saying that he's badly hurt—'

Without hesitation, Marco stepped forward and slid an arm around her shoulders. 'They are boys and they were playing,' he said, his accent thicker than usual. 'Alfie has a cut on his head, but nothing that a few stitches won't sort out. Eddie also banged his head…' He paused. 'From Alfie's description it sounds as though he might have been knocked out when he fell on the rocks. But he was starting to regain consciousness when we got to him and they've taken him to the hospital.'

'I need to get up there right away. I need to call my husband so that we can go to the hospital.' Trying to hold herself together, Mary fumbled in her bag for her phone, her hands shaking so much she dropped the bag twice. 'He's gone to help my brother take down a shed in his garden. It will take him ages to get back with the way the roads are.'

Marco stooped, picked up her bag and handed it to her. 'I'll take you in the Maserati.' He looked at his watch. 'I've got time to drive you and still be back in time for afternoon surgery. Tell your husband you'll meet him up there.'

Mary looked at him, her eyes swimming with tears. 'You'd do that for me?' She bit her lip. 'But there must be other more urgent things you should be doing.'

Marco looked directly at Amy and she knew what he was thinking. *That the thing he should be doing was giving her the conversation she'd demanded.*

So it was up to her, then, to decide. He was giving her the choice. She could insist that he stay and finish the conversation they'd started or she could let him take this frantic mother to her children.

'We can talk later,' she said quietly, slipping off his coat and handing it to him. 'My train doesn't leave until four.'

With only the briefest hesitation Marco reached into his pocket and gave his car keys to Mary. 'Go and sit in the car. I'll be with you in a minute.'

The woman walked across the car park and Amy gave a faint smile. 'Trusting someone else with your precious Maserati, Marco?'

'Only because I need to talk to you without an audience,' he growled, reaching out and removing a smudge of blood from her cheek. 'You're freezing and you need a shower. Go back to the surgery and ask Kate to sort you out with a change of clothes. Wait for me there. We'll talk later.'

'I think our conversation is doomed. We're running out of time.'

'Then stay overnight.'

She stared at him. 'That's out of the question.'

'I thought you wanted to talk? Stay the night, Amy, and then at least we're guaranteed peace and quiet. I'm not on call. You can come out to the house and we can eat, talk and then you can get the first train back tomorrow. I'll drop you at the station myself.'

'That's not—no.' She had to say no. 'I can't.'

'Amy.' His voice was impatient and he glanced towards his car where Mary was now waiting in a state of anxiety. 'We can't tie this up in a matter of minutes. We need time and we need privacy. You're the one who wants to do this. It makes sense. In fact, I can give you the house keys and you can go now and have a shower at home. That's a much better idea. Wait for me there. I'll be home by six and we can talk.'

She hadn't wanted to go to the house. It would just be too painful.

'I don't—'

'Stop arguing and looking for problems.' He dug in his pocket and pulled out his house keys. 'In that car is a woman worrying herself to death about her children and in the hospital are two young children who need their mother. They need my help and you're holding me up.'

Amy swallowed and took the keys from his hand. 'I'll see you later.'

Marco let himself into the house and walked through to the enormous sitting room that faced out to sea.

Amy was standing by the glass, staring out across the crashing waves. She was wearing the same soft wool trousers that she'd been wearing all day but she'd removed the rest of her soaked clothes and helped herself to one of his jumpers. The fact that it swamped her just increased the air of vulnerability that surrounded her.

She didn't turn when he entered the room but he could tell from the sudden increase in tension in her narrow shoulders that she was aware of his presence. 'The view is incredible.' Her voice was almost wistful. 'It was this room that sold me the house.'

Vulnerable, maybe, but still capable of wreaking havoc.

Engulfed by a fresh spurt of anger, Marco dropped his coat over the back of the sofa. 'It's a shame you didn't stay around long enough to live in it.'

She turned, pain in her eyes. 'Don't do this, Marco. This doesn't have to be an argument. Just let it go.'

'Like you did?' He watched her face, searching for some glimpse of the woman he'd married. 'You just let our relationship slip through your fingers. You never once tried to solve whatever problem it was that you suddenly found. You just walked away.'

Anguish flickered across her face and for a moment she looked as though she was going to defend herself. Then her shoulders sagged and she turned back to look out of the window as if she'd lost the will to fight. 'We wanted different things. You married me because you wanted to start a family and at first I thought I wanted that, too.' She broke off and sucked in a breath. 'But I discovered that I didn't. That sort of difference is too big to bridge, Marco.'

He stared at her with mounting incredulity.

She made herself sound both flighty and indecisive and neither adjective fitted what he knew about her. *Nothing she said made sense.*

'So you had a sudden change of heart—why didn't you discuss it with me?'

'There was nothing to discuss. You wanted one thing, I wanted another.'

Marco tried to make sense of her words. She was saying that she didn't want children and yet he'd seen her with children and had been captivated by how gentle and kind she was. Just now with Alfie, she'd been tactile and gentle. He'd seen how much she cared. In fact, he would have said that she was better with children than adults.

'You love children. You couldn't wait to be a mother,' he said hoarsely. 'That's why I married you.'

'Yes.' This time when she turned to face him, her expression was blank. 'I know that's why you married me. And that's why I knew that it would never work. I knew that there was no point in "trying again" or working at our marriage. There was no point in talking it through or having endless discussions that wouldn't have led anywhere. You married me because you wanted to settle down and have a family. You were perfectly clear about that. And I'm telling you right now that that isn't what I want. So ending our marriage is the fairest thing for both of us. You should be with a woman who wants children. That's very important to you and you can't ignore something like that.'

Marco inhaled sharply and laid himself bare. 'For me, you were that woman, Amy. What was I to you?' *She wasn't good at communicating but he'd thought he'd known what she'd felt. He'd felt utterly secure in her love. Arrogance on his part? Maybe.*

'You were—' She broke off and her eyes slid from his. 'You were a wonderful affair that never should have become anything more.'

If he hadn't been so exasperated and confused he would have laughed. 'You're trying to tell me you wanted the sex and no commitment? Do you have any idea how ridiculous that sounds, coming from you? You don't have affairs!' *It was one of the reasons he'd wanted to marry her.*

'How would you know? We were only together for three months before we married. That's not enough time to know someone. You never really knew me, Marco.'

He'd *thought* he'd known her. 'I know you're not the sort of woman to have a casual affair.'

'Maybe I *am* that sort of woman in some circumstances! I'm not the first woman to find you irresistible, Marco. You're an incredibly sexy guy. Intelligent, good company...' She shrugged as if his attractions were so obvious it was pointless naming them. 'I don't suppose there's a woman in the world who would reject you.'

He decided not to point out that *she* was rejecting him. 'So now you're saying that I seduced you?'

'Of course not. I'm just saying that...the physical side took over.'

'Physical? You married me because I'm good in bed? What about the rest of our relationship?' Finding the entire conversation completely unfathomable and beginning to wonder whether his English was less fluent than he'd previously believed, Marco ran a hand over the back of his neck and held on to his temper with difficulty. 'As I said before, we weren't teenagers, Amy. Yes, there was strong chemistry but our minds were working, too. We shared a great deal more than an incredible sex life.'

Colour bloomed in her cheeks and he remembered just how shy she'd been when they'd first met. 'We were friends, yes. But we never should have been more than that.'

'Was our relationship really that shallow? What about all those plans we made, or is my memory playing tricks? The way you're describing our life together...' he spread his hands in a gesture of raw frustration '...I'm beginning to think we're talking about a completely different relationship!'

'Perhaps we just saw it differently.'

'When we met you enjoyed your work, certainly, but your plans for the future were the same as mine. Family. We lay in bed and talked about having children. We agreed that I would work and you would stay at home with them. You thought it was important for a child to be with its mother, to know it was loved. These weren't *my* plans, *tesoro*, they were *our* plans.'

'To begin with, yes. But then I realised that it was never going to work.'

'Answer me one question, Amy. Did you love me?'

She froze and her eyes slid from his. 'No.' Her voice was so faint he could barely hear her. 'Not enough.'

Her answer shocked him so much that for a moment he didn't answer. *She'd loved him.* He *knew* that she'd loved him.

Or had he been deluding himself?

She'd left, hadn't she? She hadn't tried to mend their marriage. The only contact she'd had with him had been in relation to their separation. Were those the actions of a woman in love? No.

Which left him guilty of arrogance.

Just because attracting women had never been a problem in his life, he'd grown complacent.

He watched her for a moment, trying to make sense of it all—*searching again for the Amy he'd married.* 'So when did you first realise that you didn't love me enough?' The words almost stuck in his throat. 'Everything was fine until we moved back to Penhally. You seemed happy enough to begin with.' Scrolling through events in his mind, he watched her, still searching for clues. 'When did you suddenly decide that you wanted career, not family? And why didn't you share your thoughts with me?'

She turned back to the window. 'You were working, Marco—busy setting up the surgery with Nick. You were hardly ever home so it was hard to share anything with you. I was lonely. And I discovered that I missed working. I discovered that my own career was more important to me than I'd thought it was. Our relationship was so intense that for a short time I was totally infatuated with you. Babies—a family—that was all part of the same infatuation. But good, stable marriages aren't based on physical passion.'

Marco frowned. 'So when did you have this sudden change of heart? Not in the first few weeks, that's for sure. You spent your days going to estate agents because we both agreed we wanted a house out of town and preferably right on the cliffs. You dismissed three properties because they didn't have a garden. I still remember the day you rang me at work to tell me about this place. You were so excited! You'd even picked out the room that you thought should be the nursery. Where was the career woman then, Amy? *Where was she?*' He stared at her profile and saw the faint sheen of tears in her eyes.

The tears diluted his anger and he gave a soft curse and turned away from her, guilt tearing through him. '*Mi dispiace.* I'm sorry. Don't cry. Don't do that.' He hated it when women cried, although to be fair to her, she'd never done that to him before. He stared moodily down at the waves crashing onto the rocks, feeling as though his body and mind were under the same steady assault as the coastline. 'If you truly don't love me enough then there is nothing to be done.' This was entirely new territory for him. In the past he'd been the one to tell a woman that a relationship was over—*that he didn't love her enough.*

Only now was he discovering that it wasn't an easy thing to hear.

He glanced towards her and wondered why, if she didn't love him, she looked so utterly, utterly lost and miserable. 'You've changed so much.'

'Perhaps I have. Didn't you always say that women are sometimes difficult to understand? That we think in different ways?'

Marco gave a twisted smile, bitterly amused at his own arrogance. To think that he'd once thought that he understood women. Amy had long since proved that not to be the case.

'So, after two years of thinking in your very different way, you decided to turn up and ask for a divorce.'

'We've been apart for two years.'

'And that's some sort of magic figure? If you were expecting me to smile and sign, you picked the wrong man to marry and divorce.' His mouth tightened. 'Perhaps I should have mentioned this before, but I don't believe in divorce.'

'Surely that depends on the marriage. You don't want to be married to someone who doesn't love you. It's time to get on with our lives, Marco. I can pursue my career. You can find someone else. You can marry someone else who will give you a whole houseful of children.'

Was that what he wanted?

He'd only ever imagined this house full of his and Amy's children. *Did he want children with another woman?*

CHAPTER FIVE

THE phone rang and Marco let out a stream of Italian, clearly incensed at being interrupted yet again. His eyes glittered dangerously and he glared at the phone as if his anger alone should be enough to silence it.

'Answer it, Marco,' Amy said wearily. 'It's probably someone else whose life needs saving.'

He was angry with her. *So angry with her.*

And intellectually he was outmanoeuvring her at every step, pouncing on holes in her argument like the most ruthless trial lawyer. And there were plenty of holes. Her defence was thin and full of inconsistencies, she knew that, but she hadn't expected to be on trial long enough for it to matter. She'd expected a quick conversation and a rapid exit. She hadn't expected him to argue with her.

She hadn't expected him to *care* enough to argue and she certainly hadn't expected him to ask if she'd loved him.

That had been the most difficult lie of all.

And what now? Was he going to let her go?

Was he going to find another woman to share his heart and have his children?

The thought of another woman living in this house, living with Marco, brought a lump to her throat.

She wasn't going to think about that right now.

Grateful for the brief respite offered by the phone, she

watched as he strode across the room and lifted the handset, his movements purposeful. He was a man who was focused and didn't waste time, hence the reason he was able to cope with such a punishing workload without crumbling under the pressure.

'Nick? Problems?' He didn't even bother to disguise his impatience at the interruption and Amy winced slightly, wondering what the senior partner in the practice was thinking about her sudden unexpected return. Was he cursing her for distracting his partner when they were so busy?

It was obvious from the conversation that Nick was asking Marco about a patient and Marco sprawled into the nearest chair and gave the information that was needed.

He was never given any peace, Amy thought to herself, listening as he and Nick debated different courses of action. But he never tried to hide from his responsibilities. From the moment he'd decided to set up the surgery in Penhally with Nick, he'd been dedicated to delivering the very best health care to the local population. He was that sort of man.

The sort of man who would be an amazing father.

Feeling slightly sick, Amy tried to subdue the misery that bubbled up inside her. *Not now.* She wasn't going to think about that now. She dare not. Marco was far too astute. She had to make it look as though this was what she wanted.

'Amy?' The conversation concluded, he replaced the phone and looked at her. 'Sorry for the interruption. Since Lucy left it's been crazy. The snow hasn't helped. No one is used to having snow in the village and everyone is slipping on pavements and injuring themselves.' He ran a hand over his face. 'And it's New Year's Eve in a few days' time.'

Amy knew from experience that New Year's Eve was always busy for the local health team and being one doctor down would be a problem. 'You haven't managed to find anyone to cover Lucy?'

'We weren't exactly expecting her to deliver so early. We

didn't have time to arrange locum cover. Kate is still working on it.' He leaned his head back against the sofa and closed his eyes. His dark lashes brushed the hard, strong lines of his cheekbones and Amy stared hungrily.

The early morning had always been her favourite time of day, when he had still been asleep and she'd been able to just study his face without having to worry about what she was revealing.

'She told me this afternoon that she may have found someone, but he can't start for another month. Until then it's all hands on deck, except that the ship is sinking. I haven't even asked—how was surgery this morning?' He opened his eyes suddenly and she coloured, embarrassed that he'd caught her looking at him.

'Surgery was interesting.' *Talking about work was good.* 'Along with the usual coughs, colds and sore throats, I saw my first ever case of erysipelas and a case of ophthalmic shingles.'

'I suppose the erysipelas was one of the trawlermen; it usually is. Ophthalmic shingles?' He raised an eyebrow. 'Who was that?'

'A Mrs Duncan?'

'Paula? She's a writer. Detective novels, I think. Lives in that white house on the cliffs. You're sure it was shingles?'

Astonished that he knew so much about his patients, Amy nodded. 'Yes, she had all the symptoms and skin lesions on the side of her nose.'

'Did you refer her to the hospital?'

'Yes.'

'Poor Paula. That's the last thing she needs over the Christmas holidays. Did you give her oral aciclovir? Eight hundred milligrams?'

Amy sighed. 'Marco, if you're so worried about my skills, don't ask me to take your surgery.'

'Sorry.' He gave a faint smile, the first smile that had

touched his mouth since she'd walked back into his life that morning. 'I'm not used to delegating. And especially not to my wife.' He studied her for a moment, his dark eyes narrowed and his long legs stretched out in front of him. He looked impossibly sexy and Amy's mouth dried and she turned away from him, her heart thudding hard against her chest.

'Well—it was just the one surgery,' she muttered, feeling his gaze burning a hole between her shoulder blades.

'So what are your plans once you finally catch that train? Are you returning to Africa or are they sending you somewhere else?'

'I don't know. They've asked me to go to Pakistan.'

'But you haven't accepted?'

'Not yet.' She turned, wondering where the conversation was going. 'I wanted to get things sorted out here first.'

Marco held her gaze. 'So you're out of a job. You, who love work above everything else.' It was impossible to miss the sarcasm in his voice and Amy's tongue tied itself in a knot.

'I'm not exactly out of work.' She tried to retrace her steps. 'I'll go where I'm needed.'

'Is that right? In that case I have a proposition for you. You stay in Penhally for a month. Work in the practice. You've probably noticed that we're struggling. Nick, Dragan and I can't keep it going on our own.'

Amy stared at him for a moment, wondering if she'd misheard. 'That's out of the question.'

'Why? You've just said that you'll go where you're needed. You're needed here, Amy.'

'No.'

'You keep telling me how important it is for you to work. We need another doctor in Penhally. Urgently. You're good at what you do and you're capable of just stepping in and getting on with things. You proved that this morning. If you hadn't been here, surgery would have ground to a halt.'

'You don't want your ex-wife working in your practice.'

'My *wife*.' He emphasised the word gently. 'Actually, you're my *wife*, Amy, not my ex-wife. And why is that a problem? If you don't love me then there are no emotions involved, so working together should be easy. It's a good solution.'

Not for her.

Amy stood there in a blind panic, once again trapped by her own words. 'That's a ridiculous suggestion. We can't work together.'

'Why not?'

Because it would be too painful. *Because she wouldn't be able to hide her true feelings.* 'Marco, don't do this.'

'Don't do what? Don't talk sense? We need a doctor, you need a job. You don't love me—fine, we work together as friends and colleagues and at the end of a month I give you that divorce you want. One month, working side by side as we've done today.'

So basically she had to allow herself to be tortured for a month in order to achieve something that she didn't really want anyway.

She almost laughed.

'It would be too…awkward. Marco, how can you even suggest it?'

'We are both mature, professional people. Why would it be awkward? The only possible reason for it to be awkward would be if you still felt something for me. Is that the case, Amy? Do you feel something?'

It was like being in court in front of a deceptively gentle prosecutor determined to dig up the truth. 'I don't— That isn't what I mean.' She stumbled over the words. 'I don't feel anything for you, Marco. I'm sorry if that's hurtful but it's better that I tell the truth.'

'*Are* you telling the truth?' He was watching her closely, his gaze disturbingly intense. 'There's something going on here, Amy. Something that isn't right.'

'You're putting me in an impossible position, that's what isn't right! I can't stay, Marco.'

'Why not?' There was a hard edge to his tone. 'You've said that you never loved me and that our relationship was just a fling. Since when did a bit of hot sex need to get in the way of a sensible business arrangement? Work is all-important to you and I'm offering you work. If emotions aren't involved, there can't be a problem, can there?'

Her emotions *were* involved. But to admit that would be to admit that she was still in love with him and that would lead to complications that she couldn't handle.

Amy waded through her options and found them depressingly limited. It was obvious that if she refused he would take her refusal as an indication that she was in love with him and she just didn't want him knowing that.

Desperate now, she searched for another excuse—*anything*—that might help her extricate herself from the situation. 'I only planned to come for the day. I don't have clothes or anything.'

'All your clothes are still here. Upstairs in the wardrobe where you left them.' His tone was even. 'In case you've forgotten, you didn't take much with you.'

She'd been too upset to even bother with packing.

Amy turned away and walked over the window, her mind racing. Unlike him, she wasn't thinking clearly.

She could walk away, but then she'd just have to come back and go through all this again another time. Or she could stay and work in Penhally and prove that their relationship was truly over.

All she had to do was keep up the act for a month and then he'd give her a divorce.

She stared out to sea, watching the waves rise and fall. It wasn't as if they'd see that much of each other, she reasoned. She'd already seen how much of his life was tied up with the practice. They'd both be working. She wouldn't be spending a lot of time in his company.

How hard would it be?

'You're joining us?' Nick Tremayne stared at Amy across the desk, a serious expression on his face. 'You're going to work as a locum?'

'Just until Dr Donnelly arrives. Kate has confirmed that he can start in a month.' Exhausted after a sleepless night in Marco's spare room, Amy summoned up a smile that she hoped reflected the correct amount of enthusiasm for the situation. 'I took Marco's surgery for a while yesterday morning and I enjoyed it. I'm between jobs at the moment and you're stuck so it seemed a sensible solution.' *Did she sound convincing?*

Probably not, given that she wasn't entirely convinced herself.

But Marco had pushed so relentlessly that she'd found herself trapped between all the lies she'd told.

Nick looked at her, his gaze just a little too probing for her liking. 'I hate to point out the obvious...' he glanced towards Marco '...but you guys haven't seen each other for two years. Much as we need the help professionally, I can't risk the problems of your personal life invading practice business.'

'We're very civilised,' Marco said easily. 'Working together won't be a problem.'

Wouldn't it? Unconvinced, Amy glanced at him, trying to read his mind, but his face gave nothing away. *Was he really as relaxed about the whole thing as he seemed?*

Perhaps Nick was asking himself the same question because he studied his friend and colleague for a moment before turning back to Amy. 'Where are you going to live?'

Amy opened her mouth to reply but Marco was there first. 'In the house, with me. Where else? I'm rattling around with five bedrooms.' His emphasis on the word 'five' could have been a linguistic slip or else a gentle reminder that they'd chosen the house with the intention of filling it with their children. 'Amy missed her train so she stayed last night. We managed to get through the night without killing each other so I don't anticipate a problem.'

He was expecting her to live in the same house as him? No! That hadn't been part of the original plan. She'd been banking on the fact that, apart from the odd bit of professional communication at work, she'd be able to avoid him. Yes, she'd stayed the previous night—shivering in the spare room like an interloper—but she'd assumed that she'd be finding herself alternative accommodation at some point. Already her eyes were gritty and her head ached as a result of a night in his spare bedroom. She'd spent the entire night awake, imagining Marco just next door, probably sprawled naked in the enormous bed that they'd chosen for the main bedroom, and now she discovered that she was going to be staying there every night.

Amy opened her mouth to argue and then caught Nick's searching look and instead smiled weakly. Thanks to Marco's confident announcement she now had no choice but to stay with him. 'That's right,' she said hoarsely. 'I'm staying with him. No problem.'

Nick shrugged. 'Well, if you both think you can handle it. God knows, we need another doctor badly so I'm not likely to put up much of an argument. Welcome back, Amy, and welcome on board.' His tone was brisk. 'Well, this is a good start to the New Year. I was starting to think we might have a nervous breakdown before we found anyone to cover Lucy's maternity leave.'

'How is Lucy?' Amy tried to ignore the heavy feeling of dread that sat in her stomach. 'Is she doing all right?'

'Very well, considering the baby was premature. Annabel is still in Special Care but they're hoping to be back home for New Year.' Nick tapped his fingers on the desk, his expression thoughtful. It was clear that he was already planning, his mind on the practice and the needs of the local population. 'So, Amy, it's pretty obvious that you should just take on Lucy's patients and the antenatal clinic. I seem to remember that obstetrics was always your big love so it makes sense.'

Amy's mouth dried. 'No!' Forgetting all about the sleeping arrangements, she shook her head. 'No. I mean…could I do one of the other clinics?' *Not antenatal. Please, God, not that. Not now.* 'It would be great to do something different. Don't you do the antenatal clinic? I'd hate to take it away from you.' Aware that Marco was looking at her in astonishment, she tried to recover herself but Nick was frowning, too.

'Since Lucy left I've had to cover the minor surgery and I can't do it all. Marco does child health, of course, and Alison Myers, our practice nurse, does a fair few clinics on her own with no help. Dragan has other responsibilities that take him further afield, so he can't take on obstetrics.' Nick narrowed his eyes, studying her face carefully. 'You love obstetrics. Pregnant women were always your special interest. What's the problem? Is it something to do with your stint in Africa? I mean, it's not as if you're going to be expected to deliver the babies or anything. Just deliver the antenatal care. Have you had a drama that we ought to know about?'

'No. Nothing like that.' Her heart was galloping and her palms were damp. 'There's no problem, really,' she lied, her voice barely working. 'I just thought maybe it would be better to have a more permanent doctor doing that particular clinic. For continuity. Women like continuity, don't they?'

She wished Marco would stop looking at her. And now Nick was looking at her, too. And she had a feeling that the older doctor would be asking her questions sooner rather than later.

'Ideally, yes,' Nick said slowly, his gaze intent on her face. 'But in this case I think they'll just be delighted to have a female doctor with expertise in obstetrics. I can't imagine that anyone is going to protest.'

She was protesting. But now they were both staring at her and she knew that she'd already betrayed far too much.

'Well, if you're sure they won't mind—I'll do the clinic, of course.' She gave what she hoped was a casual smile. 'It will be fine.' Fine. Fine. Fine. She was a trained professional. She could deliver whatever medical care was required of her.

She could do antenatal.

She could switch off. Shut down her feelings. Wasn't that what she'd done for the past two years?

'Good.' Nick's eyes lingered on her face for a moment longer and then he turned back to Marco. 'So that's decided, then. I'll tell Kate and she can inform the patients. Good news. Thanks, Amy. A timely arrival on your part if ever there was one. Lucky for us.'

Not lucky, Amy thought miserably, biting her lip so hard that she tasted blood. *Not lucky at all.*

'All right, so what the hell is happening between you and Amy? Is this happy ever after?' Nick hooked his hands behind his head and rocked back on his chair. 'Are the two of you back together?'

Marco lounged in the chair opposite, his expression guarded. 'Are you asking as my friend or my colleague?'

'What difference does it make? It's a simple yes or no answer.'

'We're not back together again...' Marco paused. 'Yet.'

'But you're working on it. It's what you want, obviously.' Nick made an impatient sound. 'What about Amy? The two of you were good together. What the hell is going on? I never really understood why she left in the first place.'

Marco kept his response factual. 'Apparently she wanted a career instead of children.'

'*Amy?*' Nick looked at him in disbelief. 'That doesn't sound right. She was very excited about starting a family. I remember catching her staring at a baby outfit in a shop window one day. She went a deep shade of scarlet but she had that look in her eyes. That look that warns you to go out and buy a people carrier.'

Marco didn't laugh. 'Well, the look has disappeared. It isn't what she wants any more. She doesn't want babies and she doesn't want me.'

'I wonder why not.'

'She doesn't love me enough.' Marco gave what he hoped passed as a casual shrug. 'It happens.'

Nick laughed with genuine amusement. 'But not to you. Women always love you. It's the accent and the dark, brooding eyes. Come on, Marco! What's the matter with you? Amy loves you! Anyone can see that. She isn't a woman who is fickle in her affections! She's a one-man woman and you're that man. You always have been.'

'Apparently not.' Feeling suddenly irritable, Marco rose to his feet. 'Was there anything else we needed to talk about? Because my love life has run its course as a topic of conversation.'

'How's the car? Did you get the Maserati fixed?'

'Yesterday. Kate arranged it.'

The change in Nick's expression was barely perceptible. 'She's a wonderfully efficient practice manager.'

And she was willing to be a great deal more if Nick would only give her some encouragement, Marco thought, wondering if his colleague was truly as obtuse about Kate's feelings as he pretended to be. Or was it much more complicated than that? Was he still churned up and guilty about the death of his wife? Unable to commit to anyone else?

Marco gave a mental shrug and decided not to pursue the subject. He had enough problems of his own in that department and he certainly wasn't in a position to lecture other people on how to run their love lives. 'I've put Amy in Lucy's consulting room. I assume that's all right with you.'

'As long as she's seeing patients I don't care if she's doing it from the toilet,' Nick drawled. Then he leaned forward. 'Any idea why she was so reluctant to run the antenatal clinic?'

'She doesn't really want to be here at all.' Marco gave a grim smile. 'I used some psychological leverage to get us a doctor for a few weeks. She's here under duress, I'm afraid.'

'Well, I guessed that.' Nick frowned and tapped his pen on the desk. 'But I had a feeling that there might be something more going on. She looked…distraught at the thought of doing that clinic. Pale. Ill. Maybe she's just tired.'

Marco felt a flicker of unease. 'Yes, I think something is wrong, too. That's why I want her to stay. Once I find out what it is and help her solve it, I'll let her go. Perhaps the problem is just that she wants to be as far away from me as is humanly possible.'

'It could be that. But she's a woman…' Nick flicked the switch on his computer '…which also means that it's likely to be something a million times more complicated than that. Watch her, Marco. There's something going on. Just don't let your personal life affect the practice.'

Marco tensed and his voice was a low growl. 'I don't need that lecture from you.'

'Good.' Nick gave a cool smile. 'Then I won't give it.'

'He's getting these headaches,' the woman said, pulling the little boy onto her lap. 'Always behind the left eye and he says it's like a drilling pain.'

Amy glanced at the child's notes, checking that there was nothing in his history that she should know about. 'And what's he like when he gets the headache, Sue? Can he still play or does he have to go and lie down?'

'I give him paracetamol syrup and he lies down. Then he's

generally up and playing within about an hour and a half. The syrup works really well.'

Amy turned to the child. 'And when you have your bad headache, Harry, do you feel sick?'

'Sometimes I feel a bit churny in my stomach.'

'A bit churny.' Smiling at the description, Amy gave a sympathetic nod. 'Are you actually sick?'

'No, but when it happens at school they give me a bowl, just in case.'

Amy looked at Sue. 'And how long has he been getting headaches?'

'It's hard to say.' Sue bit her lip. 'I mean, children get headaches, don't they, so I didn't really think about it at first. Then it became more frequent and when he gets them he's sobbing and crying and it's quite scary. And I started to think—I mean—you're going to think I'm completely paranoid. A headache is just a headache isn't it? It's just that—' She broke off and glanced at the boy, clearly concerned about saying too much in front of him.

Amy leaned forward and wrote on a piece of paper. Then she leaned forward and gave it to the child. 'Harry, would you be kind enough to take this to the lady behind Reception for me? And then come back here. Thank you, sweetheart. That's really helpful.'

Eager to please, Harry left the room and Amy turned to the mother. 'I sense that there are things that you don't want to say in front of him.'

'Well, I don't want to worry him. And I'm probably just being paranoid but it's hard not to be with my history. I was diagnosed with bowel cancer two years ago and everyone told me that it couldn't possibly be anything serious. And then it was. I've had chemo and operations and—well, it's been really, really hard. And it makes you realise that things go wrong. People say, "Oh, it won't be anything," but that's what they said about me and they were wrong. It *was* something.

And when that happens you can't just look at a headache and think headache, can you? I try and do that and all the time I'm thinking brain tumour.'

'You're not alone in that and you have more reason than most to worry, given everything that has happened,' Amy said softly, feeling her heart twist with sympathy. 'You've obviously had a terrible time. I'm so sorry.'

'It's not too bad now, things have gone quiet. But now this.' Sue looked at Amy and her eyes filled. 'I can cope with anything that happens to me but if anything happens to my child—to Harry—that's it, I'm telling you that now. That's it for me. No more. If my baby is ill, then I'll…' Tears poured down her cheeks and Amy reached out and gave her hand a squeeze.

'It is very unlikely that this is anything serious, but I can understand why you're worried, so this is what we're going to do. We're going to take a very, very good look at him and if necessary we'll refer him to the paediatrician for a specialist opinion. Anything we need to do to reassure you.'

'And how long will that take?' Sue reached into her bag for a tissue and blew her nose hard. 'I'm not sleeping at night because I'm so worried.'

The door opened and Harry bounced back into the room. 'She said, "thank you."'

Sue immediately pulled herself together, her smile just a little too bright as she scrunched up the tissue and pushed it up her sleeve. 'Good boy.'

'Yes, thank you, Harry.' Amy smiled and then turned back to Sue. 'Let's start by taking some history. Does anyone in the family suffer from migraines?'

'My mother and my sister. But not for years. I did take Harry to have his eyes tested because I thought it might be that, but the optician said that his eyes are fine. I brought you the report, just in case you wanted to see it.' She rummaged in her bag and pulled out a piece of paper.

Amy glanced at the results and nodded. 'Yes, they're fine. Nothing there that should cause a headache.' She asked a few more questions, recorded the answers carefully and then smiled at the boy. 'Hop on my couch, Harry, and I'll take a look at you.'

She examined the child thoroughly, found nothing that alarmed her but saw the desperate worry in Sue's eyes.

Amy thought for a moment. 'Sue, I can't find anything that would lead me to believe this is anything other than a straightforward headache, but given your history I think it would be reassuring for you to have a second opinion. Dr Avanti is a qualified paediatrician, as you know. I think what we might do, given how worried you are, is to ask him to take a look at Harry.'

'Would he have time?'

Amy looked at the clock. 'Well, it's the end of surgery so let me just pop in and ask him and see how he's fixed.'

She left the room and found Marco in his consulting room, talking on the phone. He waved a hand towards a chair, finished the conversation and then looked at her expectantly. 'Problems?'

'I have Sue Miller in my room.'

'Sue?' His gaze sharpened. 'What's the matter with her? She was diagnosed with colorectal cancer a couple of years ago. I know Lucy did some follow-up with her.'

Amy looked at him curiously. 'Do you know everyone's patients?'

'*Sì*, if they have a history of serious illness, it's my business to know. It's important that all the partners are aware of what is going on.' He shrugged. 'She was discussed in a practice meeting a while ago. She's always a priority patient for us. So, why is she seeing you today?'

'It isn't about her. It's about Harry. He's seven and he's been having headaches.'

Marco gave a slow nod. 'And she thinks this is symptomatic of a brain tumour, no? I'm sure she is very anxious.'

'Exactly. Understandable in the circumstances.'

'Of course. And you've examined him?'

'Yes. I can't find anything, but I can see that she's very worried. I could always refer her to a paediatrician, but that would take time and given that you are a paediatrician, I thought you might look at him for me. Provide instant reassurance.' She frowned. 'Always assuming that there *isn't* anything to worry about.'

'Now who is being paranoid?' Marco said softly, a faint flicker of humour in his eyes. 'Less than one per cent of headaches are caused by a brain tumour. I think you know that statistic.'

'Yes.' Amy gave herself a little shake. 'But try telling that to a thirty-five-year-old woman who developed cancer when she shouldn't have done. I don't think she's a big believer in the relevance of statistics.'

'Point taken. Of course I will see him. Your room or mine?'

His voice was silky smooth and Amy felt the colour flood into her cheeks and cursed herself for reacting so strongly. Why couldn't she be indifferent? Why?

'You may as well come to my room. Harry is playing happily and it might be less unsettling for him.'

Marco picked up his stethoscope and auriscope and followed her out of the room.

'By the way...' He paused outside the door. 'They're having a New Year's Eve party at the Penhally Arms. We're both invited.'

'Thanks, but no.' Amy shook her head. 'I'm here to work, not to party. You go. I'll stay at home and catch up on some paperwork.'

'You need to be there. You're a member of the community now. You need to make a showing.'

'I'm only here for a short time.'

'If you don't go, people will say that we're afraid to be seen together. We need to present a united front. They don't want to think that there's dissent at the surgery.'

Feeling trapped once again, Amy paused with her hand on the door. 'I can't go to a party with you, Marco.'

'Why not?' He looked genuinely puzzled. 'We're friends and colleagues. Why wouldn't you? We can spend a pleasant evening together. What's the problem? Let's go and take a look at Harry.' And he pushed open the door of her consulting room and walked inside, leaving her staring after him with frustration.

CHAPTER SIX

HE ALWAYS seemed to get his own way.

She'd come to Penhally planning to stay for an hour and here she was, working in the surgery, living with him in their old house and now contemplating going to a party with him. It was ridiculous!

Amy watched as he spoke quietly to Sue and then dropped into a crouch next to Harry.

'Hi, there, Harry.' His voice was good-humoured. 'Good Christmas? What did Father Christmas bring?'

'The most *amazing* remote-control car. You should see it, Dr Avanti, it's so cool.'

'You didn't bring it with you?' When Harry shook his head, Marco looked disappointed. 'Shame. Never mind. Next time I see you perhaps you'll have it with you.' He asked Harry a few questions and then did the same of Sue. 'I'm going to take a look at you, Harry. Can you take off your jumper and shirt and sit on that couch, please?'

Marco listened to the child's heart and lungs and then laid him down and examined his abdomen. 'How long have you been at your school, Harry?'

'Oh…' The boy thought for a moment. 'Pretty much my whole life.'

'Since nursery,' Sue muttered, a soft smile on her face as she looked at her child. 'Age four.'

Marco felt the femoral pulse. 'And who lives at home with you?'

'Well, my mum mostly.' Harry wrinkled his nose thought-fully. 'And my dad comes home in the evenings.'

'Because he's at work all day,' Sue interjected hastily, and Marco smiled.

'Children are very literal. Any brothers or sisters, Harry?'

'Just Beth. She's two. She doesn't say much but she bites a lot. I suppose she's all right.' Harry looked a bit unsure on that point and Sue gave him a quick hug.

'She doesn't mean to bite, sweetheart. She's very little and her teeth are hurting.' She gave Marco an apologetic look. 'Beth is going through a biting phase at the moment. I'm talking to the health visitor about her in clinic next week.'

'Good idea.' Marco picked up the patella hammer and gently rolled up Harry's trouser leg. 'And what's your favourite subject at school?'

'Science.' Harry giggled as his leg jumped. 'Are you going to break my leg?'

'Definitely not.' Marco smiled and tested the reflexes in the child's feet. 'Doctors don't break legs, they fix them. Do you like your school, Harry? Are you happy?'

'Yes. Except for the lunches. The lunches are gross.'

'What do they give you for lunch?'

'Slugs and snails.'

Marco looked interested. 'Cooked or raw?'

Amy smiled. He was so good with children and they just adored him.

Harry was giggling. 'And worms. They call it spaghetti but it's *definitely* worms.'

'In Italy, where I come from...' Marco picked up the child's T-shirt and handed it to him '...we eat a lot of worms. You can get dressed now.'

'You eat worms?' Harry shuddered and pulled on his clothes. 'Weird.'

'Very weird,' Marco agreed. 'Now, I want you to sit up and play a few games with me.'

'Games? Cool.' Harry sat up cheerfully, his legs dangling over the edge of the trolley, his expression enthusiastic. 'Now what?'

Marco stood in front of him, legs planted firmly apart, supremely confident. 'I want you to touch my finger and then touch your nose—that's good. And now with the other hand. Faster. Oh, you're good at that.'

'It's easy.'

'Now look at me.' Marco held his hand to the right of the boy's head and wiggled his finger. 'Tell me if my finger is moving or still.'

'Moving.'

'And now?'

'Still.'

Marco switched sides, performed a few more tests and then reached for the ophthalmoscope. 'And now I want to look in the back of your eyes. Amy, can you close the curtains for me, please? Look straight ahead at the picture on the wall, Harry. Keep looking at it even if I get in the way.' He examined the back of both eyes and then put the ophthalmoscope down and drew the curtains.

'Can you see my brain with that light?'

Marco smiled. 'Not your brain exactly but the back of your eye tells me things about your brain. Now put your arms up.' He carried on with the examination while Sue watched anxiously and Amy watched with interest. 'Sit on the floor for me, Harry.'

Eager to please, the little boy slid off the couch and sat on the floor. 'This is fun. Now what?'

'Now stand up as fast as you can.'

The boy leapt to his feet. 'I'm the quickest at gym.'

'I can see that.' Marco walked across to him, putting his

heel directly in front of his other foot. 'Can you do this? It's like walking on a tightrope.'

'You mean like in the circus?' Harry chuckled and walked, arms outstretched like an acrobat. 'Like this?'

'Perfect. You're good at that. Better than me. So—we're finished. Good boy.' Marco sat down in the chair opposite Sue. 'All right. I don't see anything that worries me. I don't think this is what you're afraid it is, but if you want more definite reassurance I can refer him for an MRI scan.'

Sue pulled a face. 'I was scanned so many times. I wouldn't want him to have that. It's radiation, isn't it?'

'You're talking about CT scans. An MRI scan is different.' Marco's voice was calm and patient. 'There is no radioactivity, no risk to the patient and Harry is old enough to tolerate it with no problem.'

Sue looked at him and her eyes filled. 'You don't think it's…anything? Truly?'

Amy knew she was avoiding saying the word 'cancer' because the little boy was still in the room.

'I don't think so, although medicine is never an exact science, as you are well aware.' Marco's sympathetic smile indicated that he was referring to her own medical history. 'I think Harry might be suffering from migraines. Not an easy diagnosis to make in a child because the pattern of headaches is not always predictable, but what you describe—the drilling pain, the very definite episode, which is relieved by paracetamol, the fact he needs to lie down…' Marco shrugged his shoulders. 'This sounds to me like migraine and there is some family history to support the theory.'

Sue looked at him. 'If he were your child, what would you do?'

Amy felt her stomach flip. *Marco's child.*

His mind clearly in tune with hers, Marco's gaze flickered to hers momentarily and something burned, slow and hot, in the depths of his eyes. Amy swallowed, knowing that he was thinking of the plans they'd made to have a family.

'If he were mine...' Marco dragged his gaze from Amy's and glanced across at the little boy, who was playing happily on the carpet. 'If he were mine, I would watch him for a while, see how he goes. I think you should keep a diary of the headaches so that we can assess exactly how many he is getting, how long they last and whether there are any obvious triggers. Do that for six weeks and then make an appointment with one of us to go through the diary. We can look at the frequency and decide whether to refer him to the paediatricians at the hospital for them to take a closer look.'

'But you don't think—'

'No.' Marco's voice was firm. 'I don't. But we will watch him. And if you decide that you would be happier if he had an MRI scan, you have only to let me know and I will arrange it.'

Sue closed her eyes for a moment and let out a long breath. 'Thank you for that. I'll pass on the scan for the time being. But what could be causing the migraines, do you think?'

'It's hard to say.' Marco watched the child play. 'Often we underestimate children, especially very young children. We imagine that because they are young, they are somehow not aware of what is going on around them, but that is rarely the case. Most children are extremely intuitive and even if they don't pick up on conversations they pick up on atmosphere. Is he a sensitive child, would you say?'

'Very.' Sue looked at her son. 'He's a worrier. And very caring. Even in the playground at school, he's always watching out for other children.'

Marco nodded slowly. 'So—we know that the past two years have been very hard for you personally and also for your family. It would be almost impossible for that not to have had an impact.'

'I suppose so. We've done our best to protect the children,

but inevitably some of it filters through.' Sue rose to her feet and managed a smile. 'But things are going better now. I'm hoping this is going to be our lucky year. Will you be in the Penhally Arms on New Year's Eve, Dr Avanti? I hear they're planning quite an evening.'

'*Sì*. Where else would I be on New Year's Eve when the drink is free?' Marco winked at her. 'I'll be there.'

'Then we might see you. Thank you, both of you. Harry...' Sue held out a hand to her son. 'Let's go and write a few more thank-you letters for all those Christmas presents.'

Harry gave an exaggerated shudder but followed his mother out of the room with a wave at Marco.

'Sweet boy,' Amy said quietly, and then realised that Marco was watching her.

'I thought you didn't like children?'

She stiffened. 'I never said I didn't like children. I just said I didn't want any of my own. That's completely different.' Uncomfortable under his scrutiny, she turned away. *She couldn't live like this.* Couldn't be on her guard the whole time. It was exhausting and she was a useless, terrible liar. 'So we'll keep an eye on him, then. Thanks for looking at him. You really think he's all right?'

'Who?' It was as if his mind was somewhere else entirely. Then he sighed. 'Oh, Harry—yes. Amy, his neurological examination was normal, there was no evidence of poor co-ordination, ataxia or nystagmus. His peripheral nervous system was normal. His cardiovascular system was normal. Personally, I wouldn't even scan him, but if Sue carries on worrying, it's worth arranging it.'

'I'll do that. Or I suppose the locum can do it if I've gone. I'll make sure the notes are detailed. Thank you, Marco.'

He studied her in brooding silence. 'My pleasure.'

* * *

The antenatal clinic was held that afternoon and Amy spent her entire lunch hour wondering whether there was any way she could get out of it without drawing attention to herself.

Five minutes before it was due to start she was still sitting in the staffroom when Kate hurried in. 'You haven't forgotten your clinic, Amy?'

If only.

'No.' Amy forced a smile. 'Just having five minutes' rest before I start.'

'We almost cancelled this particular clinic as it's the week between Christmas and New Year, but there were so many patients that in the end I decided that we had to run it. Are you going to eat that sandwich in front of you or just look at it?' Kate flicked the switch on the kettle and waited for it to boil.

'I'm not really hungry.' *It was a shame they hadn't cancelled the clinic.*

'You have a busy afternoon ahead of you. You should eat lunch.' Kate made her coffee and added some milk. 'Is it Marco that's made you lose your appetite? What's going on with the two of you?'

Amy hesitated. Kate was a friend, but she wasn't used to confiding in people. All her life she'd made her own decisions and relied on herself. To begin with she'd had no choice, and then it had become a way of life. 'We're— Well, let's just say our relationship is still over. We're just working a few things out.'

'That must be hard.' Kate put her mug on the table and sat down. 'You're very pale, Amy. Are you ill? Or is it just the stress of seeing Marco again?'

Could she pretend she was ill?

It would get her out of doing the clinic and it wasn't altogether a lie. The mere thought of spending an afternoon talking to pregnant women was enough to make her ill. But if she said she was ill, Marco would be on to her, trying to find out what was wrong.

'I'm not ill.'

'Then it must be stress. Do you honestly think the two of you are going to be able to work together?' Kate slowly stirred sugar into her coffee. 'I know that Nick's worried about it. He thinks that the history between you is going to make things difficult.'

'It will be fine. Nick has nothing to worry about. Marco and I are not planning to discuss the demise of our marriage at work.'

'No—all the same, it was good of you to stay and help us. I'm guessing that you didn't want to but Marco is very persuasive, as we both know. He has a way of getting a person to say yes to all sorts of things.' Kate's voice was gentle. 'Whatever you say to the contrary, I know this can't be easy for you, Amy. I never really understood what went wrong between the two of you but if you want someone to talk to, you have a friend in me. I just wanted to remind you of that.'

'Thanks. Thanks, Kate.' Unbelievably touched, Amy rose to her feet quickly before she was tempted to blurt out the truth about the current situation. 'Love is complicated, isn't it? And painful.' She had no doubt that Kate knew firsthand how painful love could be. Hadn't she lost her husband in a tragedy at sea that had left her to bring up a child alone?

'Yes. It's both those things.'

'How are things with you? How is Jeremiah?'

'Jem? He's fine. Really good. He's eight now. Unbelievable, really, how time passes.' For a moment, Kate stared blankly into the distance and then she cleared her throat and reached for her coffee, suddenly brisk and efficient. 'I envy you doing the antenatal clinic. At least pregnant women are healthy and cheerful.'

Amy's smile froze. 'Yes.'

'There are days when I miss midwifery.'

'I'd forgotten that you're a trained midwife.' *This was a conversation she didn't want to be having.* 'I'd better get on. I'll see you later, Kate.'

She had a clinic to run. A clinic that she didn't want to take.

And she needed to prepare herself.

Amy worked on automatic, barely registering the identity of each patient.

It was as if a part of her mind was shut off.

By four o'clock, she only had one pregnant woman left to go and she poured herself a glass of water and drank deeply, promising herself that she was going to go straight home after the clinic. She was going to go straight home and hide under the duvet.

The door opened and her last patient walked in, a blonde woman in her late twenties, carrying a baby in a car seat.

'I know, I know, you're thinking I'm in the wrong clinic.' The woman laughed and sat down on the chair. 'Can you believe it? This little one is only four months old and I'm pregnant again! It's done wonders for my husband's ego. He thinks he's some sort of stallion. So much for the contraceptive effects of breastfeeding! I didn't believe it at first but I've done the test three times so I don't think there's any doubt. I rang for an appointment and they told me to come along this afternoon. They like you to get checked out as soon as possible these days, don't they?'

'That's right. You did the right thing to come.' Amy's mouth dried. 'Congratulations. Are you pleased?'

'Oh, yes. Well, Geoff, that's my husband, always wanted a large family so it's not a problem. We hadn't quite planned on having them so close together but it's quite good when they're close in age, isn't it?' The baby started to cry and she bent down, undid the straps and gently lifted the baby from the car seat. 'Oh, now I've woken him up with my loud voice. Are you ready for your milk? Ridiculous, isn't it? Breastfeeding while you're pregnant. I mean, that's one of the things I wanted to talk to you about. Is it OK? I don't want to deprive the new baby of nutrients or anything.'

Amy watched as the woman lifted her jumper and skilfully attached the baby to her breast. The baby greedily clamped its jaws around her nipple and then closed his eyes and started to suck, a blissful expression on his face.

What did it feel like?

'Are you all right, Dr Avanti?' The woman frowned at her. 'You look a bit pale, yourself.'

'I'm fine,' Amy said tonelessly.

'And you're married to the other Dr Avanti. Lucky you. Now, that's a man any woman would want to make babies with.'

The pain inside her was so vicious that it took Amy a moment to find the breath to speak. 'It shouldn't be a problem to continue breastfeeding.' Somehow she forced herself to deliver the facts. 'Your biggest problem is likely to be that you'll feel very tired. Make sure you get plenty of rest and eat well. The taste of the milk might change and the baby might object to that for a while…' With difficulty she got through the consultation, saying what needed to be said and carrying out the tests that needed to be done.

By the time she finally closed the door on her consulting room at the end of clinic she felt emotionally drained. Sliding back into her chair, she felt the hot sting of tears behind her eyes.

Appalled at herself, she took a huge gulping breath and tried to control her emotions, but her misery was just too great to be contained and the tears spilled down her cheeks as the dam broke.

Sobs tore through her body and she put her head in her arms and gave in to it, crying like a child, consumed by the emotion that had been building inside her for so long.

She didn't hear the door open—wasn't aware of anything apart from her own misery until she felt a gentle hand on her shoulder and the sound of her name.

She gave a start and lifted her head to find Nick standing there, a look of concern on his face. 'Amy? What's happened?'

'Nothing.' Mortified, she sat up instantly and rubbed her palms over her cheeks, trying to compose herself. 'Well, this is embarrassing. I'm so sorry. *Really* sorry. I'm just tired or something. It's been a bit of a long week.' Her voice was thickened by crying and she knew that she must look a mess.

'Tired?' He studied her for a moment and then pulled up a chair and sat down next to her. 'No one cries like that just because they're tired. Are you depressed?'

Depressed?

Sodden with misery, Amy just stared at him. Clearly he wasn't going to leave her alone without an explanation and she was worn out with searching for new explanations that would keep people satisfied. 'Honestly, I'm not depressed. I'm sorry, Nick.' She yanked a tissue out of the box on her desk and blew her nose hard. 'That was very unprofessional of me. I can assure you that I was fine in front of the patients. I didn't—'

'Amy.' His tone was gruff as he interrupted her anxious apology. 'At this precise moment I don't give a damn about the patients. I'm not thinking about the patients. It's you that I'm worried about.'

'That's kind of you.' She blew her nose again and then gave him a smile. 'But there's no need to worry. I'm fine. Really.'

'Fine doesn't make you sob your heart out on the desk. Does this have something to do with the antenatal clinic? You really didn't want to run it, did you? And we didn't listen.'

'It's not the antenatal clinic.'

Nick watched her. 'Did you lose a baby, Amy?'

'No!' She shot him an anguished look, the pain twisting inside her. 'No, I didn't.'

'Then what's this about? Tell me.'

Amy teetered on the edge of confession and then suddenly remembered just who Nick was. 'I can't.' The tears threatened to start again and she gritted her teeth. 'I— It wouldn't be fair to you.'

'So it's something to do with your relationship with Marco and you're afraid that telling me would put me in a difficult position. You're also not sure that you trust me not to tell him. He mentioned that you'd changed your mind about having a family. Is this related?'

'Don't ask me. I can't talk to you, Nick.'

'I'm your doctor. You can talk to me and it's confidential.'

She blew her nose again and gave a watery smile. 'You're not my doctor. I've only been back in the country for five minutes. I don't have a doctor.'

'Well, you clearly need one, so from now on I'm officially your doctor. Kate will take care of the paperwork.' There was a faint trace of humour in his eyes. 'I need new patients. In case you hadn't noticed, we're nowhere near busy enough around here. I want to know why you were crying, Amy.'

She looked at him, her reluctance dissolving under the kindness she saw in his eyes. 'I find the antenatal clinic difficult.'

'Yes. I gathered that.' His voice was soft. 'Tell me why, Amy. Tell me why you find it difficult.'

She waited a heartbeat. 'Because I can't have children. I'm infertile.'

Nick was silent for a moment and then he sat back in his chair and gave a slow nod. 'All right. Now things are starting to make more sense. And this, presumably, is why you ended a relationship with a man you love?'

'I had no choice.'

'What about Marco? Didn't you think he deserved to know?'

'Don't judge me, Nick!' Her voice sharp, she rose to her feet and paced across the consulting room. Then she turned and wrapped her arms around her body, rubbing her hands up her arms to try and warm herself. 'I did what had to be done.'

'Can we take this a step at a time? When the two of you first arrived in Penhally, you were planning to start a family, I know. That's why you didn't bother finding a job. You were chasing around looking for suitable houses. You'd only been together for a few months. Given that you were in your early thirties, I wouldn't have expected you to become pregnant immediately. It often doesn't work like that, as you well know.'

'I know.' Should she tell him the truth? 'I went for tests.'

'After three months?'

'It was longer than that. By the time I had the tests, we'd been together for six months. No contraception. No pregnancy.' She started to pace again. 'To begin with I thought what you thought. I said all those things women always say to themselves when they're trying to get pregnant. Six months is nothing. I'm over thirty, it might take a while. And then I bumped into an old friend I was in med school with and she turned out to be an infertility specialist at a clinic in Exeter. I decided I may as well have some tests.'

'You didn't tell Marco?'

'No.' She stopped pacing. 'I wanted to find out for myself.'

'So what did the tests show?'

'Scarring.' Such a simple word for something that had had such a massive impact on her life. 'Mild endometriosis. Not enough to need treatment but quite enough to interfere with my fertility. The doctor said that my Fallopian tubes are completely gummed up.'

Nick listened carefully and then he stirred. 'Well, the first thing to say is that infertility is a particularly inexact science. No doctor would ever be able to be one hundred per cent sure that you were infertile.'

'She said that if an egg ever made it along my Fallopian tube, she'd be surprised.'

'Well, we've just had snow in Cornwall.' He gave a wry smile. 'So life is full of surprises, Amy.'

'I know that miracles happen. I know all that, Nick.' She was touched by his kindness. Often with his colleagues Nick was brusque and sometimes even sharp-tongued. But there was no doubting his concern for her at that moment. 'But I couldn't risk our marriage and Marco's happiness on a hope. The chances are that I will never be able to get pregnant.'

'And that was enough for you to decide to end your marriage?'

'It was enough for me.' *More than enough.*

'Let's assume for the sake of argument that your Fallopian tubes are blocked—there are still other options. IVF? Adoption?'

Amy stilled. 'Those aren't options for me.'

'Why not?'

'I have my reasons.' And she wasn't going to share those reasons with anyone. She'd already said more than enough. 'So now you see why I had to leave.'

'Well, not really, no. I see why you *think* you had to leave. You managed to convince yourself that Marco would be better off without you. So you spun a story about choosing a career over a family and about not loving him enough.'

'I had to give him a reason.'

'Why not give him the truth?'

'Because then he would have felt an obligation towards me. I was already his wife. I decided that the easiest way was just to end the relationship. It would have ended at some point anyway, so I didn't do anything except bring forward the inevitable.'

'That's a very negative attitude. Why would it have ended anyway?'

'Because infertility wrecks marriages. It tears them apart.' She stared out of the window, her expression bleak. 'Even strong marriages, and ours wasn't that strong. We hadn't known each other long. He didn't love me enough.'

'Didn't he? That's interesting,' Nick said calmly. 'So why did he go completely off the rails when you left?'

Startled, Amy turned to him. 'What do you mean, "off the rails"?'

'I'll spare you the details but let's just say that he wasn't a happy man.' Nick's eyes narrowed. 'I've known Marco for years, as you know. I can honestly say that you were the first woman he ever really loved.'

'He didn't love me. He couldn't have done.'

'Why not?'

'Because we were together such a short time.'

'But you loved him in that same short time,' Nick pointed out calmly, and she gave a reluctant nod.

'Yes, but…he didn't love me.' Amy frowned and shook her head. 'He never said.'

'Ah. Didn't he?' Nick gave a wry smile. 'Well, we men are terrible at saying what women want to hear, you should know that. But just because the words aren't there doesn't mean that the emotions aren't.'

'He didn't love me, Nick.' She clasped her hands in front of her. 'He didn't try and stop me going.'

'He was in shock. You'd just bought a house to move into together and then suddenly you changed overnight. He assumed you'd met someone else and were just throwing excuses at him.'

Amy felt the colour drain from her face. 'There was no one else. There's never been anyone else.'

'I'm just telling you what he assumed. He couldn't think of anything else that would explain the sudden shift in your behaviour.'

'Is that why he didn't come after me?'

'He's a proud man, Amy. He assumed that you wanted to get away from him so he wasn't about to follow you. And after he calmed down—well, that was when things fell apart here.' Nick's face was expressionless as he referred obliquely to the death of his wife. 'I expect he felt he couldn't leave.'

'Of course he couldn't. I understand. It must have been a horrendous time for you. And I didn't want, or expect, Marco to follow me.' She closed her eyes for a moment. 'I'm so, so sorry about your wife, Nick.'

'We're talking about you, not me.'

'I think we've said all there is to say. I can't have a child, Nick. I can't give Marco the family he wants so badly. And he *does* want it badly—you of all people should know that. He's Italian. He wants a big, noisy, busy family with at least four children as beautiful as he is, fighting over the large bowl of spaghetti in the middle of the table.'

'I don't understand why you're so black and white about this.' Nick stood up and rubbed his forehead with the tips of his fingers. 'There are other options, Amy. If it's so important to you both, you could look for a solution.'

The past clawed at her and she gave a little shake of her head, trying to dispel the memories. *It was always there in the background.*

'I'm not interested in any of those options. I've seen what—' She broke off but Nick's questioning gaze was enough to tell her that she'd already said too much.

'What have you seen, Amy?'

'Nothing.' Her voice was hoarse. 'Nothing. I just know that those aren't options.'

Nick studied her face for a moment but he didn't push her

for more information. 'Well, at least now I understand why you didn't want to do the antenatal clinic.'

'It was difficult,' she said honestly, 'but you don't come to terms with something by ignoring it, so I'm sure that taking that clinic will do me good in the long term.'

'Some things are more difficult to come to terms with than others. Marco can do that clinic from now on, Amy. Or I will. You can do child health or minor surgery.'

'If we swap things around then he'll ask questions that I don't want to answer, and anyway he should do child health—he's a paediatrician. I'll be fine, Nick. I can do the clinic.' Amy walked back to her desk and picked up her coat and bag. 'I'm sorry to dump all over you like this. I can't think what came over me.'

'If a problem is big enough then it eventually finds its way out,' Nick said softly, and Amy slipped on her wool coat and belted it.

'Maybe.'

'My guess is that you've bottled this up for two years. You should talk to someone about it. Talking can help.'

She picked up her bag. 'Do you talk to anyone, Nick?'

His gaze held hers for a moment and then he gave a humourless laugh. 'I'm not sure if you win that point or not. It's different. I'm a man.'

'And you know as well as I do that talking doesn't always help anything. Sometimes it makes things worse. I'd be grateful if you didn't say anything to Marco.'

'He'd want to know, Amy.'

'It would make everything a thousand times more complicated and painful and it wouldn't change the outcome.'

'He loves you.'

Amy felt as though her heart was being squeezed by a vice. 'Even if that were true, it wouldn't change the outcome either,' she said quietly, walking towards the door. 'Thanks, Nick, for listening. Actually, it *was* good to tell someone. I feel better now. More in control. I can do this. I can work as a locum and then walk away and pursue a career.'

'And is that what you want?'

She paused with her hand on the door. 'No. But life doesn't always give you what you want, does it?'

'No. It doesn't.'

She left the room and immediately bumped into Marco in the corridor. Knowing that the evidence of her distress would still show on her face, she kept walking. 'I've finished the clinic. I'll see you at home.' She kept her head down but he caught her arm.

'You're always in such a hurry! I just spoke to the hospital. Eddie doesn't have a skull fracture and they're happy with him. He's coming home tomorrow.'

'That's good. Really good. His mother must be relieved.' She glanced at her watch. 'I've got to dash.'

'Why?' He slid a hand under her chin, lifted her face and then swore softly. 'You've been crying.'

'No, of course I haven't.' She tried to ease her arm away from his grip but he held her firmly.

'Your eyes are red.'

'I think I'm getting a cold.' She sniffed to prove the point. 'It's that time of year. Germs everywhere.'

'Germs don't give you swollen eyes. You've been crying, Amy. Why?'

Given the determined pressure of his fingers, she had no choice but to look into his eyes and this time there was no trace of anger. Just concern. And the concern brought the lump back to her throat.

Oh, for goodness' sake, what was the matter with her? Why did her body have to pick this particular moment to release all the tension that had been building inside her? She'd had two years to break down and she'd chosen the most inappropriate moment possible and the most public place.

With a determined effort she freed herself from his grasp

and stepped away from him. 'Honestly, I'm fine. I'm really, really pleased about little Eddie. I'll see you at home.' And she turned and hurried away from him.

CHAPTER SEVEN

'SHE was crying.' Marco followed Nick back into his consulting room, anger shaking his powerful frame. 'Amy has been crying and you were with her! What did you say to her?'

'I can't discuss it.'

'You *will* discuss it!' Marco slammed the door shut with the flat of his hand and gave a low growl. 'This is my wife we're talking about.'

'You're separated.'

'She's *my wife*.'

'Why would you care if she's upset?' Nick's tone was even. 'You've been angry enough with her for the past two years.'

'She left me. I'm human. Yes, I was angry. But that doesn't stop me caring about her.'

Nick sat down in his chair. 'How much do you care about her?'

'What sort of a question is that? So now you are—what do they call it?' His English momentarily abandoning him, Marco switched to Italian and then back again. 'A marriage counsellor?'

'Do you still love her?'

Thrown by the intimacy of the question, Marco prowled across the consulting room and stared blankly at the wall displaying a poster on the dangers of smoking. 'Yes. I still love her.' He turned sharply. 'So now will you tell me why she was crying?'

'I can't do that. Our talk was confidential.'

'So you *do* know what's wrong.' Exasperated, Marco spread his hands in question. 'Tell me what she said! How could it be confidential?'

'Because she spoke to me as a doctor.'

'It was a consultation?'

'Yes.'

'She's ill?' Anxiety replaced anger, but the emotion was just as sharp. 'Is something the matter with her?' He'd wondered. It might explain why she'd lost weight and why she was looking so pale.

'She isn't ill.'

Marco let out a long breath. For a moment he'd been afraid that— 'Well, if she wasn't ill, why did she need to talk to a doctor?'

Nick was silent for a moment. 'How well do you know Amy?'

Marco frowned and rubbed a hand over his face. 'Well enough to love her. I know the sort of person she is. She's shy with people she doesn't know, she finds it quite hard to talk about her feelings but underneath she's very loving and giving. She loves children, or at least I always thought she did.' Marco broke off, wondering why he was revealing so much to his partner. 'I don't understand what you're getting at.'

'How much do you know about her past? Her background? Before she met you?'

'I don't know. Not much. I never really worried about it. It's not that relevant, is it?' His gaze sharpened. 'You think it's relevant?'

'I don't know.' Nick's voice was thoughtful. 'I think it could be. If you want my advice, and frankly I wouldn't blame you if you didn't take it because advice on the matters of the heart isn't exactly my strong suit, I'd get to know her better. I mean the Amy underneath. What makes her tick? What made her believe the things she believes? Find that out and you might find the answers you're looking for.'

'You can't tell me more than that?'

'No. I can't.' Nick leaned forward and switched on his computer. 'That's already far more than I should have said.'

Amy took a hot shower but it didn't stop the shivering. Desperate for warmth, she dressed in a pair of jeans and a warm jumper, her hair hanging damp and loose to her shoulders.

Her head throbbed from crying and outside the wind had picked up. The sky was grey and threatening and the word among the villagers was that there was more snow on the way.

Still shivering, she walked down to the kitchen to make herself a hot drink. The conversation with Nick had left her feeling raw and vulnerable. She felt slightly odd, having exposed so much of herself to another person. And yet, despite that, telling Nick had made her feel better. He was the first person she'd confided in and she felt lighter.

Or did she feel lighter because he'd told her that Marco had been so badly affected by her departure?

He'd cared.

And she'd so badly wanted him to care. Not that it changed anything, she reminded herself miserably. It didn't change anything at all. No relationship was strong enough to withstand such a bitter blow—she knew that better than anyone.

Thoughts flew into her head and clashed, a cacophony of childhood memories that unsettled and disturbed her.

Not now. *She wasn't going to think about any of that now.*

Hearing the unmistakable sound of the Maserati, Amy tensed.

Marco was home.

Which meant more questions.

She was just debating whether to go up to the spare room and close the door when she heard his key in the door and moments later he walked into the kitchen.

'It's freezing out there and as for the wind...' He gave a shudder that more eloquently described his views on the weather than his words did. 'They were planning fireworks on New Year's Eve but they won't be able to do them if this wind keeps up. It will be too dangerous. We will be treating burn victims.'

Amy found herself looking at the curve of his mouth and then at the dark shadow of stubble on his hard jaw. She turned away quickly. 'It will be a shame if we have to cancel. The fireworks are always a highlight of New Year in Penhally. I used to love them when I was a child.' *Why did she still have to feel like this?* It was so unfair!

Marco reached for a bottle of wine. 'You stayed with your grandmother?'

'That's right.'

'In the cottage? I've often wondered why you sold it.'

'It would have been too small for us.'

'*Sì*, but I would have thought it had sentimental value.' He jerked the cork out of the bottle and reached for a glass. 'Wine?'

'No, thanks.'

'You look tired.' His eyes lingered on hers for a moment and then he turned away and poured wine into his own glass.

Her heart pumping hard, Amy closed her eyes briefly, hoping that he couldn't sense her body's response to him. Everything suddenly felt confused. She'd arrived with one clear objective and an iron resolve, but now everything was clouded. Suddenly what she had to do and what she wanted to do seemed a million miles apart.

It was just because she was living and working with him, she thought helplessly. Marco didn't exactly melt into the background. He was a very confident, very physical man. Even now, with his powerful shoulders and long, strong legs, he seemed to fill the room, and suddenly the large, beautiful kitchen seemed claustrophobically small.

'So, your grandmother's house—was it full of memories?'

Full of memories, many of them not good. 'I didn't want to keep it.' Why was he watching her so closely? *Had Nick said something to him?*

'You're very tense,' he said softly. 'Is something wrong?'

Of course she was tense. She was so aware of him that it was almost impossible to breathe.

'Amy?' He stepped towards her and lifted a hand, stroking her hair away from her forehead with the tips of his fingers. 'Do you have a headache?'

This was insane. She had to move away now. The brush of his fingers set her body on fire, even though she knew that his touch hadn't been sexual in nature.

Her gaze lifted to his and she saw the hot burn in his eyes, the look they exchanged an intimate meshing of their thoughts.

Terrified that he'd see too much, Amy moved away from him, ignoring the instinct that was telling her to move closer. 'I do have a slight headache. Do you have any paracetamol in the house?'

His eyes didn't leave hers. 'Go and lie on the sofa. I'll bring you something.'

Relieved to put some space between them, she did as he suggested and moments later he reappeared with a glass of water and the tablets.

'Thank you.' She took them gratefully and then leaned her aching head against the back of the sofa, hoping that the tablets wouldn't take long to work. 'Sorry. Long day.'

'I can imagine.' He took the water from her, put it on the table and then moved behind the sofa.

The next thing she felt was the touch of his hands in her hair. 'Marco—'

'This will ease the pain of your headache far more effectively than medication,' he murmured softly, sliding his fingers into her hair and gently massaging her scalp. 'I remember that you often had headaches when we first met.'

'Like little Harry. Poor thing. I wouldn't wish this on anyone.' She knew she ought to move but she couldn't. His fingers were firm and rhythmic as they moved over her scalp. 'That feels good.'

'Tell me about the Penhally fireworks. Tell me about your grandmother.' His voice was deep and soothing and her eyes drifted shut.

'I stayed with my grandmother every Christmas and New Year, right through the holidays. There was a window-seat in my bedroom and on New Year's Eve I'd kneel there and watch the fireworks—they were fantastic. Then we'd have hot chocolate together. When I was older, I was allowed to go along and watch.'

'And that was fun?'

'Yes. Everyone was very friendly.' For a short time she'd felt as though she'd belonged somewhere.

'You spent every holiday with your grandmother?'

'Because my mother was working right through and she couldn't look after me.'

'And your father?'

The question disturbed the calm flow of her thoughts. 'My father spent every Christmas with his twenty-four-year-old secretary.'

'Ah…' Marco's fingers stopped moving. 'He had an affair?'

'It started as an affair, but then he married her and at the last count they had four beautiful children, two boys and two girls.' The tension flowed back into her veins and she sat up. 'Why are we talking about my father?'

'Why not?' He walked over to the table and picked up his wine. 'You said that we didn't know each other well enough and I'm starting to think that perhaps you were right. I want to know more about your life before I met you. It must have been tough, spending every holiday with your grandmother.'

'I loved it,' she said honestly. 'She was a wonderful woman.'

'You didn't miss your home? Your mother?'

Her heart beating rapidly, Amy rose to her feet. 'No, not really. What is this? The Spanish Inquisition?'

'Calmo, tesoro.' His voice was soft. 'Suddenly your voice is rising and you're very tense. Why does a simple question feel like an inquisition? Is the subject matter that painful?'

'Painful? I didn't say it was painful,' she said quickly. 'I just don't see how my past is in any way relevant to our current situation. You don't *need* to know any more about me, Marco. It's irrelevant. Our marriage is over, we both know that.' She regretted the words instantly, knowing that such a declaration simply invited the very response on his part that she was trying to avoid.

'It is over? Ah, yes.' His tone was deceptively casual as he strolled across the room towards her. 'I remember now. It is over because you feel nothing for me, isn't that right?'

She didn't dare look at him and she didn't need to because his slightly husky, lazy drawl revealed his feelings all too clearly. Amy ceased to breathe. 'I think I'll go upstairs and—'

'You're not going anywhere.' Without allowing her time to move, he curved an arm around her waist in an unmistakably possessive gesture and pulled her against him, ignoring her soft gasp of protest.

'What are you doing?'

'What I should have done two years ago. When you talk, nothing makes sense so the obvious solution is to try a different method of communication.' She was breathlessly aware of the dangerous glint in his eyes and then his mouth came down on hers and they were kissing, their mouths hungry, the pleasure hot and instantaneous.

It was like a storm breaking and Amy sank her fingers into the hard muscle of his shoulders to stop herself sliding to the floor. Her legs shook, her whole body trembled and the heat of his mouth coaxed a response from her, even though she was dimly aware that what they were doing now was going to make everything much more complicated later.

She didn't care about later. She only cared about *now*, and anyway it was impossible to think or concentrate when his skilful hands were reacquainting themselves with her body. They slid under her jumper and stroked the warm skin of her back and then they moved back to her waist and one thumb circled her navel. And all the time he kissed her, his mouth and hands creating sensations that threatened to consume her.

She'd missed him so much.

The hot, desperate kiss was briefly interrupted as he pulled her jumper over her head and then her shirt followed and her bra until she stood only in her jeans, shaking and shivering in his arms.

'You are cold?' He muttered the question against her mouth and she shook her head, wondering how she was expected to answer when she could barely stand.

'No. Not cold.'

Hot. *Dangerously, deliciously hot.*

Marco kissed her again and she clung to him as he pulled her gently off balance and lowered her onto the thick rug. Next to them the fire flickered but neither of them noticed or cared.

Amy could hardly breathe and she gave a low moan as his mouth moved to her breast, his tongue teasing her nipple to hardness. He seduced and tormented until the sensation that shot through her body was almost agonising in its intensity.

And then he shifted his attention to her other breast and Amy writhed and gasped, her body arching against his as he used all his skill and experience to drag a response from her.

Oblivious to everything except her own need for him, she reached down to touch him and only then realised that he was still fully clothed. With a whimper of frustration she tugged at the belt of his trousers and he covered her hand with his and swiftly helped her.

Amy felt her mouth dry as Marco dragged off his own clothes, revealing a body that was hard and fit. Had she really thought she'd ever be indifferent to this man? He had an amazing physique, the muscles of his shoulders and arms curved, his stomach flat and the movement of his body fluid.

Then he turned back to her and lowered his head, his mouth hot and hard and the touch of his fingers skilled and impossibly intimate. He wasn't slow or gentle but she didn't care because this wasn't about seduction—it was about wild, desperate need. And when he finally parted her thighs she gave a whimper of assent and wrapped her legs around him. Nothing mattered any more. Nothing except this. *Nothing except him.*

She felt the thickness of his arousal and then he paused for a moment and looked straight into her eyes, strands of inky black hair falling over his forehead, his breathing uneven. 'Amy?'

'Don't stop, Marco.' She virtually sobbed the words, her hands sliding over his warm skin, urging him forward. 'Please...'

He hesitated for just a moment and then moved his hips and entered her in a single, smooth thrust that joined them completely.

It had been so long.

The sudden intimacy overwhelmed her and then he started to move and each powerful stroke felt shockingly delicious. All she was aware of was him, the intoxicating scent of him, the skilled touch of his fingers, *the hard male pulse of his body*. He didn't take it slowly and she didn't care. Frantic, desperate, she urged him faster and he drove his body into hers with ruthless, reckless hunger until the tingle and burn inside her grew into something that couldn't be contained and her body exploded.

Her climax was shockingly intense and she heard his harsh groan and knew that her body had driven through his control and tipped him over the edge. He exploded inside her and her fingers dug hard into the slick muscle of his shoulders, clinging as they rode the storm, oblivious to everything around them.

Eventually the wildness eased and they lay for a moment, their bodies still joined and their minds still numb.

And then Marco rolled onto his back, drawing her against him. 'That was incredible. *You* are incredible.'

Amy closed her eyes tightly, waiting for the aftershocks to pass.

What had they done? What had *she* done?

For a moment she lay there, her body still weak and drugged from the after-effects of his love-making. 'We shouldn't have done that.'

'Why not? We're still married, *tesoro*. Sex is part of a relationship.'

'We don't have a relationship, Marco, not any more.' More than a little confused, she sat up and immediately felt the hot burn of his gaze on her body. Horribly self-conscious, she reached for her jumper and pulled it over her head. 'Nothing has changed.'

It took him a moment to answer and he rubbed a hand over his face, as if forcing himself to concentrate. 'You can't truly believe that.' His voice was soft and when he finally looked at her, his gaze was dark. '*Everything* has changed, *amore*.'

'No, it hasn't.' She reached for her jeans and wriggled into them. 'I— The sex was great, Marco, you know that. But it doesn't change the fact that we no longer have a relationship.'

He lifted a brow in silent mockery. 'A moment ago, when I was inside you, did that not feel as though we had a relationship?'

She felt her face turn scarlet. 'Don't talk like that.'

He gave a soft laugh. 'How can you still be shy with me? You are the most complex, confusing woman I've ever met. You don't mind indulging in hot, mindless sex but you don't want to talk about it. Don't pretend that nothing has changed between us, Amy. That would be foolish. And a waste of time. I'm not stupid and neither are you.'

She rose to her feet, unable to resist a sideways glance at his naked body. He was magnificent—his body lean and muscular, his stomach taut and flat, his olive skin liberally dusted with a pattern of dark hair that emphasised his virility and masculinity.

'Marco, don't do this. Please, don't do this.'

He rose to his feet, completely unselfconscious. 'You've lost weight.' Ignoring her plea, he slid a hand around her waist and drew her against him. 'But you're still beautiful.'

Amy put a hand on his chest. 'No.'

'Yes,' Marco purred softly, sliding his hands inside her jumper and smoothing her spine. 'Let's go upstairs to bed. This time we take more time. *Lentamente. Gentilmente.*'

Slow. Gentle.

Amy felt the smooth masculine tones connect with her insides. 'That would just confuse things even more and I'm confused enough already.'

'I am not at all confused.' He brushed her hair away from her neck, lowered his head and delivered a lingering kiss to the base of her throat. 'I am entirely clear about everything. And now we have the whole weekend ahead of us to make up for lost time.'

'No!' Dizzy from his touch, Amy gave him a push and

forced herself to step backwards. 'No, Marco! I meant what I said—nothing has changed. You're not listening to me! I'm talking and you're *just not listening*!' Not trusting herself to be so close to him and not touch him, she walked over to the window and stared out into the darkness. Beyond the glass came the faint sound of the sea crashing onto the rocks below the house. 'All right, so we had sex—good sex—but it doesn't change the facts. We want different things. You still want a family and I still want a career.'

'Ah, yes.' He sounded unperturbed. 'A career. You don't love me enough, isn't that right?'

'That's right.' After what they'd just shared, she couldn't look at him. 'I don't.'

'And you always have sex with men that you have no feeling for, no? That is so typical of you, isn't it, *tesoro*?'

How did he know so much about her when they'd spent so little time together? She forced herself to turn, noticing in a glance that he'd pulled on his trousers but his torso was still bare. 'I can understand why you might read more into what just happened but, please, don't. It really was just sex, Marco. And it wasn't that surprising. The chemistry between us always led us into trouble.'

His gaze was brooding. 'Talking of trouble—since you are still so set on following this career path and not having a family, we probably ought to talk about contraception.'

'There's no need. It won't happen again.'

'I wasn't talking about the future,' he said gently, reaching for his jumper, 'I was talking about the past. We just had unprotected sex, *amore*. Do you want the morning-after pill? I have some in my bag.'

She froze. 'No.' Her mouth was so dry she could barely answer the question. 'No, that won't be necessary.'

'Why not?' He moved towards her, his eyes intent on her face. 'You have decided that you will take your chances? If you become pregnant, you will have a family and abandon your ideas of a career? You are leaving the choice to fate perhaps?'

'None of those things. There just isn't any way I could get pregnant.' She kept her tone casual, assuming that he'd take her comment to mean that it was the wrong time of the month, but he swore softly in Italian and his eyes darkened with anger.

Amy watched him, confused by his reaction. Only a moment ago he'd offered her contraception. Surely he wouldn't want her to get pregnant, given the mess that their marriage was in?

So why did he look as though he wanted to put his fist through the window?

Marco ran out of the back door and onto the coast road. It was dark but he didn't care because he knew the road as well as he knew his own kitchen and he needed to burn off his anger.

She'd turned down the morning-after pill.

There was no way she could get pregnant. Wasn't that what she'd said?

So what did that mean? That she was already taking contraception?

They'd been apart for two years so there was only one reason why she would be using contraception.

Jealousy dug its claws in deep and he increased his speed, pounding along the road, ignoring the punch of the wind and the bite of the cold as he tried to outrun his demons.

Obviously it was as he'd first suspected.

She'd found someone else.

Was that why she'd been crying? Was that why Nick had encouraged him to find out more about her past? Was this man an ex-lover? Someone she'd known before she'd met him?

Marco pounded along the road, his mind full of questions.

Was this mystery man the reason she'd been so intent on ending their marriage?

He ran until the breath tore through his lungs and then he stopped, breathing heavily, forcing his mind to work.

This was Amy. *Amy.* Not any other woman. She wasn't a woman to take a string of lovers. Despite the evidence, it didn't fit with what he knew of her.

Amy would only indulge in a physical relationship with a man if she cared deeply.

But if she didn't have another man, why was she using contraception?

Marco ran a hand over the back of his neck, remembering the way she'd clung to him and urged him on, *remembering the sort of woman he knew her to be*, and knew that he wasn't mistaken in her feelings for him.

She cared deeply. For him. After what they'd shared that afternoon, he knew that she was still in love with him. So why was she so intent on denying it?

Why did she want to end their marriage?

Amy lay on the bed with her eyes wide open, staring at the ceiling, full of regrets. She should have kept her distance from Marco. She should have known that she wouldn't be able to resist him.

If only she'd walked away from him the moment she'd felt the tension sizzling between them.

If only she had more self-control.

If only—the two most useless words in the human language.

The slam of the door downstairs announced that Marco was back from his run, but judging from the violence of the sound his temper hadn't improved.

Hardly surprising perhaps, running in the freezing wind in the darkness.

Amy closed her eyes, feeling nothing but sympathy for

him. Their impulsive love-making session had left her feeling equally confused and frustrated. That was what happened when you gave in to chemistry.

It produced complications.

It was some consolation that he had no more self-control than she did.

The door to her bedroom opened and she turned her head and saw him standing in the doorway, broad-shouldered and powerful. There was a sheen of sweat on his forehead and he'd clearly pushed himself to the limit physically.

His eyes glittered darkly and his mouth was set in a grim line. 'Is there someone else?'

'I'm sorry?' The question was so surprising that she sat up instantly, her eyes wide. 'What do you mean, someone else?'

'It's a plausible reason for you to end our marriage.'

'Marco, I've told you why I ended our marriage. There isn't anyone else in my life.' And there never would be. She had nothing to offer any man.

'So why are you taking contraception?'

'I never said that I was—' She broke off, realising too late that she'd revealed far too much yet again. How did people ever lie and cheat? She was hopeless, absolutely hopeless.

'You said that there was absolutely no chance that you could possibly become pregnant.'

Her heart pounded against her chest. 'It's just not the right time of the month.'

'Nature isn't that predictable, as you and I both know. If you are truly this career person now, why would you want to risk having a baby?' He strode into the room, his eyes fixed on her face. 'I've been thinking about this, going through the facts, sifting through the options, and I've only come up with one possible explanation for the way you're behaving. You don't think you *can* become pregnant, is that right?'

She felt the colour drain from her face. 'Marco...'

He watched her and nodded slowly. 'That's it, isn't it? You can't have a baby.'

Amy shrank back on the bed, her arms around her knees like a child. 'Go away, Marco.' She was shivering again and the headache was back. 'I want to be on my own.'

'Well, that's tough, because when you're married there are two people involved.' His voice soft, he sat down on the edge of the bed. 'An honest woman makes a hopeless liar, Amy, and you are an honest woman. Since the day you told me you were leaving, nothing you have said has made sense.'

'Marco, please—'

'You are a mass of inconsistencies. You keep telling me that you want a career and although you are undoubtedly an excellent doctor, it's always been clear to me that what you really long for is a family. You say you don't want children and yet I see you with them and you are warm and kind. And you say that you don't love me but when we are together...' he reached out and slid a hand under her jaw, gently insisting that she look at him '...you give everything, *tesoro*. What we shared earlier—that wasn't sex, it was love.'

She sucked in a juddering breath. 'Don't do this. The truth is that none of the reasons matter. The end is the same. I can't be with you.'

His thumb gently stroked her jaw. 'We both know that is nonsense. We were meant to be together.'

'No.' Tears welled up and spilled onto her cheeks. 'Don't let's have this conversation! I've already cried more today than in my whole life!'

'Emotion is a good thing. Only the English treat emotion as if it were a dangerous animal.' His faintly humourous analysis of her countrymen would have made her smile at any other time.

But she was a long way from smiling.

She wiped one cheek with the back of her hand. 'Emotion gives you a headache.'

'*Cucciola mia.*'

She sniffed and tried to ignore the insistent brush of his fingers on her face. 'That's what you called Michelle. I don't even know what it means.'

'Literally?' He slid his hand behind her neck, leaned forward and kissed her gently on the mouth. Then he lifted his head and gave a slow smile. 'It is a puppy.'

'So now you're calling me a dog?'

He laughed softly. 'So now I finally see the Amy I used to know. For a long time she was afraid to come out, but I knew she was tucked away in there somewhere. I want to ask you something and I want an honest answer—probably the first one you've given me for a long time.'

'I don't want to talk about this.'

'Shh…' Amusement in his eyes, he pressed his fingers to her lips. 'You need to stop arguing with me. It's bad for you, *amore*, and it gives me indigestion. A good Italian wife should agree with everything her husband says.'

Her heart aching, she gave a wobbly smile. 'I don't think I'm a good Italian wife, that's what I've been trying to tell you.' Her smile faded. 'I can't do any of the things that a good Italian wife is supposed to do. For a start, I don't even speak the language.'

'This could be good! Most Italian men would kill to have a wife who couldn't answer back!' His eyes gleamed but this time she didn't manage a smile in response. How could he be so good about it all? Did he understand what she was telling him?

'You're refusing to take me seriously.'

'*Sì*, that's right, I am.' Suddenly his voice was deadly serious. 'Because you are talking nonsense. What is this about? Who is this "good Italian wife"? I didn't pick an Italian for my wife—I picked you.'

It was time to spell it out. 'But I can't have children, Marco. You're right about that. I'm infertile.' There. She'd said it.

Finally, after two long years of anguish and misery, she'd said it. Such a small word for something so big.

There was a moment of silence and she saw a muscle flicker in his lean cheek but when he spoke his voice was calm and even. 'I understand that. What I *don't* understand is why this made you leave. Why would this have an impact on our marriage? Why didn't you share it with me?'

'Because I was afraid you'd say that it wouldn't make a difference.' She pulled away from him and hugged her knees tighter.

'It doesn't make a difference. A relationship starts with two people, *amore*. Later on more may be added but always it starts just with two.'

'I know how much you want children.'

'Look at me, Amy.' His voice was firm and he nodded when she lifted her head. 'That's better. Yes, I would like children but I am not a child myself. I know that life doesn't always give us what we want or plan for and being an adult is about making choices. When I asked you to marry me I made a choice, *tesoro*. You were my choice.'

She struggled with the tears again. 'Pretty lousy choice.'

'Certainly it's true I would have preferred to have a wife who didn't run away to a different continent for two years,' he said mildly, 'but you are back now and everything is sorted. That's all that matters.'

'How can you say that? Nothing is sorted.'

'*Belissima…*' His voice infinitely gentle, he cupped her face in his hands and forced her to look at him. 'You are determined to make life so complicated.'

'You can't pretend that this is nothing, Marco!'

'No, I'm not going to do that. But neither am I going to sacrifice our relationship for it. And neither should you isolate yourself.' He said something in Italian and she looked at him expectantly.

'In English?'

He slid his fingers through her hair in an unmistakable gesture of affection. 'I said that this didn't happen to you, it happened to us. And now we will deal with it. There are lots of options.'

Unable to help herself, Amy leaned against his chest and felt his arms close around her. She felt his warmth, his strength and she closed her eyes for a moment, greedy for the comfort even though she knew it could only be temporary.

For her there were no options. None.

Marco locked the bathroom door securely and then crossed to the washbasin, his breathing unsteady as he struggled with the emotion that he'd been holding back.

Two years.

They'd wasted two years.

His jaw tensed and he gripped the edge of the basin so hard that his knuckles whitened.

When he'd finally realised the truth, it had taken all his self-control not to erupt with anger. But then he'd seen the torment in her eyes and realised that she'd made the decision to leave him based on a set of beliefs of which he had absolutely no understanding.

Was that what Nick had meant when he'd hinted that he should find out more about her past?

And what exactly was it in her past that made Amy so sure that their marriage couldn't survive the blow of infertility? Why did she think there were no options?

Inhaling deeply, Marco turned on the taps and splashed his face with cold water.

'Marco?' Amy's voice came from outside the bathroom, tentative and unsure. 'Are you all right?'

Marco reached for a towel and stared at his reflection in the mirror. *Was he all right?* He was angry, frustrated and disappointed, but he knew that displaying those emotions wouldn't help his cause.

What he needed to do was prove to Amy that their marriage had a future. And to do that he needed to understand why she was of the opposite opinion.

And she didn't need his anger. She needed his patience.

'I'm fine.' He kept his voice even. 'I'll be out in a moment, *amore.*'

And they were going to do some talking.

CHAPTER EIGHT

THE following morning Marco was no closer to answers despite having spent a long and sleepless night examining that question in detail.

He'd *known* she wasn't a career woman.

He'd *known* she'd loved him.

Why hadn't he managed to unravel the problem sooner?

Since when had he been so obtuse?

All he had to do now was convince her that it didn't make a difference to their marriage.

He heard a noise behind him and turned to find her standing in the doorway to the bathroom. She'd borrowed one of his T-shirts to sleep in and she looked impossibly young and slender, her face free of make-up and worryingly pale.

'*Buongiorno, tesoro.* I'm sorry if I woke you. I have surgery this morning.'

'So do I. I agreed it with Nick.' Her eyes slid from his and she gave an awkward smile. 'I'll go and use the other bathroom, shall I?'

'Go back to bed.' He splashed his face and reached for a towel. 'You're not in a fit state to do surgery. Yesterday was a huge trauma for you and you've had no sleep. I'll take your patients and I'll explain to Nick.'

'I'll be fine when I've had a shower.' After a moment's hesitation she reached into the shower cubicle and turned on the water. 'You're not doing the surgery on your own, Dr Avanti. Who do you think you are? Superman?'

'Superdoctor, actually.' He watched hungrily as she pulled the T-shirt over her head and stepped naked into the shower. Her breasts were high and firm, her waist tiny and her hips gently curved. Gripped by a vicious attack of lust, Marco stood for a moment, feeling himself grow hard. Then he gave a soft curse and stepped into the shower with her.

She gave a gasp of shock and turned, clearing the water from her eyes. 'What are you doing? You've had your shower.'

'I decided I needed another one.' He stroked a hand down her smooth, silky skin and gave a groan of masculine appreciation. 'I've been deprived of your body for too long.'

'I thought you said I was too thin.'

He smiled and curved her body against his, ignoring the relentless sting of the water. 'My beautiful Amy, so much a woman. Always insecure and with no reason.'

'Marco…' She sounded breathless. 'We don't have time for this.'

'I can always make time for something important.'

'Things are complicated enough already—'

'If life isn't complicated, I become bored.' He buried his head in her neck and slid his hands over the soft curve of her bottom. Then he gave up on English and spoke only Italian.

'Marco, no…' But her words were insincere and her head fell back and her eyes closed. 'We really can't—*non posso*—' Then she gasped as she felt the intimate stroke of his fingers.

'You have been learning Italian for me?'

'Marco…' She stroked a hand over her face to remove the water. Her hair was dark and sleek under the jet of the shower, her eyelashes spiky. *And she'd never looked more beautiful.*

Unable to hold himself back a moment longer, Marco brought his mouth down on hers. He felt her arms come round his neck, felt the tantalising brush of her firm breasts against his chest hair, and then he was pressing her back against the wall of the shower, his need for her so great that it bordered on the primitive.

With no preliminaries he slid his hands over her thighs and lifted her, winding her legs around his body and sinking inside her in a series of hard, determined thrusts.

'Marco…' She cried out his name and he felt the scrape of her fingernails on his shoulders, and then they were moving together, the pleasure so wild and intense that there was no holding back.

He felt her tighten around him, the involuntary spasms of her body driving him forward to his own savage release. As he tumbled over the edge into paradise he gave an agonised groan and thrust hard, his fingers biting into her soft flesh, his mouth locked on hers as he swallowed her cries.

It took him several moments to realise that he was probably hurting her and that water was still thundering down his back. He lowered her carefully and then stroked her soaking hair away from her face.

'Did I hurt you, *amore*?'

'No.' Her voice was a whisper and drops of water clung to her lashes and to her lips. 'You've never hurt me. But I've hurt you, I know I have. I'm sorry for everything, Marco.'

He held her face gently. 'Pain is part of every relationship.'

'I'm sorry,' she whispered again. 'Really sorry that it turned out this way for us.'

'Hush.' He pulled her against him, feeling her tremble, acutely aware of her fragility and vulnerability. 'Everything will be all right, I promise. You will trust me, *tesoro*.'

She stayed like that for a moment, her head against his chest, and then she pulled away. 'We have less than ten minutes before surgery starts.'

He flashed her a smile and reached for a towel. 'Then it is fortunate for both of us that I have an Italian sports car.'

* * *

Throughout the whole of Saturday surgery, Amy couldn't stop thinking about Marco. Her body ached from their encounter in the shower and she knew that even though he now understood the real reason for her departure, nothing had changed.

Her last patient of the morning was a mother with a young baby.

'Helen?' Amy smiled and forced herself to concentrate. 'What can I do for you?'

'It's Freddie. I'm so worried about him. He's always been a really sicky baby, but it's getting worse and worse.'

'And how old is he now?' Amy quickly checked the records. 'Six weeks?'

'Yes. He always has brought up milk at the end of his feed.'

'Lots of babies do that.'

'I know but—' Helen broke off and bit her lip. 'I just feel as though something is wrong. He just isn't right, I know he isn't.'

'Let me examine him and see whether I can find anything.' Knowing better than to dismiss a mother's worries, Amy washed her hands and gently lifted the baby out of the car seat. 'I'm sorry to wake you, sweetheart,' she crooned, 'but I want to have a good look at you.'

The baby yawned and stretched then closed his eyes again.

'Is he always this lethargic?' Amy gently undid the poppers on the sleepsuit and undressed the baby down to his nappy.

'Yes. He sleeps all the time.'

Amy examined the baby's abdomen. 'When did you last have him weighed?'

'Last week. He'd lost some weight. The health visitor told me to increase the feeds, but if I increase the feeds then I just increase the sick. It's got to the point where he's barely keeping anything down.'

Amy slid her hand over the baby's scalp, examining his

fontanelle and finding it slightly sunken. 'He seems a bit dehydrated, Helen. Has he been having plenty of wet nappies?'

'Actually, now you mention it, no.' Helen frowned. 'They used to be quite heavy, but now I sometimes don't even bother changing it because it seems dry. What does that mean?'

'It could mean that he isn't getting enough fluid.'

'Because he's bringing it all up?'

Amy finished the examination, popped him back into his sleepsuit and handed the baby back to Helen. 'You're still breastfeeding?'

'Yes.'

'Wait there just a moment, Helen. I'm going to ask my colleague to have a look at him.'

She tapped on Marco's door and found that he had already finished surgery. 'Can I grab you for a minute?'

'*Sì*.' He leaned back in his chair and gave her a slow, sexy smile. 'Do you want to grab me here or wait until we are home?'

Remembering his performance in the shower, she felt the colour ooze into her cheeks and clearly he read her mind because he raised an eyebrow and his eyes mocked her gently.

'Any time you are ready for a repeat performance, you just have to say the word. Or don't even speak—just switch on the shower and strip naked.'

'Marco!' She glared at him, flustered by the sudden intimacy in his gaze. 'I—I wanted to talk about a patient.'

'I know, but I love to tease you because you always blush. You are the only woman I've ever met who can be hot and shy at the same time.' He leaned back in his chair. 'I am listening, *tesoro*. You need the advice of the master? Superdoctor?'

She looked at him. 'Has a woman ever hit you really, really hard?'

'Such passion.' His smile widened. 'My little English Amy is becoming *al*most Italian.'

'Marco—be serious.'

'I'm serious.' He leaned forward. 'What is your problem, *amore*? Tell me and I will solve it.'

'I have this little baby in my consulting room.'

His smile vanished and he rose to his feet. 'And seeing the baby has upset you? It is too difficult for you emotionally? You want me to handle it?'

Touched by his protectiveness, she shook her head swiftly. 'No, it's nothing like that. It's just that I'm worried about him and I wondered if you'd look at him. He's dehydrated, vomiting after every feed and very, very lethargic. I think he has pyloric stenosis.'

Marco frowned. 'Unlikely. It isn't that common.'

'That's why I wanted you to check him. And you're the one who always taught me to remember the uncommon, particularly when faced by a worried mother.'

'True enough.' He shrugged. 'Have you examined the baby feeding?'

'No.' She shook her head and frowned. 'I didn't think to do that.'

'So—we will do it together.'

They walked back to her consulting room and Marco smiled at Helen. 'You had a good, relaxing Christmas? Plenty of food and wine?'

'I was cooking for twelve so it wasn't exactly relaxing.' Helen gave a wry smile. 'I must admit I'm pretty exhausted. I wondered if that was why Freddie had lost weight. I can't believe my milk is much good at the moment.'

Marco washed his hands. 'You shouldn't have been cooking. Your family should have been pampering you with a little one this age.' He leaned forward and stroked a gentle hand over the baby's head. 'Can I take him?'

Helen nodded and Marco scooped the baby up confidently. 'Are you giving your mother worries?' He gazed down at the baby and gave a faint smile. 'Amazing that something so small can be so much trouble.'

Amy swallowed hard, wishing it wasn't quite so hard watching him with babies.

His gaze shifted from the baby to her and she knew instinctively that he'd followed the direction of her thoughts. He gave her a warm, reassuring smile and her stomach shifted.

What was he thinking?

His eyes searched hers for a moment and then he handed the baby back to Helen. 'Amy is right that the baby is a little dehydrated. You say that he is vomiting after every feed. Is he ready for a feed now?'

'He's a bit sleepy.'

'That might be because he hasn't had enough fluid. Dehydration can make him sleepy. We will undress him a bit—make him a bit less comfortable.' Marco's fingers moved over the baby, undressing, tickling, waking him up, and eventually Freddie yawned. 'So—now try and feed him. He is a man after all, so his stomach is probably a priority for him.'

Helen smiled and put the baby to her breast. Freddie played with the nipple doubtfully and Marco curved a strong hand over the back of the baby's head and guided him gently.

'You are starving hungry, you know you are.'

The baby latched on and Helen looked at Marco. 'He's feeding. Now what?'

'Now I want to look at his tummy.' Marco crouched down and looked at the baby's abdomen. Then he gently felt the stomach. 'Amy? Can you see?' He trailed a finger over the stomach. 'The muscles are straining. They're moving from left to right as they try and push milk through the pylorus. And on the right side I can feel a small, hard lump. You're right, I think. Clever girl.' He rose to his feet and washed his hands.

Helen looked between the two of them. 'So what's wrong with him?'

Amy reached for a piece of paper and a pen. 'We think

he has something called pyloric stenosis. Basically it means that the passage between the stomach and the small bowel is narrowed and that stops milk passing into the bowel.' She drew a simple picture to illustrate what she was saying and Helen stared at it.

'But why would that happen?'

'No one really knows. It tends to affect more boys than girls. Has anyone else in your family had the same problem?'

Helen shook her head and Freddie let go of the breast and vomited violently. It cleared Helen's lap and landed on Amy's feet. 'Oh!' Mortified, Helen lifted the baby and reached for a cloth. 'I'm so, so sorry.'

'It's fine, really.' Amy smiled and mopped up the mess with paper towels. 'But I think our diagnosis has just been confirmed.' She looked at Marco. 'Projectile vomiting?'

Helen cuddled Freddie tightly. 'So what happens now?'

'We refer him to the hospital,' Marco said. 'They may want to do more tests—an ultrasound scan, possibly, to get a picture of the muscle.'

'Will that hurt him?'

Marco shook his head. 'It is like the scan they give you in pregnancy.'

'And then what?'

'He will need a small operation to cut through the thickened muscle so that food can then pass into the bowel.'

'An operation?' Helen looked horrified. 'Is it a big one? How long will it take?'

'Probably about half an hour, no more than that. And afterwards he will be given painkillers.'

'I can't bear the thought of him having an operation.' Helen's eyes filled. 'He's so little.'

'But at the moment he can't digest his food,' Amy said gently. 'He needs help, Helen.'

'What a Christmas this has been.' Helen brushed away

the tears and sniffed. 'All right. Well, if that's what he needs—when will he have to have it done?'

'Soon, because he is dehydrated.' Marco walked over to Amy's computer. 'We will call the hospital now and talk to the doctors. You should take him straight to the paediatric ward.'

'But it's Saturday!'

'And they will probably put up a drip and give him some fluid.' Marco swiftly completed a referral letter. 'That way they can correct the dehydration before they operate.'

'And when is that likely to be?'

'They will need to check that his blood has the right balance of minerals and salts and then they will operate as soon as possible.'

Helen strapped Freddie back into the car seat and lifted it. 'All right. I'll take him up to the hospital right away. Thank you, both of you.'

'Try not to worry,' Marco said gently, his eyes warm and kind. 'It will all be fine in the end.'

Helen gave a wobbly smile. 'I hope so. Thanks again.'

She left the room, clutching the letter in her hand and Amy sighed. 'Poor thing. What a worry.'

'Yes. Having children also comes with an ocean of worries,' Marco said quietly, walking towards the door. 'Call Paeds. I'll be waiting in the car park for you.'

She sat down at her desk and reached for the phone. 'Why?'

'I need to give you a lift home. We have the rest of the weekend off.'

'And?' *What did he have in mind?*

He smiled. 'First I am going to take you home and wash the vomit off you, then we are going for a bracing walk and finally we are having dinner at the Smugglers' Inn.'

She opened her mouth and closed it again. 'Has anyone ever told you that you're controlling?'

His smile widened. 'I'm a man who knows what he wants, that's true. Don't forget it, *amore*. Now, ring the hospital.'

'I always loved this part of the North Cornish coast.' Amy stared ahead of her, the wind whipping her hair across her face. 'It's wild, isn't it? You can so easily imagine wrecks and smugglers.' She tensed as she felt Marco's arms slide round her.

'It is wild yes, but—' He broke off and gave a shrug that betrayed his Mediterranean heritage. 'Truly? I prefer the beauty of the Amalfi coast. I like to admire the coastline without risking frostbite. One day I will take you to Positano and you will understand what I mean. Positano is a little town that clings to the cliff like a jewel in a necklace. You would love it. And it's very romantic.'

'Positano.' She turned, a smile on her face. 'You sounded so Italian when you said that.'

'*Sì*, because I *am* Italian. So, of course, I sound Italian.' He lowered his mouth to hers and she felt her body melt under the pressure of his kiss. 'Are you ready to go back?'

Still in the circle of his arms, she glanced out to sea again. 'I suppose so.'

'You came here with your grandmother?'

'No. On my own. I used to sit and stare at the waves for hours.'

'That sounds lonely.'

Her whole childhood had been lonely. 'I was used to it.'

'Tell me what made you think you might be infertile.'

Surprised by the sudden change of subject, she looked up at him. 'I had tests.'

'Without telling me?' His eyes darkened ominously and she sighed.

'At the time I didn't think there was anything to tell. To be honest, I didn't really think anything would be wrong.' She wriggled out of his arms, finding it impossible to talk about such a difficult subject when they were so closely entwined. 'We hadn't used any contraception for months—'

'No time at all.'

'I know that.' She took a deep breath. 'But I just had…a bad feeling. It was always a worry of mine.'

'Why would you worry about it? Had you ever tried for a baby before?'

'No.' She threw him a puzzled glance, surprised by the question. 'You know I hadn't.'

'I don't know that. I know very little about your past before you met me.' He reached out, caught a strand of hair that was blowing in front of her face and tucked it behind her ear. 'If I'm honest, I wasn't very interested in your past.'

And she wasn't interested in talking about it.

The touch of his fingers made her stomach tumble and Amy had to force herself to concentrate on the conversation. 'I bumped into a friend of mine who runs an infertility clinic. She suggested I have some tests, so I did.'

'And you didn't think it worth mentioning to me?' Some of the warmth had left his voice and she turned to him.

'You have every right to be angry with me but you have to try and see it from my point of view. If I'd told you, you would have said that it was too soon to worry.'

'It was.'

'No! As it turns out, it wasn't! And I was able to end our marriage quickly.'

'And I'm supposed to be grateful for that?'

'No. Yes.' She wrapped her arms around herself to keep out the cold. 'I don't know. I just know that I ended something that would have ended anyway.'

'You think I would have divorced you for being infertile?' His tone was incredulous. 'Is that truly what you think of me?'

'No, actually.' She turned to him, her voice flat. 'I think you probably would have stayed with me because for all your arrogance and self-confidence you're a decent man and I think you would have felt an obligation. I didn't want that. Only one of us can't have children in this relationship, so there was no need for both of us to suffer.'

His hands closed over her arms and he jerked her against him. 'You think I didn't suffer, *tesoro*?' His eyes blazed into hers. *'You think I didn't suffer when you walked away from me?'*

'I'm sure you did.' The wind howled angrily around them but she ignored it. 'I'm sure you suffered. But nowhere near as much as we both would have suffered if we'd limped along in our marriage.'

He stared down into her face for a moment, as if trying to work something out. Then he released her and his voice was flat. 'It's cold. Let's go home.'

He didn't understand.

And she couldn't expect him to.

Because she hadn't told him who she was or where she'd come from.

Their marriage was doomed, she knew that.

But she'd promised to help out in the practice so she'd work these few weeks and then end it properly. By then she would have been able to convince Marco that it was the right thing for both of them.

They returned from their walk and Marco dragged her into his arms and kissed her, his mouth demanding and passionate. Then he released her suddenly and took a step backwards. 'Let's go to the Smugglers' Inn.'

'Now?' Still dizzy from his kiss, she looked at him, trying to focus. 'You want to go out?'

'I think it's a good idea. We need to talk. And if we stay here…' he smiled the smile of a red-blooded male '…we won't talk. Even I won't be tempted to make love to you in front of the locals so we'll talk on neutral territory.'

'There's really nothing left to say, Marco. We don't have to go out. I could cook something.'

'Out of what?' He gave a humourless laugh. 'Have you checked in the fridge, Amy? Housekeeping isn't exactly my strong point at the best of times and these certainly aren't the best of times. Unless you nipped out between patients, I'm guessing that you haven't been to the supermarket either?'

His accent was more than usually pronounced and she gave a soft smile. 'No, I haven't. And you don't have to tell me that housekeeping isn't your strong point. You've always been a very traditional Italian male. You want your woman in the kitchen.'

And she'd loved that.

She'd loved the fact that she had finally been able to create a home.

She glanced around her, at the house she'd chosen, *the place she'd wanted to raise their children.*

His eyes trapped hers and he inhaled deeply. 'Not *that* traditional,' he said huskily. 'I was more than happy for you to pursue a career if that was truly what you wanted. But it wasn't, was it?'

She shifted. 'Do you want to argue about this now or shall we go to the pub?'

'Subject avoidance appears to be your favourite activity at the moment.' He gave a shake of his head. 'Let's go to the pub. Give me five minutes to change.'

Deciding that jeans were perfectly acceptable for a casual supper at the Smugglers' Inn, Amy didn't bother changing but went into her bathroom, splashed her face with cold water and applied some make-up. Remembering everyone's comments on how pale she was, she gave her cheeks an extra swipe with the blusher brush and then decided that she looked like a clown and rubbed it off again.

She was pale, yes. But apart from that she looked quite normal. Nothing like a woman whose insides were in turmoil and whose heart was breaking.

'Ready?' Marco stood in the doorway, a black jumper brushing the hard lines of his jaw, his eyes glittering dangerously. There was fire and confrontation in his eyes and Amy swallowed, remembering the passion that had exploded between them that morning. *And the previous evening.*

Perhaps they were right to go out.

They couldn't just carry on making love, could they? What did that solve? Nothing. If anything, it made things worse. They were becoming more and more entwined in the emotional web they were spinning and before long it would be almost impossible to extricate themselves.

Realising that the evening wasn't going to be easy, Amy gave a sigh as she followed him out of the room and waited while he locked the front door.

It was dark and cold and she snuggled deeper into her coat.

'Do you think it's going to snow again?' She slid into the Maserati, enjoying the warmth and the smell of leather.

'I have no idea.' Marco waited while she closed the door. 'I hope not. The car hates it. I hate it. The only place I want snow is when I'm skiing and there isn't much of that on the North Cornish coast.'

Amy smiled at the thought of skiing in Penhally. 'The car is still working, then, despite the cold?'

'*Sì*, occasionally.' Humour in his voice, Marco leaned across and fastened her seat belt then slid his hands over the steering-wheel in a gesture of affection. 'Except when she wants to make my life difficult. Which, of course, she does quite often.' The engine gave a throat roar and Marco steered the car onto the coast road.

'Why is it a "she"? Why does it have to be a woman?'

'Of course she is a woman.' Smoothly he changed gear, his eyes fixed on the road. 'You only have to look at her temperament. She's moody sometimes. Unpredictable. Determined to frustrate. And then other times—she is a dream.' He spoke with such affection that she looked at him with disbelief.

'Marco Avanti, you're a qualified doctor, not a little boy with a toy. You're just a little bit crazy, do you know that?'

He turned his head quickly and gave her a sexy smile. 'Crazy is good, no? Sensible is…' He removed one hand from the wheel and slid it over her knee. 'English? No passion. No emotion.'

Feeling the sudden rush of heat inside her body, Amy coloured, relieved that it was dark. Everything she knew about passion and emotion she'd learned from him. Her response to him had always astonished her. It was as if he drew out a part of her that she hadn't known existed.

'We're so different. How did we ever end up together?'

'Because what we have is powerful.' He increased speed and she gripped the edge of the seat and gasped.

'Marco! Are you planning to end the year with a speeding ticket?'

'Calm down. This car spends so long in the garage that she needs a run occasionally. And, anyway, the police have better things to do than check my speed.' Marco swooped into the car park and turned off the engine.

Feeling relieved that they were still alive, Amy undid her seat belt. *If he were less macho, would it be easier to resist him?*

Or was it his blatant, unashamed masculinity that was so attractive?

Marco was red-blooded male, through and through. Women sensed it within moments of meeting him. *She'd* sensed it.

She shivered as she slammed the car door and felt the wind whip round her body. 'It's cold.' She felt his arm slide round her and then he was urging her across the car park and into the welcoming warmth of the pub.

'*Buenas noches*, Marco,' Tony called out from the bar, and Marco sighed.

'You just wished me goodnight in Spanish, my friend. *Buona sera* is Italian. Don't you ever listen to anything I tell you?'

'Depends what it is.' Tony reached for a glass, a smile on his face. 'If you're telling me to eat less fat, no, I don't listen. If you're ordering a drink, my hearing improves.'

Marco glanced around the pub. 'It's quiet.'

'Early yet. Most folks are still tucked up indoors, away from the weather. It'll be crowded later. Always is. What will it be? Amy?'

'I'll have fizzy water.'

Tony lifted an eyebrow at Marco. 'Is she going to be decent company on fizzy water?'

Marco gave a slow, masculine smile. 'Unlike most of you Englishmen, I don't need to get my women drunk in order to seduce them. My company alone is enough.'

His comment was so outrageously arrogant that Amy couldn't hold back her laughter and he turned towards her, his attention caught, his expression curious. 'What is funny?'

'*You're* funny. You make me laugh. You always did.' Realising that paying him compliments wasn't going to help create distance between them, she turned away quickly and settled herself at the table by the fire. 'Nice fire, Tony.'

'Are you two eating? Specials are up on the board.'

Amy stared at the scrawl on the blackboard, wondering if she dared admit she wasn't hungry. There was something about being in love with Marco that just drove her appetite away.

'I'll have the goat's cheese salad,' she muttered, and Marco frowned.

'She'll have lamb hotpot. And I will, too.' He sat down opposite her and Amy gaped at him.

'I don't want lamb hotpot!'

'Amy.' His voice was patient. 'You look as though you've eaten nothing for the past two years. This morning you missed breakfast. The sandwich that Kate gave you at lunchtime came back uneaten. You are eating less than that baby we referred to the hospital. Tonight you're having lamb hotpot and you're eating it, even if I have to fork it into your mouth myself.'

'But I'm not—'

'Not hungry?' He finished the sentence for her and gave a nod of understanding. 'So—something is the matter? You are off your food because you are so in love with me you can't see straight, no?'

'Don't start, Marco. I don't love you. And you don't love me. Not enough.'

He studied her face in silence. 'All right. Because I need you to recover your appetite, we'll play a different game for the time being.' He leaned back, his dark eyes glittering in the light of the fire. 'I tell you one thing you don't know about me and you tell me one thing I don't know about you.'

'I don't like lamb hotpot. There.' She smiled innocently. 'That's my one thing. Now it's your turn.'

'I don't like really skinny women?'

She laughed. 'You should do an article for the local paper. It would help soothe all those poor women sobbing over the extra pounds they gained over Christmas.'

'Only women think that thin is attractive. All men prefer curves.'

Tony delivered the hotpot to the table and Amy sighed as she picked up her fork and looked at it without enthusiasm. 'Why is it that you always get your own way, Marco?'

'Because I'm always right?' His expression grew serious. 'I didn't get my own way when you left, Amy. That wasn't what I wanted.'

She stilled, the fork balanced in her fingers, her heart in her throat. 'I thought we weren't going to talk about this now.'

'You made the decision for both of us, just as I did with the hotpot.' His eyes challenged her. 'You didn't like it when I chose your food.'

'That's not the same thing at all.'

'You're right, it isn't. To select someone's meal for them…' he waved a hand dismissively '…that is nothing, I agree. But to choose someone's whole future—now, that's entirely different, *amore*.'

'That's not fair, Marco. A relationship can't work if one of the people involved doesn't want it to work. And I didn't—it wasn't what I wanted.'

'You're lying. You wanted it but you were afraid.' He leaned forward. 'My beautiful, cowardly Amy. You were afraid that infertility would wreck our marriage. So you wrecked it anyway. That is woman logic.'

'Woman logic?'

'*Sì.*' He dug into the hot pot. 'A man would not wreck something just in case.'

She inhaled deeply. 'It wasn't "just in case."'

'Eat.'

'But—'

'Eat, Amy, or I will have to force-feed you.'

She sighed and stabbed a small amount of food with her fork.

Marco sighed. 'Now put it in your mouth—yes, like that. Good. And now another mouthful. These tests you had done—I want to know what they told you.'

Amy stopped chewing and put down her fork. 'I had the usual done. The laparoscopy—'

'You had a laparoscopy?' He interrupted her, his tone rough. 'When? How? Where was I?'

'Busy. Working.' She shrugged. 'I don't know.'

The breath hissed through his teeth. 'All right—carry on. You had a laparoscopy. And then?'

'I had mild endometriosis. Nothing that needed treating. Just enough to have completely blocked my Fallopian tubes.' Her hand shaking, Amy picked up her fork again.

'So the laparoscopy suggested that your Fallopian tubes were not patent, is that right?'

'That's right.'

'Eat.'

Amy stared at the food on her fork. 'I really don't think I—'

'Eat.'

Aware that the pub was filling up and that a few people were glancing towards them, Amy dutifully took another mouthful of food. 'I'm not hungry.'

'Then you need to do more vigorous exercise, *amore*, increase that appetite of yours,' Marco purred softly, and her eyes flew to his.

'No, we mustn't. We mustn't do that again,' she whispered softly, and he lifted an eyebrow.

'And why not?'

'Because it is just confusing things.'

'I'm not confused.' He gave a slow, sexy smile and reached across the table and took her fork from her hand. 'I know exactly what I want. And I know exactly what you want, too, *tesoro*.'

'I want a divorce.' She heard his sigh and bit her lip. 'Marco, I know that we have fun together and I know that the sex is good.' She glanced swiftly towards the crowd at the bar but no one was paying them any attention. 'But our relationship can't carry on. It's over.'

The humour was gone from his eyes. 'It isn't over. We met

and the chemistry was so powerful that for three days we didn't get out of bed. We made love almost continuously. Do you remember that, *amore*?'

Of course she remembered that. 'Perhaps that was the problem. We let the sex cloud our judgement. Sharing a bed is very different from sharing a life.'

'So you're still pretending that there is no emotional connection between us and never was?'

Trying to ignore the faint sarcasm in his tone, she straightened her back and didn't look at him. 'I like you, of course—'

'Amy, a woman doesn't lose her appetite over a serious case of "like". You were in love with me and you are still in love with me. Please, at least admit that.'

Her stomach churned. 'Answer me one question, Marco.' She pushed her plate away from her. 'How many times has a woman ended a relationship with you?'

'Never.'

Finally she looked at him. 'That's what I thought. So perhaps it's just very difficult for you to accept that I want to end the relationship.'

'You're implying that this is all about my ego?' He let out a long breath and shook his head in blatant disbelief. 'Sometimes, Amy, you are more trouble than the Maserati and that, as you say in English, is really saying something. Now, eat and forget our problems.'

Reluctantly Amy took a few more forkfuls of food. 'It's quite good,' she conceded, 'for hotpot.'

'*Sì*. And you are going to eat all of it. You're a good cook. Who taught you? Your mother?'

'No, my grandmother. She loved cooking, especially baking. Her cakes were amazing. She was quite a homely, domestic person. My mother wasn't.' Discovering that she was hungrier than she'd thought, Amy slowly ate her way through the bowl of food.

'Why did you stay with her on your own? Did your mother never join you?'

'She was always working and she needed somewhere for me to go during the holidays. And, anyway, they didn't get on. They had a difference of opinion.'

'About what?'

'About me. My mother never really wanted children.' Talking about herself felt uncomfortable and with a flash of panic she swiftly she changed the subject. 'How's Michelle Watson? Is she home from hospital?'

'Yes, and they have changed her asthma medication.' He gave a twisted smile. 'Poor Carol worries so much about her. I'm planning to call and see her tomorrow.'

'It's Sunday.'

'Sunday is the only day I have time to fit in that sort of visit. I need to check on her. She needs the support. And I also want to check on Lizzie.'

'They certainly didn't seem like a perfectly harmonious family.' Amy glanced around to check that no one was listening to them and then lowered her voice. 'I wondered whether Lizzie might be suffering from more than teenage tantrums.'

'Me, too. But it wasn't right to tackle the subject when the focus was on her sister.'

'Half-sister.'

'You think that might be the root of the problem?'

'I don't know. I suppose I'd start there.'

He nodded agreement. 'I will find a way of spending time with her tomorrow.'

Amy felt a warm rush of pride. 'You're a good doctor, Marco Avanti,' she said softly. 'You care about the children so much, I know.'

'And with that comment you have brought us back to our own problems. You are imagining that my life would be empty without my own children and that I'd therefore be better with a different woman.' He finished his food and put down his fork. 'Despite the fact you are an intelligent woman, you are putting two and two together and coming up with the wrong answer.'

She knew it wasn't the wrong answer.

She knew that from personal experience just how child-lessness could affect a marriage, but she wasn't ready to share that with him.

She'd never shared it with anyone. 'Do you miss paediat-rics?'

'Sometimes. But I see a great number of the children in the practice and it is nice to have that long-term relationship so...' he shrugged '...in many ways I am very happy as a family doctor.'

'You've done a good job with the practice, you and Nick. It must have been awful after Annabel died.' She bit her lip. 'I—I didn't know or I would have written sooner.'

'He managed. I managed.' Marco shrugged again. 'The surgery carried on.'

'Kate's such a good practice manager.'

'Yes.' Marco finished his drink. 'Although I'm not sure how long she'll stay.'

'Really? She's thinking of leaving? Why?'

'I don't know that she's thinking of leaving. It is just a sus-picion and I might be wrong. I just sense that things aren't altogether good for her at the moment.'

'Well, being a single mother must be hard,' Amy said quietly, and Marco nodded, his eyes on hers.

'And losing someone you love is even harder. All the more reason not to throw it away when you find it. Let's go home, *amore*. It is more comfortable to argue at home.'

But they didn't argue.

They made love and then talked long into the night. And Marco didn't mention loving or leaving. He just seduced and possessed her until she was no longer capable of rational thought.

Until she'd forgotten why it was that she had to leave.

CHAPTER NINE

ON MONDAY Amy worked her way through a steady flow of patients, but couldn't stop thinking about the visit she and Marco had made to see little Michelle the day before. There had been no sign of Lizzie and Carol had told them in an embarrassed voice that the teenager had come in drunk the night before and was sleeping it off. So Marco had merely checked on Michelle and reassured Carol, but Amy knew that he was still determined to spend some time with Lizzie.

'Amy?' The door opened and Nick walked into her consulting room. 'I've been thinking about the conversation we had on Friday afternoon. I think you need to tell Marco the truth.'

Still wondering about Lizzie, Amy pulled her mind back to the present. 'I've told him.'

'Ah.' He looked at her expectantly. 'And?'

'And nothing. It doesn't change anything just because he knows. Our marriage is still over.' She almost laughed as she listened to herself and recalled the passion of the weekend. For a marriage that was over, the relationship was intensely passionate.

And she was making trouble for herself, she knew she was. The web was tightening.

Nick looked startled. 'That's what Marco wants?'

'Well, no, not exactly.' Amy fiddled with her pen, 'He

doesn't think he wants it, but I know it's the best thing for both of us.'

'You're deciding for both of you again? On what basis?'

On the basis of her past. On the basis that she had firsthand experience in this area.

Dark memories oozed into her brain and she pushed them away resolutely. 'Yes,' she croaked, 'I am deciding for both of us. Once Kate finds a locum, I'll be off.'

'Does Marco know you still feel like this?'

'I keep telling him. He doesn't seem to be listening.'

Nick grimaced. 'That sounds like Marco. He has a way of ploughing through obstacles that get in the way of what he wants. He did it when we were setting up this place. You might find he changes your mind yet.'

'That isn't going to happen.' *She couldn't let it happen.* 'In the meantime, I'll do the job you're paying me to do.'

Nick stood for a moment. 'This must be very hard for you, Amy. If you need a shoulder…' He gave a wry smile and raked a hand through his hair. 'I'm not sure that relationship counselling is my forte, but—'

'I'm fine, Nick,' she said quietly, 'but thank you. I'll manage on my own.'

The way she'd always managed. It was what she did. The way she lived her life.

The whole of Penhally came to life on New Year's Eve.

Despite another small flurry of snow and the drop in temperature, the shops were crowded as people rushed around, preparing for the celebrations. The off licence did a steady trade as people bought bottles of champagne and then picked their way home along the snowy pavements, bottles clanking in plastic bags, their breath clouding the freezing air.

The surgery was also busy and it was almost the end of the day before Amy managed to find time to nip to the staffroom for a cup of tea.

'You, too?' Kate followed her into the staffroom and filled the kettle. 'If I don't have a cup of tea this minute, my throat is going to collapse in protest. The pavements are icy and we've had several people in after falls, but at least the wind has dropped, which is good news. The firework display should be able to go ahead. They've brought it forward to six o'clock so that the children can enjoy it. Everyone will have time to go home and get changed before the party at the Penhally Arms. What are you wearing?'

Amy hesitated. 'I'm not going.'

Kate gaped at her. 'Not going? Amy, you *have* to go. It's *the* event of the year. Well, maybe not quite the year, but it's certainly the event of the winter.' She gave a rueful smile. 'Not that that's saying much around here. We're a bit short of entertainment on the long, dark nights, as you well know.'

'I can't go, Kate.' Amy took two mugs from the cupboard and Kate dropped a tea bag in each. 'It would just be too awkward.'

'Why? What's awkward about it?' Kate poured water into the mugs. 'You're working here, aren't you? You're living with Marco. Everyone knows you're together—'

'We're not together. Not in the way you mean.'

'Oh. I hoped…' Kate finished making the tea and took it with her to the nearest chair. 'Well, anyway, it's just a party, Amy. I don't understand the problem. Do you have a dress?'

'No.' Amy thought about the contents of the wardrobe. *The wardrobe she'd abandoned along with that whole part of her life*. 'Well, yes, I suppose I do have a dress, but it isn't really suitable. I mean, it isn't me any more.'

Kate sipped her tea. 'Was it you once upon a time?'

Without thinking she answered. 'Oh, yes. It was Marco's favourite. Whenever I wore it we never actually managed to—' She broke off, suddenly embarrassed by how much she'd revealed, but Kate simply chuckled.

'You never actually managed to leave the house in it? If it was that good, you should definitely wear it to the party tonight. In fact, I insist on it. If you don't turn up wearing it I'm going to drive you home myself and force you to change.'

Amy sighed and shook her head. 'I don't think the dress sends out the right message.'

'What does that matter?' Kate's tone was dry. 'Since when did men take any notice of the messages we give them, anyway? Especially men like Marco. Whatever the dress is saying, Marco will hear what he wants to hear, take it from me. He's that kind of guy.'

Amy's stomach lurched alarmingly and she wondered fleetingly just how well Kate knew Marco. *Kate was an attractive woman.*

And then she pushed the thought away. Kate and Marco had been colleagues for two years. It was natural that they'd know each other quite well.

And she had no right to be possessive. She was letting him go. 'I honestly don't think a party is the right way to spend an evening.'

'Are things that bad?' Kate's voice was gentle. 'I was really hoping that the two of you might have patched up your marriage.'

'We haven't.'

'I'm sorry. And surprised. You're so good together and you've been laughing and you make a great team. I thought you were getting on well.'

'We *are* getting on well.' Amy thought of their passionate love-making and blushed. 'But we haven't patched up our marriage.'

Kate studied her. 'Why not? You're so in love with him, anyone can see that. And he's in love with you!'

Amy frowned. 'Nick said the same thing—'

Kate tensed slightly, her eyes suddenly wary. 'Did he?' Her tone was suddenly cool. 'You've discussed this with Nick?'

'He's surprisingly intuitive, don't you think?'

'Sometimes. With patients.' Kate stood up so suddenly that her coffee sloshed over the table. 'Oh, now look what I've done.' She walked across to the sink and picked up a cloth and Amy watched, mystified by the sudden tension in the air. Everything had been fine until she'd mentioned the senior partner's name.

'Has something happened between you and Nick?' *Had they had a row?* Or was it something more than that?

'Nothing. You know what this place is like. We're in each other's pockets all the time.' She wiped the table. 'So, if Marco *was* in love with you, would you stay?'

'No. I'd be leaving even if he was in love with me.' Amy paused. 'I can't have children. That's why I left and it's why I'll be leaving again. I can't give Marco the family he needs.' Swiftly, removing as much of the emotion as possible, she told Kate the facts and the older woman sank back onto the chair, her expression sympathetic.

'Oh, Amy, I'm so sorry. Why didn't you tell me any of this before? You must have gone through so much and all on your own!'

'I couldn't talk to anyone about it,' Amy murmured. 'I—I'm not really used to talking about problems and this, well, this was just too big.'

'But there are so many options these days and even if none of them worked, there's always adoption.'

Amy tightened her grip on her mug.

Why did people always say that?

Why did they throw it in like some sort of consolation prize with no emotional value?

'That wouldn't be a solution. It's hard to understand, I know.' She rose to her feet quickly. 'I'd better get back. Surgery was very busy. I have some notes to tie up and some referral letters to write.'

'If I've upset you, I'm sorry.' Kate's voice was soft. 'I

probably understand more than you think, Amy. Not about the infertility, no. I don't pretend to know what that must be like. But I know all about finding the man you truly love and then not being able to be with him. Life has a warped sense of humour. Whoever said that it was better to have loved and lost than never to have loved at all, had obviously never loved. Either that or he was on drugs when he wrote that. Love is agony.'

Amy stood for a moment, unsure what to say. Was Kate referring to the tragic loss of her husband years earlier? Or something else entirely?

She opened her mouth to ask a probing question but then the door opened and Alison walked in.

'Is that kettle hot? My tongue is sticking to the roof of my mouth.'

Amy looked at Kate for a moment longer and the practice manager gave a tired smile.

'Go and finish your paperwork, Amy, or I'll be forced to nag you.'

In other words, this wasn't the right time for a deep conversation. Knowing that Kate was right, Amy smiled at Alison.

'Kettle is hot.'

'Aren't you getting ready to go out? The party started half an hour ago.' Marco paused in the doorway, looking at Amy who was curled up on the sofa with a book that she wasn't reading.

She couldn't concentrate on anything. When she wasn't working, all she did was think about Marco. 'You go.'

'We're both going.' He reached out a hand and pulled her to her feet.

'I'm tired, Marco.'

He gave a slow smile and stroked a hand over her cheek. 'Too much sex perhaps. Tonight, *tesoro*, I will let you sleep. I promise.'

She blushed. 'Marco, I just don't want to go to the Penhally Arms! Everyone will be there.'

'*Sì.*' He pulled her towards the stairs. 'That is why we are going. We're part of this community.'

'You are. I'm not.'

He jerked her against him. 'You're my wife,' he breathed, his eyes holding hers. 'Remember that.'

'Marco—' She broke off and sighed. This wasn't the time to start that argument again. 'All right, I'll come to the party if it means so much to you.'

'Good.' He lowered his head and delivered a lingering kiss to her mouth. 'We leave in ten minutes.'

Amy waited for him to walk into the shower and then opened the wardrobe and took out the dress. It was scarlet, daring, and didn't match her mood at all.

If she were dressing for her mood then it would have been black, she thought gloomily, looking in the wardrobe to see what else there was.

But there was nothing.

Only the vivid red dress.

With a little shrug she slipped it on, wondering if it would even still fit.

'*Molto belissima,*' Marco breathed from behind her, sliding his hands slowly over her hips and then drawing her zip upwards in a smooth movement. 'I always *loved* you in this dress.'

'It isn't— I don't—'

'It is and you should.' He turned her to face him. 'Tonight let's just go out and have a good time. Forget everything. No mention of problems. Agreed?'

She hesitated and then nodded. It sounded good to her. She was exhausted. 'All right.'

The Penhally Arms was decorated with clusters of balloons and rows of twinkling lights and the dining room had been cleared to accommodate a dance floor. Although it was still relatively early, the place was already crowded.

'So now you will see all my moves and be unable to resist me.' Smiling wickedly, Marco hauled her straight onto the dance floor and spun her round.

'What are you doing?' Half laughing, half embarrassed, she moved closer to him and he shrugged.

'Dancing. Your dress has a very sexy split at the side. When I spin you round I get a better view of your legs.'

'Marco, that's dreadful!'

'Not from where I'm standing.' He pulled her against him and ran a possessive hand over the curve of her bottom, leaving everyone in no doubt that their marriage was alive and well.

'People are watching everything you do.'

'Let them watch. The only way to survive in a small community is not to fight it. Don't be so English.' He smiled down at her, his eyes glittering dark and dangerous in the dim light. 'Relax and let go. All the people here wish us well.'

And, indeed, everyone seemed happy and contented, mingling, drinking and eating. Amy joined Marco as he weaved his way through them, exchanging a few words of greeting here and there, stopping to have a longer conversation with some people.

And then she saw Kate standing in the doorway, a look of such utter yearning on her face that Amy stopped dead. Puzzled, she followed the direction of Kate's gaze and gave a soft gasp of enlightenment.

Marco turned from his argument about Italian wines. 'What?'

'I just— I didn't…' She drew him to one side, her voice soft. 'Kate. Did you see the way she looked at Nick?'

'No, but I can imagine.'

Amy looked up at him. 'I think she's in love with him.'

'I *know* she's in love with him.'

'You *know*?'

'I have worked with both of them for over two years,' Marco said wearily. 'I may be a man, but even I can pick up on tension and atmosphere if it surrounds me for long enough.'

'Well, but— That's great.' Amy smiled, genuinely delighted for Kate. 'I mean, they're both widowed and—'

Marco pressed a finger over her lips. 'I think the situation is perhaps more complicated than it might first appear to be,' he drawled softly, removing his finger and giving her a gentle kiss instead. 'Say nothing to either of them.'

'But Kate is my friend—'

'All right, then say nothing to Nick,' Marco said quietly, his gaze resting on his colleague who was standing at the bar, talking to several other locals. 'Nick is a man with a lot of issues.'

'You mean he still hasn't got over Annabel's death?'

Marco was silent for a moment. 'That, yes. And more, I suspect. Come on, let's eat.'

They helped themselves to food, chatted to some of the villagers and then everyone started the countdown to midnight.

'Ten, nine eight…' everyone chanted in unison, and then the church bells started to chime and they all let out an enormous cheer.

Amy smiled and suddenly she was glad she'd come. Just because you knew that tomorrow was going to be difficult, it didn't mean that you couldn't grab hold of today and enjoy it.

'*Felice Anno Nuovo.*' Marco took her in his arms and kissed her. 'Happy New Year, *amore.*'

Amy closed her eyes, her happiness bitter-sweet. '*Felice Anno Nuovo*, Marco.'

She didn't have any reason to believe that the new year would be any happier than the last two, but Marco had insisted that tonight wasn't about their relationship and she had to admit that it had been nice to get away from the subject for a while.

All around her people were hugging and kissing and letting off party poppers, and then she saw Kate and Nick. And there was something about the way they stood—*so close but neither touching nor talking*—that made Amy catch her breath.

Across the lively crowd, she could almost feel their agony.

Couldn't anyone else feel it, too?

She glanced around her to see if anyone else had noticed but everyone was dancing and singing and whooping.

And suddenly, Nick finished his drink, picked up his coat and strode out of the bar, his handsome face strained and his mouth grim. He had his car keys in his hand and one glance at the misery in Kate's eyes told Amy that he was going home alone.

Moments later Kate picked up her bag and followed, clearly too distressed to stay at the party.

Amy watched the door of the pub close behind her and hesitated.

Should she follow? Or should she stay out of it?

She'd seen the tears in Kate's eyes and knew that she was close to breaking down. Who did she have to turn to?

Around her everyone was celebrating noisily and Marco was in conversation with a group of people, so Amy quietly slipped away, intending to offer Kate some support.

Outside, the winter wind bit through her thin dress and suddenly she wished she'd stopped to pick up her coat.

Then she saw Kate, hurrying across the car park towards Nick. 'Nick! Wait.' Her voice carried and Amy watched as Nick paused, his hand on the door of his car, the collar of his coat turned up against the bitter chill of the wind.

Laughter burst from inside the pub but the two of them didn't even look round.

Were they talking?

What were they saying?

Amy knew she should go back into the pub but she just couldn't look away and she gave a soft intake of breath as she saw Nick's hand lift towards Kate's shoulder as if he was going to pull her against him. For a moment his hand hovered, and then his fingers curled into a fist and his hand dropped to his side.

Without saying another word to Kate, he slid into his car and slammed the door.

Nick drove off with an ominous squeal of tyres and Kate stood for a long, tortured moment, her back to Amy.

And then finally she turned and Amy saw tears glistening on her face.

'Why did you go outside?' Marco slid his coat over Amy and turned up the heater in the car. 'Were you hoping for hypothermia?'

'I was worried about Kate.' Her teeth chattering, Amy snuggled under his coat. 'She looked…desperate. Do you think we should call on her?'

'We can't solve everyone's problems, Amy.' He drove carefully on the icy roads. 'We don't even seem to be managing to solve our own.'

'There's nothing to solve.'

'We have a major difference of opinion. You love me, Amy. Admit that at least.'

Exhausted with lying, Amy looked at him. 'All right, I love you. There, I said it. Are you satisfied?' She turned her head away from him. 'I said it and it still doesn't change a thing. We can't be together.'

'Because you think you can't have children? We're not the first couple to face this and it doesn't have to be the death of our relationship.'

The conversation continued all the way home and followed them into the house.

'If the whole children thing bothers you that much, let's talk about it.' Marco dropped his keys on the table and strode through to the kitchen. 'There are any number of options. IVF. Adoption.'

'That isn't an option.'

'Why not?'

She hesitated. 'Because it still wouldn't be your child.'

'I want you, Amy. You. I take you as you are.' Marco jammed his fingers into his hair and let out a stream of Italian that was completely incomprehensible, but the gist of it was clear even to her. He was frustrated and exasperated. '*What* do I have to do to convince you?'

'Nothing. You'll never convince me. That's why I left, Marco.' Her voice was soft. 'There was really nothing left to say.'

CHAPTER TEN

THE first two weeks of the new year were flat and bleak. Children scurried along the pavements wearing hats and scarves on their way back to school, everyone removed the Christmas decorations and all that was left of the festive period was icy cold weather and frosty streets.

In the Penhally Bay Surgery, the atmosphere was tense. Amy woke up feeling exhausted every day and was beginning to wonder whether she'd contracted a virus in Africa. Marco refused to listen to her reminders that she was leaving in just two more weeks. Nick seemed more aloof than ever and although Kate was her usual efficient self, her face was pale and she hardly ever seemed to smile.

Unable to forget the scene she'd witnessed on New Year's Eve, Amy tried to talk to her, but they were so busy that it wasn't until the third week of January that Amy finally caught her on her own as they were leaving work.

'Do you fancy a coffee?'

'Now?' Kate glanced at her watch. 'I suppose I could. My babysitter doesn't leave for another hour. All right. Why not?'

They went to the nearest coffee-shop and found a small table in the window. 'You're sure you're leaving at the end of the month?' Kate unwound her scarf and picked at the foam on her cappuccino. 'I had a call from Adam Donnelly today, confirming his arrival date.'

Amy felt her stomach drop. It was one thing to know that she was leaving, quite another to actually do it. 'Yes. I have no choice.'

'For what it's worth, I think you're wrong. What you have with Marco is strong enough to withstand everything.'

Amy shook her head. 'I don't want to talk about me. I want to talk about you. Kate…' she leaned forward, her eyes gentle '…how long have you been in love with Nick?'

Pain flickered in Kate's eyes. 'Is it worth me uttering a denial?'

'No. Because I saw the two of you together on New Year's Eve.'

'Ah…' Kate gave a twisted smile. 'That was a particularly bad evening. Nick at his least communicative. Believe me, that's saying something.'

'He doesn't communicate? But you're always talking. You and he.' Amy frowned, confused. 'You're *always* planning and laughing.'

'That's business. Never personal.'

'But you'd like it to be personal.'

Kate stared down at her coffee. 'It's complicated, Amy. I can't tell you all of it. But…' She hesitated. 'I will tell you that I've decided to leave. I can't do this any more. I just can't work alongside him, it hurts too much. There. You're the only person I've said that to. I'd be grateful if you didn't repeat it until I've decided for sure what I want to do.'

'You want to leave? No! You can't do that!' Amy reached across the table and took her hand. 'You love your job. You love working with Nick. You're a great team.'

Kate pulled her hand away. 'There's only so much torture a woman can stand, Amy. I've reached my limit.'

'Are you quite sure he doesn't feel the same way about you?'

Kate stared blindly into her coffee. 'Does Nick feel anything for me? Yes, I think he probably does. Is he going to do anything about it? No, definitely not. He isn't that sort of man.'

'Has he dated anyone since Annabel died?'

'Oh, yes.' Kate gave a bitter laugh. 'Quite a few women, actually. Just no one who is remotely interested in creating an emotional connection. That isn't Nick.'

'Does he know you're thinking of leaving?'

'No.' Kate picked up her coffee. 'I'm going to tell him soon, though. I need to do something different. Goodness knows what. Get a life, as my son would say. Stop brooding. Nick's only a man after all.'

'But some men are harder to get out of your system than others.'

Kate looked at her and gave a sad smile. 'Yes. And you'd understand that, wouldn't you, Amy?'

'Kate tells me that Adam Donnelly is starting in a week.' Wondering why she was always so exhausted, Amy slid her bag onto her shoulder. 'Finally you'll have a proper replacement for Lucy.'

'You're still intent on leaving, then? Despite everything?' Marco's glance burned a hole in her conscience and she forced herself to carry on walking towards the car.

'Yes. Of course. I've told you that all along.'

His phone buzzed and Marco gave a tired sigh and answered it. 'Marco Avanti.' He listened for a moment and then his jaw tightened. 'We'll come over now.'

'What?' Amy looked at him as he dropped the phone back into his pocket and strode towards his car.

'That was Carol. Lizzie is screaming with a headache and she has spots. She's worried that she has meningitis.'

'Meningitis?'

Marco shrugged and unlocked the car. 'We will see. Are you coming?'

'Of course! Why wouldn't I?'

'Because you're leaving, Amy, remember? In another week the inhabitants of Penhally will no longer be your responsibility.'

They sat in silence, Marco's hands gripping the steering-wheel tightly as he drove the short distance to the terraced cottage that Carol shared with her husband and the two girls.

'Thank you so much for coming.' Carol's voice was thick with tears as she let them into the house. 'I always seem to be ringing you. My phone is programmed to ring your number.'

'How long has she had the headache?'

'Well, she was out with her friends last night and they were obviously drinking. Again.' Carol's mouth tightened. 'She's grounded, but that's another story. Last night when she came in she was really drunk—slurring her words and really, really stroppy. Worse than ever. I left her to sleep it off and, of course, she woke up with a headache. Nothing surprising there. I assumed it was a hangover but it's just got worse and worse and about an hour ago she started complaining that the light hurt her eyes. That's when I noticed this rash on her face and I panicked.'

'She is in the bedroom?' Marco was already on the stairs and Amy was right behind him.

'She can't get out of bed because her head is so bad. Her bedroom is the second door on the right.'

The teenager was lying on her side, crying softly, and little Michelle was curled up on the bed next to her sister.

''Izzie sick,' she muttered, and Carol hastily scooped the child off the bed.

'You shouldn't be there. You might catch something. Go downstairs to Daddy, sweetheart. Pete? Can you come and take the baby?'

Reluctant to be parted from her sister, Michelle reached out her arms. ''Izzie sick.'

Marco slid a hand over her cheek. ''Izzie is going to be fine, *cucciola mia*. Go with your mama.'

'I'll be right back,' Carol said, but Marco shook his head.

'I'd like to examine Lizzie and talk to her on my own first. Amy will help me.'

Carol hesitated and then gave a nod. 'All right. I'll be downstairs with Michelle if you need me.'

'Where she always is,' Lizzie sniffed, her forearm across her eyes as she rolled onto her back. 'If you ever want to find Mum, just look for Michelle.' Her face was red and blotchy from crying and Amy noticed the spots on her face. 'My head is killing me. It's like a bomb is exploding in it every minute. Am I dying?'

Marco sat down on the edge of the bed. 'You're not dying,' he said gently, 'but I'll take a look at you and then we'll talk.'

'Oh, don't you start,' Lizzie groaned, rolling onto her side again. 'When adults say "talk" they mean "nag". Don't drink, don't stay out late, don't spend time with those friends because they're not suitable—who the hell does she think she is, anyway, picking my friends? Life is just a load of bloody "don'ts".'

'Is that how it seems?'

'It's how it is.' Lizzie screwed up her face and started to cry. 'God, my head hurts. Mum said I might have meningitis. That's why she got Michelle out of here. She doesn't care about me, but she doesn't want her baby hurt.' The teenager put her hands over her face but Amy saw tears find their way through her fingers.

'You're her baby, too.' Marco opened his bag and took out a stethoscope and an ophthalmoscope.

'No, I'm just a reminder of Dad. They got divorced, remember? Mum can't stand him and she can't stand me either because I'm exactly like him.' Lizzie let her hands drop. 'If she'd had her way I would have gone and lived with him. Neither of them wanted me.'

Amy felt her heart twist. 'Lizzie, I'm sure that isn't true.' She dropped onto her knees beside the bed and took the girl's hand. 'You and I are going to talk about that, but first we need to check you over to see why you've got this headache. When we've got the physical check out of the way, we'll deal with the rest of it.'

Lizzie rolled onto her back, her eyes closed. 'Go on, then. Get it over with. If I'm going to die, I might as well know.'

'You're not going to die, *angelo mia*.' As kind and gentle as he always was with little Michelle, Marco examined her thoroughly and closely checked the rash around her mouth. 'Amy, what exactly were you doing out with your friends last night?' His tone was casual as he put the stethoscope back into his bag and swiftly checked her blood pressure.

'I dunno.' Lizzie didn't open her eyes. 'We were just hanging out. Having fun. Drinking. You heard Mum.'

'What were you drinking?'

'Stuff.'

'Have you or your friends tried sniffing glue?'

Lizzie's eyes flew open and colour flooded into her face. 'No.'

'Lizzie.' Marco gently unwound the blood-pressure cuff and put it away, 'I'm your doctor, not your mother. You need to be honest with me.'

'Why? So that you can lecture me?'

'So that I can help you.'

Lizzie looked at him for a moment and then covered her face with her hands and started to cry again. 'They were doing it and I didn't want to be different. They're always saying I'm posh and stuck up. So I tried it. And I felt really happy and part of everything. And then afterwards I felt totally crap. Dizzy and sick. How did you guess?'

'I'm a doctor. And I suspected it when you came to the

surgery last week. You were short-tempered, your mother mentioned that your school work had gone downhill and I noticed that you had an oil stain on your jumper.'

Lizzie gaped at him. 'What are you, a detective?'

'Sometimes, yes.' Marco gave a wry smile. 'That's exactly what my job is.'

'What about the spots on my face?'

'Same thing.'

Lizzie swallowed. 'Not meningitis?'

'Not meningitis,' Marco said gently. 'Glue sniffing.'

Lizzie groaned and closed her eyes. 'It's no big deal,' she muttered. 'I mean, I've only done it occasionally.'

'It *is* a big deal. Sometimes it can kill, sometimes it causes organ damage.' He talked to the teenager, dishing out cold, hard facts until Lizzie sat up and covered her ears with her hands.

'All right, stop! I've messed up, I know I have, but—you have no idea what it's like. Mum just *hates* me.' She started to cry again and Amy gave a murmur of sympathy and slid a hand over the girl's shaking shoulders.

'I don't think your mum hates you, Lizzie.'

'What would you know, anyway?' Lizzie wriggled away from her moodily. 'You, with your perfect life.'

'Actually, I know quite a lot about how it feels to be un-loved,' Amy said calmly, 'because my mother didn't want me at all.'

Lizzie looked at her. So did Marco.

'Family life is complicated, Lizzie, but I know your mum loves you.' Amy's voice was firm. 'She's worried about you and she doesn't know how to handle you, but she loves you. All the signs are there.'

'What? She spends all her time with Michelle.'

Amy nodded. 'Yes, that must be hard. Michelle is a toddler and toddlers are always time-consuming, and on top of that she has asthma. I can quite see how it might seem that your mum doesn't have time for you.'

'She doesn't even notice me except when it's to nag about something.'

'If she's nagging, then she's noticing,' Amy said quietly. 'My mother didn't care where I was or who I was with. When I was seven she sent me to boarding school. I would have given a great deal for her to nag me about something because at least it would have showed that she minded about something.'

Lizzie was silent. 'I hadn't thought of it like that.' She looked at Amy. 'We never talk or anything.'

'Do you talk to her?'

Lizzie's gaze slipped from hers. 'No.' She plucked at the duvet. 'I don't suppose I do. Not any more.'

'Then perhaps you should try. She might surprise you.'

Lizzie pulled a face. 'She's going to kill me when she finds out I've been sniffing glue. Are you going to tell her?'

'*You're* going to tell her,' Marco said gently, closing his bag, 'along with all these other things that you've been telling us. I think she needs to know how you feel, don't you?'

'It won't make a difference.'

'Why don't you tell her and we will find out?'

Lizzie curled her arms round her knees, suddenly looking very young and lost. 'Will you stay while I talk to her?'

Amy nodded immediately. 'I will.'

'I didn't really want to do it, you know? The glue stuff.' Lizzie's eyes filled. 'But those girls were like so cool and kind of superior and they look at you like you're *nothing* if you don't go along with what they say. I just wanted to fit in but at the same time I always knew that I didn't.'

'If they don't respect your right to make your own choices, maybe they're not good friends,' Amy said quietly, and Lizzie nodded.

'I know.' She wiped her nose on her sleeve. 'I think I just

wanted Mum to notice me and when I hung out with them, Mum noticed. She hates them. So what happens now?'

'To start with, you talk to your mother. Hopefully she can give you the support you need.' Marco rose to his feet. 'If necessary I can refer you to the hospital for some help but I don't think you'll need it. Eat healthily, get plenty of sleep and let's see how you go. I'll go and call your mum.'

'Poor Lizzie. And poor Carol.' Marco drove towards home, a frown on his face.

'They'll be all right. They love each other and they'll work it out.' Amy glanced out of the window. 'Where are we going? This isn't the way home.'

'I want to talk to you.' He pulled up in a small car park that overlooked the jagged coastline. 'Here, we shouldn't be disturbed.'

Amy felt her heart sink. 'Marco, we're not going over this again.'

'No. We're exploring something entirely different. You are going to tell me about your childhood.'

'That's irrelevant. And it's not my favourite subject.'

'But you mentioned it just now to help a very confused, sad teenager. Doesn't our marriage deserve the same consideration?'

'Talking about the past won't make any difference to the future, Marco.'

'At least let me understand why you're walking away.' His voice was rough and his eyes were tired. 'At least give me that much, Amy. None of this makes sense to me. I'm sure that all your beliefs about marriage and children come from your own experiences. Clearly your mother didn't want children, but why does that affect your own perception of parenthood?'

'My mother *did* want children. But she wanted her own children.'

Marco was silent for a moment. 'This I don't understand.'

'I'm not her child,' Amy said wearily. 'I'm adopted, Marco. She adopted me because she was infertile and she couldn't have children. I was supposed to be the solution to her problem. Instead, I made the problem a thousand times worse.'

The only noise in the car was the sound of Marco breathing. 'You are adopted?'

'That's right. And now can we move on? There's really nothing else to say and it makes no difference to our relationship.'

'It makes a difference to me.' His voice was a low growl and he slid a hand behind her neck and forced her to look at him. '*Ti amo*. I love you. You love me.'

Amy swallowed and spoke with difficulty. 'That doesn't make a difference either.'

'How can you say that!' Visibly frustrated, his mouth tightened. 'Of course it's relevant. Our love is strong enough to survive anything.'

'No.' She shook her head. 'That isn't true. You want children. I can't give you children. I've seen firsthand what that can do to a relationship.'

'So tell me.' His voice was soft but the pressure of his hand prevented her from looking away. 'Tell me what it can do, I want to know. I want to know what you have seen that I am so blind to.'

'My father wanted children. My mother couldn't have them. So she adopted me, thinking that that would solve the problem. It didn't. My father never saw me as his and my mother blamed me for that. She believed that had I been different, he would have loved me.' Amy kept her voice level as she recited the basic facts. 'If I'd been prettier, cleverer, more outgoing—the list was endless. By the time she finally sent me to boarding school, I was so afraid of doing and saying the wrong thing, I barely spoke.'

'Amy.' Marco breathed her name and then gave a groan and pulled her against him. 'I had no idea. Why did you never tell me this before?'

'Because I try and forget it. I have a different life now. It isn't relevant.'

'If it's destroying our relationship, it's relevant. And your father paid you no attention either?'

'My father's ego was badly damaged by the lack of children. He thought it made him less of a man. He had an affair with his secretary and she became pregnant almost immediately. There was no question of keeping it a secret because my father wanted everyone to know that he'd fathered a child, as if it were somehow confirmation of his masculinity. So he divorced my mother and married the secretary. They had four children in quick succession, each one another bitter blow to my mother. I rarely ever saw her. During term time I was at school and in the holidays I stayed with my grandmother in Penhally.'

'I can't believe that she never tried to build a relationship with you.'

'You don't understand.' Amy gave a faint smile. 'She didn't really want me, Marco. I was just a solution to her problem. She needed to produce a child and she couldn't. So as a last resort she produced me. I'm sure the authorities would have thought that they were a perfect couple to qualify for adoption. Nice home, good income and my mother was very, very excited about having me. But not because she wanted me. Because she thought I'd save her marriage.'

'And when you didn't, she sent you away.'

'That's right.'

'So now I begin to understand you.' Marco stroked a hand down her cheek. 'You think that perhaps I am like your father and I need children to prove my manhood, no?'

'I know you're nothing like my father.' She felt exhausted.

And sick again, really, really sick. 'But I also know that you want a family and you deserve one.'

'Did your parents love each other?'

'Why is that relevant?'

'It's totally relevant.' His eyes held hers. 'You see, you are the one I want to spend my life with. And maybe our life together will come with problems, because life always does. Perhaps for us it will be infertility. But we will still be together and that is what I want. That is what I choose. A life with you.'

'Marco—'

'No, it is your turn to listen to me. All this time you have focused only on the fact you can't have children, not on our relationship.'

'Because it matters!'

'Of course it matters, I'm not pretending that it doesn't matter. I'm just saying that it can't be allowed to destroy what we have.'

'You don't understand—'

'No, *you* are the one who doesn't understand,' he said firmly. 'You don't understand how much I love you. If you understood that, you wouldn't ever think of leaving me again.'

'You really love me? Why?' Amy's eyes filled. 'I can't give you want you want.'

'Amy, *tesoro*.' He gave a gentle smile and lowered his mouth to hers. '*You* are what I want. How can I make you see that? I want my life to be with you and I will take whatever problems come along with that.'

She stared at him, her heart beating hard against her chest. 'We got married in a hurry.'

He gave a wry smile. 'Amy, I had successfully avoided commitment for thirty-nine years until I met you. Are you seriously suggesting that I didn't know my own mind? I married you because you were the woman I wanted to spend the rest of my life with, and it took me very little time to work that out.'

'You said that you wanted me to be the mother of your children.'

He grimaced. '*Sì*. In the circumstances I can see how you would have arrived at your totally false belief that our marriage couldn't work. But what I was trying to say was that you were the only woman for me. The only woman I wanted to marry. The only woman I wanted to have children with.' His voice softened. 'Or not have children with, if that is what fate dictates for us. I love you.'

Amy stared at him, not daring to believe that he meant it. Then she felt her eyes fill. 'I didn't believe that you loved me.'

'I married you,' Marco said softly. 'Wasn't that proof enough of my love?'

'You didn't come after me when I left.'

He breathed out heavily. 'To begin with I was in shock. I couldn't believe what had happened because we went from being happy to you leaving in the blink of an eye. I would have come but then Annabel died and Nick needed me here. Time passed—'

'And I didn't come back because I just couldn't see how our relationship could survive. After everything I saw at home. Even now, I can't really believe that we can be different from my parents.'

'We *are* different. No two people are the same, remember that. And no relationship is the same. Have a little faith.' He brushed away her tears. 'If we weren't already married, this is the moment when I would propose. And you would say yes.'

'Would I?' She felt hope unfold inside her like the petals of a flower. 'What if—?'

'Life is full of what ifs. Let's deal just with what is. I love you. You love me. We stay together. And don't even think of arguing because I'm not going to listen. And don't think of leaving because I'll come after you.'

'Oh, Marco.' She flung her arms round his neck and felt his hand smooth her back.

'You are tired, *tesoro*. I need to take you home.'

'I love you.'

'I know. And I love you, too. And now you are going to rest because this has all been very traumatic for you. You are looking so, so tired at the moment.'

'It's probably just the worry. I've been dreading the thought of leaving you again.'

'You're not leaving. Not ever.'

'Do you mean it? You think everything can work?'

'I know it can.'

Amy leaned against him, feeling truly loved for the first time in her life. The feeling warmed her and she gave a soft smile.

If only she didn't feel so completely exhausted, everything about her life would be perfect.

The following morning Amy woke up with a churning stomach and only just made it to the bathroom before being violently sick.

'Amy?' Marco followed her into the bathroom, stroked her hair away from her face and then sat down on a chair and lifted her from the cold tiles onto his lap. 'Are you hot? Have you eaten something?'

'Obviously. Or maybe this is why I was so tired yesterday,' she murmured, sinking against his chest. 'I must have picked up a bug.'

'You weren't just tired yesterday,' Marco said gently. 'You are always tired.'

Amy felt a sudden flicker of unease. It was true. She *was* always tired.

What was the matter with her?

Was this another of life's cruel tricks? Had she finally found someone who truly loved her, only to become seriously ill?

'It's just a bug,' she said firmly. 'I feel better now I've been sick. I'll get dressed in a minute. We don't want to be late for surgery.'

'Don't be ridiculous. You can't take a surgery, feeling like this.'

She closed her eyes, wishing her stomach would settle. 'I'll be fine.'

'Amy.' Marco slid a hand over her forehead, checked her temperature and then gave her a smile. 'Spend the morning in bed. I'll be back to see you at lunchtime.'

She knew she ought to argue, but she just felt too tired to utter a protest so she allowed him to tuck her into bed and lay there, sleeping all morning until he reappeared.

'Do you feel any better?' He sat down on the bed next to her and stroked her face, his fingers cold from his short walk from the car. 'Have you been sick again?'

'No, just the once this morning.' She sat up. 'How was surgery?'

'Fine.' He hesitated. 'Amy, I'm going to say something and I hope you won't be upset.'

Her stomach dropped. 'You've changed your mind?'

'About what?' He looked baffled and she blushed.

'About spending your life with someone who can't have babies.'

His mouth tightened. 'I'm spending my life with you, that's what I want. But what I have to say does have to do with babies and I'm afraid you may misinterpret—' He broke off and let out a long breath. 'Amy, I want you to do a pregnancy test.'

'What?' She stared at him. 'Are you mad? Haven't you listened to a single thing I've said to you?'

'Look at your symptoms. Every day you're exhausted—'

'We're working hard!'

'You were sick this morning.'

'So? I've picked up a bug!' She pushed her hair away from her face and glared at him, her insides churning again. 'You're imagining it, Marco, just because you want it to happen. Wishful thinking. This is just what I was afraid of! You say it doesn't matter, *but it matters, Marco.* I can see that it matters to you.'

'No!' His voice was sharp. 'I knew this was going to be difficult because I knew you would make that association, but it isn't true. This isn't about our relationship. I'm a doctor, Amy, and I'm looking at your symptoms.'

'Well, you obviously haven't looked very closely because there's no way I…' Her voice tailed off and she looked at him. 'I can't be. You *know* I can't be.'

'I don't know that. I do know that fertility is an unpredictable thing. I know that we've been making love for almost a month now with no contraception.'

'I can't be pregnant!'

'Then do the test and we will know. Don't cry, please, don't cry.' He cursed softly and pulled her into his arms. *'Mi dispiace, tesoro.* Don't cry.'

Amy pulled away from him and wiped her hand over her face, furious with herself for being so emotional. What was happening to her? She'd never been the hysterical, weepy type. 'All right. I'll do it. Of course I'll do it if that's what you want me to do.' She sniffed and held out her hand. 'Do you have it?'

He hesitated and then reached into his jacket and pulled out the test. 'I'll come with you.'

She stared at the test in her hand. 'Would you mind if I did it on my own?' Her voice shook and he gave a sigh.

'Don't push me away, Amy. Don't push me away, *tesoro.* Not now when we are just learning how to share.'

Amy hesitated. She wasn't sure that she could actually do a pregnancy test in company, even when that company was Marco. 'The thing is,' she said honestly, 'even though I know it can't be positive, I want it to be, so badly. I—I just need a few moments…'

'I understand that.' Marco hugged her tightly. 'We'll compromise. Do the test and then call me.'

So that he could offer comfort.

And she was going to need comfort, she knew she was.

Amy closed the bathroom door and sat on the edge of the bath, the packet in her hand unopened. Why was she even hesitating? It wasn't as if she didn't know the answer, because she did. So why was she treating the test as if it were a bomb that was going to blow her life apart?

She didn't really think she was going to be pregnant, did she? Surely she wasn't really that stupid? *That delusional?* Had she really, somehow, allowed a tiny flicker of hope to creep in and contaminate her common sense?

With an impatient sound she stood up and unwrapped the test.

A few minutes later she was still staring at the stick, tears trickling unnoticed down her cheeks. The tiled bathroom floor was cold under her bare feet but she didn't notice that either.

'Amy?' His tone impatient and concerned by equal degrees, Marco pushed open the door without waiting for an invitation. 'Talk to me, *amore*. I'm sorry. I shouldn't have even suggested that you do that test. It was thoughtless of me and—'

'I'm pregnant.' Her voice was a hoarse whisper and she felt suddenly dizzy. 'Marco, I'm pregnant. I'm having our baby.'

She heard him swear softly and then felt his arms slide around her and support her as her legs gave way.

'So now I believe in happy endings.' Nick glanced between them and smiled. 'I'm pleased for you both. Really.'

Marco laughed in disbelief. 'I just told you that I want to leave the practice and return to Italy. It's not exactly a happy ending for you.'

Nick looked at him for a long moment and Amy saw something pass between the two men. An understanding. They'd shared so much. Loss. Pain. Pride at the way the practice had developed.

'Life moves on. Things change and we have to change with them.' Nick shrugged. 'We set this place up together and a lot of the success is down to you, Marco. The practice will go on without you. Grow. Change. I can understand that you and Amy want to go back to Italy.'

'Penhally will always remind Amy of her past.' Marco slid a protective arm around her and Amy looked up at him.

'And you miss Italy.'

'*Sì*. That is true.' He smiled at her. 'I miss Italy. I feel like the Maserati. In this weather, my engine suffers.'

'Well.' Nick cleared his throat. 'On a practical note, Adam Donnelly is due to start tomorrow, as you know, so we won't be left high and dry.'

'We can stay for a few months if that would help.'

Nick shook his head. 'I don't want you to do that. You've managed to sort things out and I'm pleased about that. You've no idea how pleased. Now I want you to go and get on with your lives. Get ready for that baby.'

'You're very generous.' Marco's voice was gruff. 'Thank you.'

'*Prego.* Isn't that what I'm supposed to say?'

'And what about you, my friend?'

A shadow flickered in Nick's eyes. 'I carry on building the practice. Supporting the community. Kate's resigned.'

'Oh, no!' Despite the conversation they'd had, Amy couldn't help feeling shocked. She hadn't actually believed that Kate would do it.

'And you accepted her resignation?' Marco's gaze was steady and Amy held her breath. It was the nearest any of them had come to asking Nick directly about his relationship with Kate.

'It's disappointing for the practice but she wants to take a new direction in her career. It would be wrong of me to talk her out of it.'

Work. He only talked about work. Nothing personal. *Nothing about missing Kate or feeling anything for Kate.*

For a moment Amy was tempted to step forward and shake him. Didn't he know how Kate felt about him? And was he really pretending that he felt nothing for Kate? She knew that wasn't true. Not after the scene she'd witnessed on New Year's Eve.

'Nick—'

'People are complicated,' Marco said quietly, closing his hand over Amy's to silence her. 'Relationships are complicated. And not all the obstacles to happiness come from outside and can be solved. Sometimes they are inside us and only time can shift them.'

For a moment Nick didn't respond. 'And sometimes time just isn't enough. Good luck, the two of you. Stay in touch. I look forward to holidays in Italy.'

They walked away from the surgery and Marco turned to look back.

'You're going to miss it, aren't you?' Amy slid her hand into his and he turned and smiled at her.

'I'm ready to move on. Do something else. I suppose I feel a little guilty about leaving Nick, especially as Kate is leaving, too. Whatever is going on between them, she has been a big part of the Penhally Bay Surgery for a long time.'

'She would have stayed if he'd told her that he loved her.'

'Nick has far too many issues after Annabel's death. He isn't ready to think about another relationship. Perhaps he never will be.'

Amy sighed. 'Why didn't you make him admit that he is in love with Kate?'

'I'm not sure that he knows it himself. And I'm not a doctor of relationships.'

Amy slipped her arm into his. 'I think you are. You cured ours. I can't believe this has happened. I arrived in Penhally a month ago to ask you to give me a divorce and now here I am back with you and pregnant. It's like a dream.'

'But a good dream.'

'Of course.' She reached up and kissed him. 'It's like being given a second chance. When I first met you I was so in love and then it all went so wrong. I didn't believe our relationship could work if I was infertile because I'd seen what it did to my parents.'

'It isn't about fertility, it's about love. Your parents didn't share the love that we have for each other.'

'No. I think you're right about that.'

'You know I'm right.' He slid his arms around her waist. 'I'm always right.'

'And so modest. So what happens now?'

'We make our home in Italy. The sun will put some colour in your cheeks and you will grow so accustomed to being loved that there will be no room for doubt in your mind. And you will speak Italian and learn how to make pasta from scratch.'

Amy laughed. 'And Penhally?'

He glanced around him, his eyes warm. 'This place has been a part of our lives. But it's time to move on.' His gaze moved back to hers. 'Will you move on with me, *tesoro*? Build a new life? Do you trust me enough to give up everything you know?'

'Yes.' She answered without hesitation. 'The only thing I don't want to give up is you. You're all that matters.'

Marco gave a slow smile of satisfaction. 'Finally, we agree on something.'

And he bent his head and kissed her.

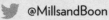

MILLS & BOON

THE HEART OF ROMANCE

A ROMANCE FOR EVERY KIND OF READER

MODERN

Prepare to be swept off your feet by sophisticated, sexy and seductive heroes, in some of the world's most glamourous and romantic locations, where power and passion collide.
8 stories per month.

HISTORICAL

Escape with historical heroes from time gone by. Whether your passion is for wicked Regency Rakes, muscled Vikings or rugged Highlanders, awaken the romance of the past.
6 stories per month.

MEDICAL

Set your pulse racing with dedicated, delectable doctors in the high-pressure world of medicine, where emotions run high and passion, comfort and love are the best medicine.
6 stories per month.

True Love

Celebrate true love with tender stories of heartfelt romance, from the rush of falling in love to the joy a new baby can bring, and a focus on the emotional heart of a relationship.
8 stories per month.

Desire

Indulge in secrets and scandal, intense drama and plenty of sizzling hot action with powerful and passionate heroes who have it all: wealth, status, good looks…everything but the right woman.
6 stories per month.

HEROES

Experience all the excitement of a gripping thriller, with an intense romance at its heart. Resourceful, true-to-life women and strong, fearless men face danger and desire - a killer combination!
8 stories per month.

DARE

Sensual love stories featuring smart, sassy heroines you'd want as a best friend, and compelling intense heroes who are worthy of them.
4 stories per month.

To see which titles are coming soon, please visit

millsandboon.co.uk/nextmonth

JOIN US ON SOCIAL MEDIA!

Stay up to date with our latest releases, author news and gossip, special offers and discounts, and all the behind-the-scenes action from Mills & Boon...

 millsandboon

 millsandboonuk

 millsandboon

It might just be true love...